CatStronauts

RACE TO MARS

CatStronauts

RACE TO MARS

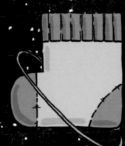

BY DREW BROCKINGTON

LB

Little, Brown and Company ·
New York Boston

Little, Brown and Company

Hachette Book Group
1290 Avenue of the Americas, New York, NY 10104
Visit us at lb-kids.com

Little, Brown and Company is a division of Hachette Book Group, Inc.
The Little, Brown name and logo are trademarks of Hachette Book Group, Inc.

The publisher is not responsible for websites (or their content) that are not owned by the publisher.

First Edition: April 2017

Library of Congress Cataloging-in-Publication Data
Names: Brockington, Drew, author, artist.
Title: CatStronauts : race to Mars / by Drew Brockington.
Description: First edition. | New York : Little, Brown and Company, 2017. |
Summary: "With national pride and valuable scientific research on the line, the CatStronauts race against the CosmoCats and others to be the first cats to Mars"— Provided by publisher.
Identifiers: LCCN 2016042317| ISBN 9780316307482 (hardcover) | ISBN 9780316307505 (trade pbk.) | ISBN 9780316307499 (ebook)
Subjects: LCSH: Graphic novels. | CYAC: Graphic novels. | Astronauts—Fiction. | Space flight to Mars—Fiction. | Cats—Fiction.
Classification: LCC PZ7.7.B76 Caw 2017 | DDC 741.5/973—dc23
LC record available at https://lccn.loc.gov/2016042317

10 9 8

1010

Printed in China

FOR
SIMON & MARCELINE

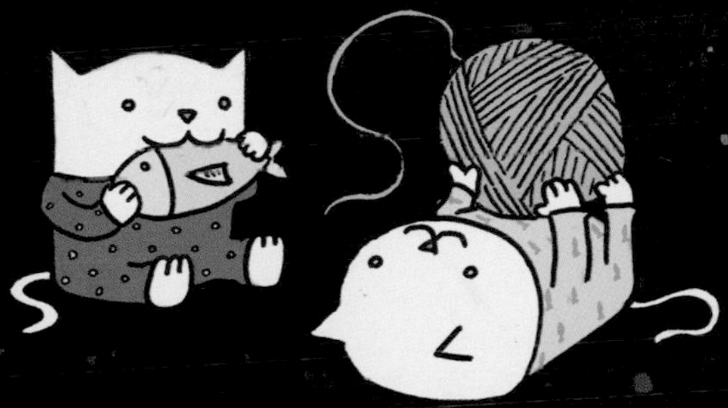

CatStronauts

RACE TO MARS

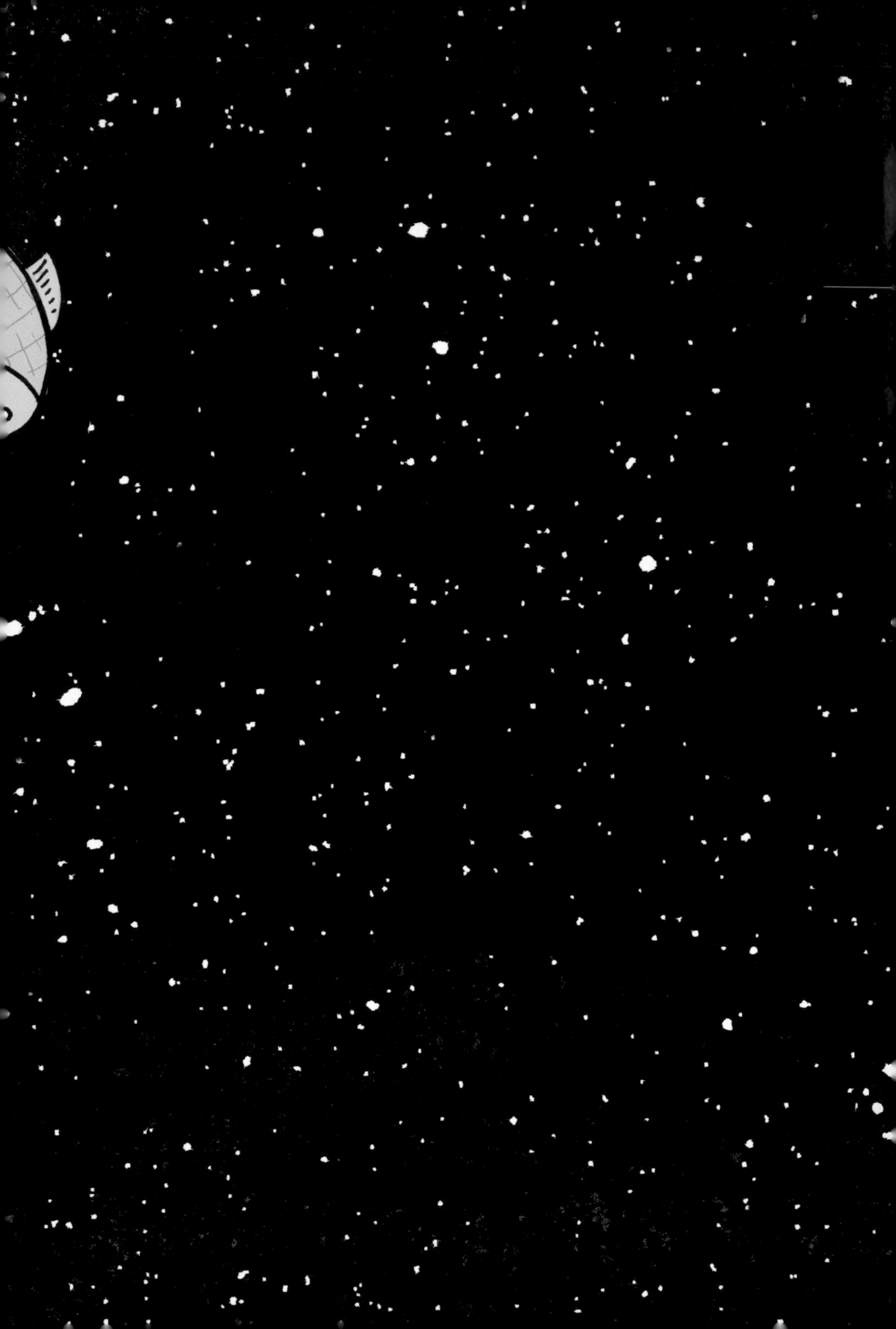

CHAPTER 1

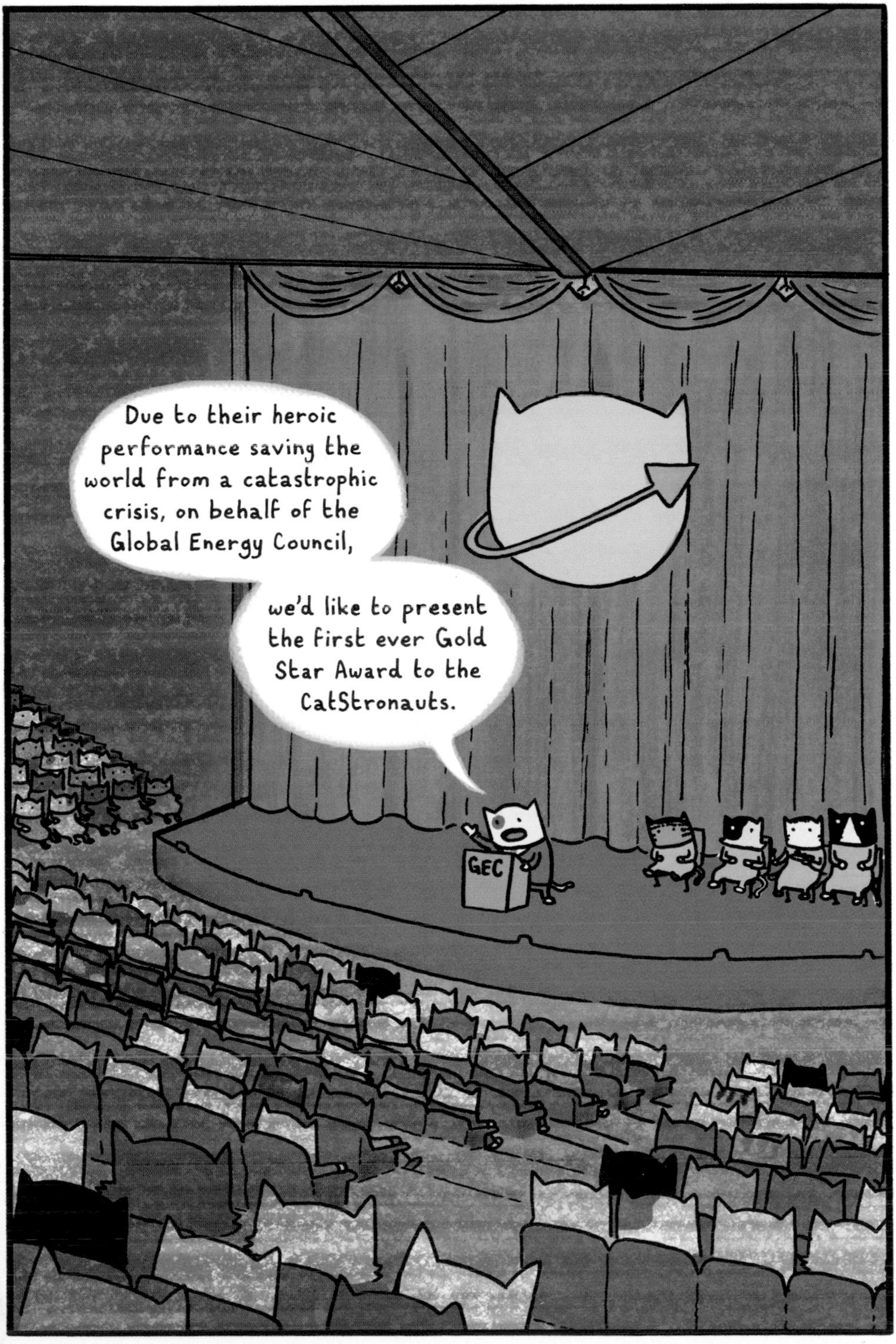
Due to their heroic performance saving the world from a catastrophic crisis, on behalf of the Global Energy Council,
we'd like to present the first ever Gold Star Award to the CatStronauts.
GEC

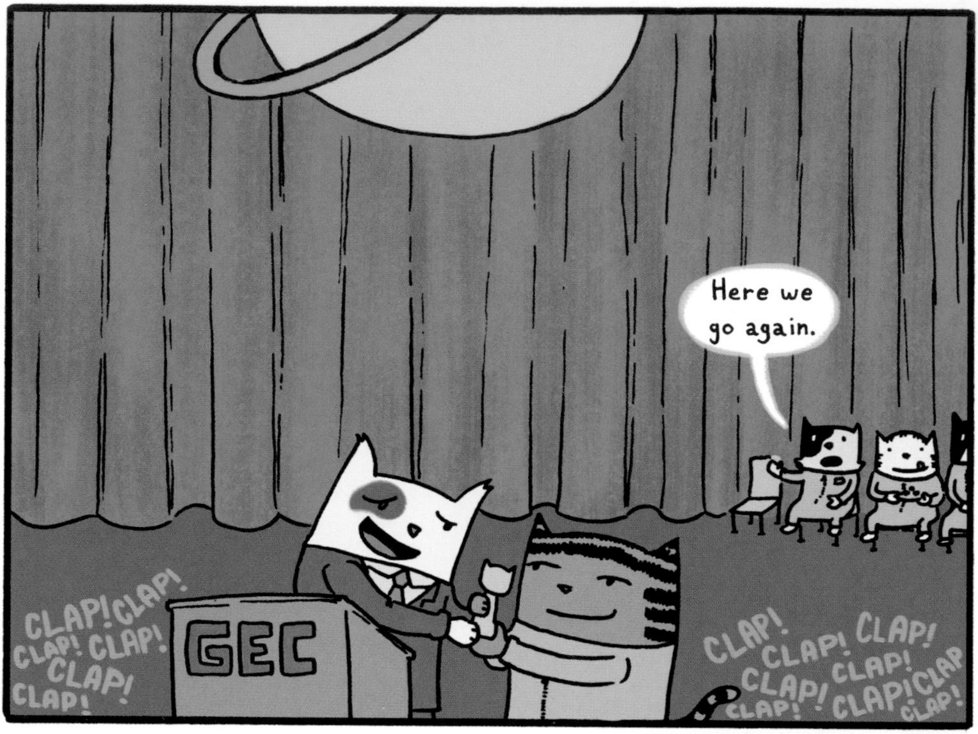
Here we go again.
CLAP! CLAP! CLAP! CLAP! CLAP! CLAP!
GEC
CLAP! CLAP! CLAP! CLAP! CLAP! CLAP! CLAP! CLAP! CLAP!

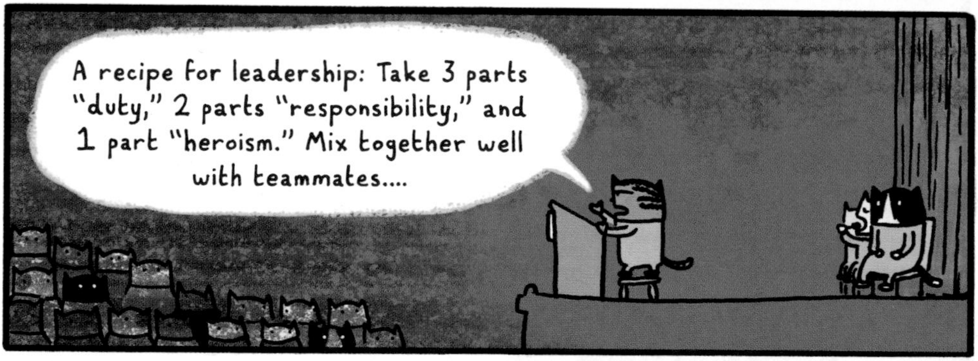
A recipe for leadership: Take 3 parts "duty," 2 parts "responsibility," and 1 part "heroism." Mix together well with teammates....

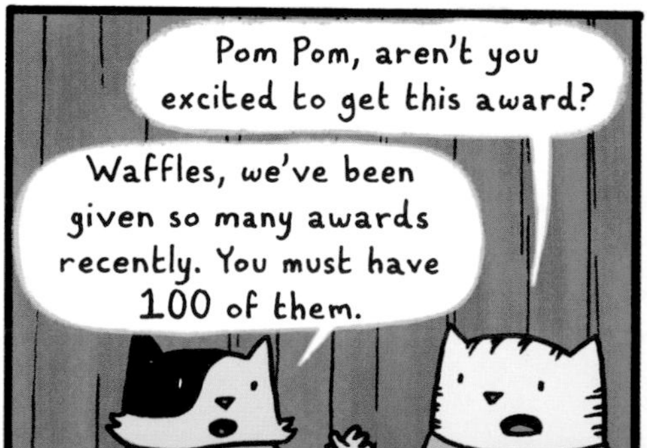
Pom Pom, aren't you excited to get this award?
Waffles, we've been given so many awards recently. You must have 100 of them.

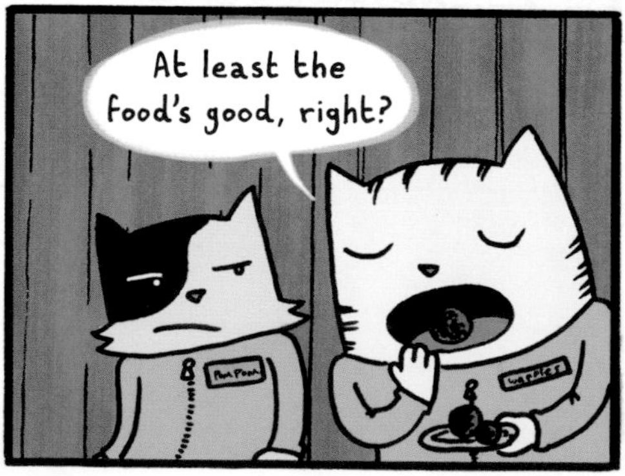
At least the food's good, right?

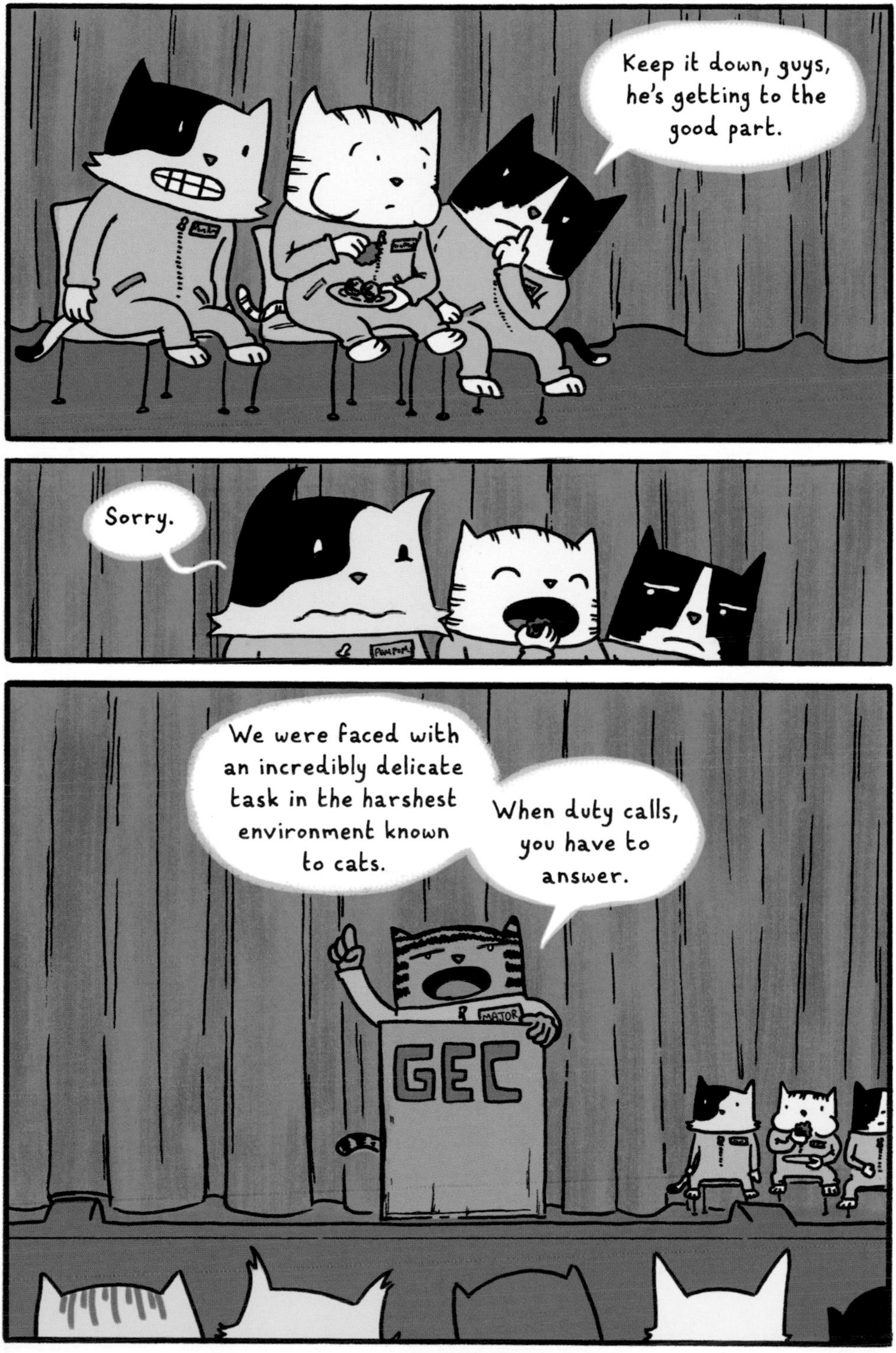
Keep it down, guys, he's getting to the good part.
Sorry.
We were faced with an incredibly delicate task in the harshest environment known to cats.
When duty calls, you have to answer.
MAJOR
GEC

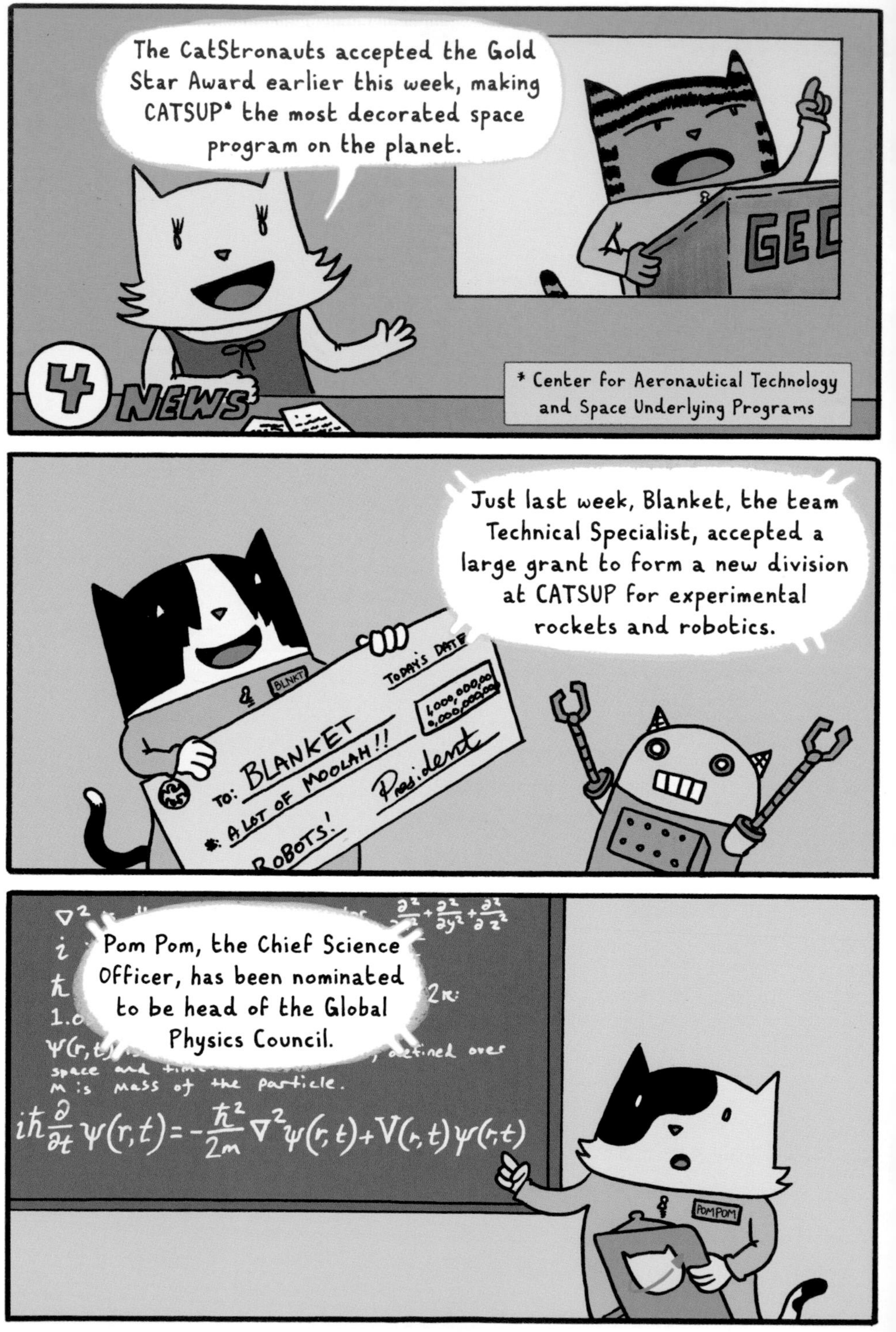
The CatStronauts accepted the Gold Star Award earlier this week, making CATSUP* the most decorated space program on the planet.
GEC
4 NEWS
* Center for Aeronautical Technology and Space Underlying Programs
Just last week, Blanket, the team Technical Specialist, accepted a large grant to form a new division at CATSUP for experimental rockets and robotics.
BLNKT
TODAY'S DATE
TO: BLANKET
A LOT OF MOOLAH!!
President
ROBOTS!
Pom Pom, the Chief Science Officer, has been nominated to be head of the Global Physics Council.
m is mass of the particle.
$i\hbar \frac{\partial}{\partial t}\psi(r,t) = -\frac{\hbar^2}{2m}\nabla^2\psi(r,t) + V(r,t)\psi(r,t)$
POM POM

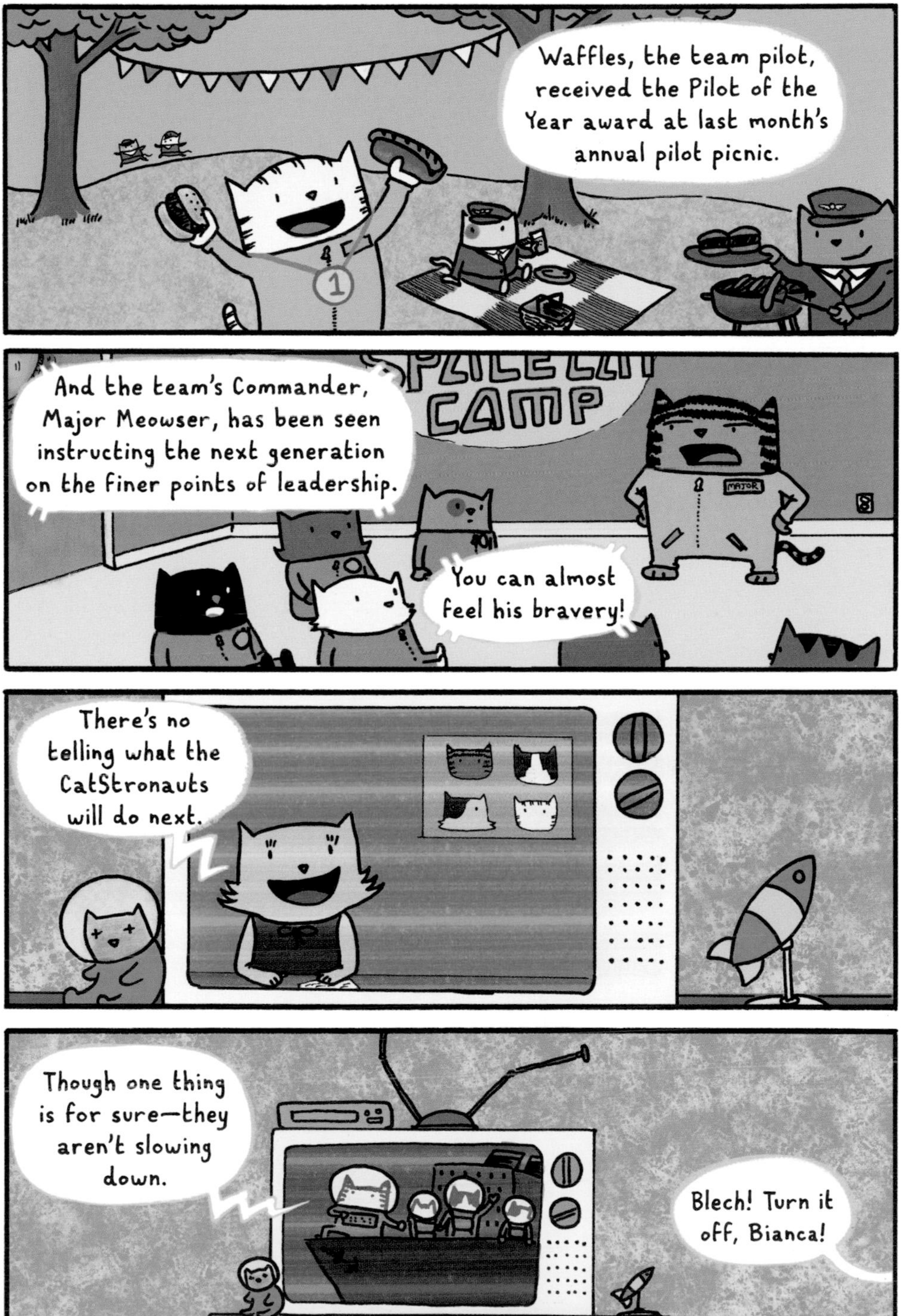
Waffles, the team pilot, received the Pilot of the Year award at last month's annual pilot picnic.
And the team's Commander, Major Meowser, has been seen instructing the next generation on the finer points of leadership.
CAMP
MAJOR
You can almost feel his bravery!
There's no telling what the CatStronauts will do next.
Though one thing is for sure—they aren't slowing down.
Blech! Turn it off, Bianca!

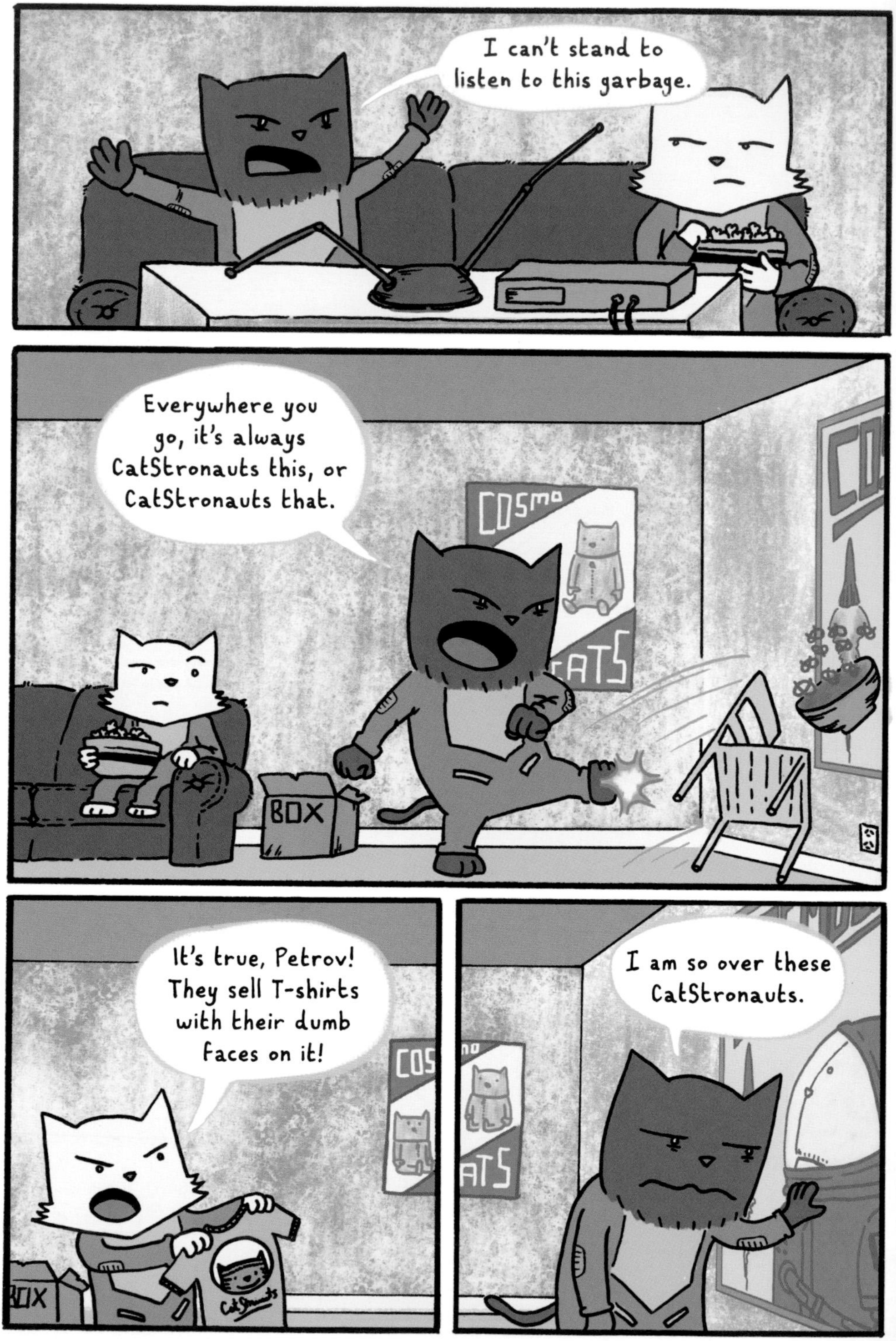
I can't stand to listen to this garbage.
Everywhere you go, it's always CatStronauts this, or CatStronauts that.
COSMO CATS
It's true, Petrov! They sell T-shirts with their dumb faces on it!
BOX
I am so over these CatStronauts.

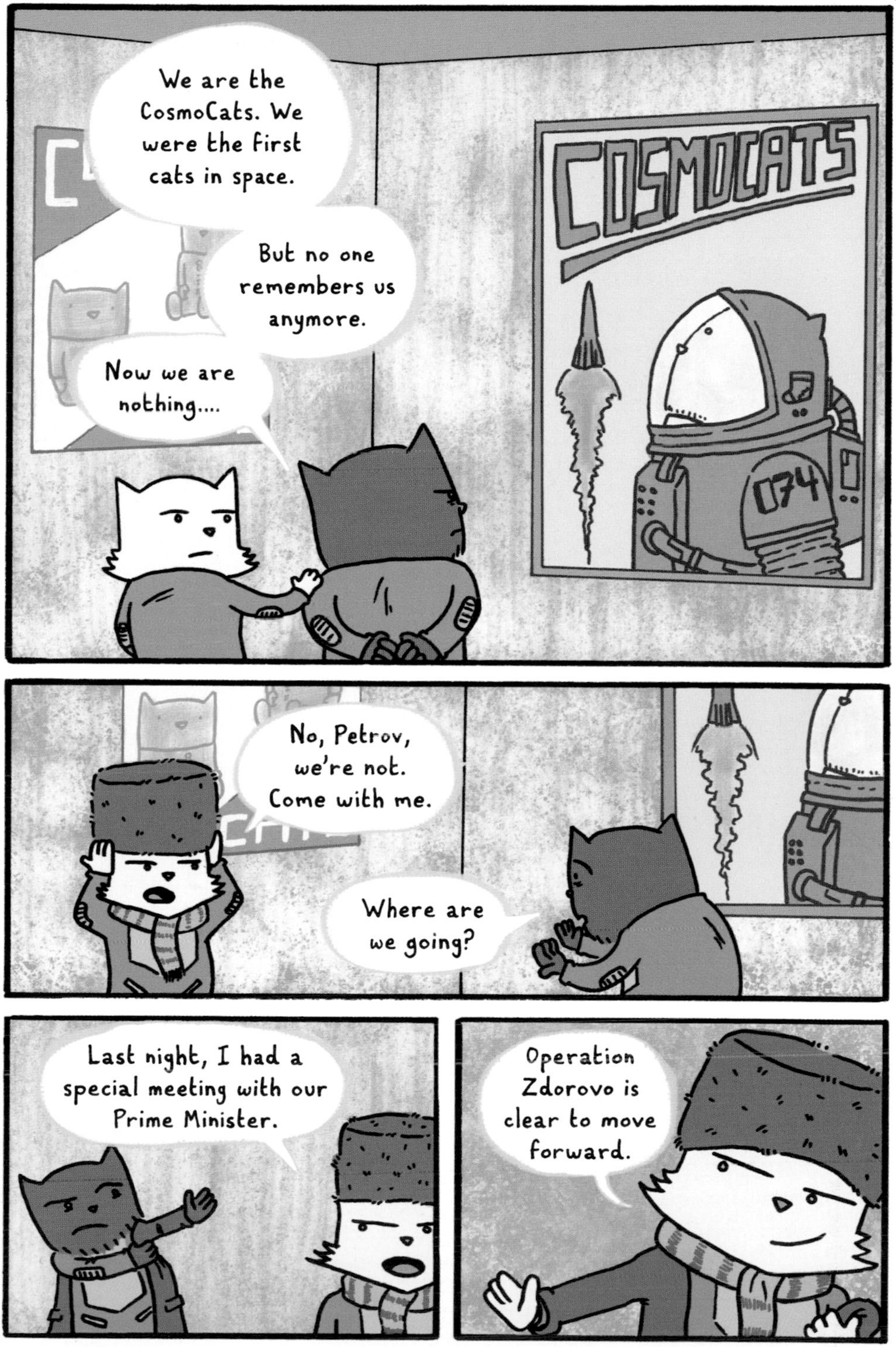
We are the CosmoCats. We were the first cats in space.
But no one remembers us anymore.
Now we are nothing....
COSMOCATS
074
No, Petrov, we're not. Come with me.
Where are we going?
Last night, I had a special meeting with our Prime Minister.
Operation Zdorovo is clear to move forward.

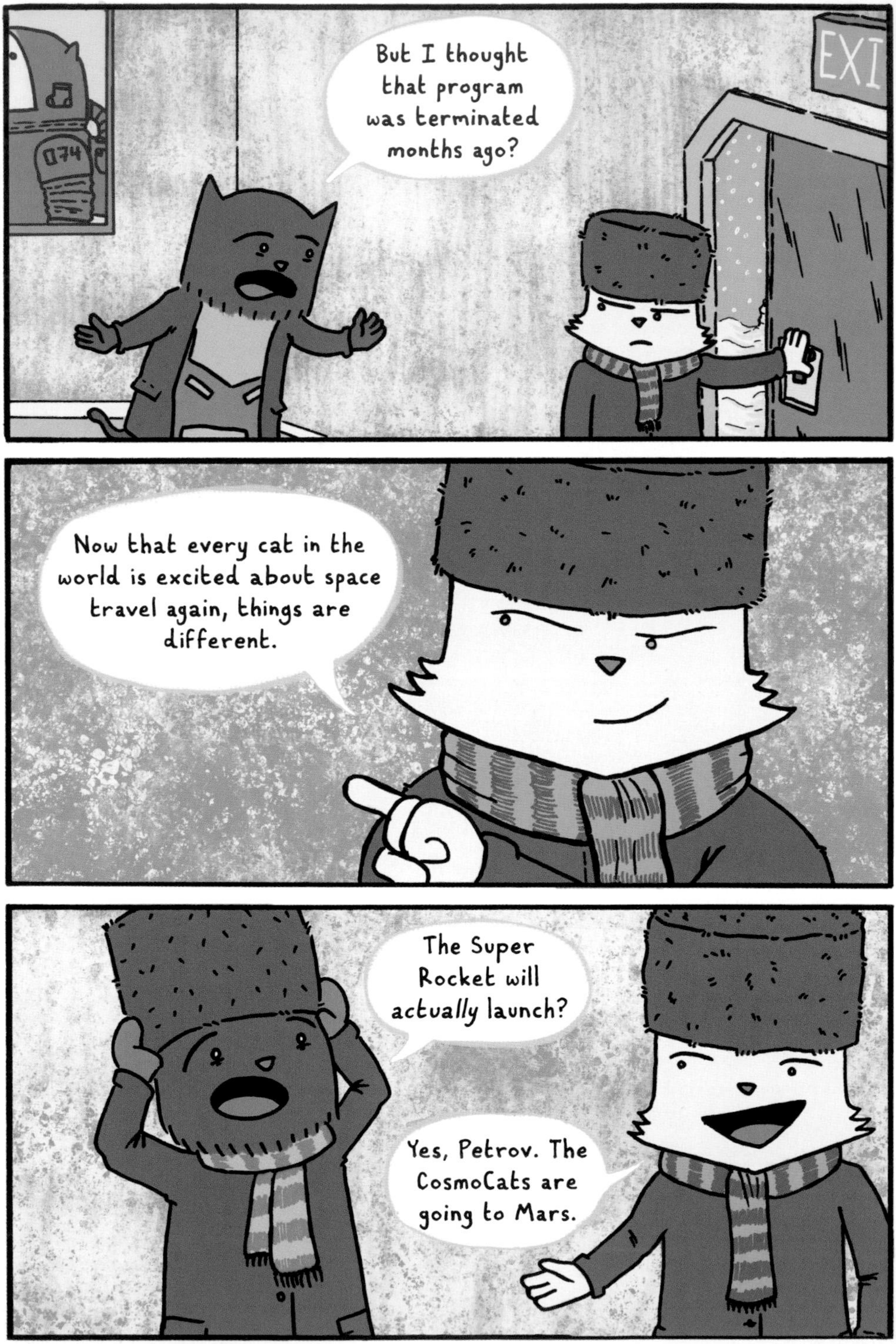
EXI
074
But I thought that program was terminated months ago?
Now that every cat in the world is excited about space travel again, things are different.
The Super Rocket will *actually* launch?
Yes, Petrov. The CosmoCats are going to Mars.

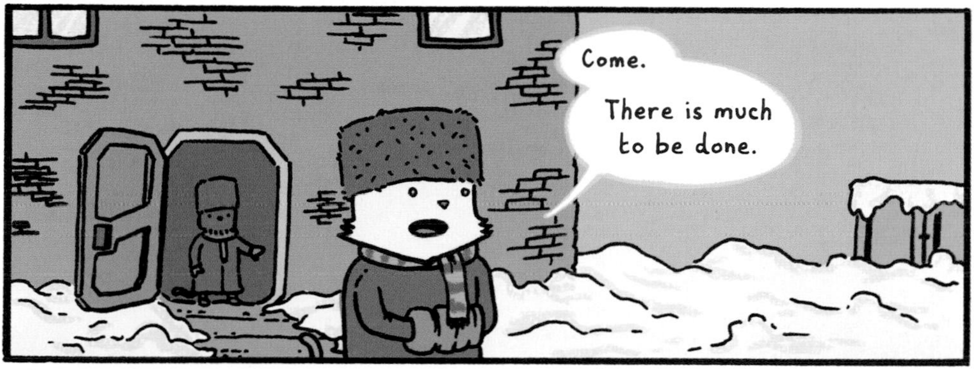
Come.
There is much to be done.

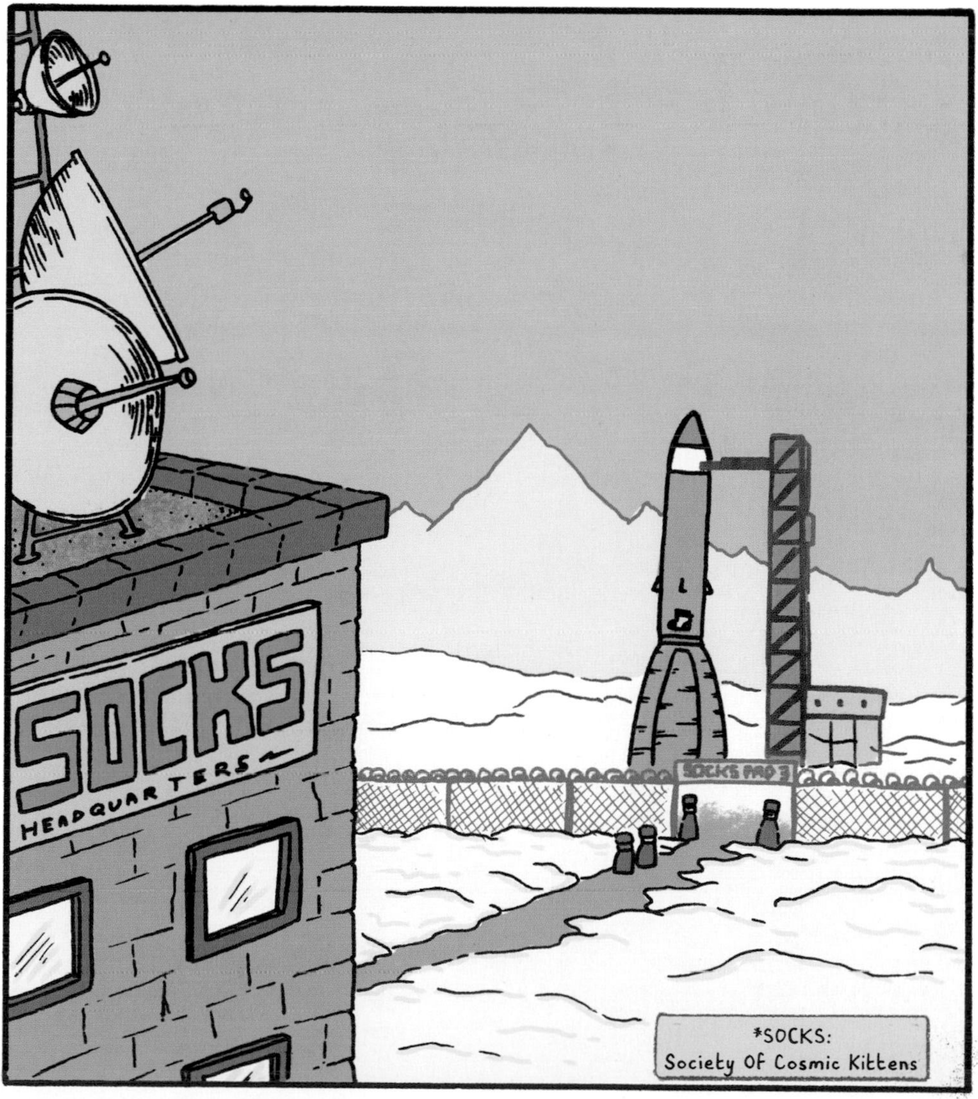
SOCKS
HEADQUARTERS
SOCKS PAD 3
*SOCKS: Society Of Cosmic Kittens

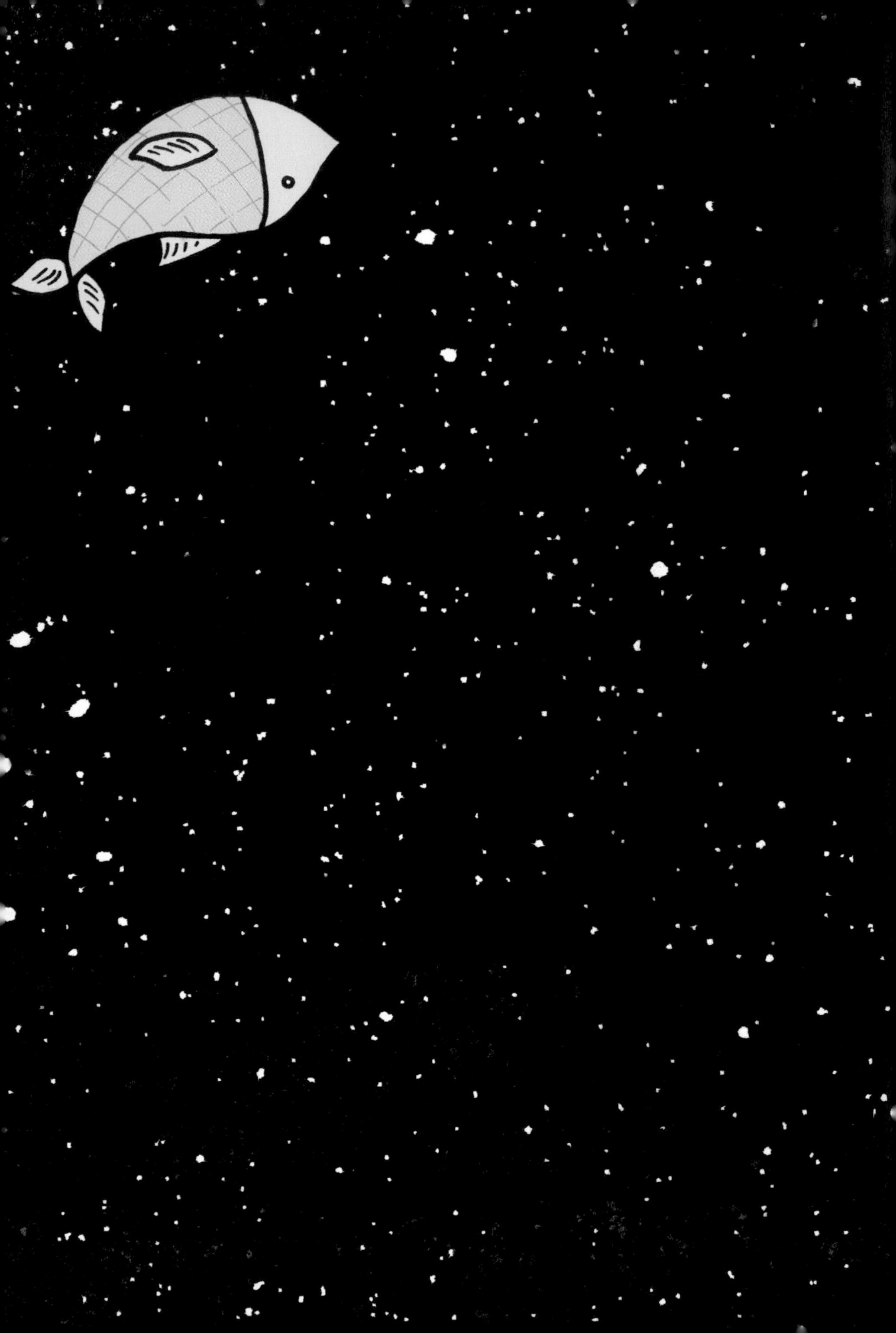

CHAPTER 2

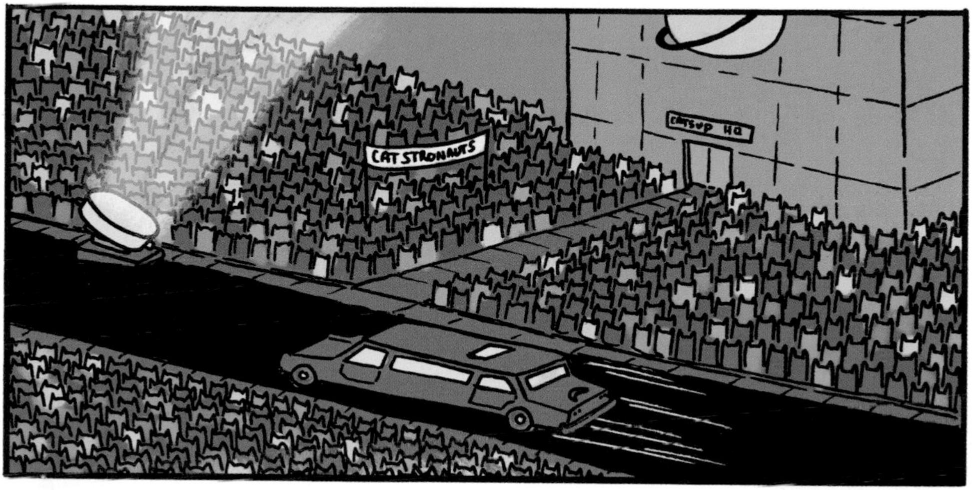
CATSTRONAUTS
CATSUP HQ

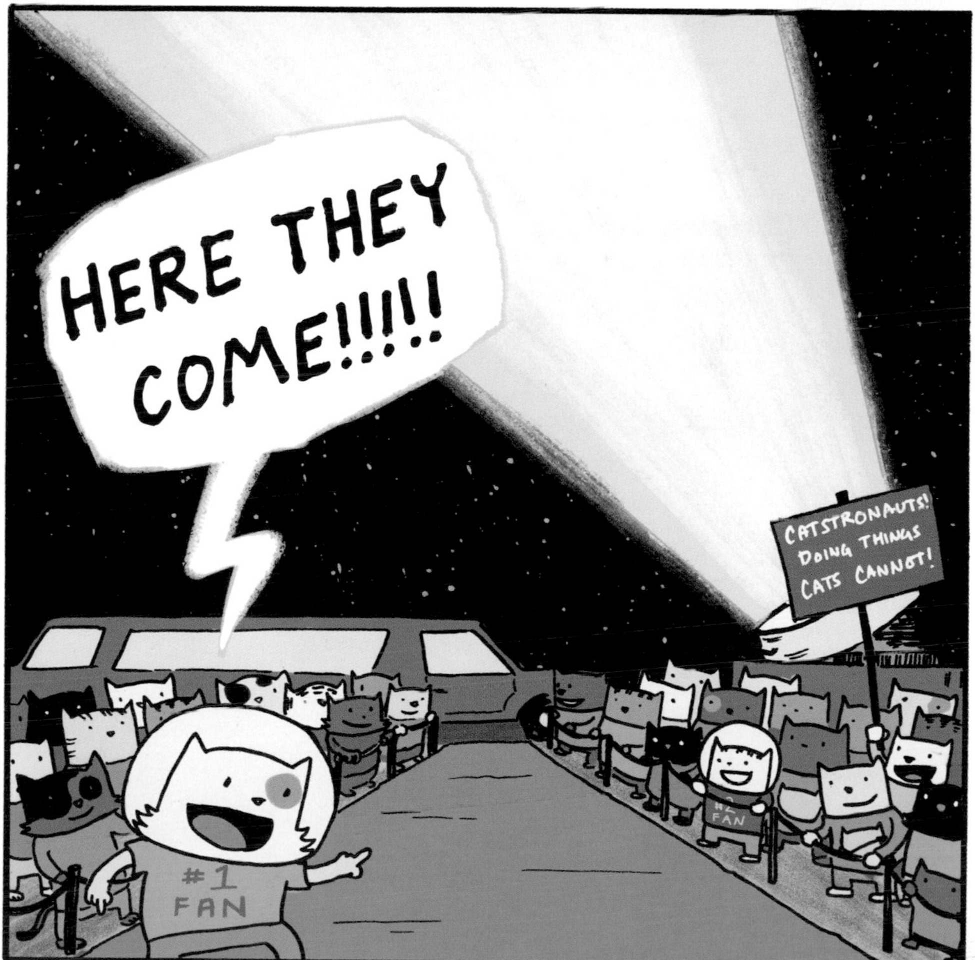
HERE THEY COME!!!!!
CATSTRONAUTS! DOING THINGS CATS CANNOT!
#1 FAN
#2 FAN

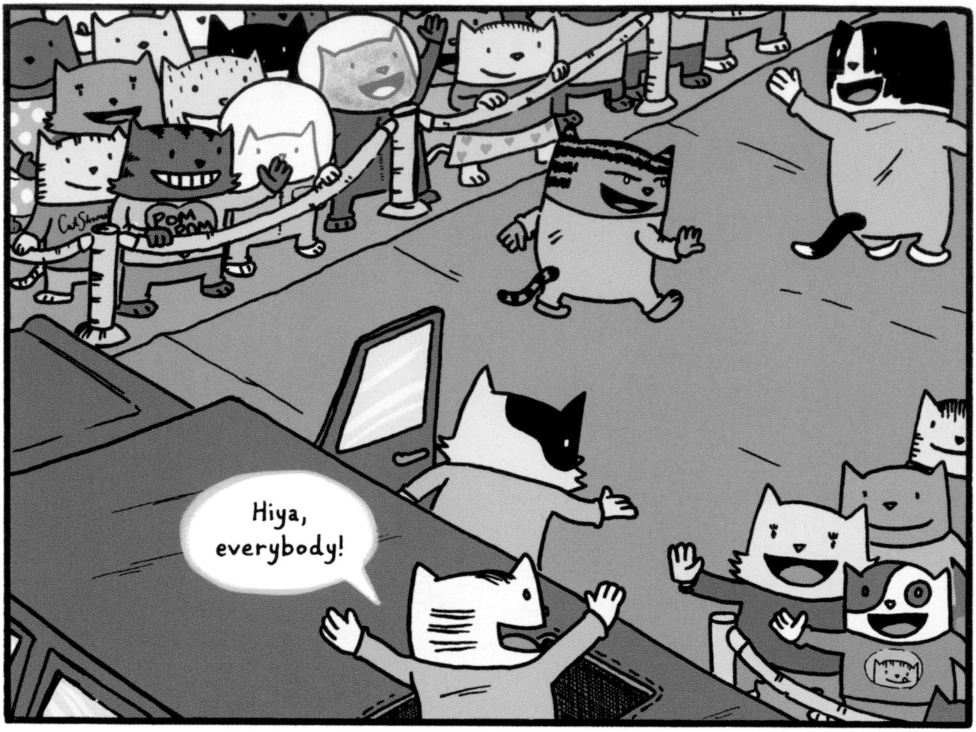
Hiya, everybody!

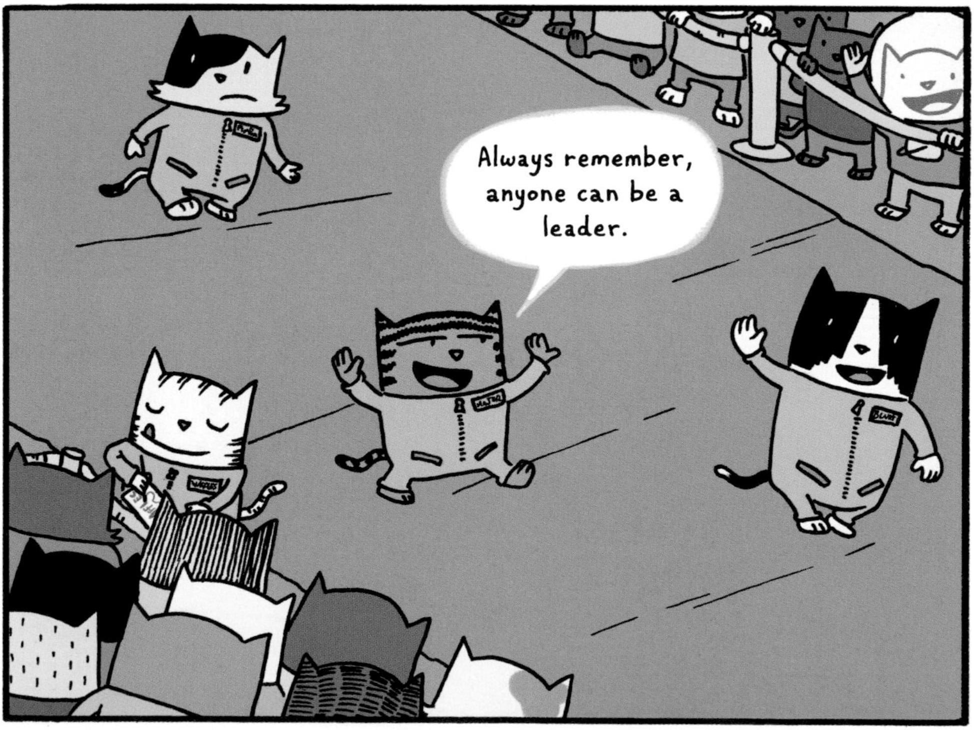
Always remember, anyone can be a leader.

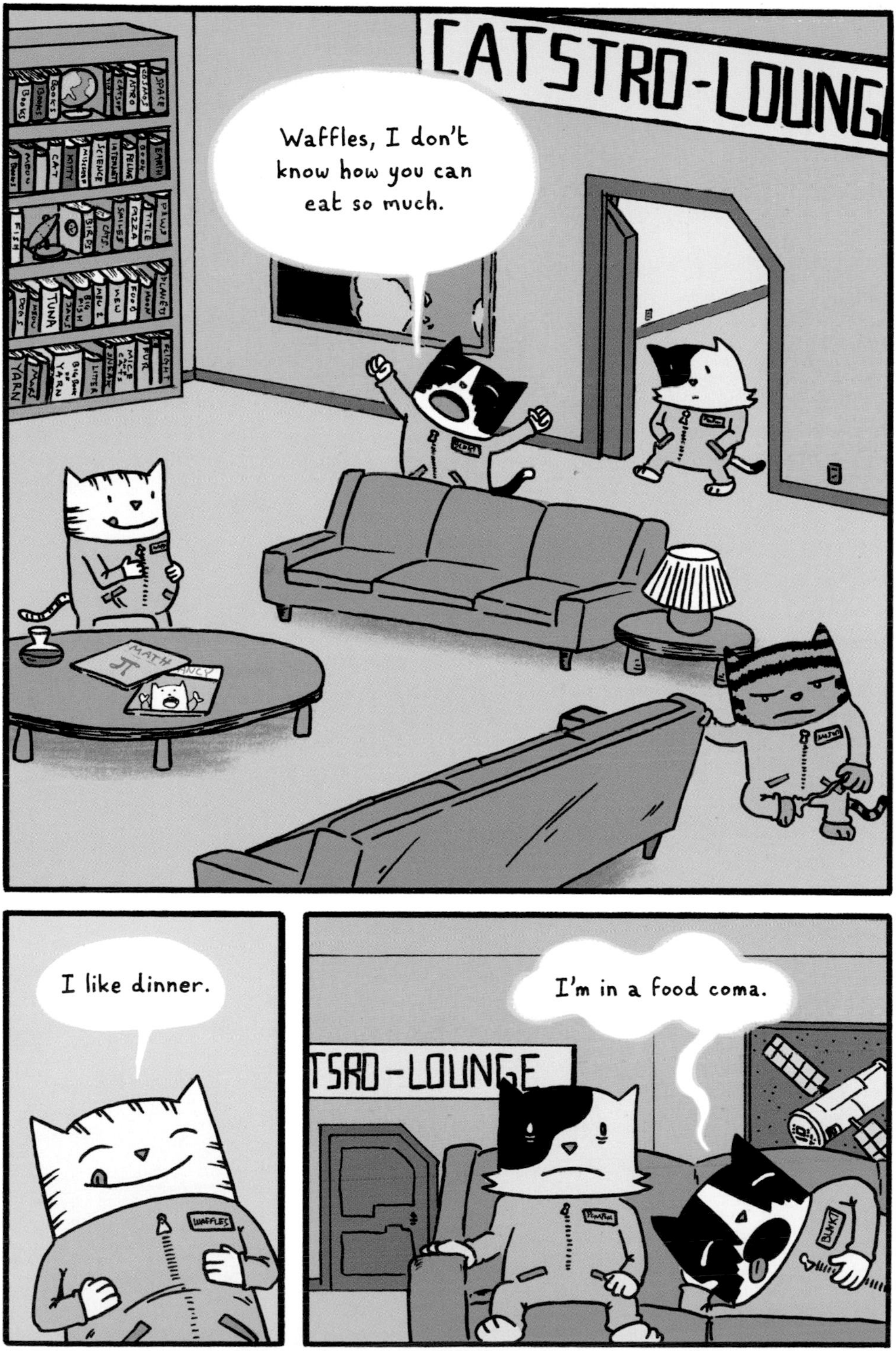
Waffles, I don't know how you can eat so much.
I like dinner.
I'm in a food coma.

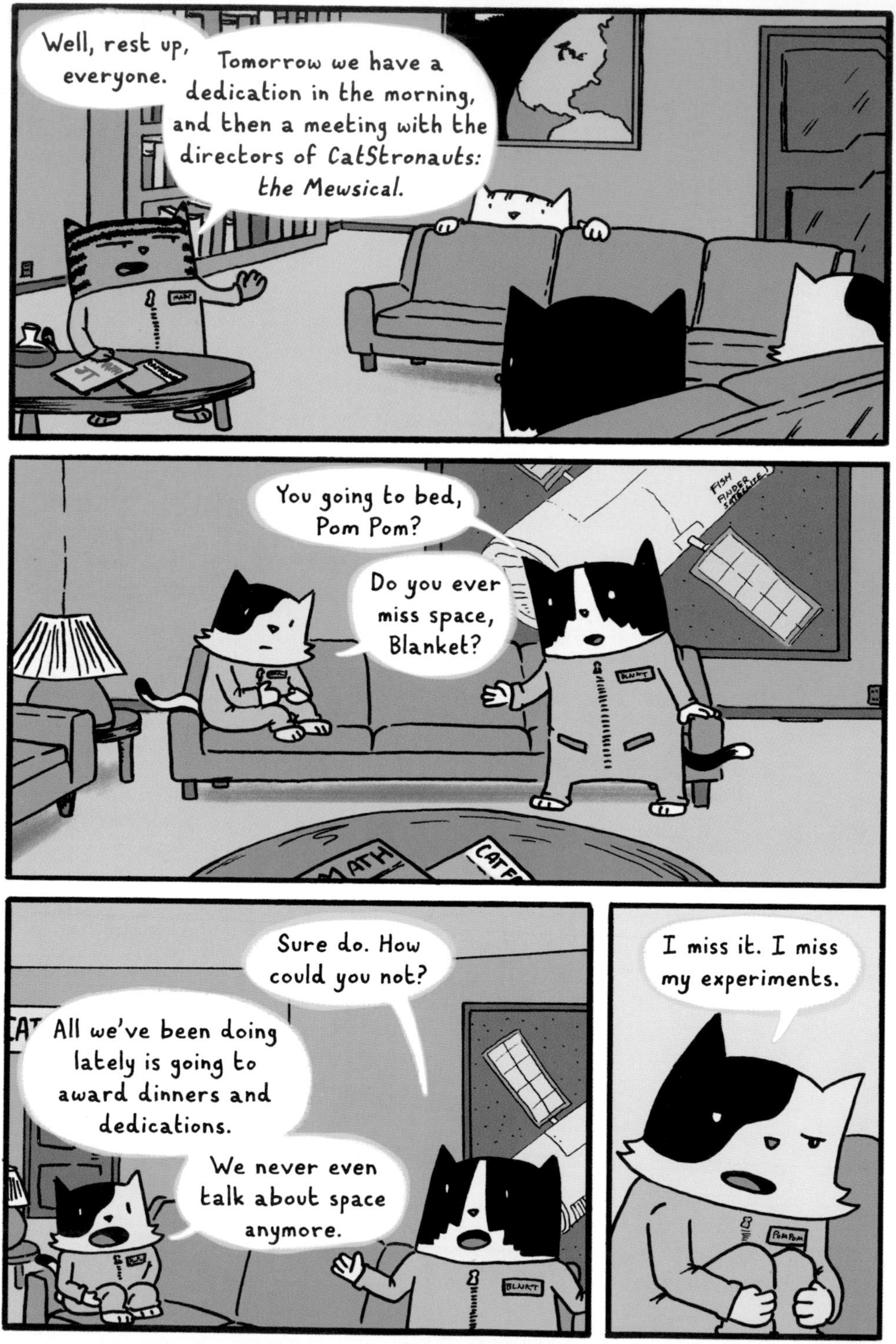
Well, rest up, everyone.
Tomorrow we have a dedication in the morning, and then a meeting with the directors of CatStronauts: the Mewsical.
MATH
FISH FINDER SATELLITE
You going to bed, Pom Pom?
Do you ever miss space, Blanket?
BLNKT
MATH
Sure do. How could you not?
All we've been doing lately is going to award dinners and dedications.
We never even talk about space anymore.
BLNKT
I miss it. I miss my experiments.
POMPOM

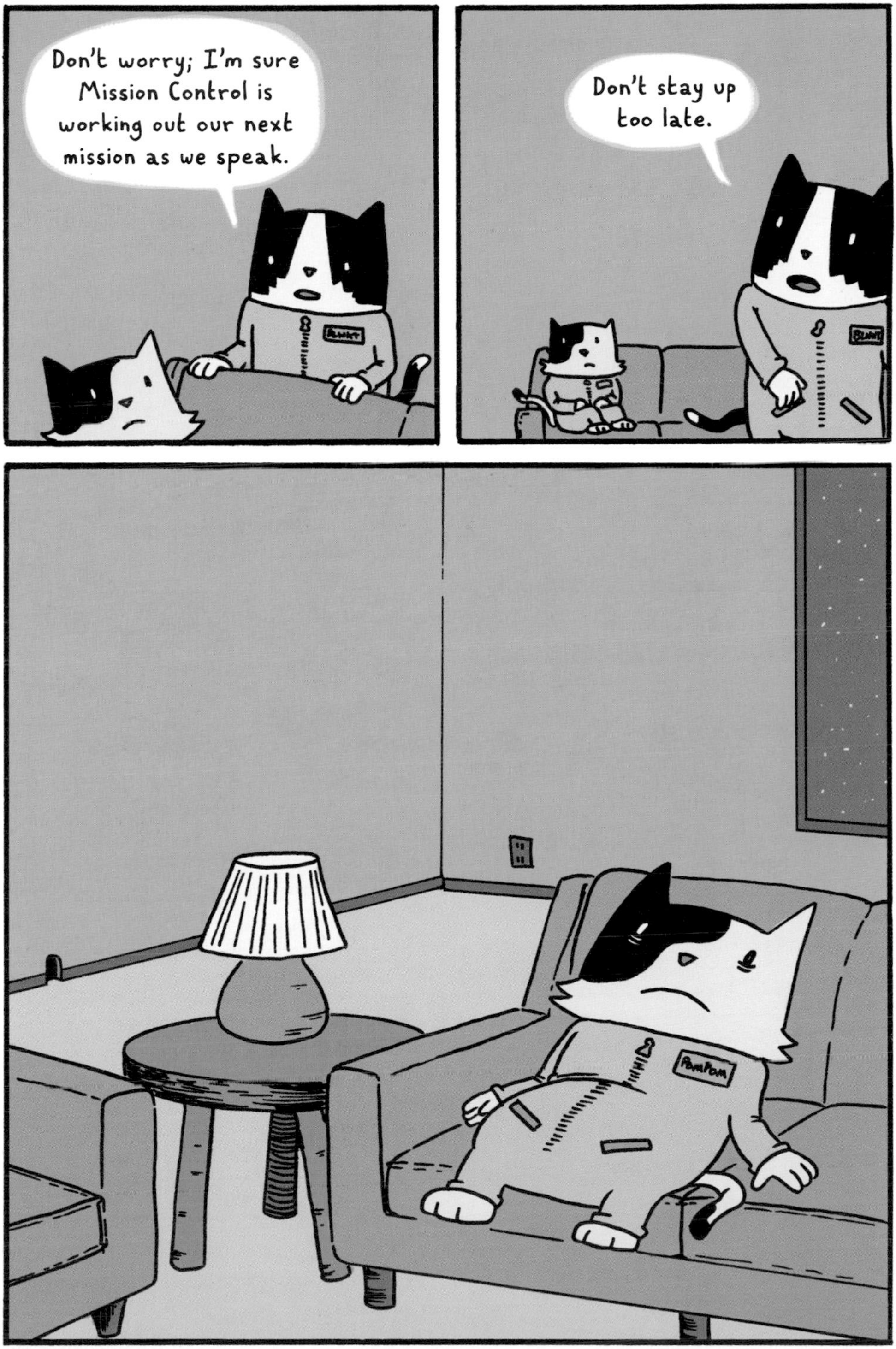
Don't worry; I'm sure Mission Control is working out our next mission as we speak.
Don't stay up too late.
PomPom

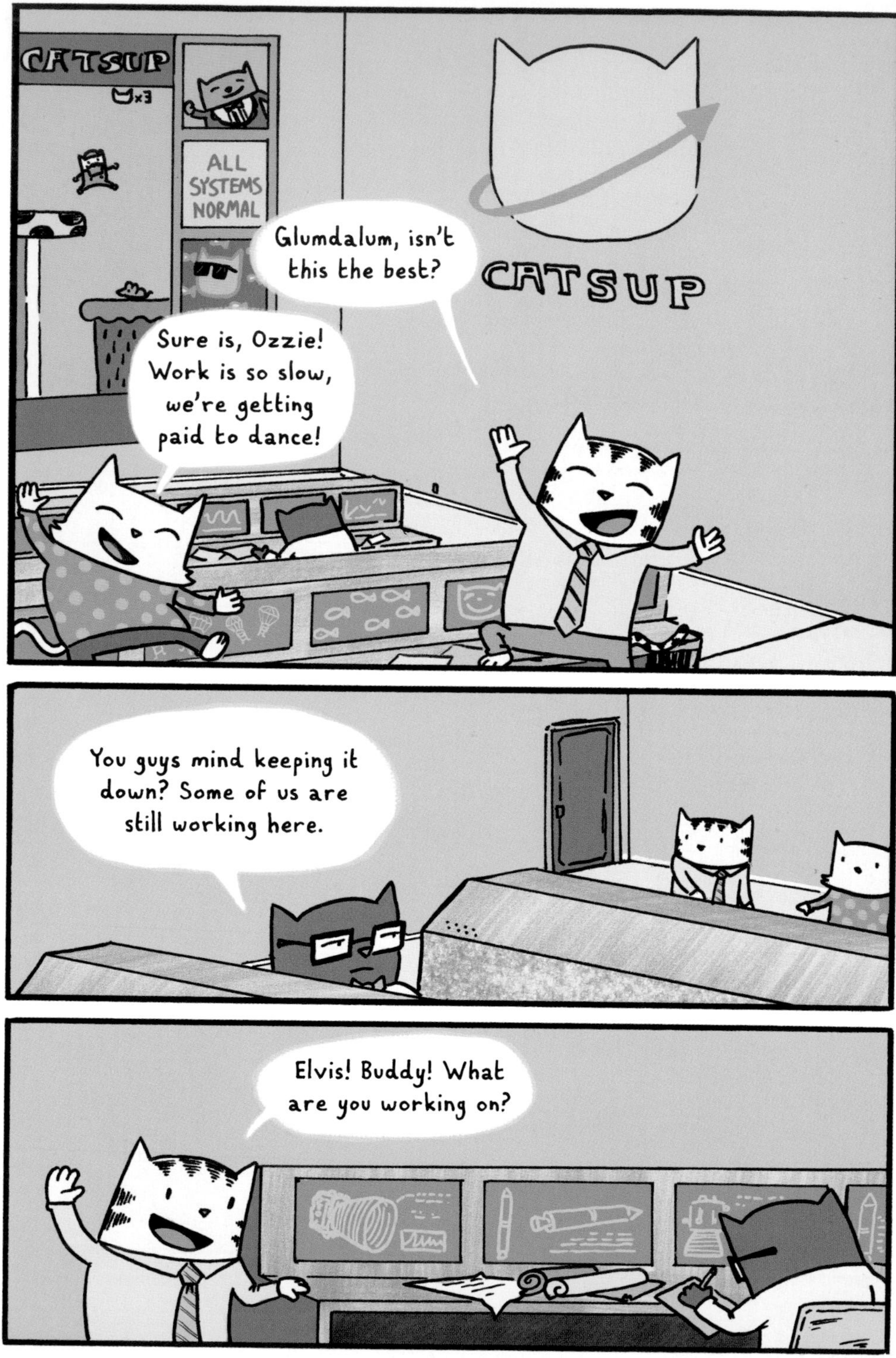
CATSUP
ALL SYSTEMS NORMAL
Glumdalum, isn't this the best?
CATSUP
Sure is, Ozzie! Work is so slow, we're getting paid to dance!
You guys mind keeping it down? Some of us are still working here.
Elvis! Buddy! What are you working on?

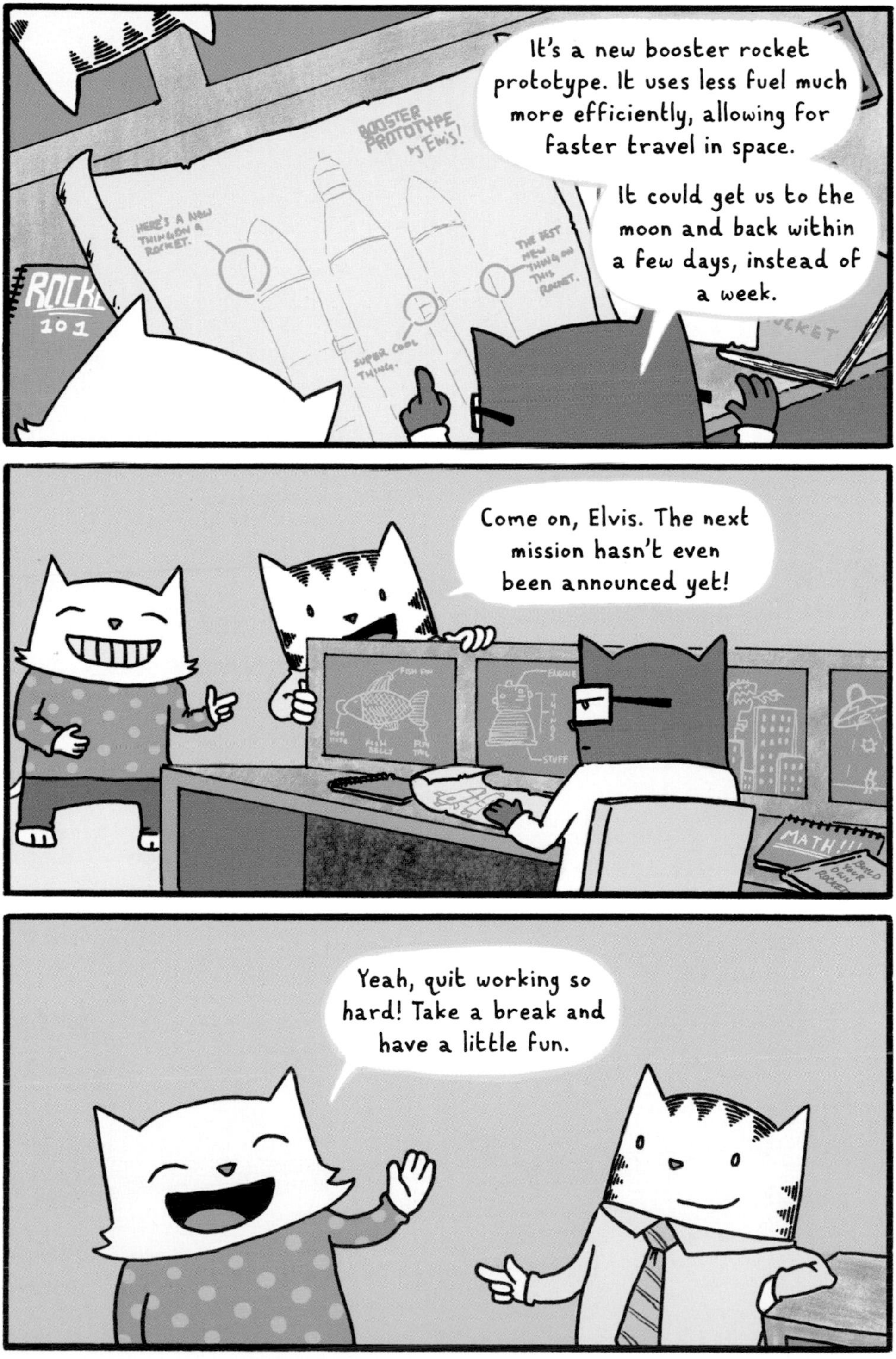
It's a new booster rocket prototype. It uses less fuel much more efficiently, allowing for faster travel in space.
It could get us to the moon and back within a few days, instead of a week.
BOOSTER PROTOTYPE
HERE'S A NEW THING ON A ROCKET.
THE BEST NEW THING ON THIS ROCKET.
SUPER COOL THING.
Come on, Elvis. The next mission hasn't even been announced yet!
FISH FIN
FISH BELLY
FISH TAIL
ENGINE
STUFF
MATH!!!
Yeah, quit working so hard! Take a break and have a little fun.

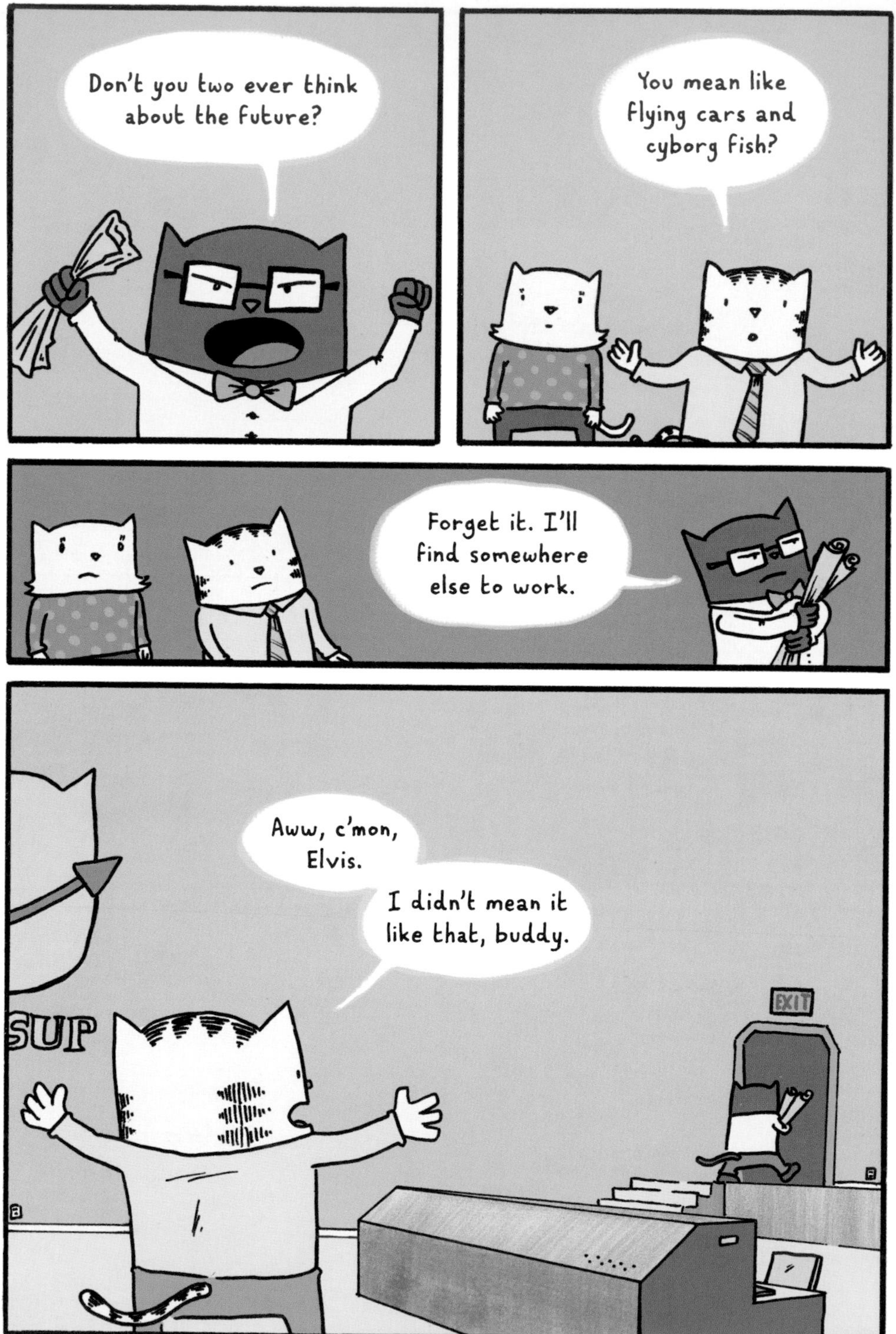
Don't you two ever think about the future?
You mean like flying cars and cyborg fish?
Forget it. I'll find somewhere else to work.
Aww, c'mon, Elvis.
I didn't mean it like that, buddy.
SUP
EXIT

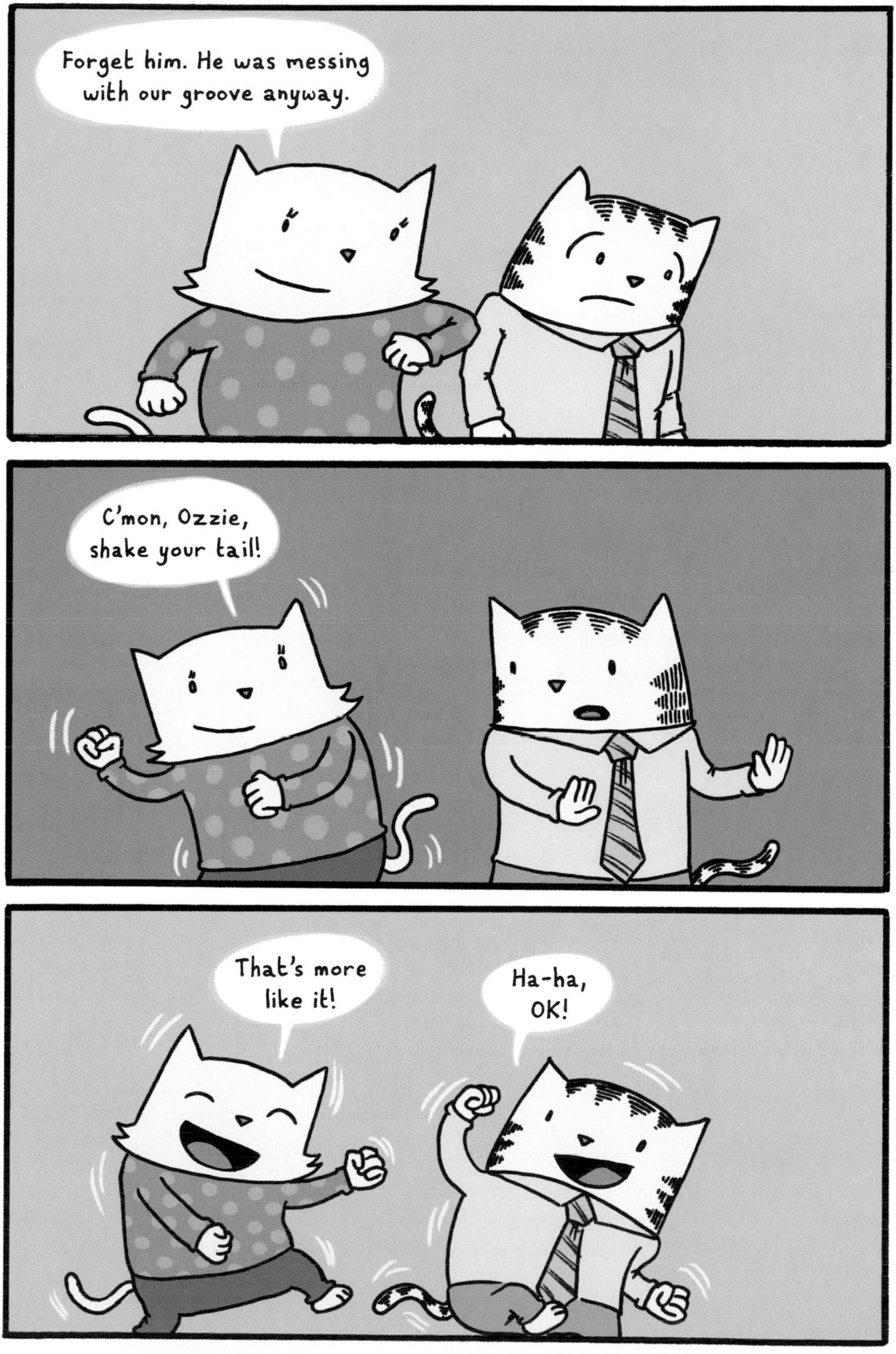
Forget him. He was messing with our groove anyway.
C'mon, Ozzie, shake your tail!
That's more like it!
Ha-ha, OK!

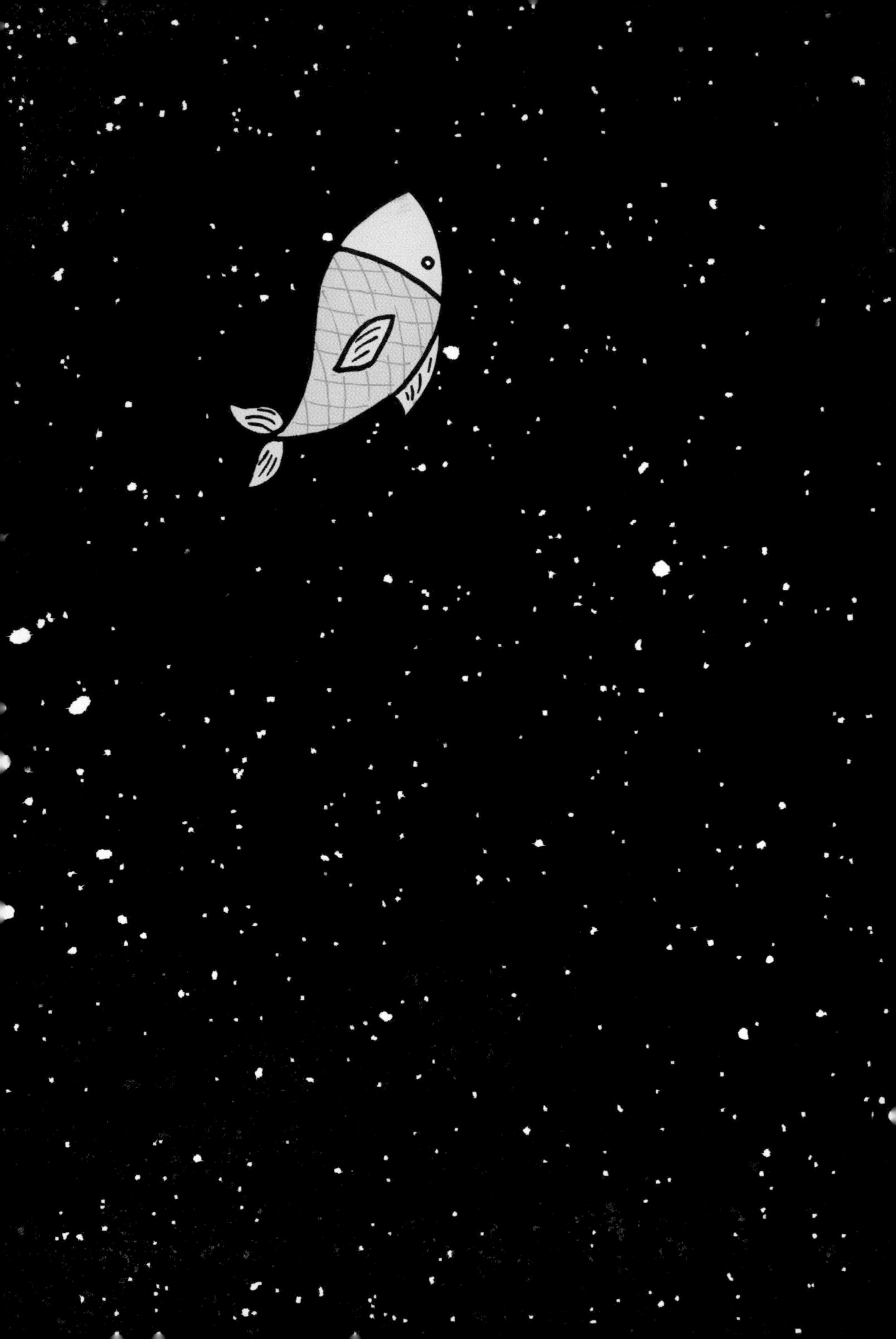

CHAPTER 3

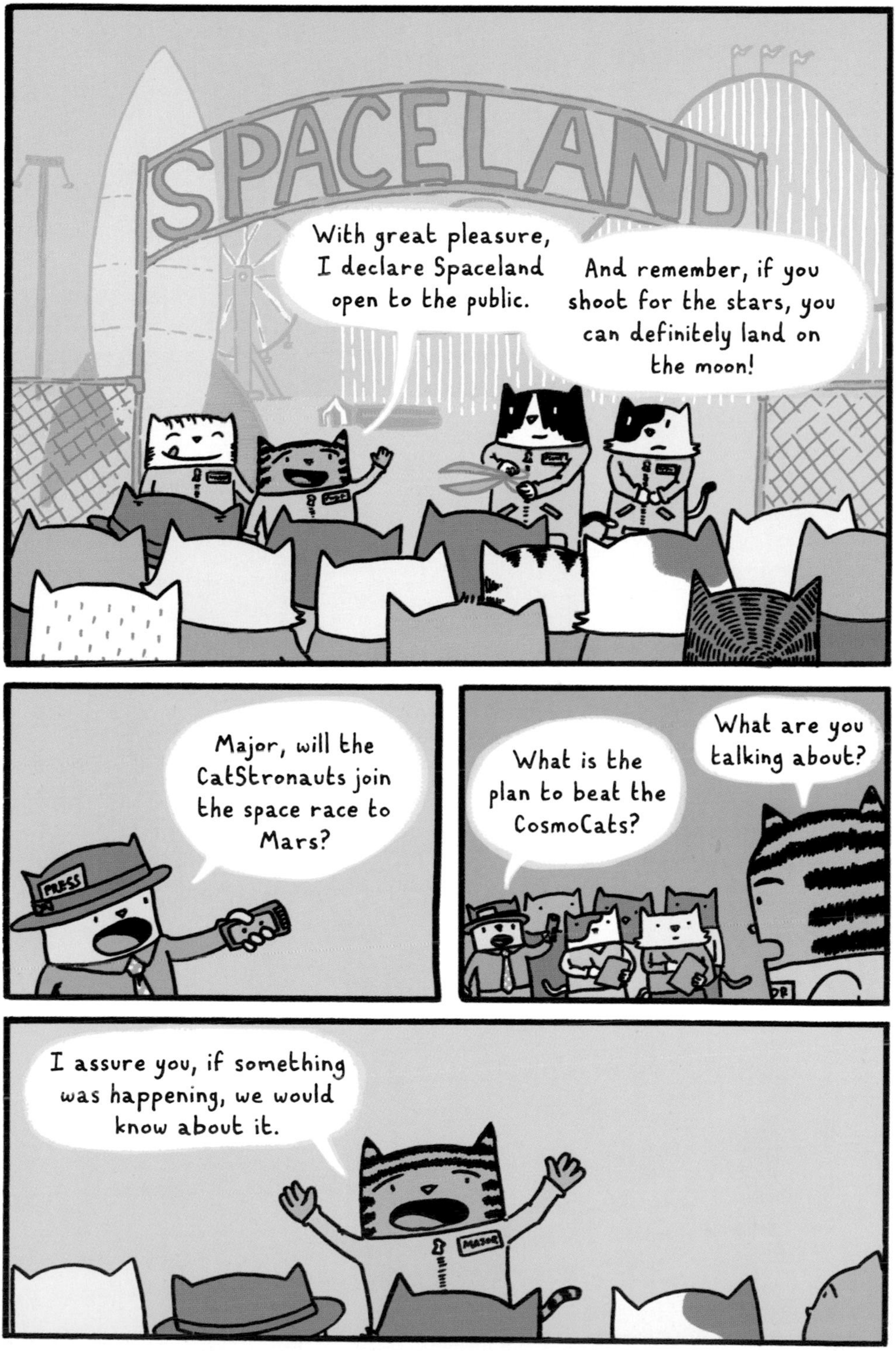
SPACELAND
With great pleasure, I declare Spaceland open to the public.
And remember, if you shoot for the stars, you can definitely land on the moon!
PRESS
Major, will the CatStronauts join the space race to Mars?
What is the plan to beat the CosmoCats?
What are you talking about?
I assure you, if something was happening, we would know about it.
MAJOR

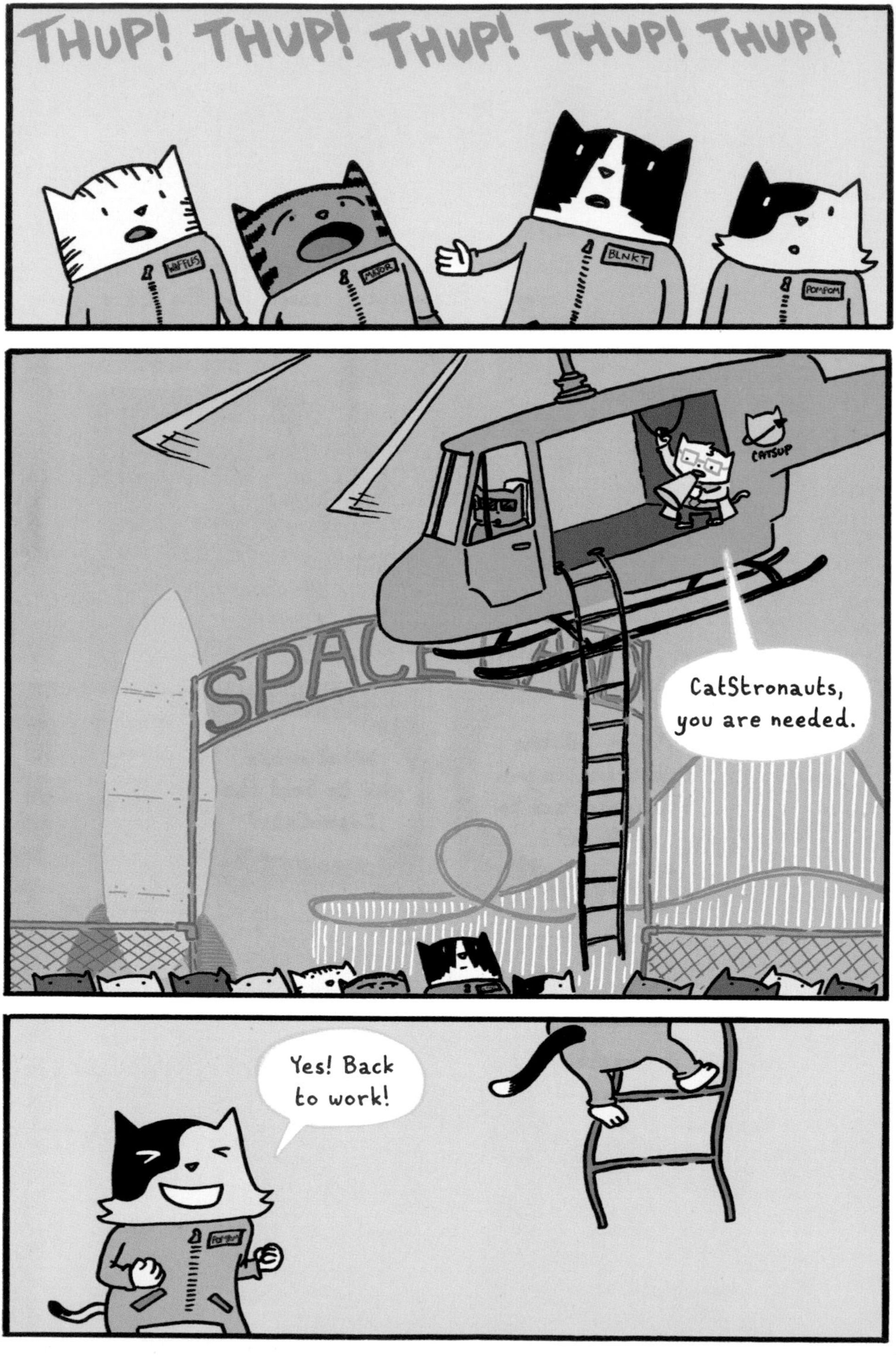
THUP! THUP! THUP! THUP! THUP!
WAFFLES
MAJOR
BLNKT
POMPOM
CATSUP
SPACE
CatStronauts, you are needed.
Yes! Back to work!

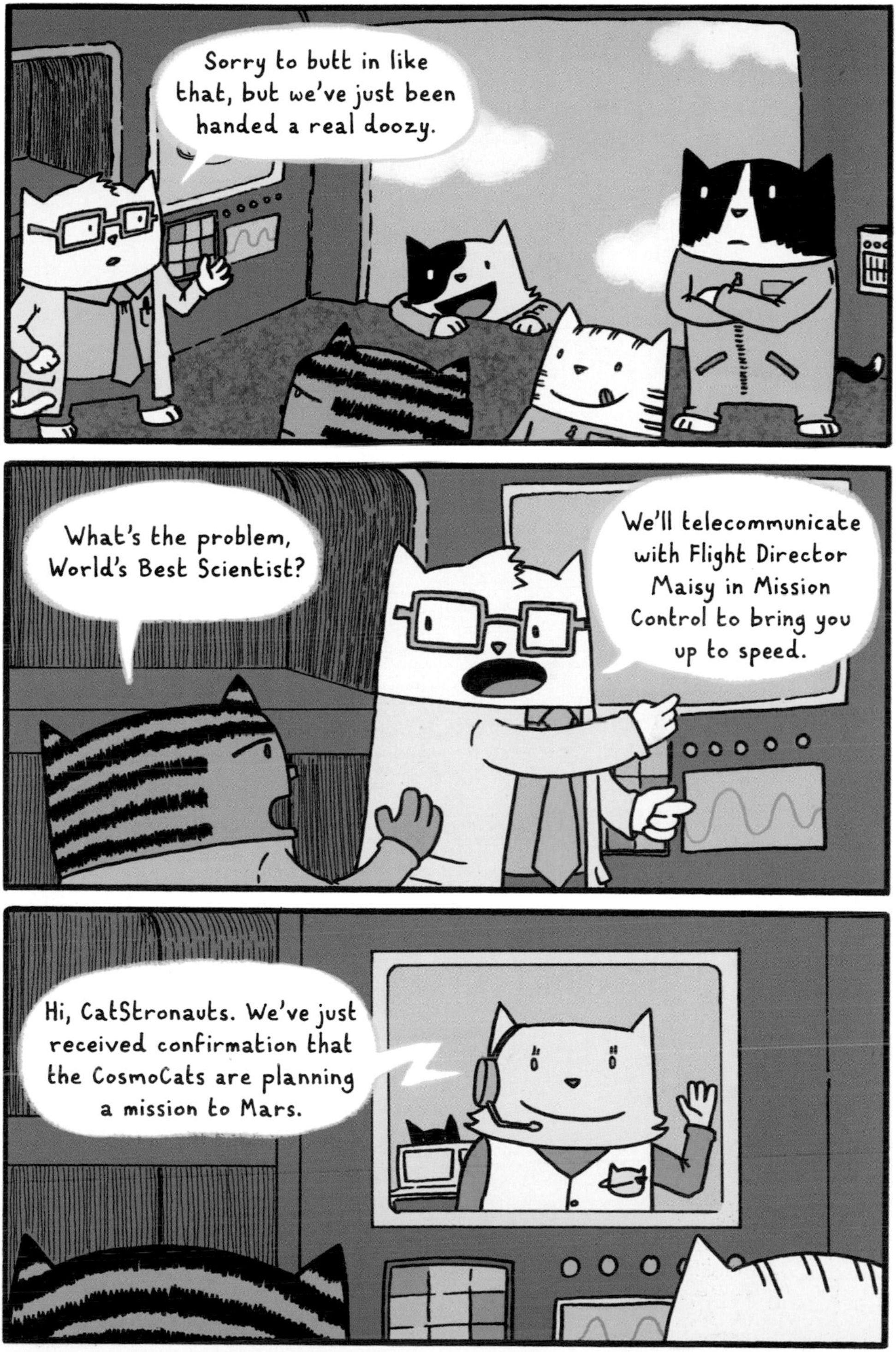
Sorry to butt in like that, but we've just been handed a real doozy.
What's the problem, World's Best Scientist?
We'll telecommunicate with Flight Director Maisy in Mission Control to bring you up to speed.
Hi, CatStronauts. We've just received confirmation that the CosmoCats are planning a mission to Mars.

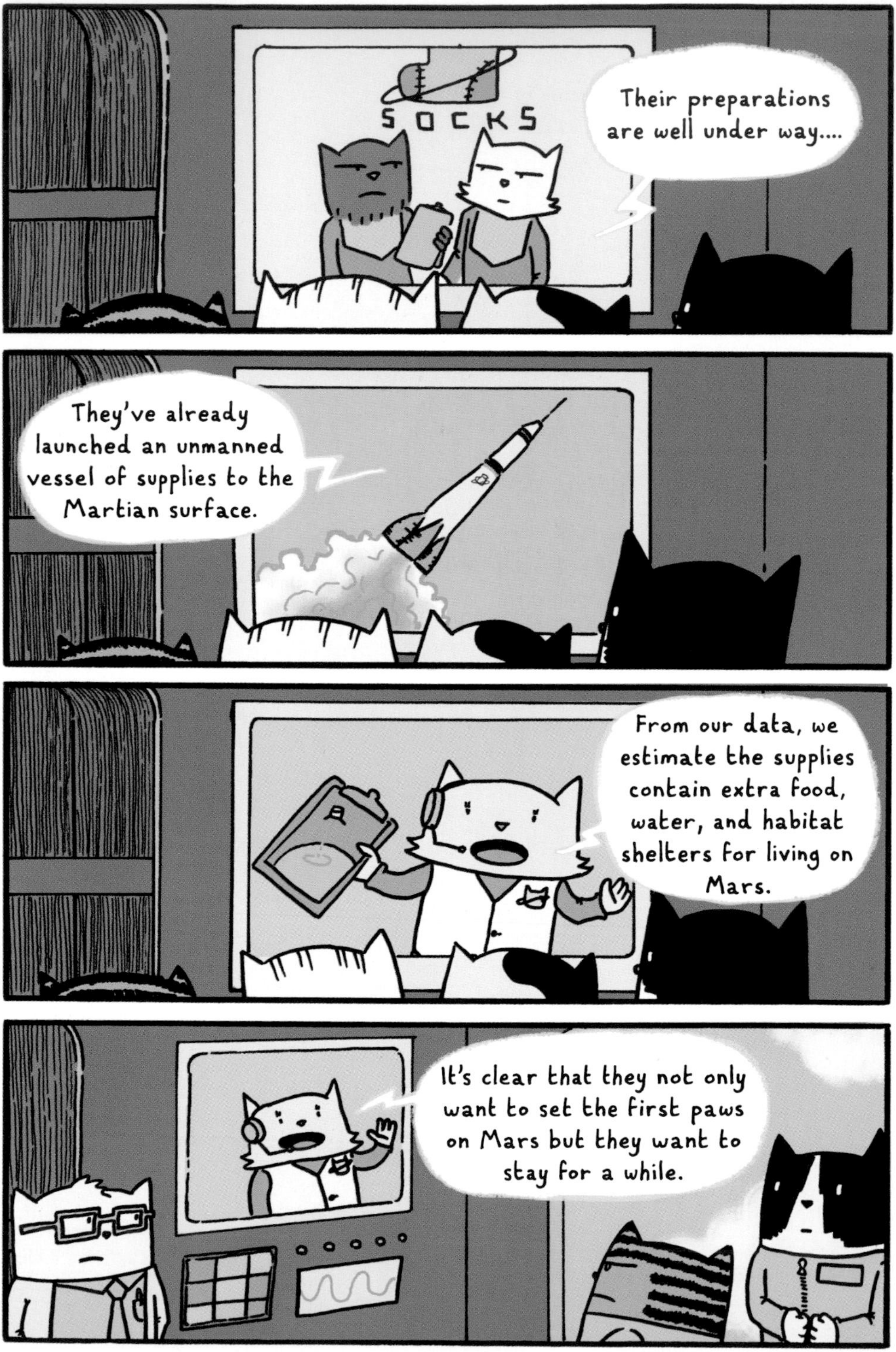
SOCKS
Their preparations are well under way....
They've already launched an unmanned vessel of supplies to the Martian surface.
From our data, we estimate the supplies contain extra food, water, and habitat shelters for living on Mars.
It's clear that they not only want to set the first paws on Mars but they want to stay for a while.

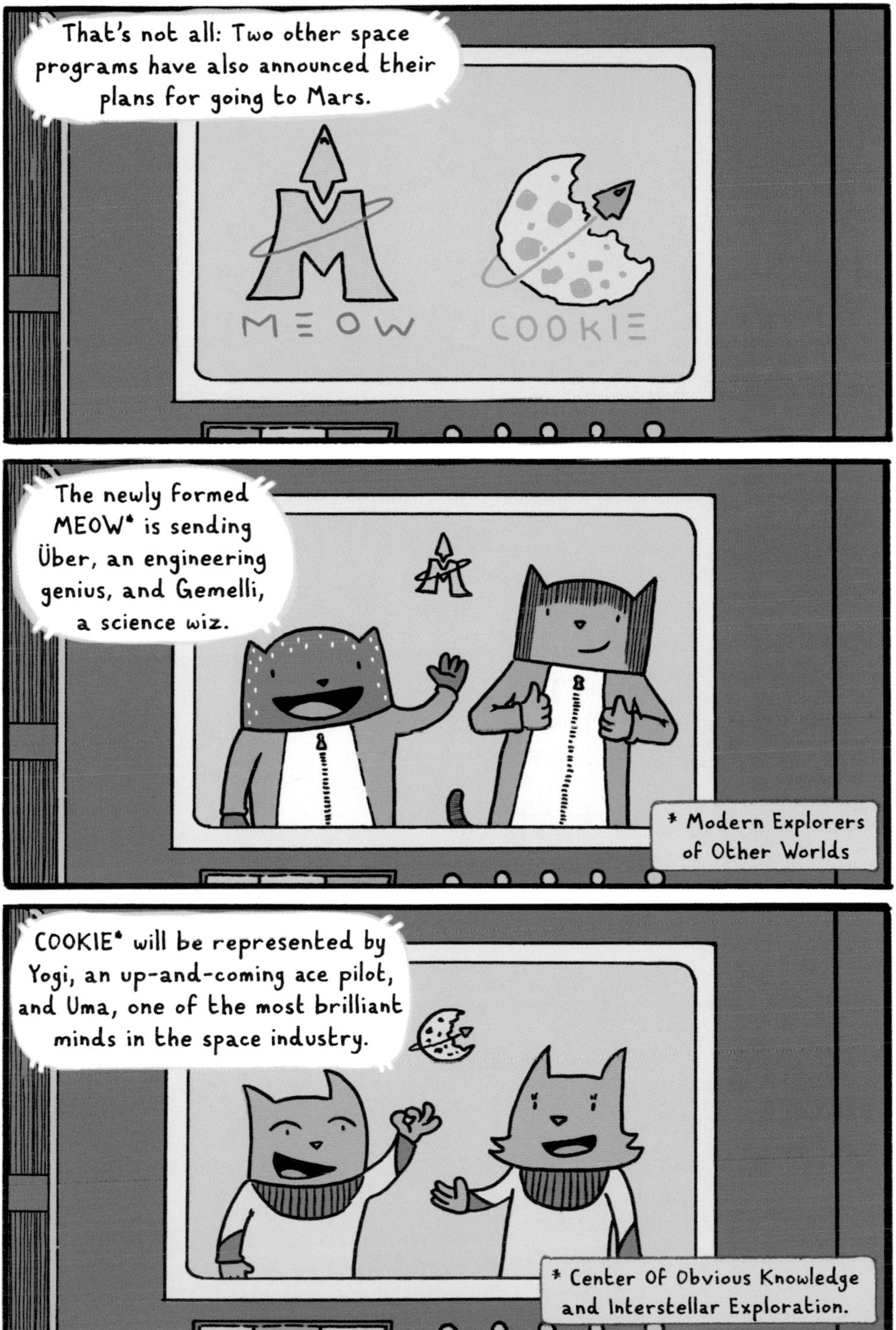
That's not all: Two other space programs have also announced their plans for going to Mars.
MEOW
COOKIE
The newly formed MEOW* is sending Über, an engineering genius, and Gemelli, a science wiz.
* Modern Explorers of Other Worlds
COOKIE* will be represented by Yogi, an up-and-coming ace pilot, and Uma, one of the most brilliant minds in the space industry.
* Center Of Obvious Knowledge and Interstellar Exploration.

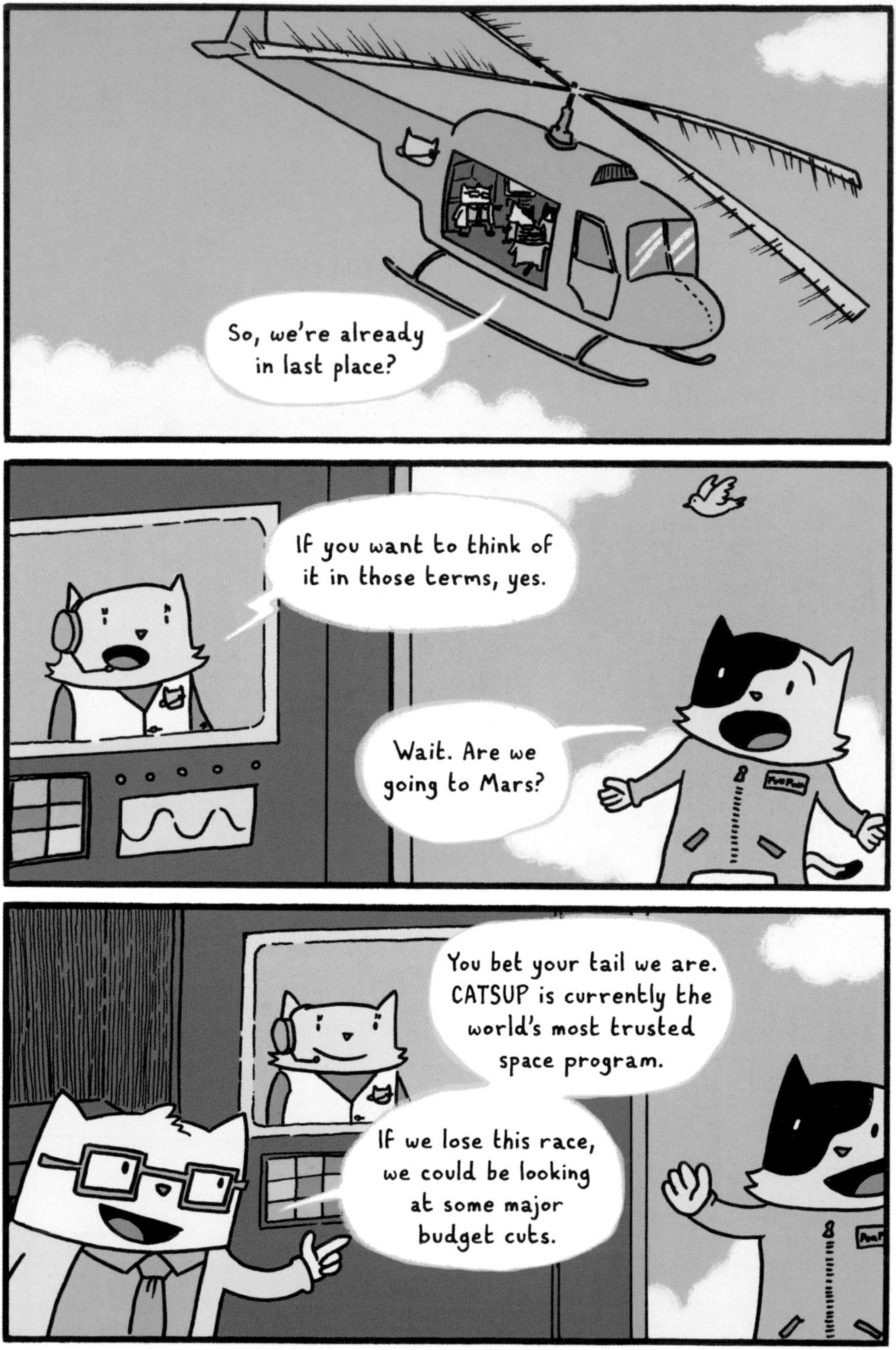
So, we're already in last place?
If you want to think of it in those terms, yes.
Wait. Are we going to Mars?
You bet your tail we are. CATSUP is currently the world's most trusted space program.
If we lose this race, we could be looking at some major budget cuts.

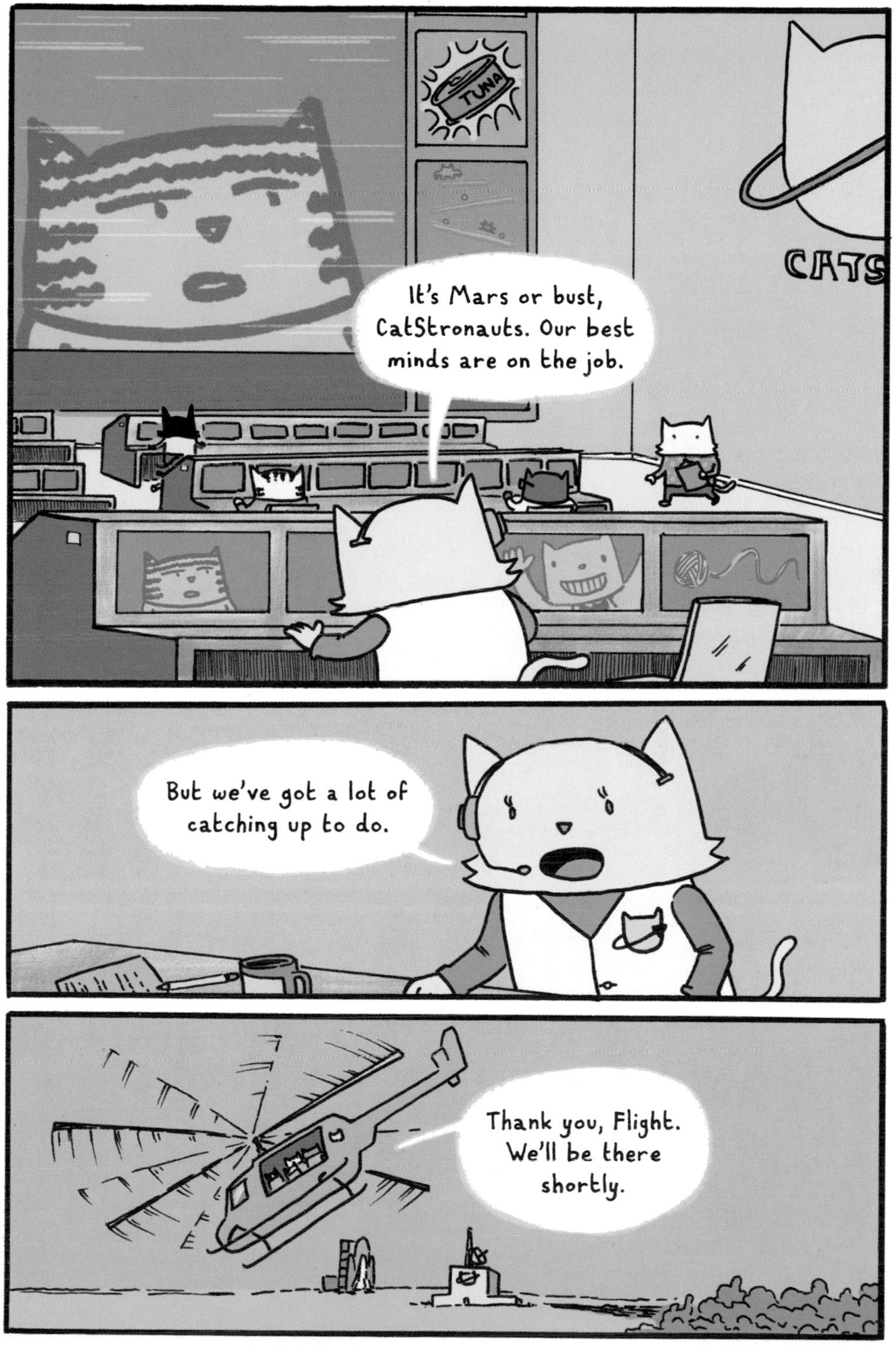
TUNA
CATS
It's Mars or bust, CatStronauts. Our best minds are on the job.
But we've got a lot of catching up to do.
Thank you, Flight. We'll be there shortly.

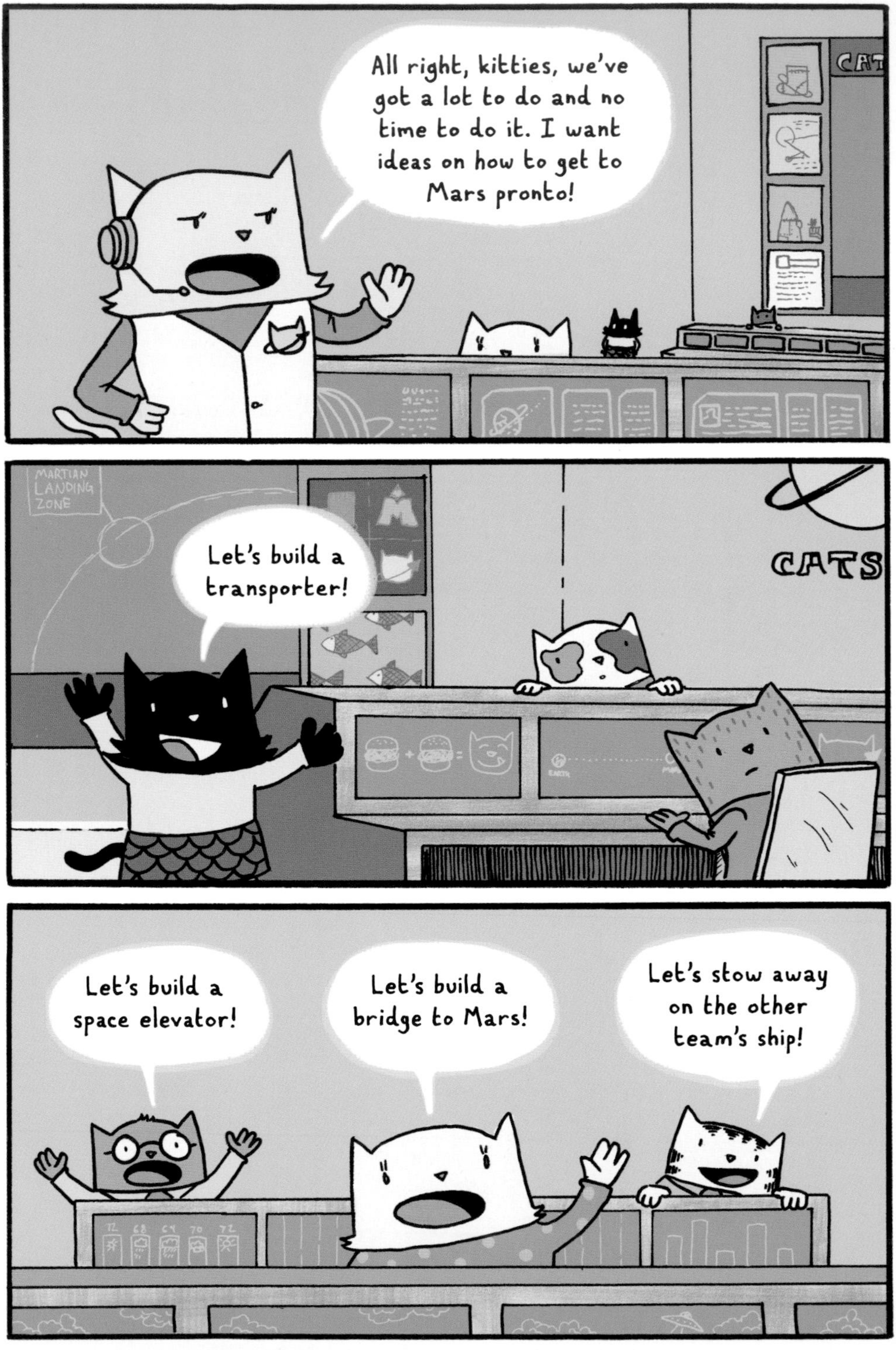
All right, kitties, we've got a lot to do and no time to do it. I want ideas on how to get to Mars pronto!
MARTIAN LANDING ZONE
CATS
Let's build a transporter!
Let's build a space elevator!
Let's build a bridge to Mars!
Let's stow away on the other team's ship!

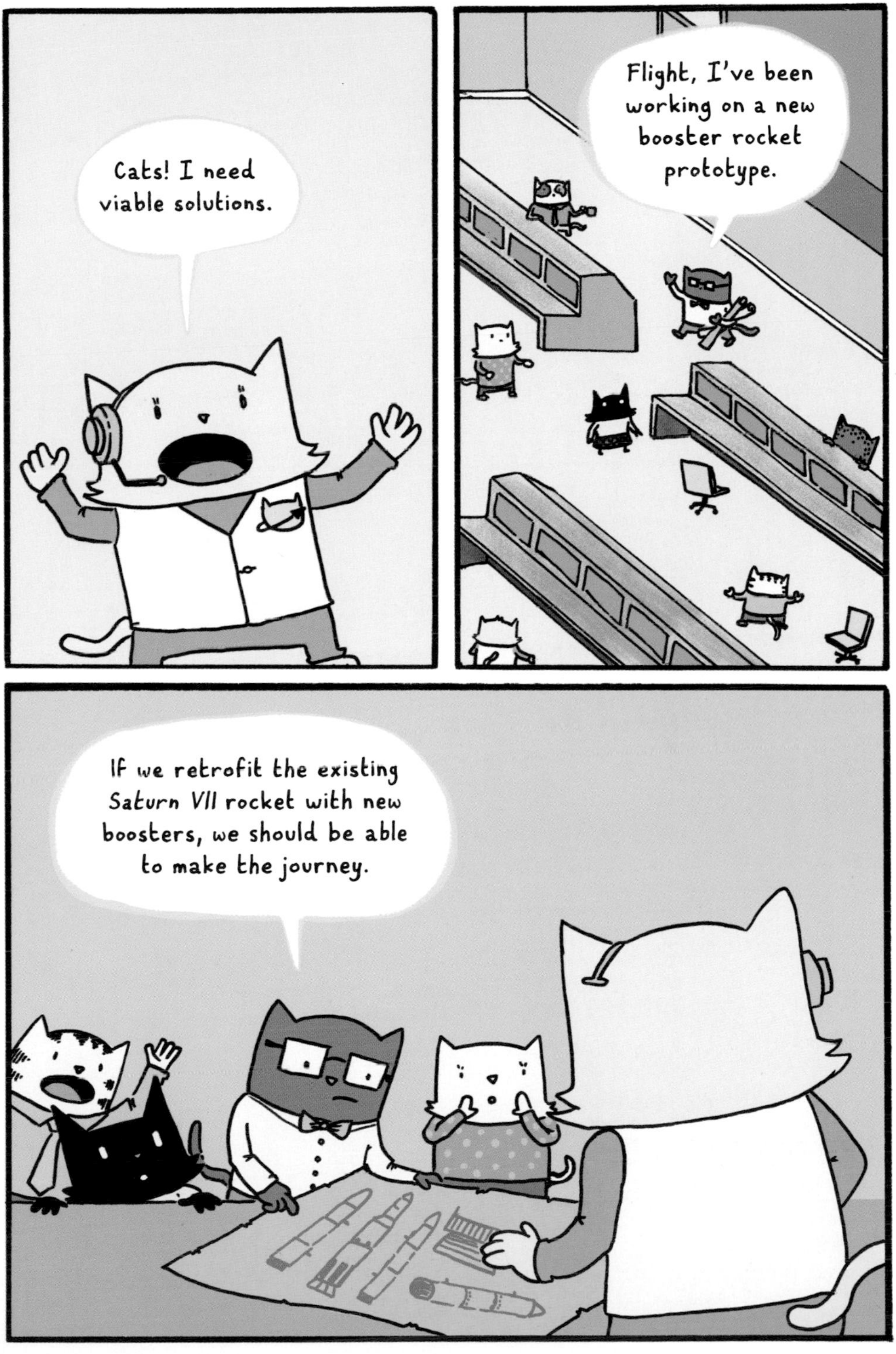
Cats! I need viable solutions.
Flight, I've been working on a new booster rocket prototype.
If we retrofit the existing Saturn VII rocket with new boosters, we should be able to make the journey.

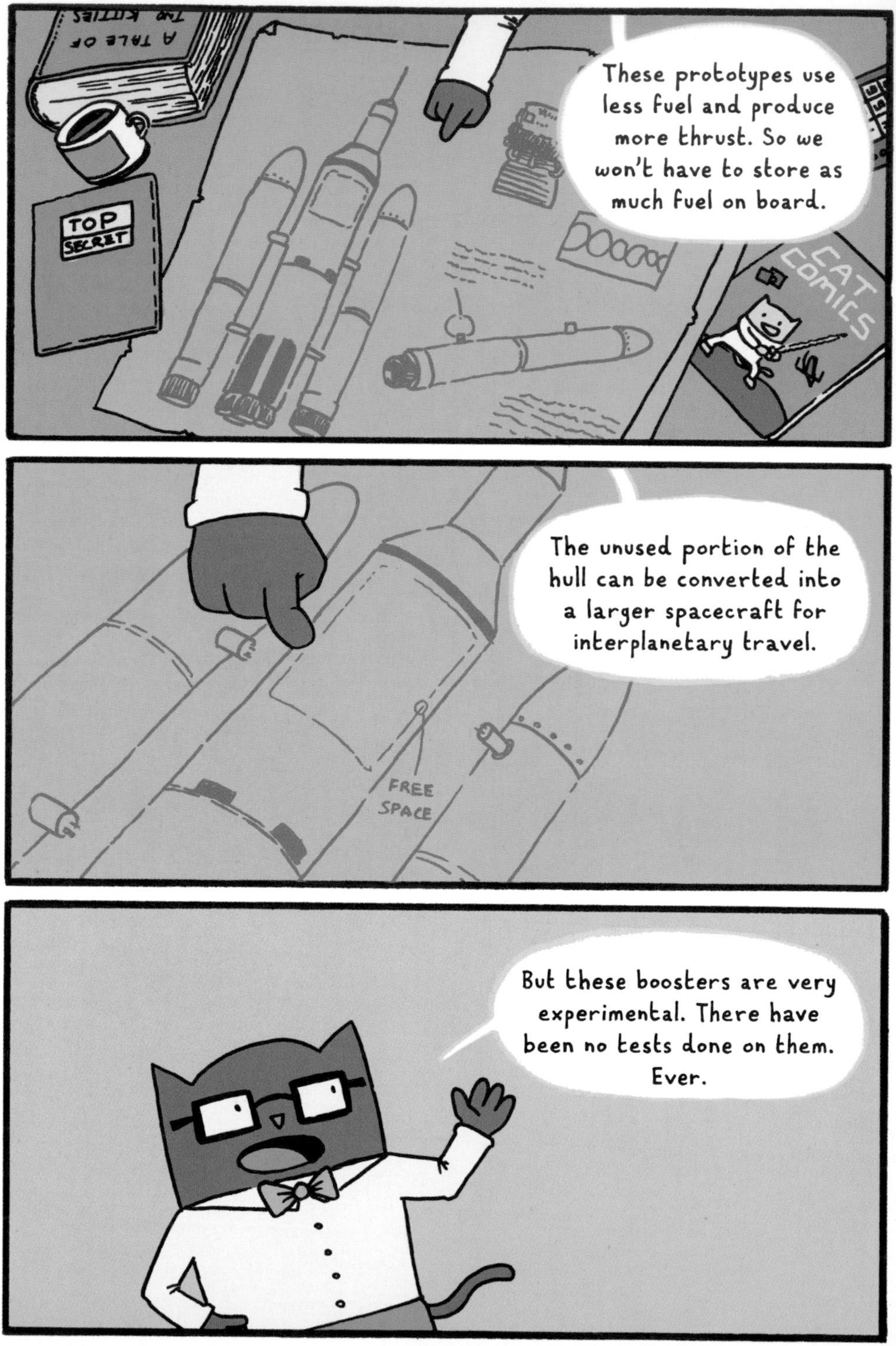

A TALE OF TWO KITTIES
TOP SECRET
These prototypes use less fuel and produce more thrust. So we won't have to store as much fuel on board.
CAT COMICS
The unused portion of the hull can be converted into a larger spacecraft for interplanetary travel.
FREE SPACE
But these boosters are very experimental. There have been no tests done on them. Ever.

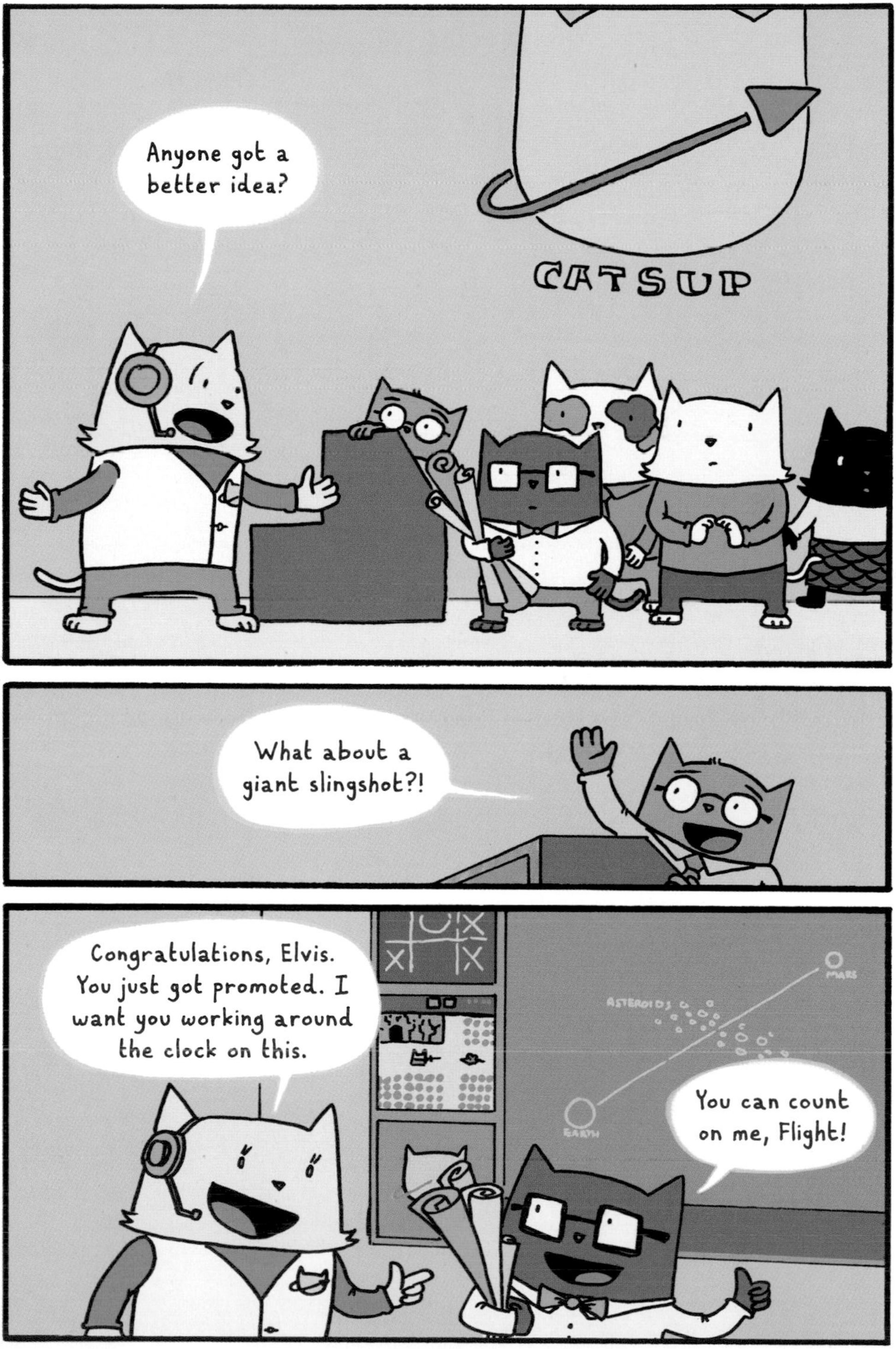
CATSUP
Anyone got a better idea?
What about a giant slingshot?!
Congratulations, Elvis. You just got promoted. I want you working around the clock on this.
MARS
ASTEROIDS
EARTH
You can count on me, Flight!

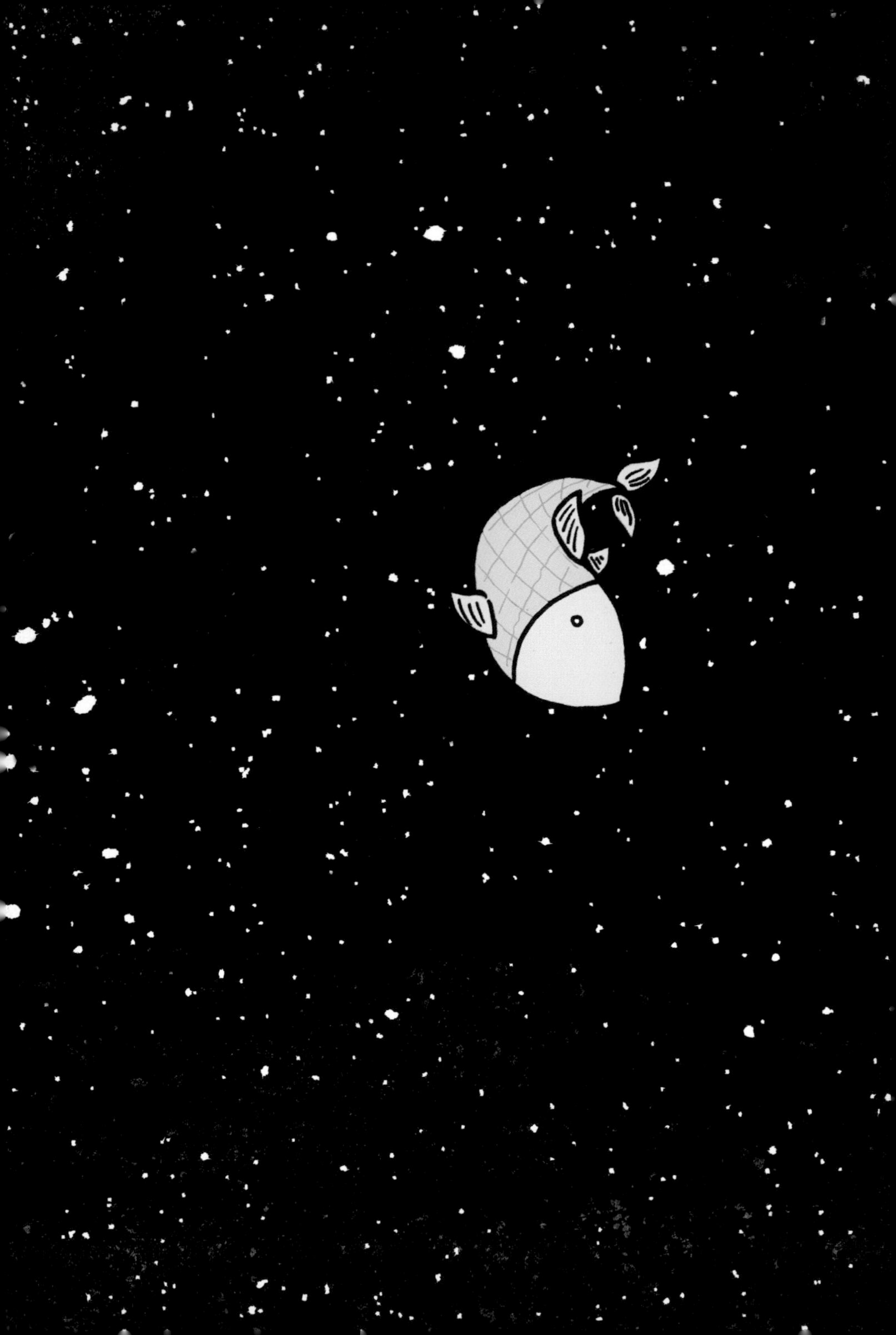

CHAPTER 4

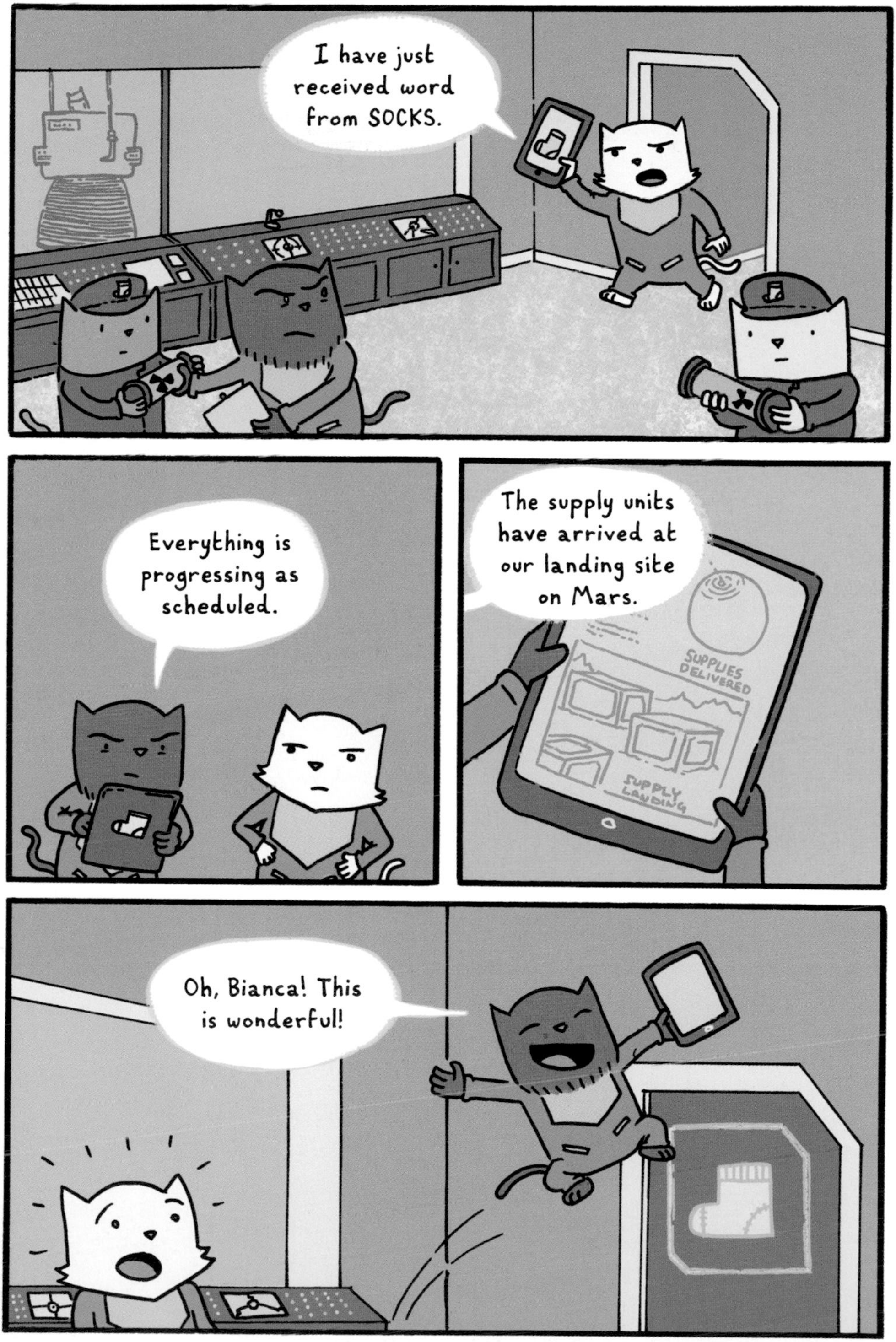
I have just received word from SOCKS.
Everything is progressing as scheduled.
The supply units have arrived at our landing site on Mars.
SUPPLIES DELIVERED
SUPPLY LANDING
Oh, Bianca! This is wonderful!

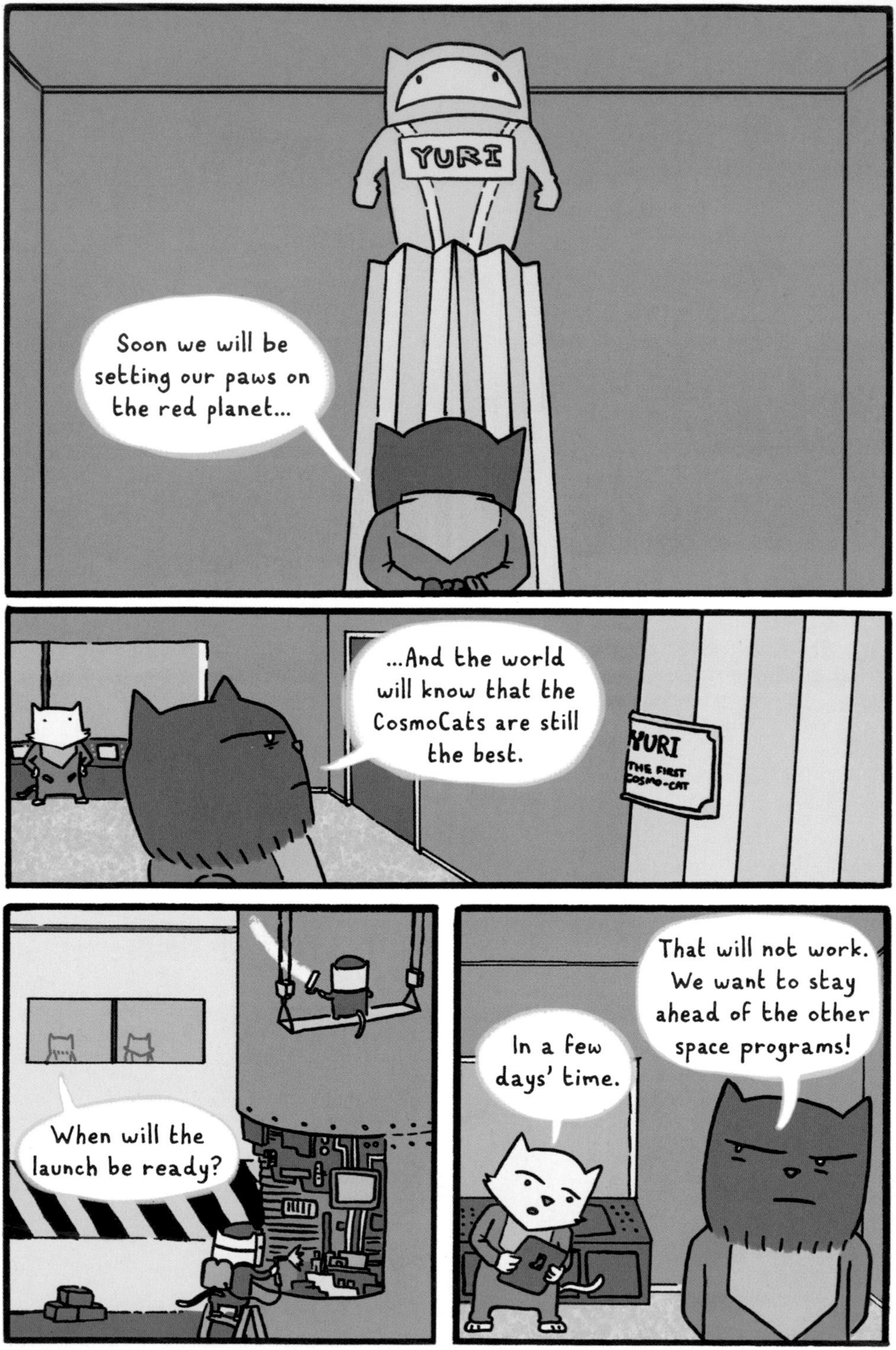
YURI
Soon we will be setting our paws on the red planet...
...And the world will know that the CosmoCats are still the best.
YURI
THE FIRST COSMO-CAT
When will the launch be ready?
In a few days' time.
That will not work. We want to stay ahead of the other space programs!

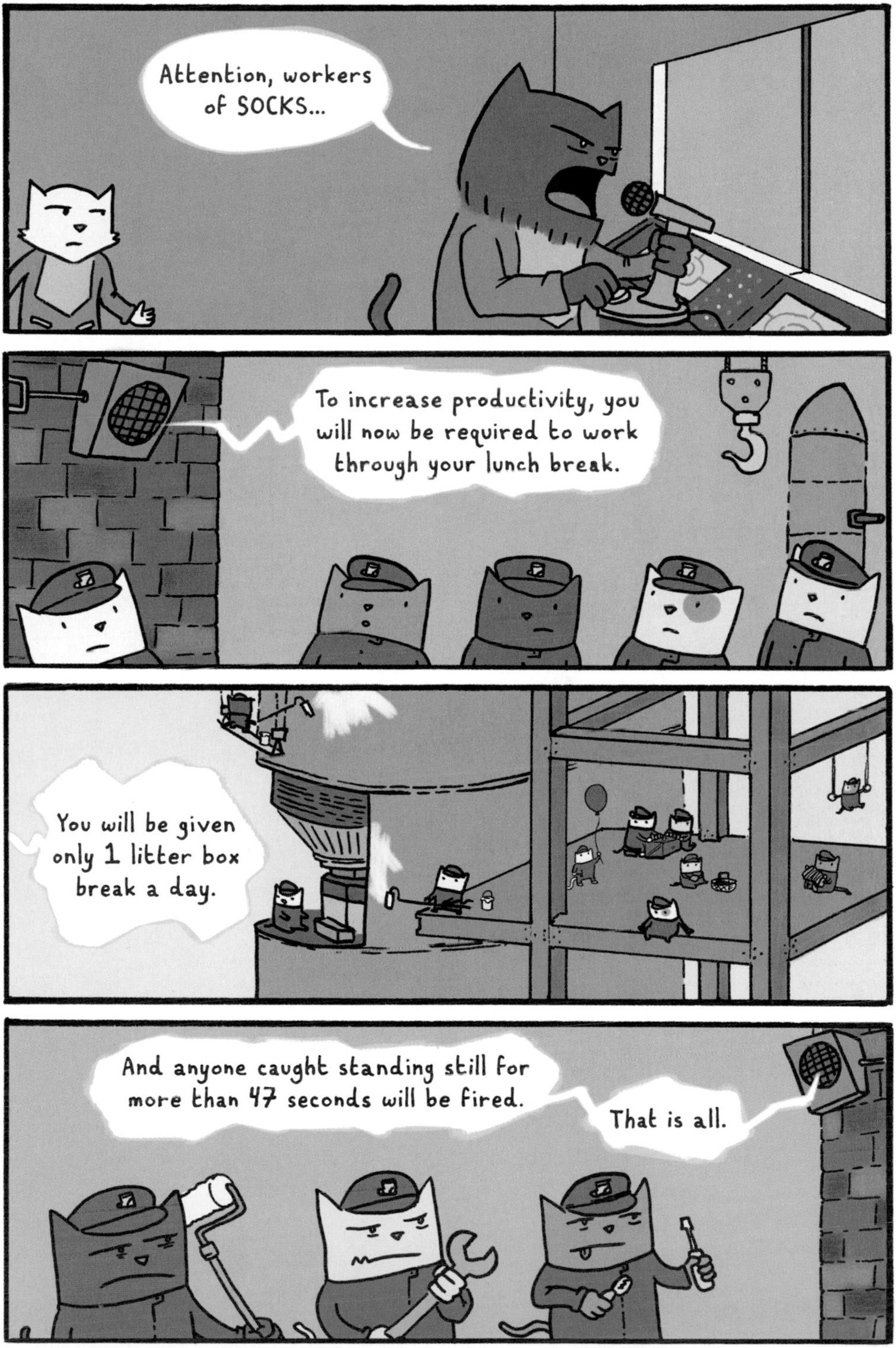
Attention, workers of SOCKS...
To increase productivity, you will now be required to work through your lunch break.
You will be given only 1 litter box break a day.
And anyone caught standing still for more than 47 seconds will be fired.
That is all.

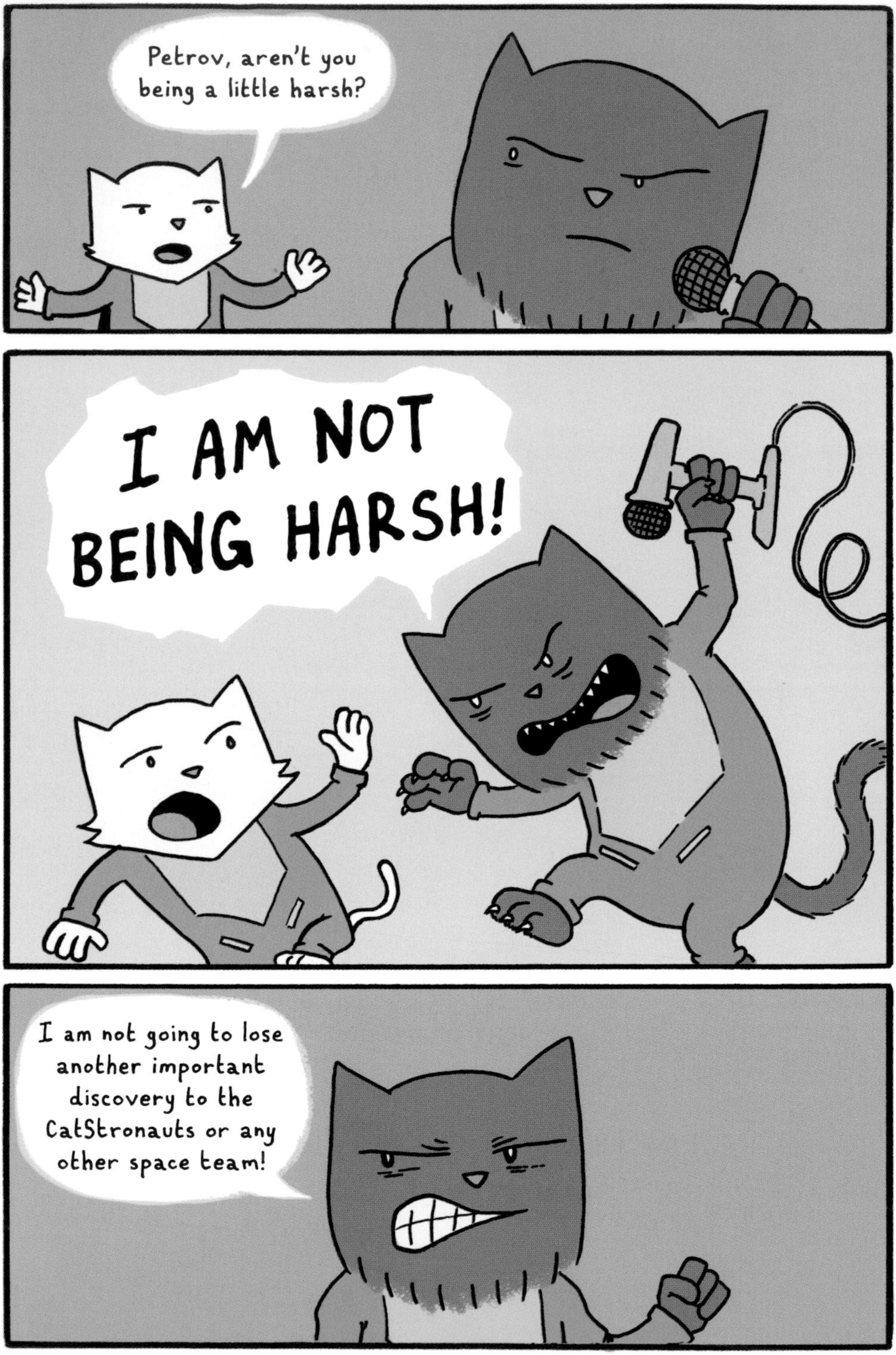
Petrov, aren't you being a little harsh?
I AM NOT BEING HARSH!
I am not going to lose another important discovery to the CatStronauts or any other space team!

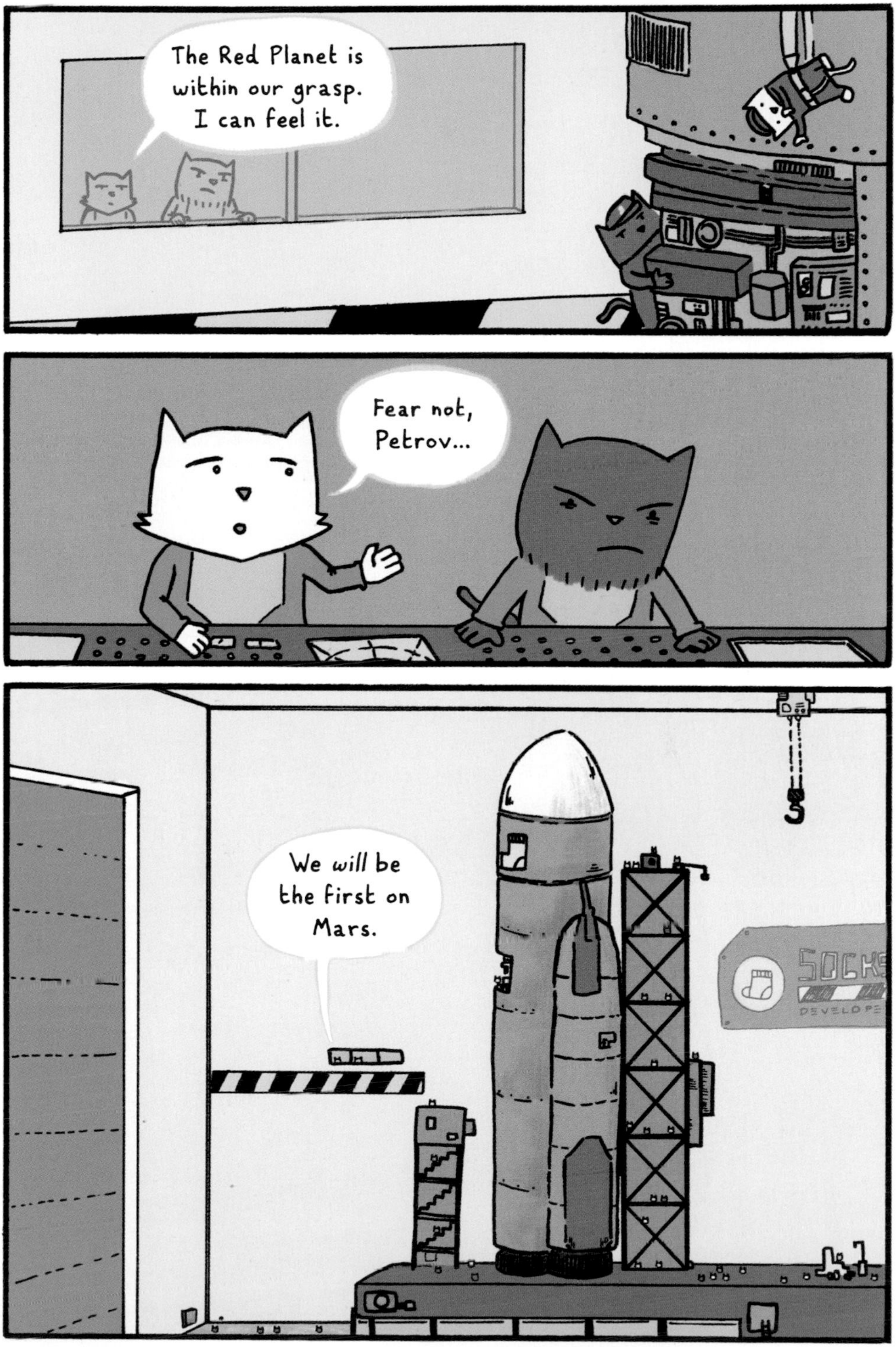
The Red Planet is within our grasp. I can feel it.
Fear not, Petrov...
We *will* be the first on Mars.

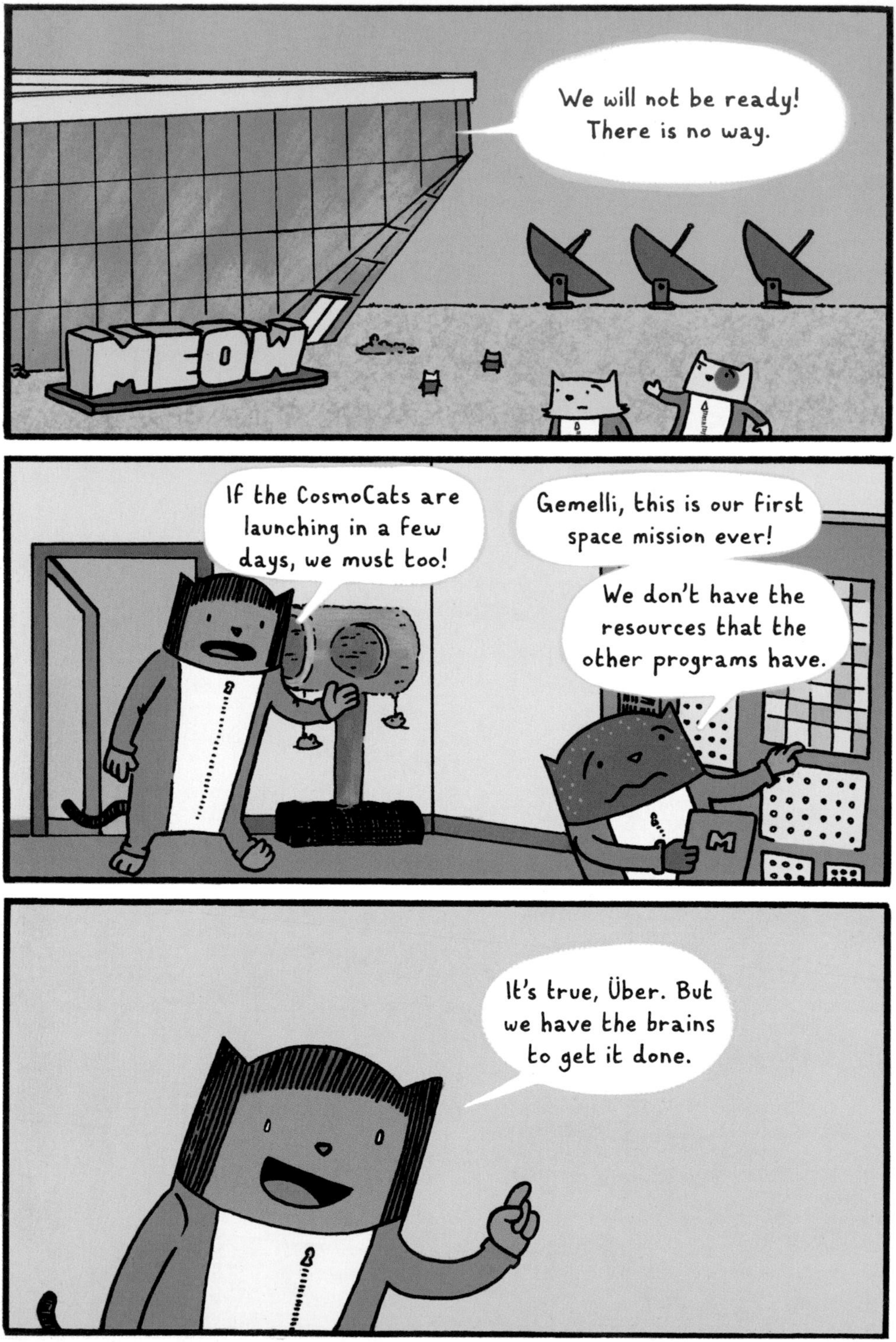
We will not be ready! There is no way.
MEOW
If the CosmoCats are launching in a few days, we must too!
Gemelli, this is our first space mission ever!
We don't have the resources that the other programs have.
M
It's true, Über. But we have the brains to get it done.

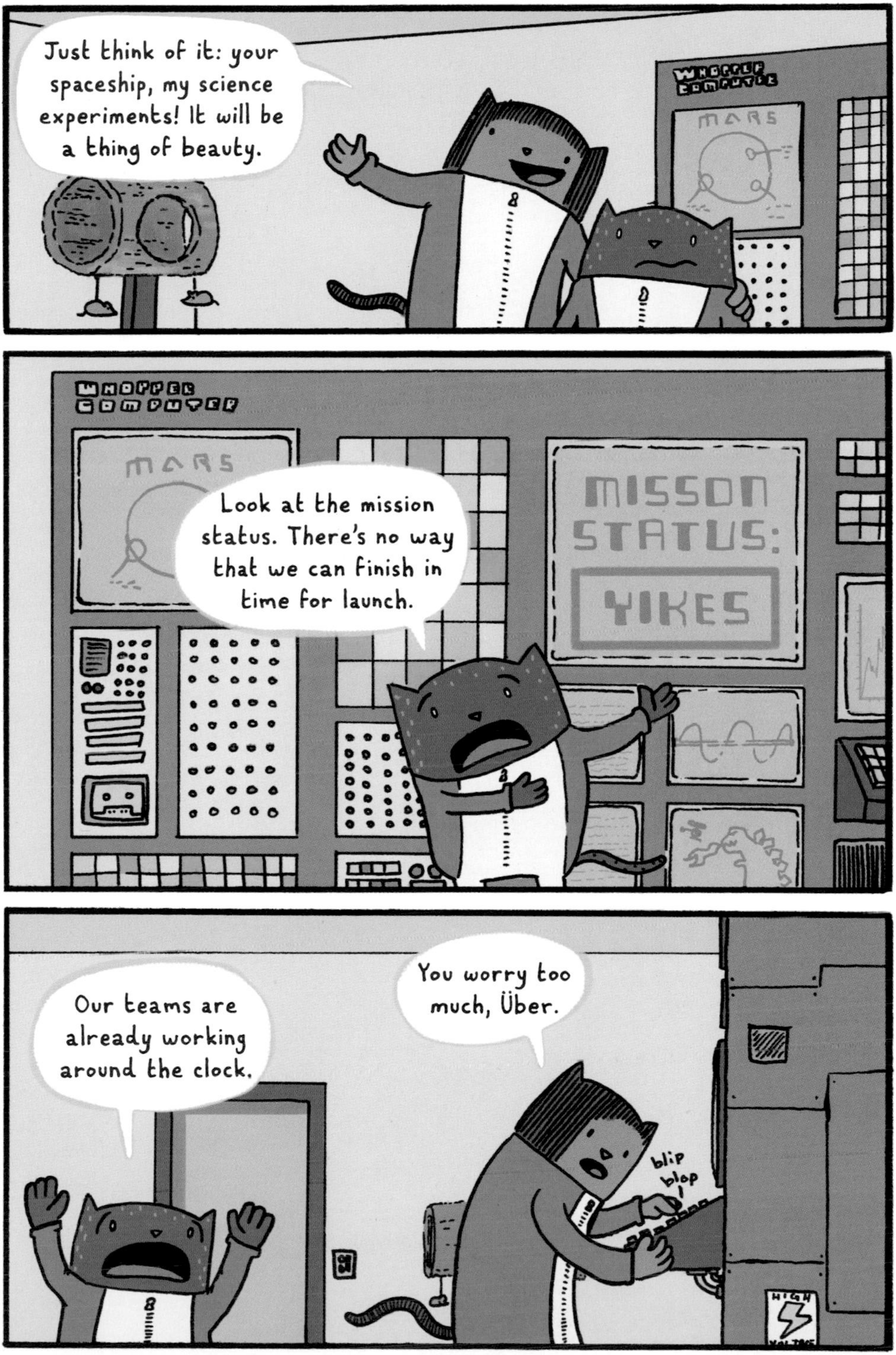
Just think of it: your spaceship, my science experiments! It will be a thing of beauty.
MARS
MARS
Look at the mission status. There's no way that we can finish in time for launch.
MISSON
STATUS:
YIKES
Our teams are already working around the clock.
You worry too much, Über.
blip
blop
!
HIGH

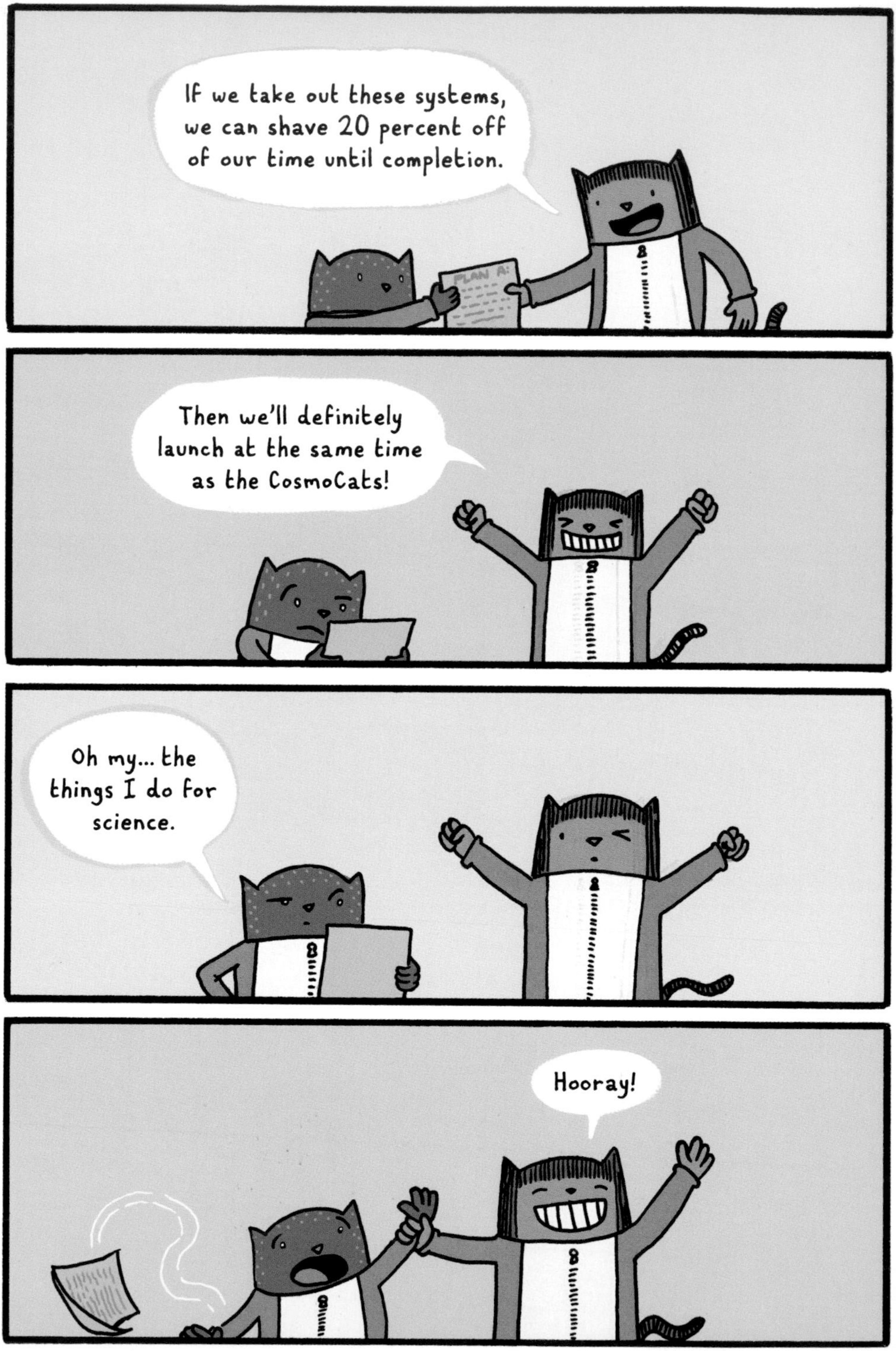
If we take out these systems, we can shave 20 percent off of our time until completion.
PLAN A:
Then we'll definitely launch at the same time as the CosmoCats!
Oh my... the things I do for science.
Hooray!

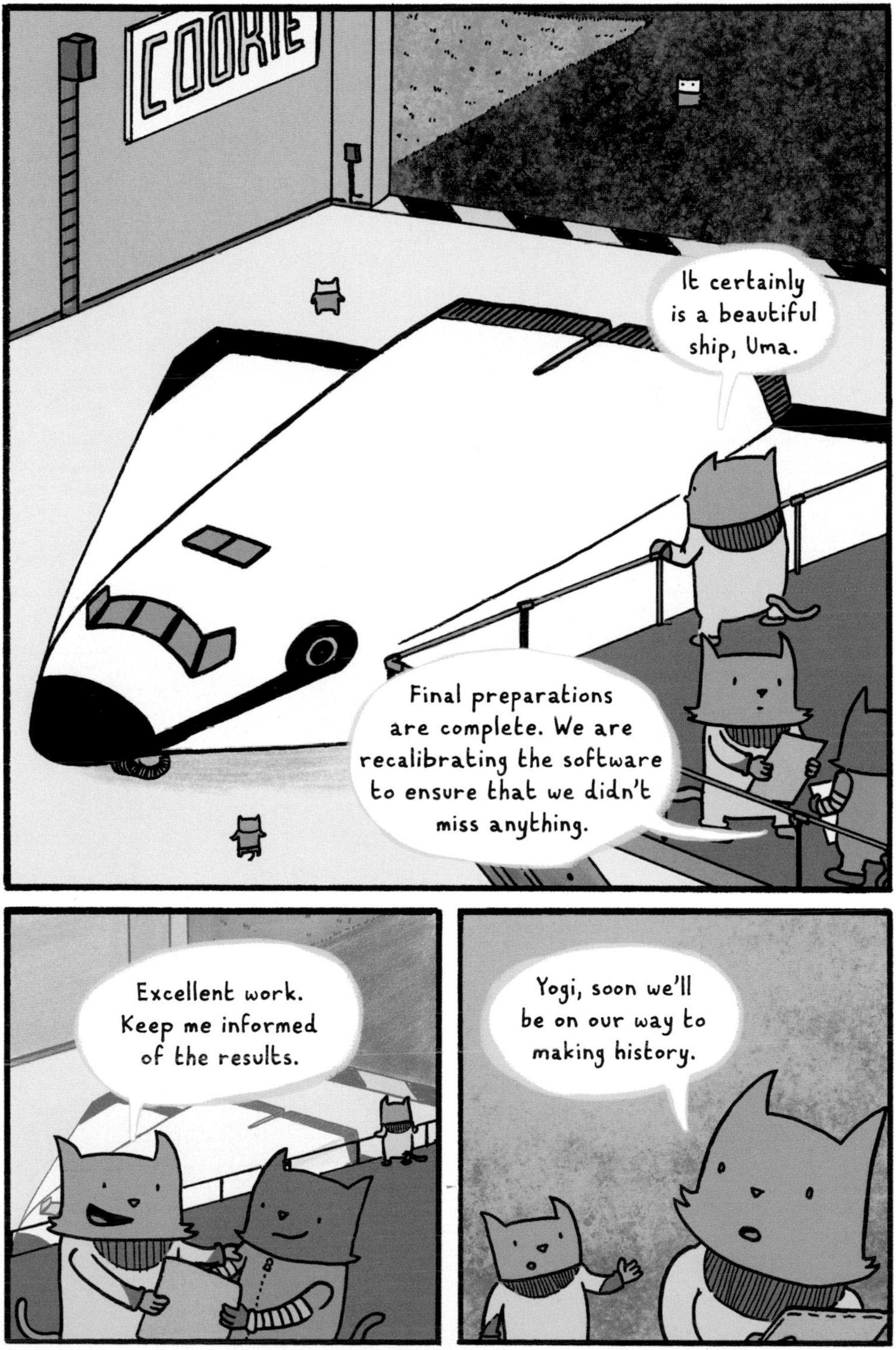
COOKIE
It certainly is a beautiful ship, Uma.
Final preparations are complete. We are recalibrating the software to ensure that we didn't miss anything.
Excellent work. Keep me informed of the results.
Yogi, soon we'll be on our way to making history.

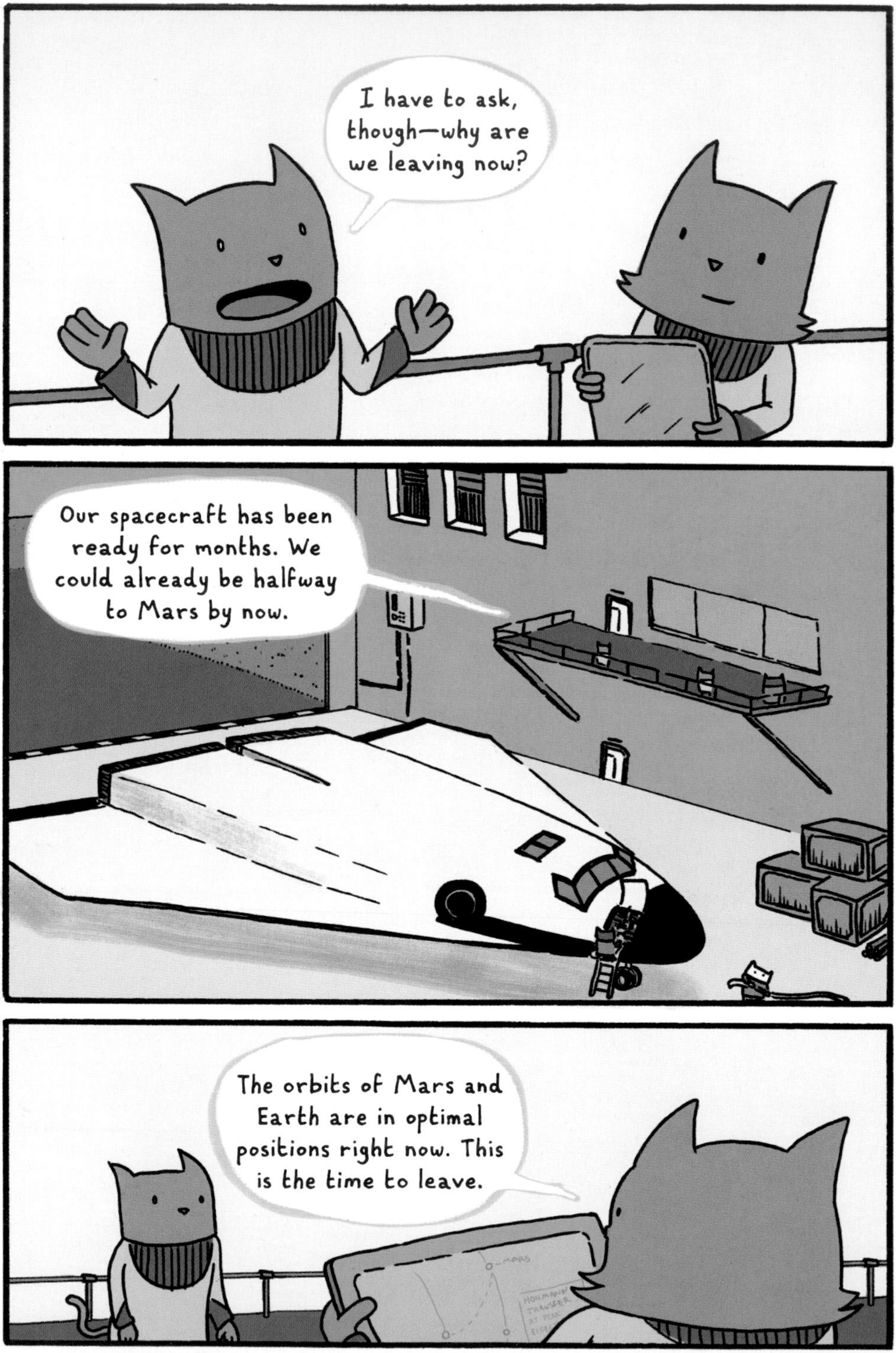
I have to ask, though—why are we leaving now?
Our spacecraft has been ready for months. We could already be halfway to Mars by now.
The orbits of Mars and Earth are in optimal positions right now. This is the time to leave.

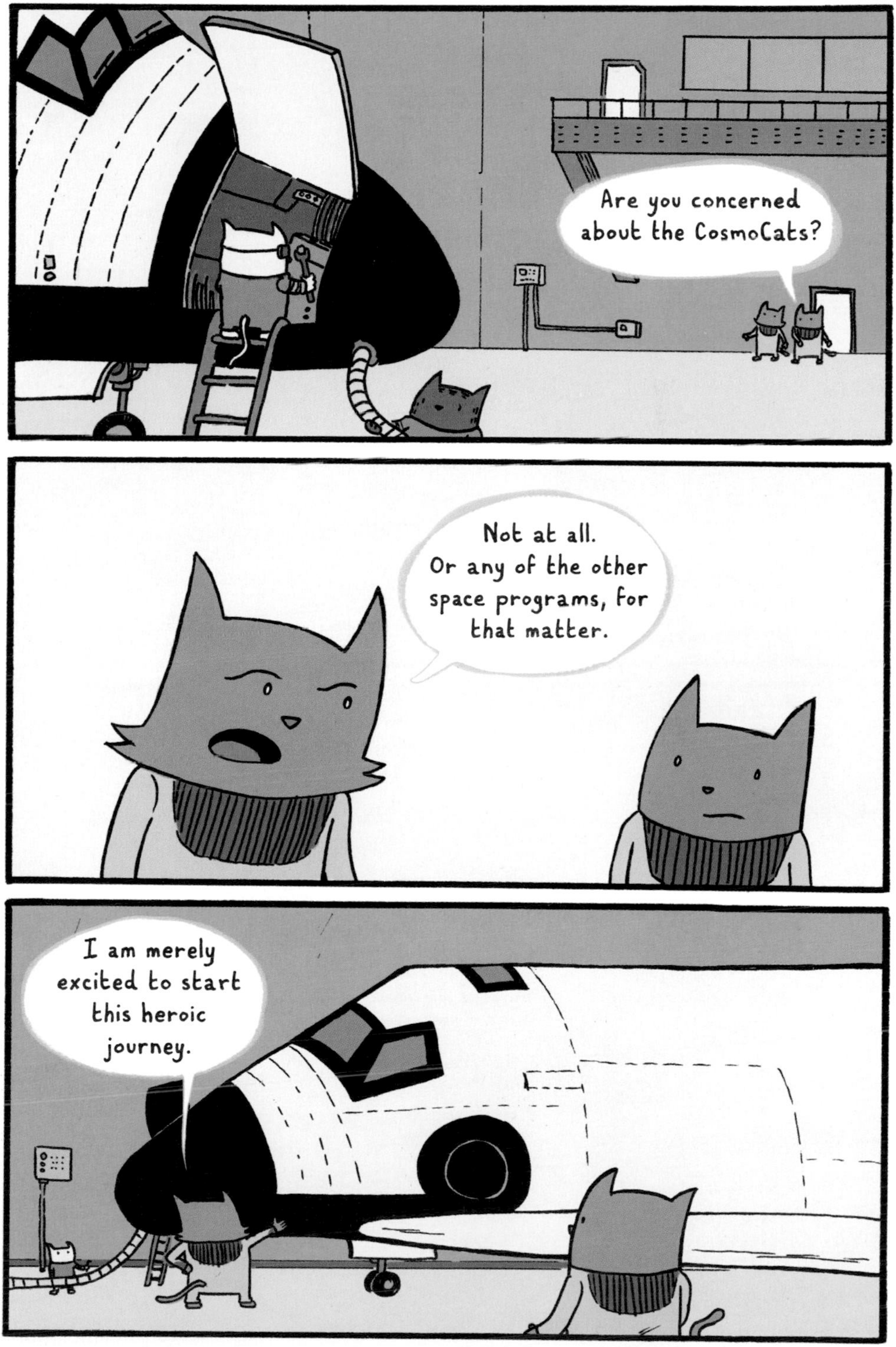
Are you concerned about the CosmoCats?
Not at all. Or any of the other space programs, for that matter.
I am merely excited to start this heroic journey.

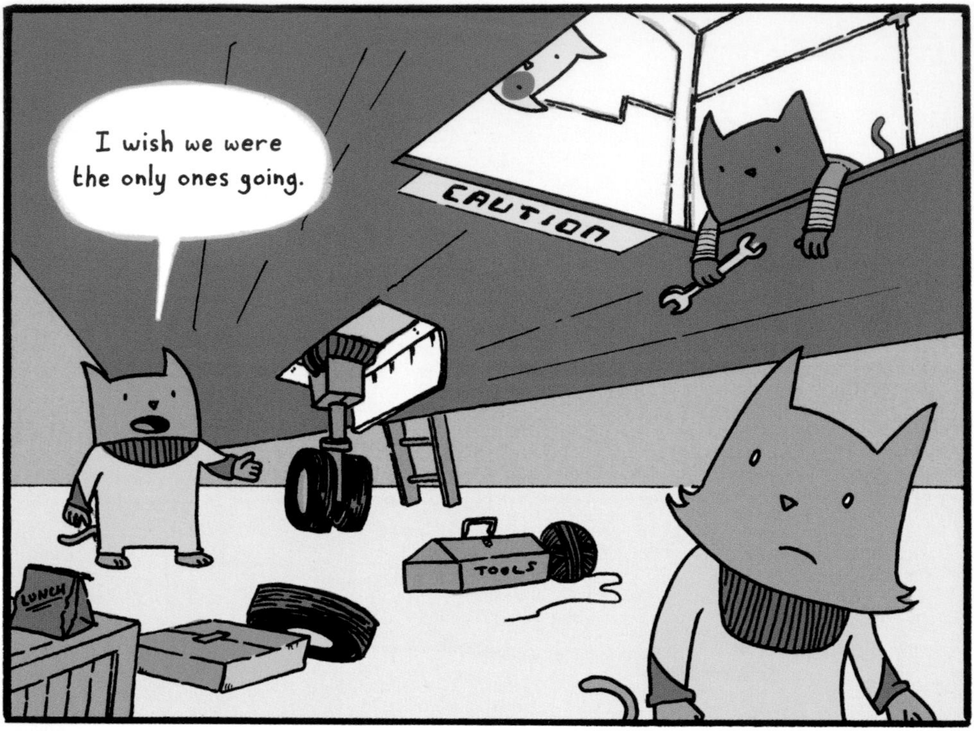
I wish we were the only ones going.
CAUTION
LUNCH
TOOLS

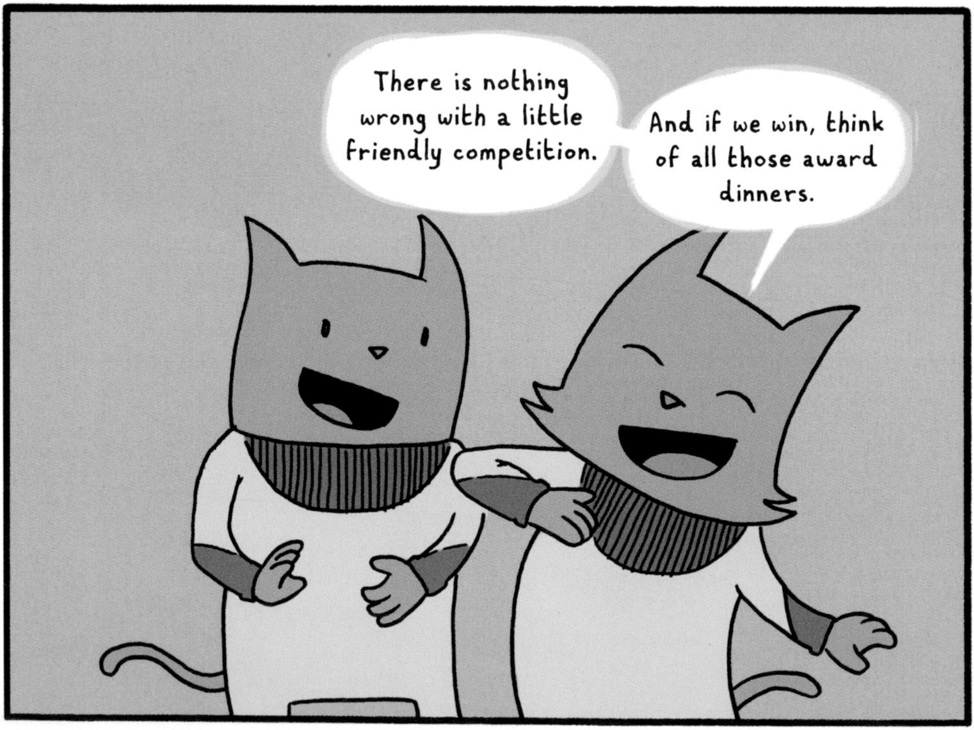
There is nothing wrong with a little friendly competition.
And if we win, think of all those award dinners.

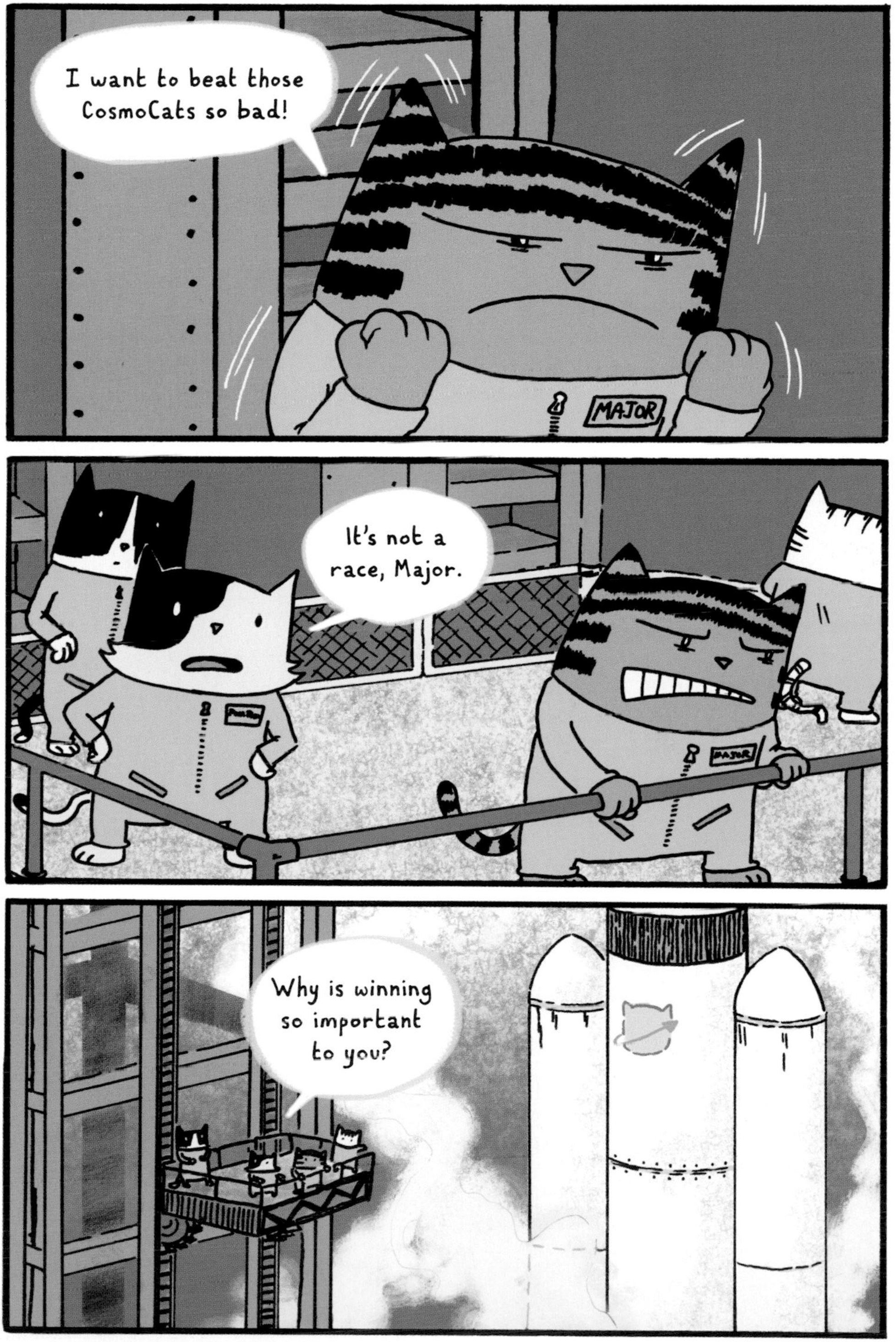
I want to beat those CosmoCats so bad!
MAJOR
It's not a race, Major.
Why is winning so important to you?

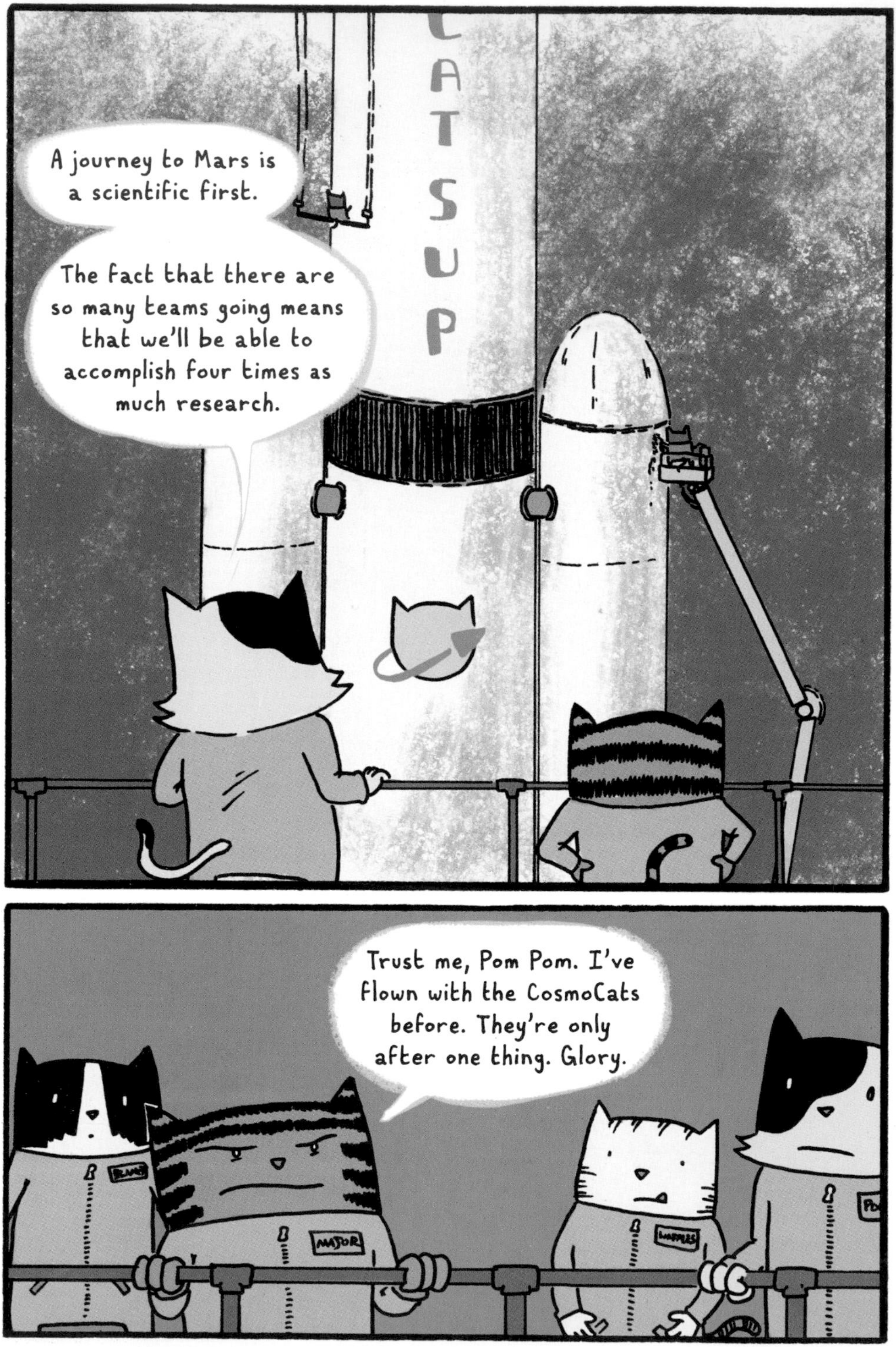
A journey to Mars is a scientific first.
The fact that there are so many teams going means that we'll be able to accomplish four times as much research.
Trust me, Pom Pom. I've flown with the CosmoCats before. They're only after one thing. Glory.
MAJOR

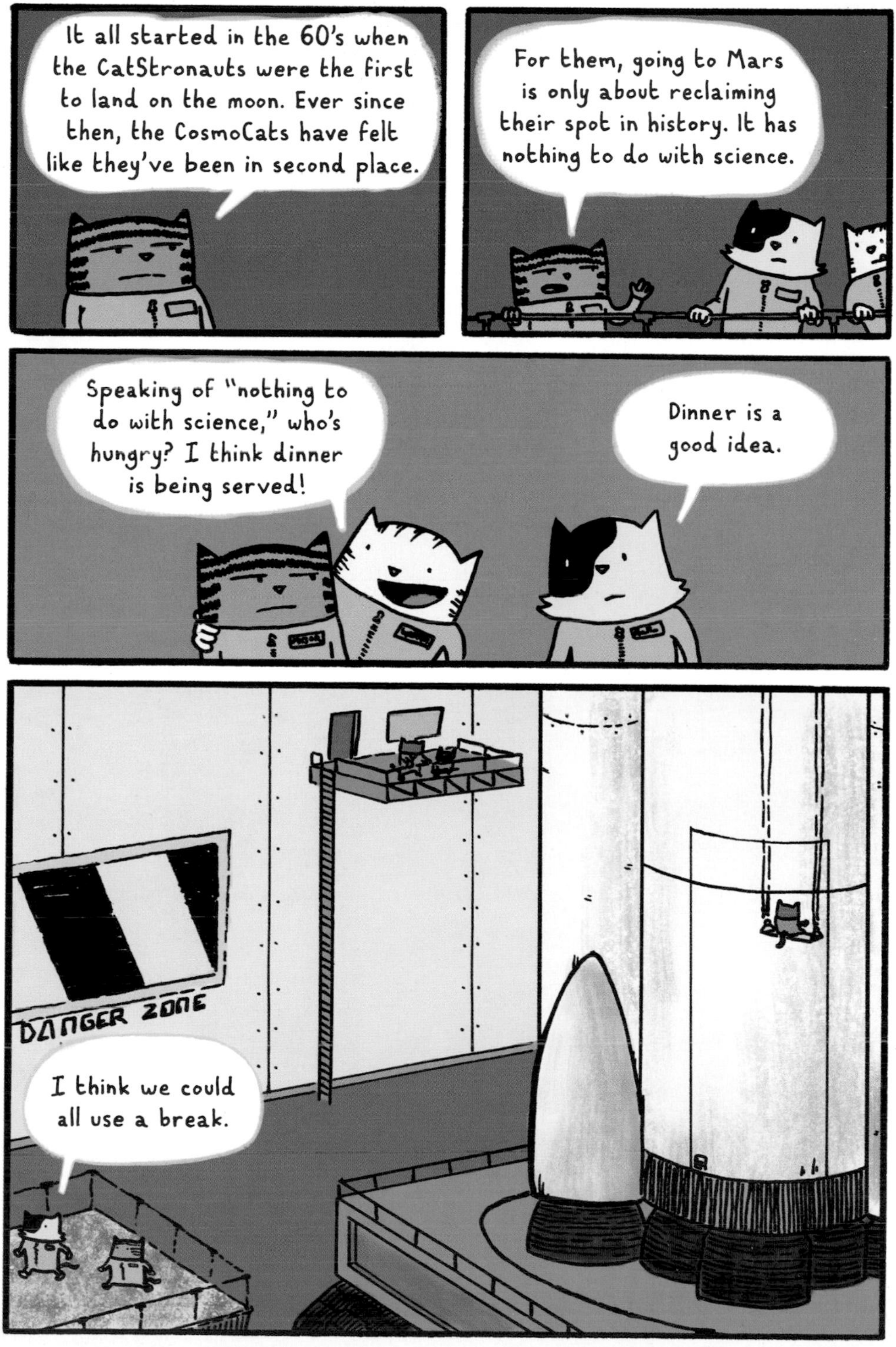
It all started in the 60's when the CatStronauts were the first to land on the moon. Ever since then, the CosmoCats have felt like they've been in second place.
For them, going to Mars is only about reclaiming their spot in history. It has nothing to do with science.
Speaking of "nothing to do with science," who's hungry? I think dinner is being served!
Dinner is a good idea.
DANGER ZONE
I think we could all use a break.

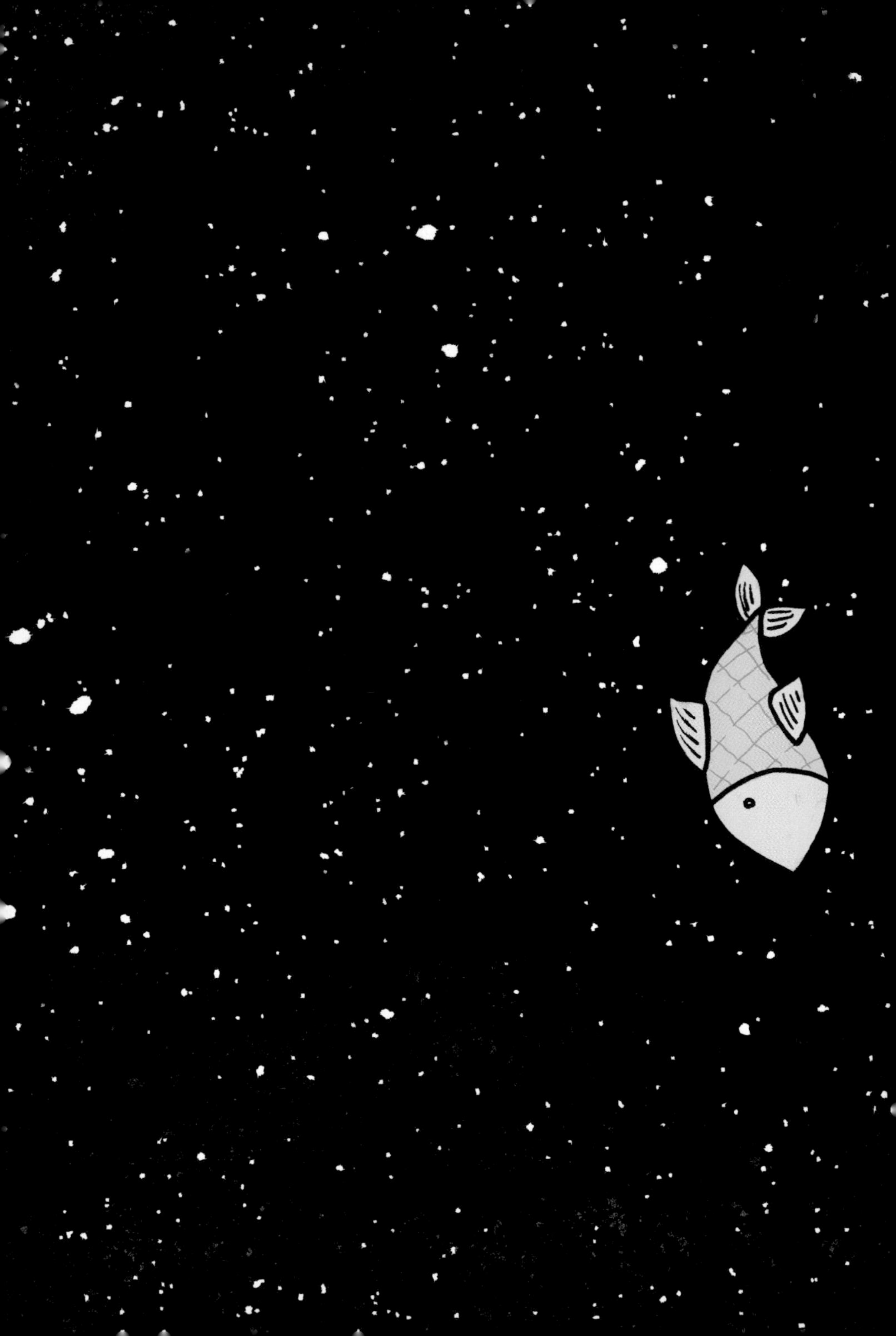

CHAPTER 5

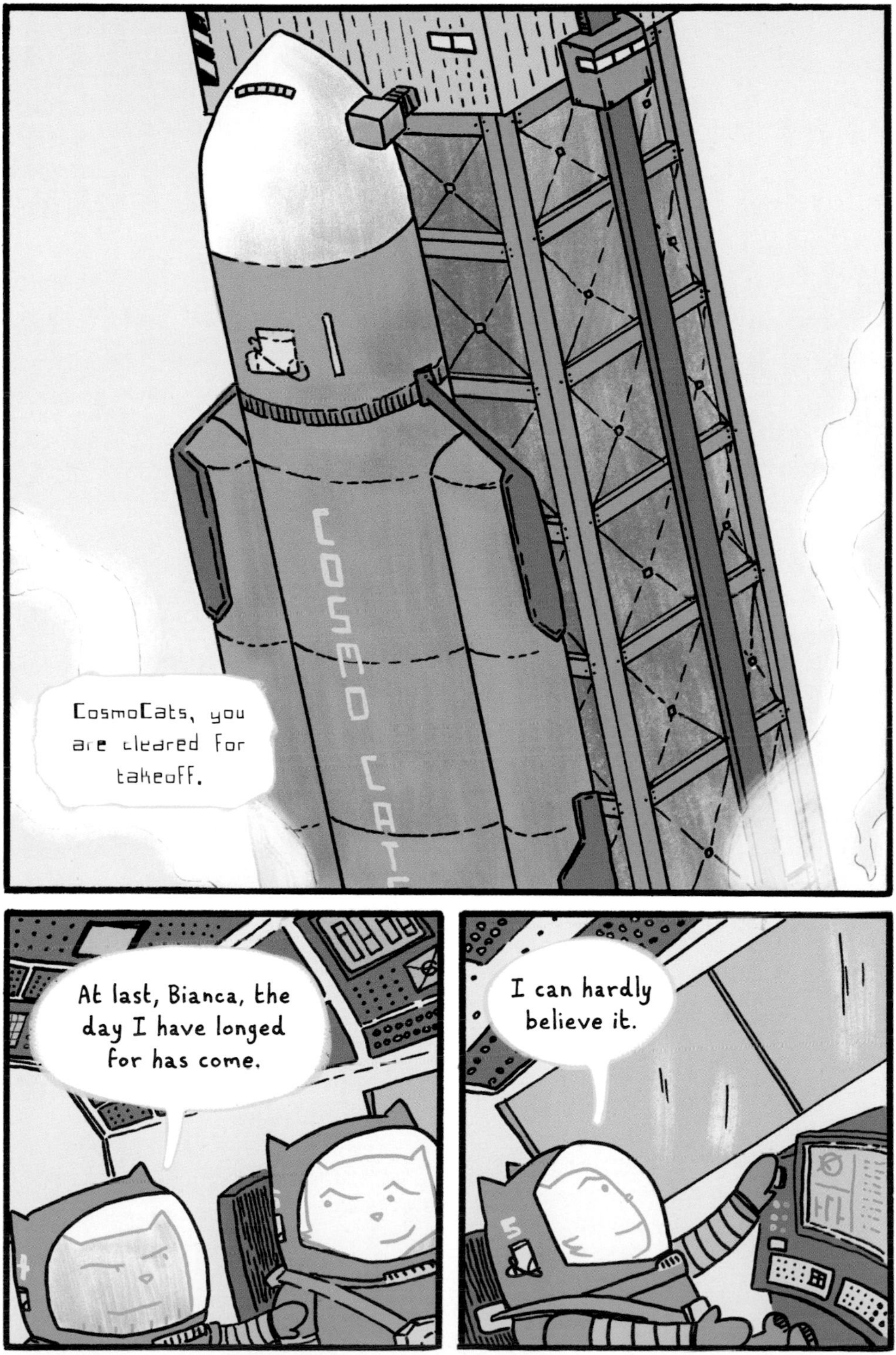
CosmoCats, you are cleared for takeoff.
At last, Bianca, the day I have longed for has come.
I can hardly believe it.

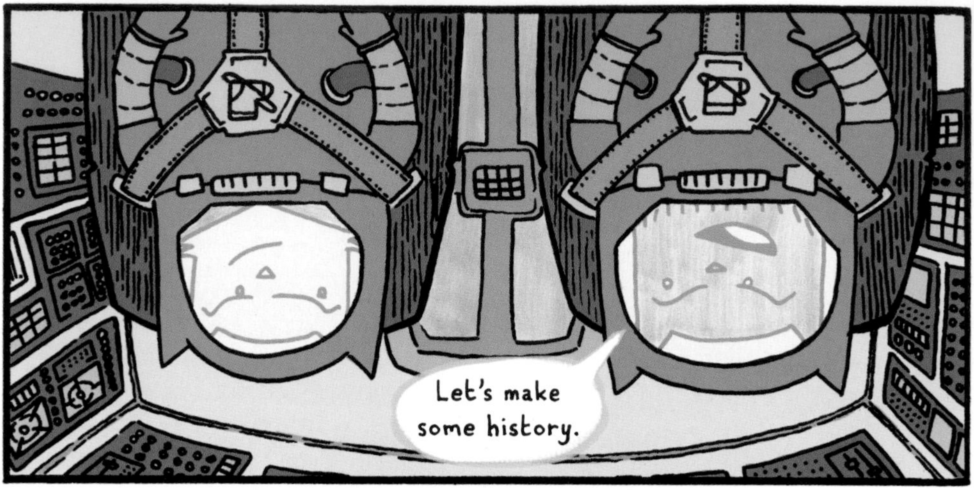
Let's make some history.

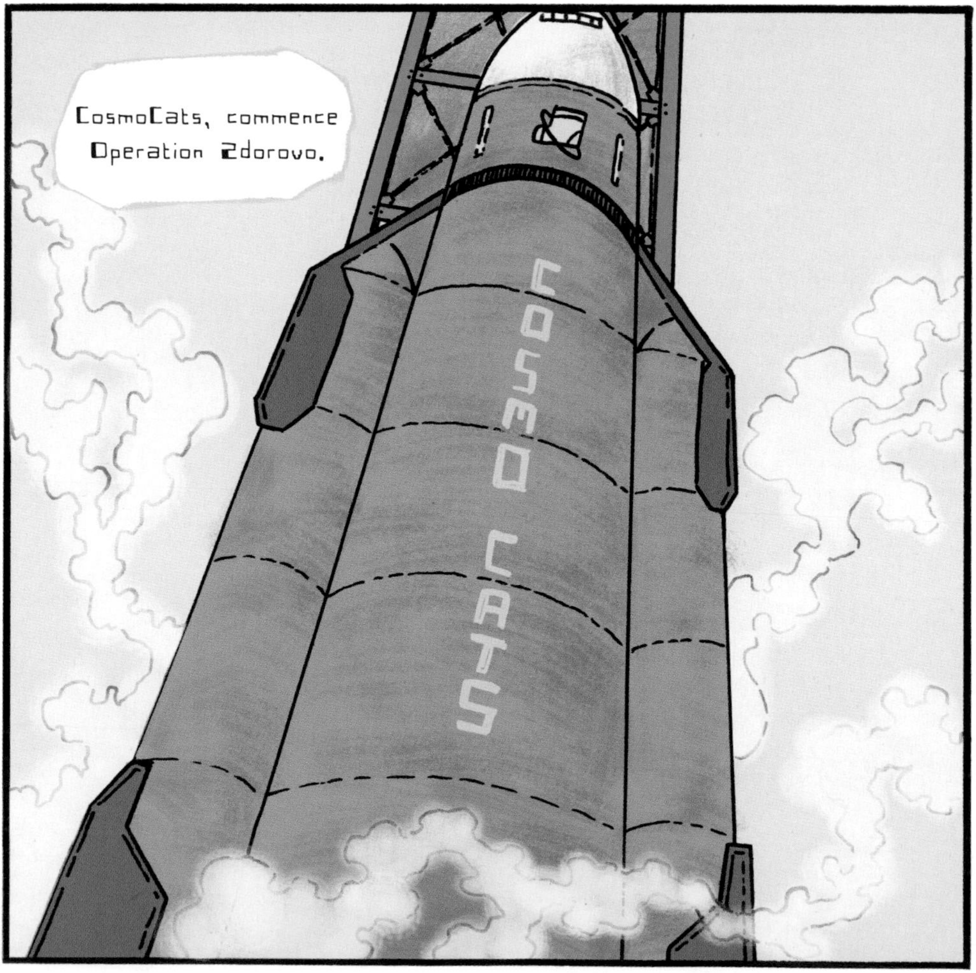
CosmoCats, commence Operation Zdorovo.
COSMO CATS

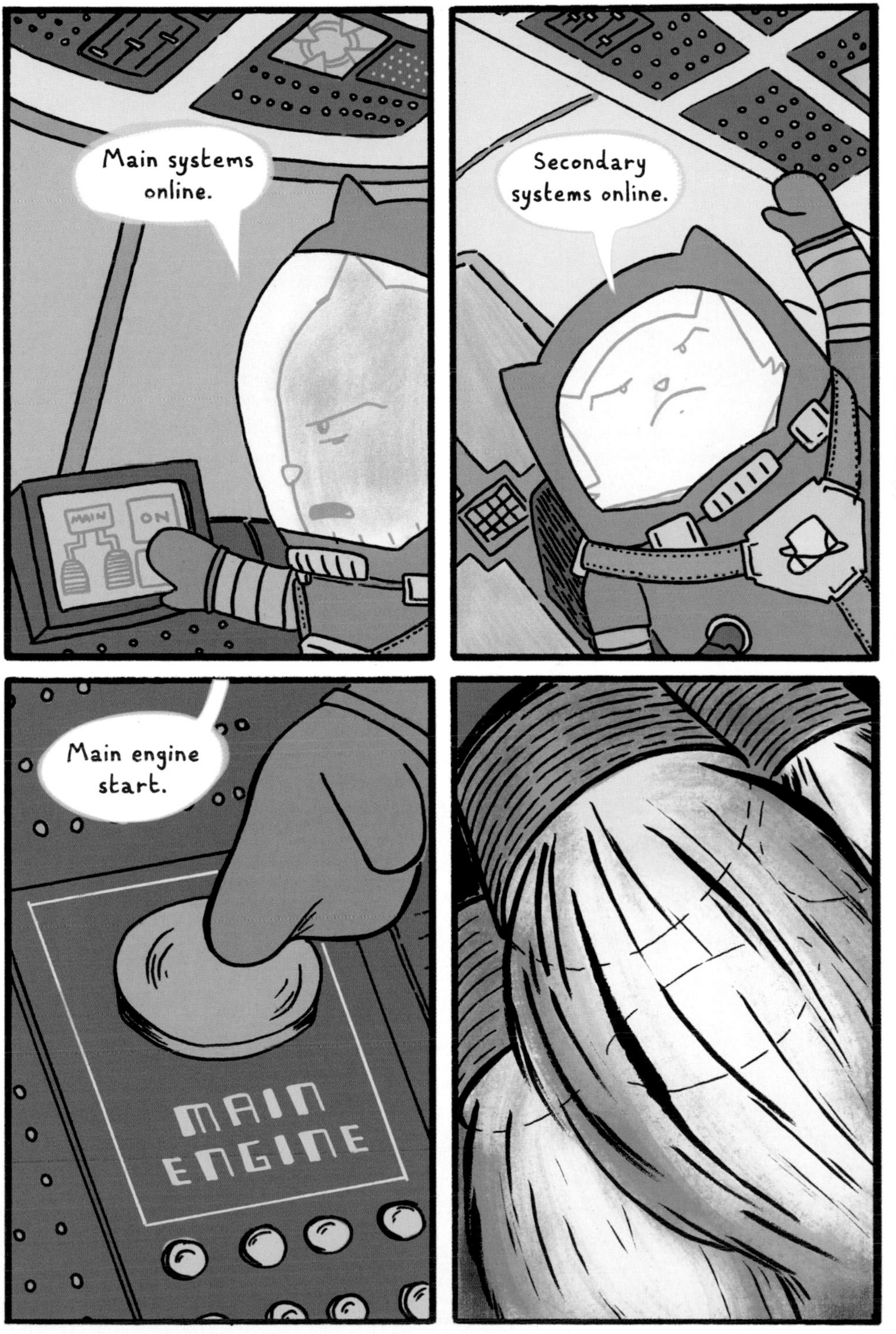
Main systems online.
MAIN
ON
Secondary systems online.
Main engine start.
MAIN ENGINE

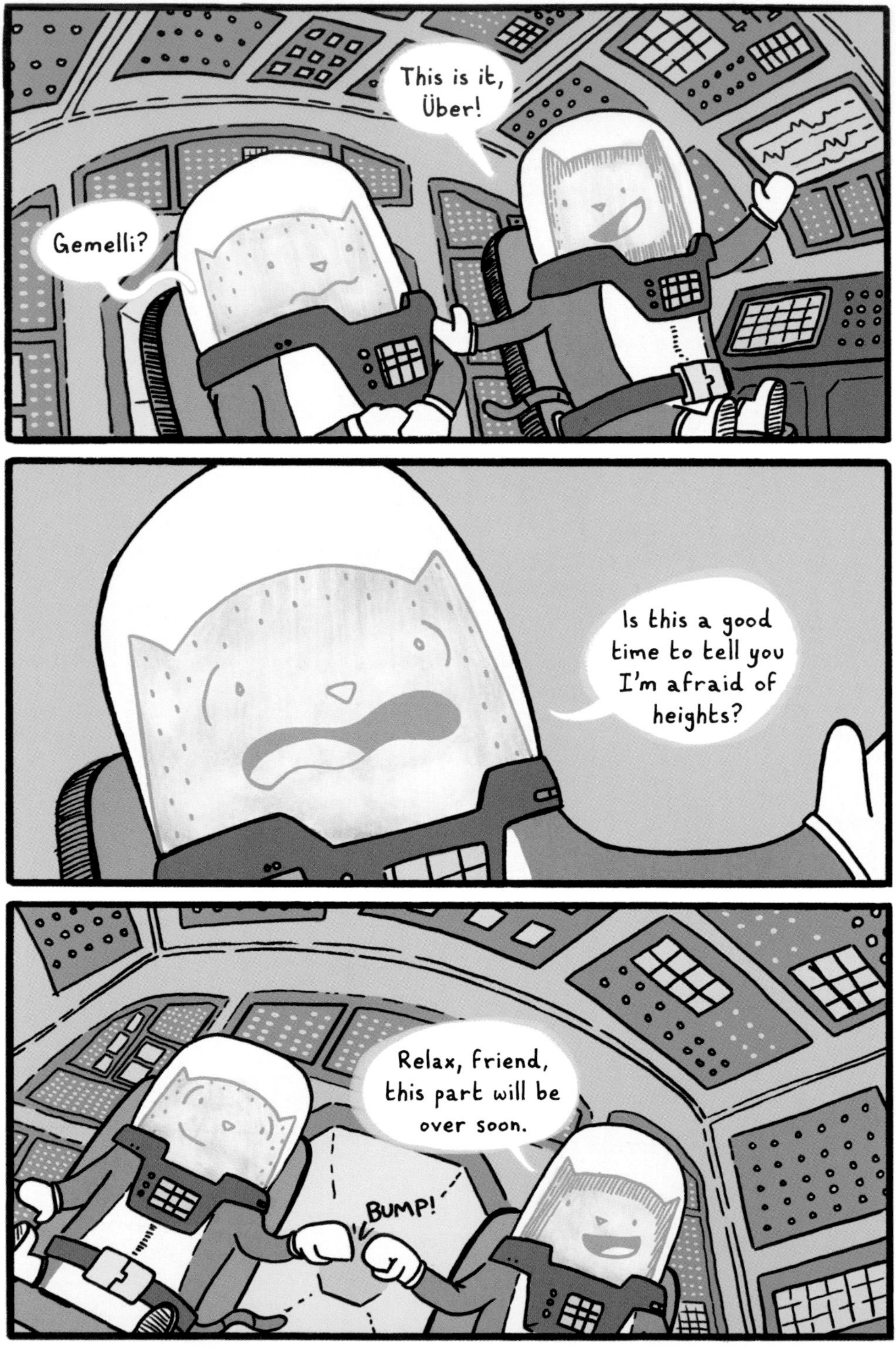
Gemelli?
This is it, Über!
Is this a good time to tell you I'm afraid of heights?
Relax, friend, this part will be over soon.
BUMP!

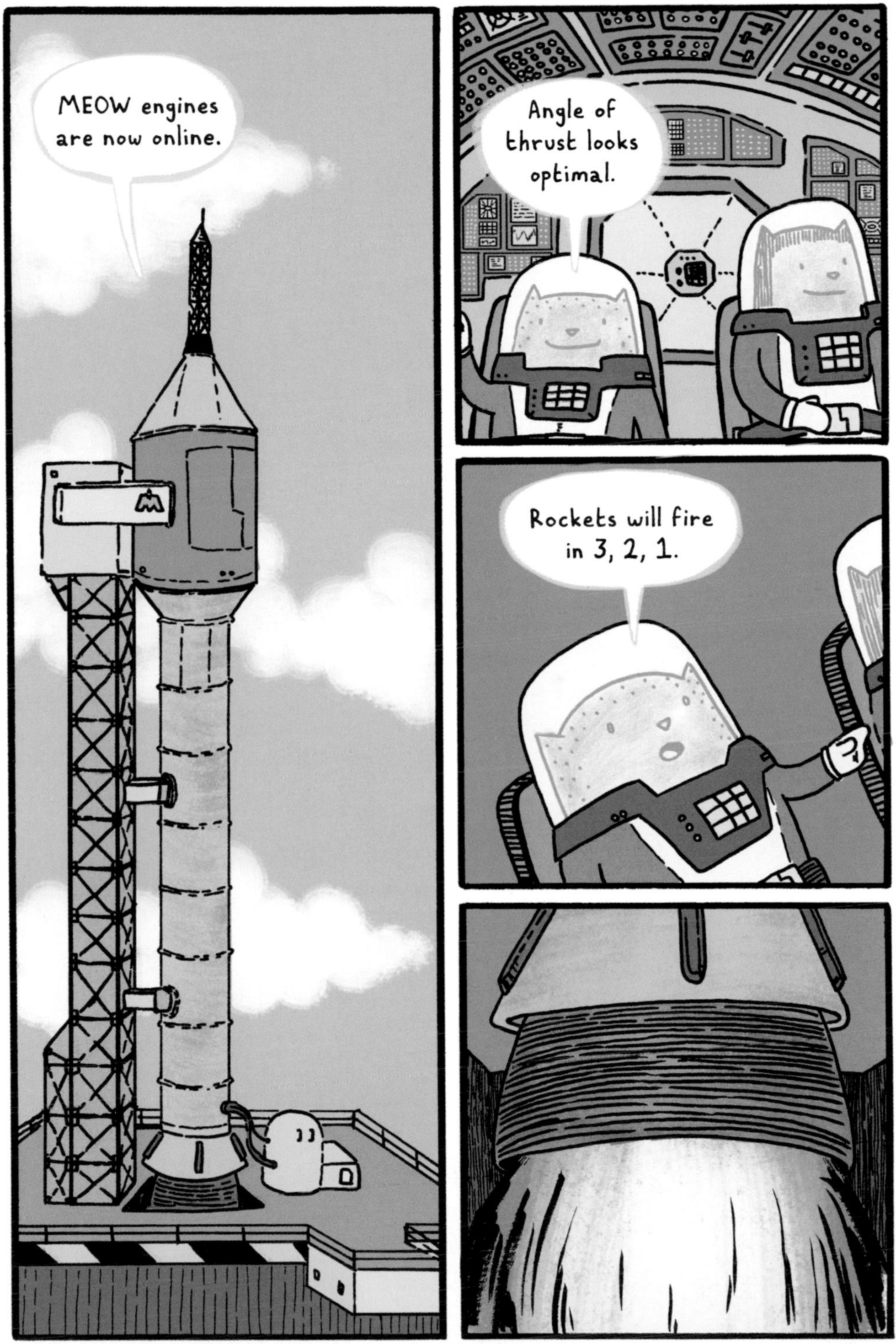
MEOW engines are now online.
Angle of thrust looks optimal.
Rockets will fire in 3, 2, 1.

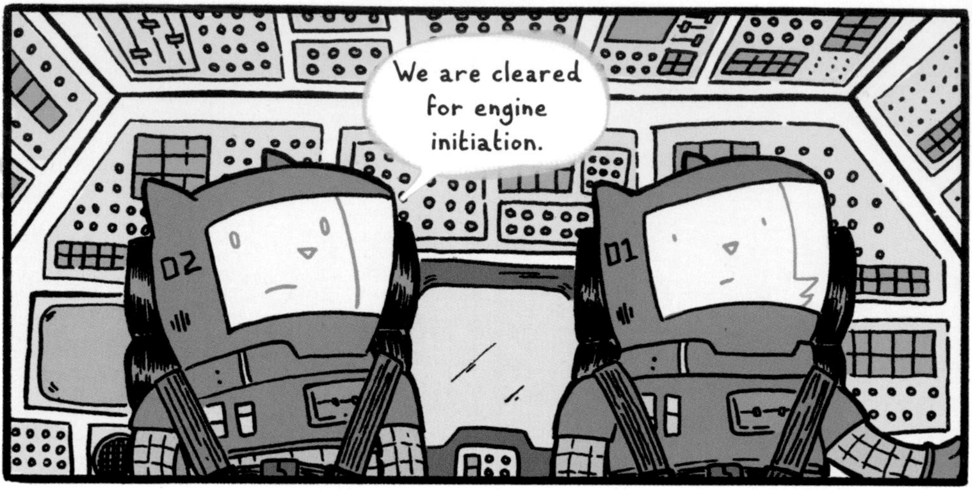
We are cleared for engine initiation.
D2
D1

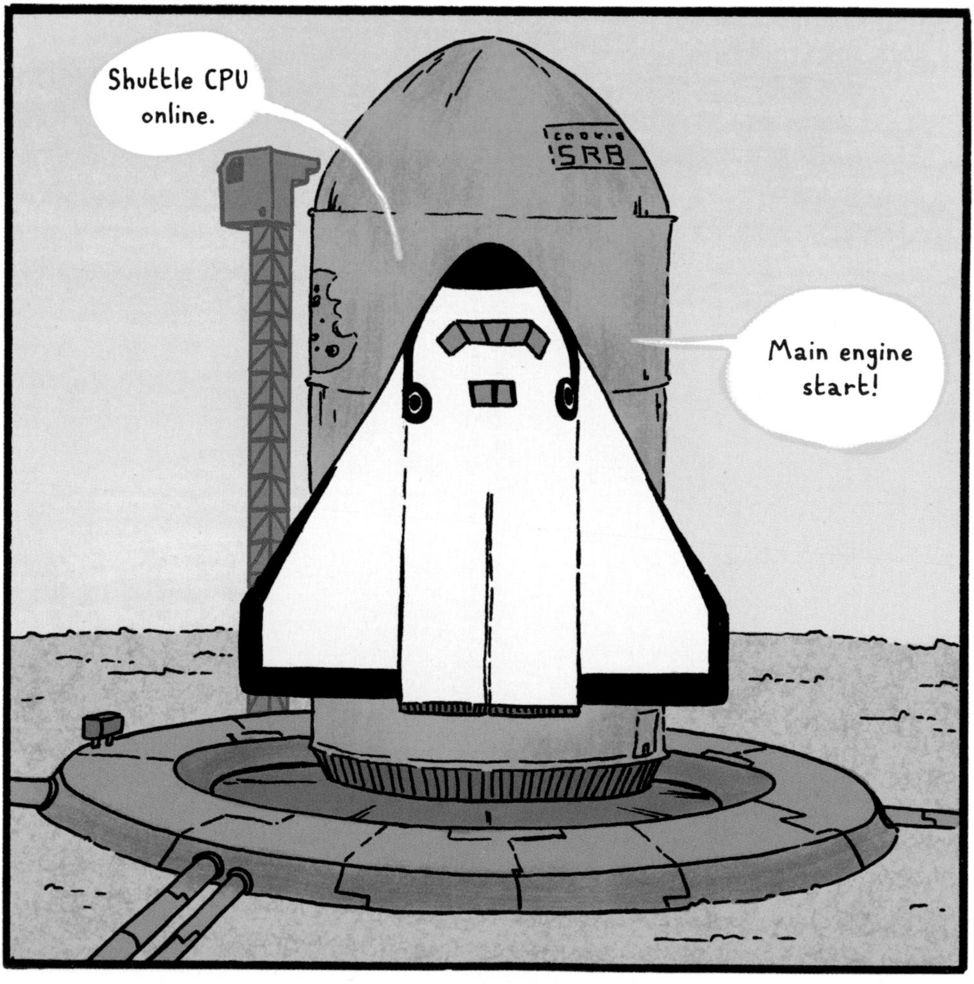
Shuttle CPU online.
SRB
Main engine start!

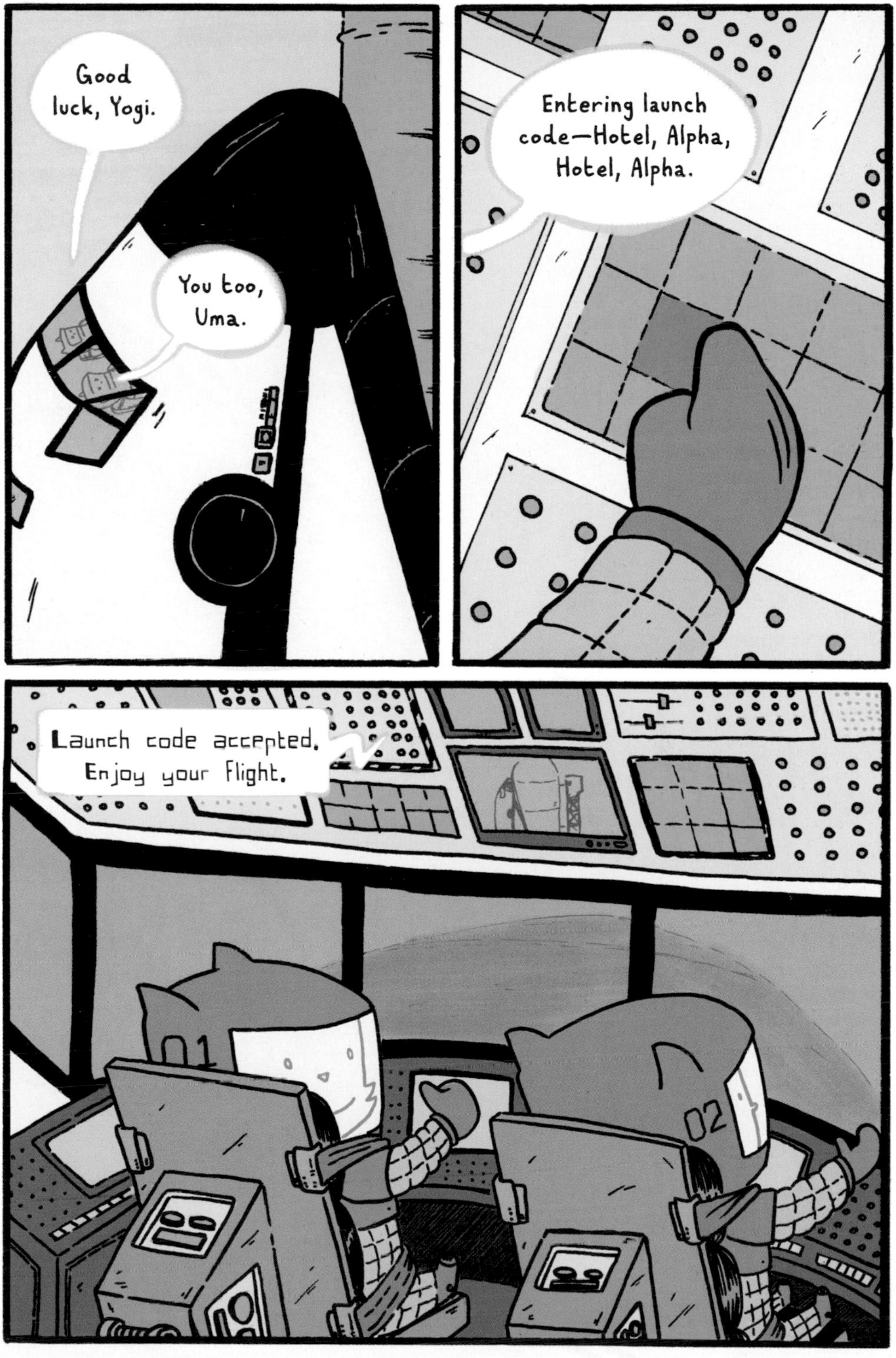

Good luck, Yogi.
You too, Uma.
Entering launch code—Hotel, Alpha, Hotel, Alpha.
Launch code accepted. Enjoy your flight.

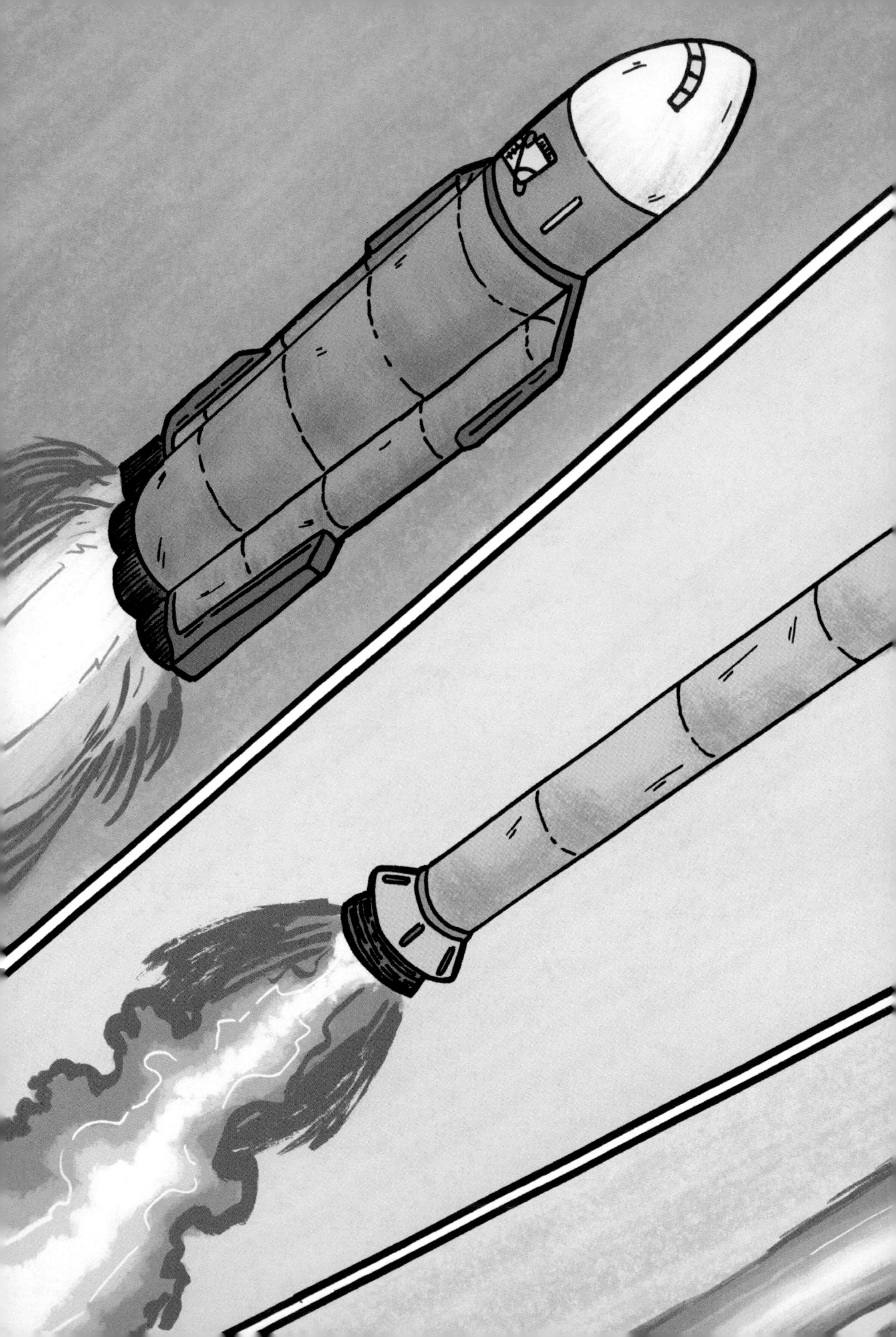

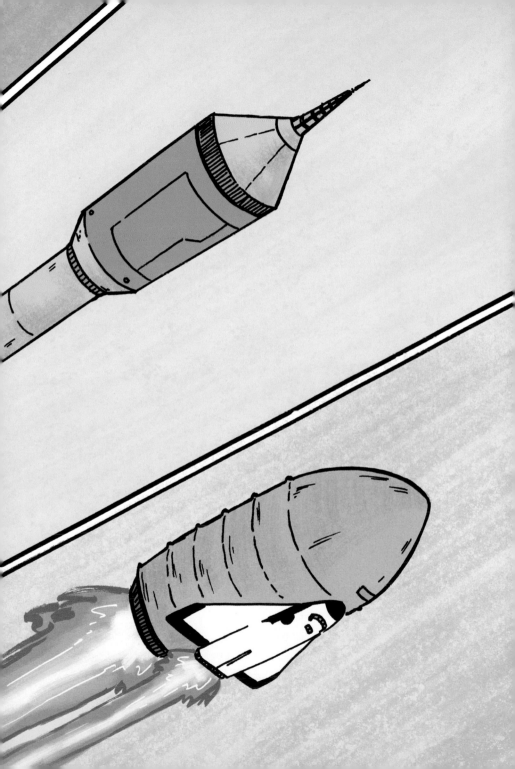

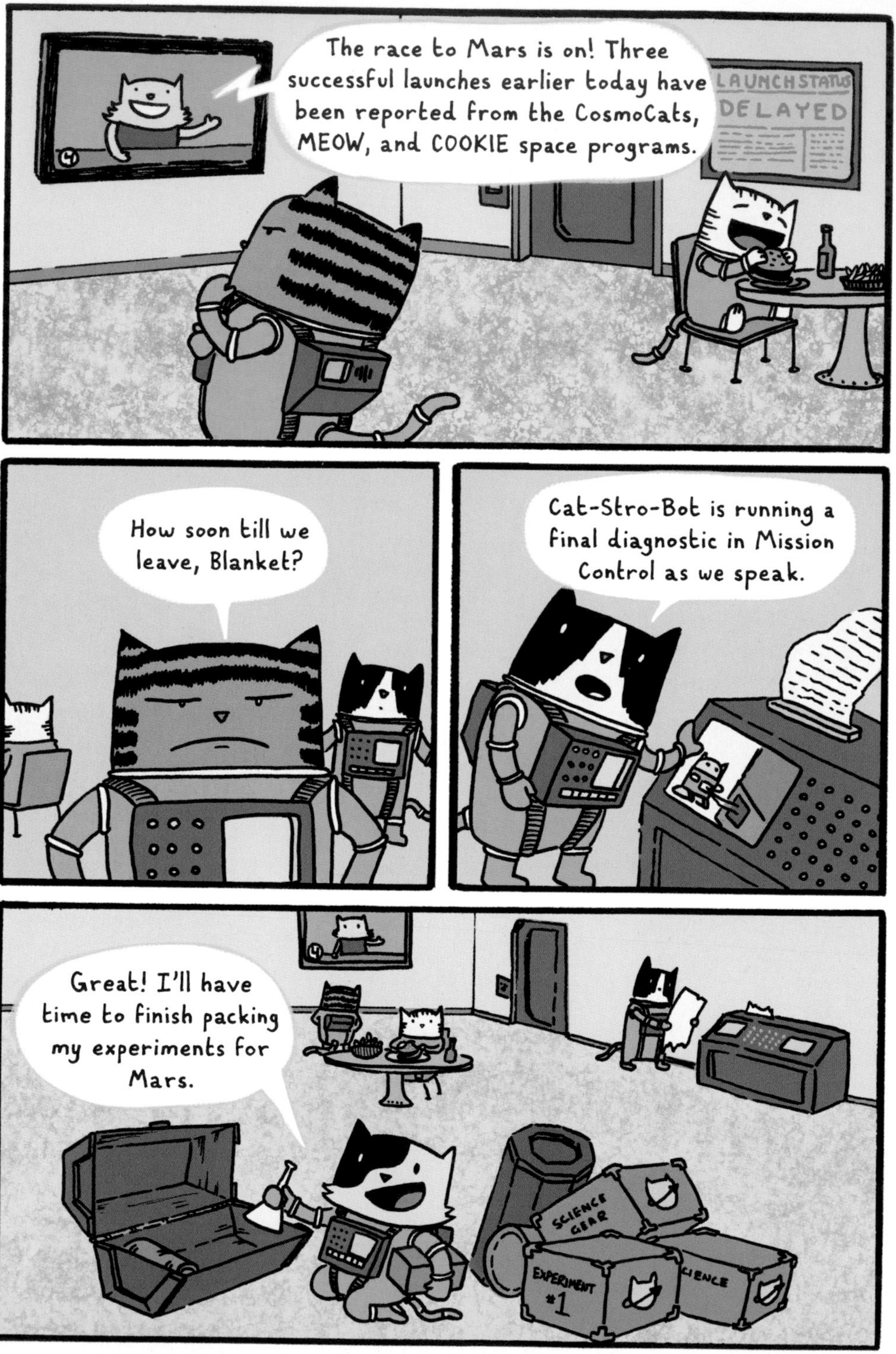
The race to Mars is on! Three successful launches earlier today have been reported from the CosmoCats, MEOW, and COOKIE space programs.
LAUNCH STATUS
DELAYED
How soon till we leave, Blanket?
Cat-Stro-Bot is running a final diagnostic in Mission Control as we speak.
Great! I'll have time to finish packing my experiments for Mars.
SCIENCE GEAR
EXPERIMENT #1
CIENCE

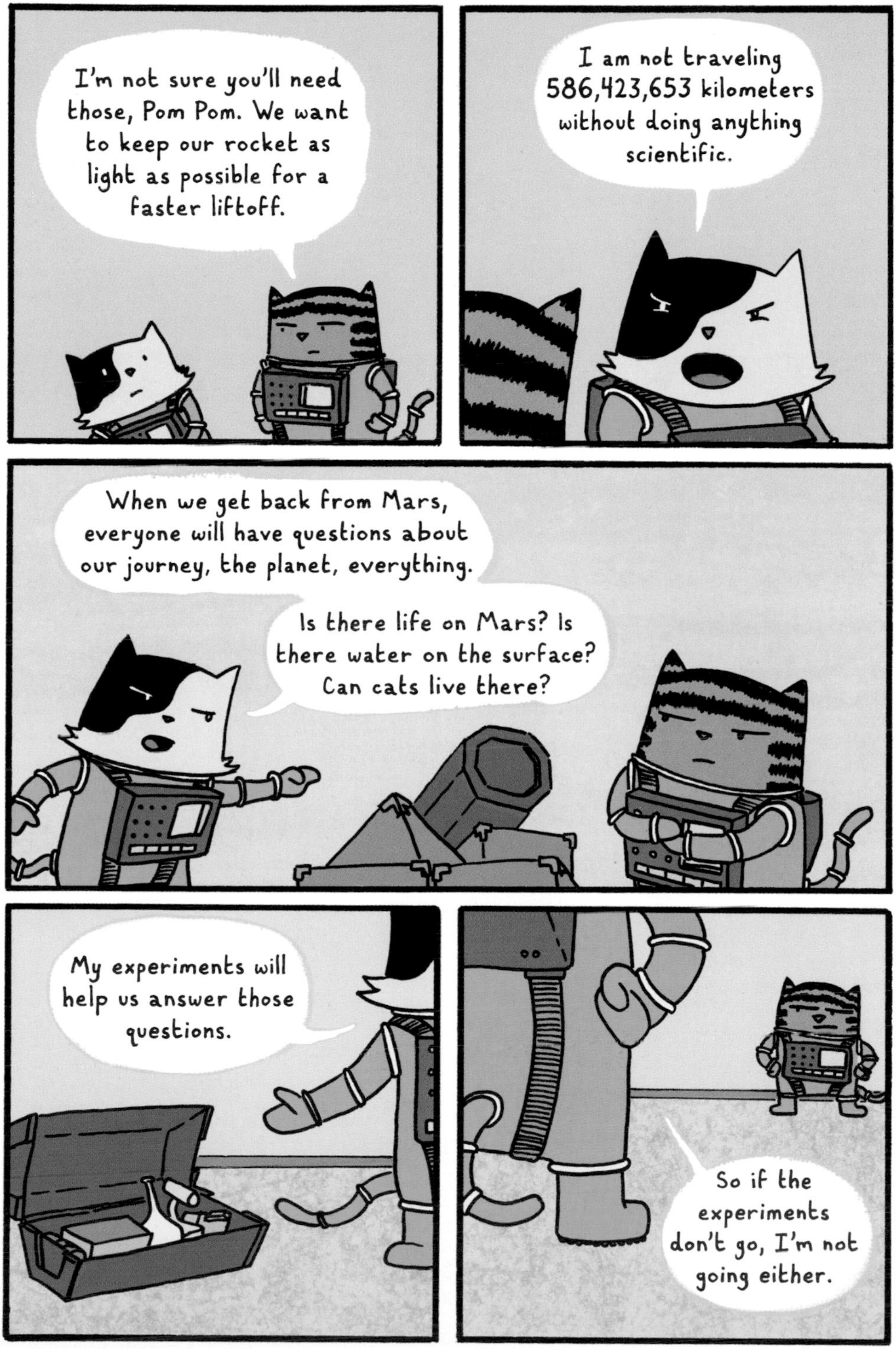
I'm not sure you'll need those, Pom Pom. We want to keep our rocket as light as possible for a faster liftoff.
I am not traveling 586,423,653 kilometers without doing anything scientific.
When we get back from Mars, everyone will have questions about our journey, the planet, everything.
Is there life on Mars? Is there water on the surface? Can cats live there?
My experiments will help us answer those questions.
So if the experiments don't go, I'm not going either.

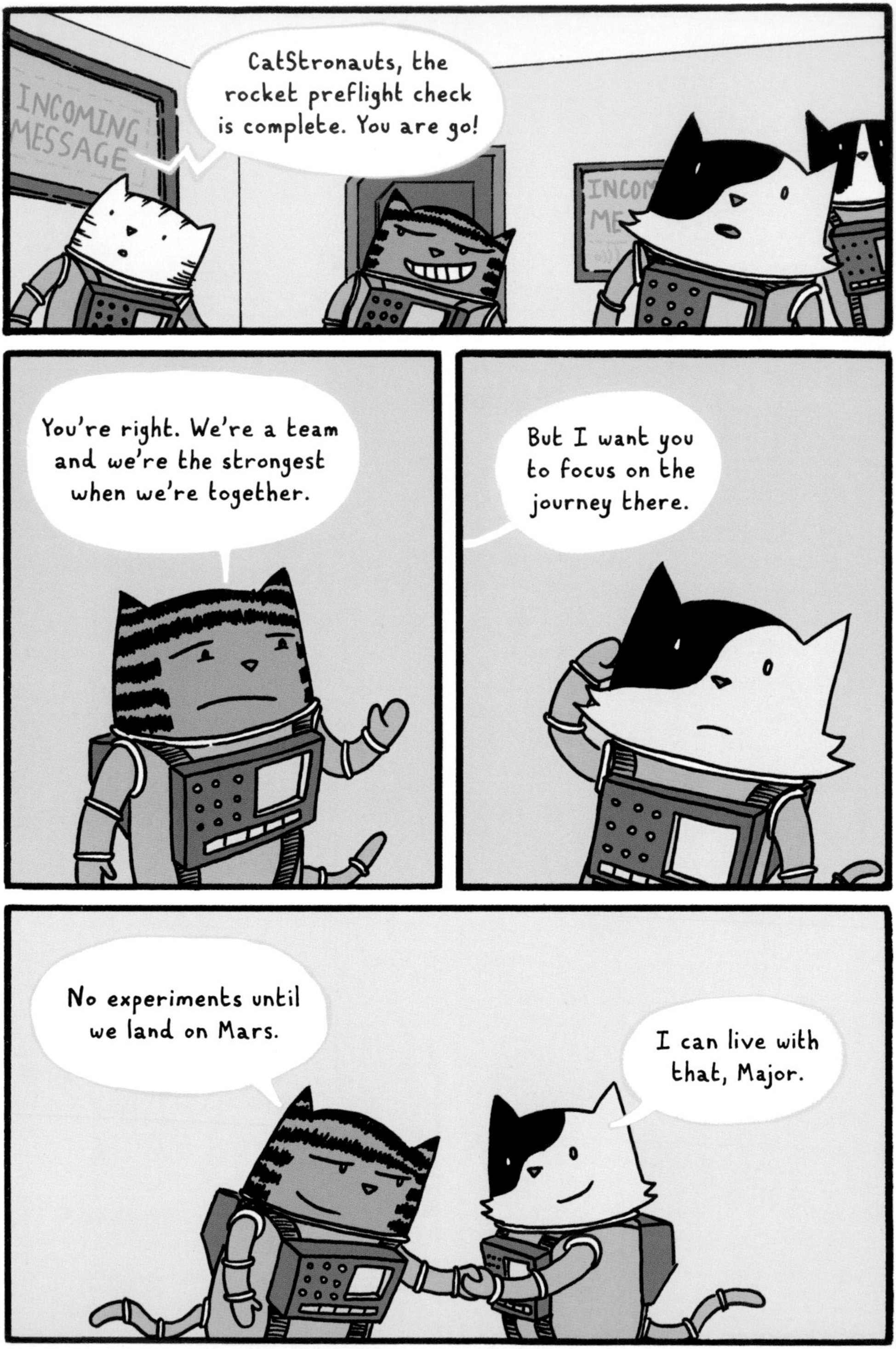
INCOMING MESSAGE
CatStronauts, the rocket preflight check is complete. You are go!
You're right. We're a team and we're the strongest when we're together.
But I want you to focus on the journey there.
No experiments until we land on Mars.
I can live with that, Major.

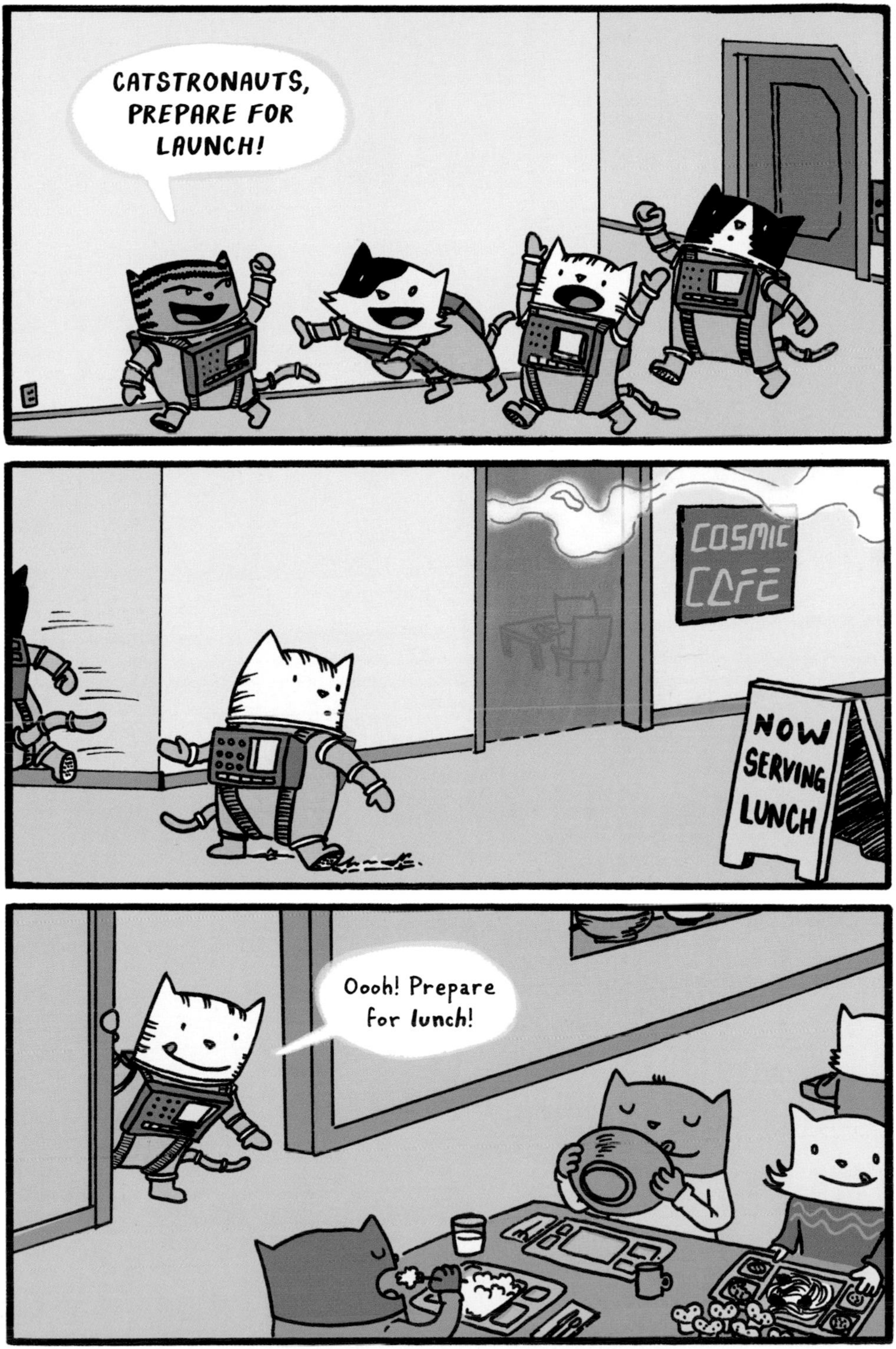
CATSTRONAUTS, PREPARE FOR LAUNCH!
COSMIC CAFE
NOW SERVING LUNCH
Oooh! Prepare for lunch!

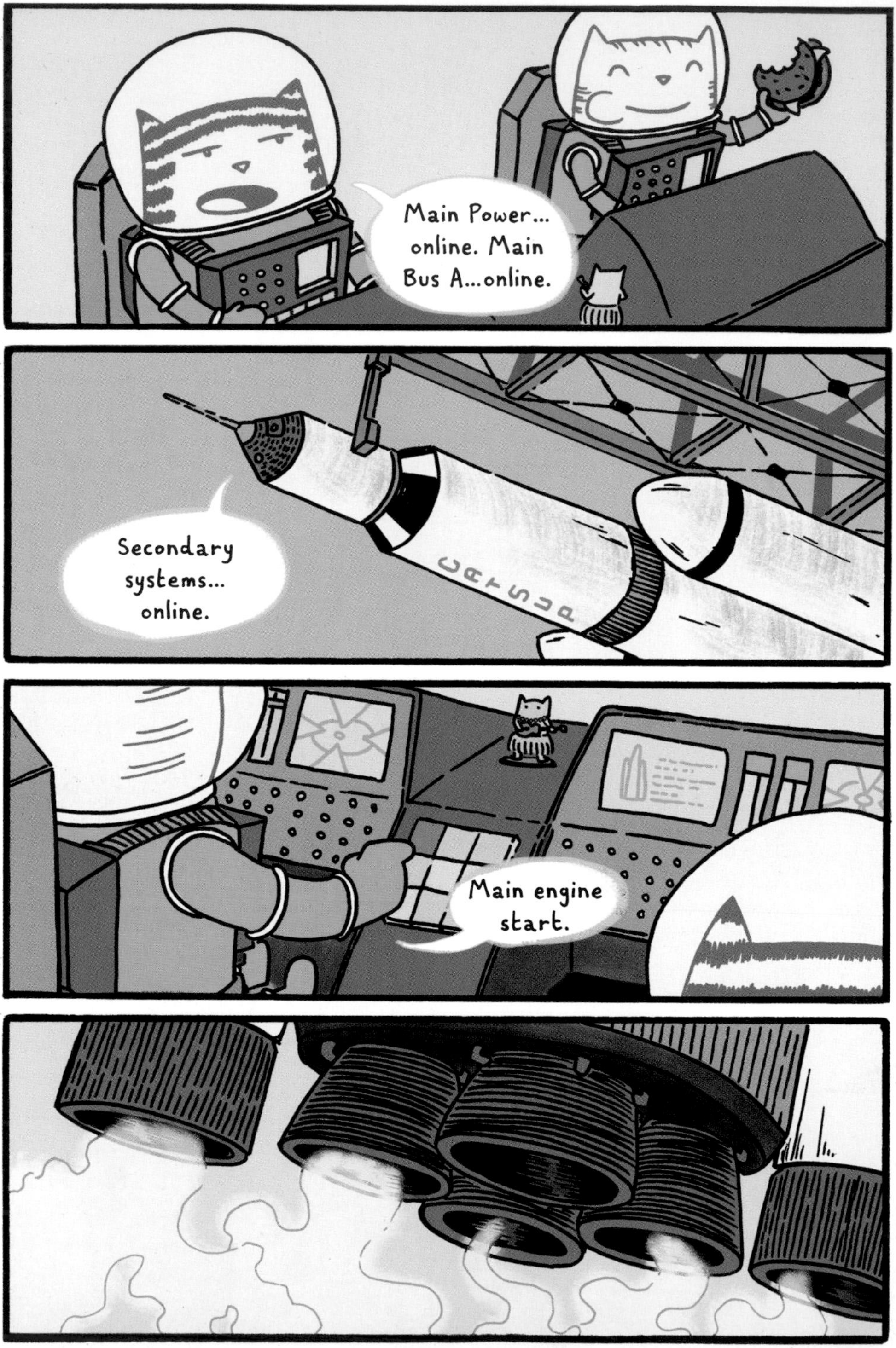
Main Power... online. Main Bus A...online.
Secondary systems... online.
Main engine start.

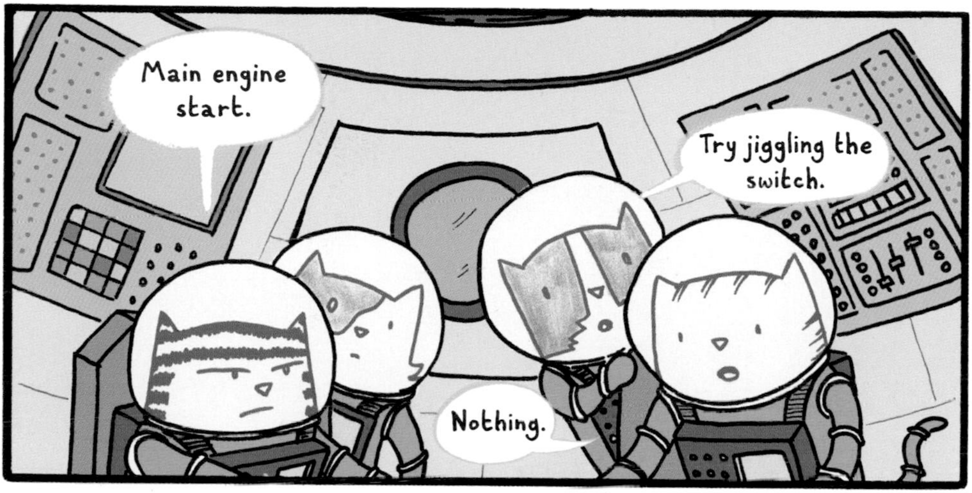
Main engine start.
Try jiggling the switch.
Nothing.

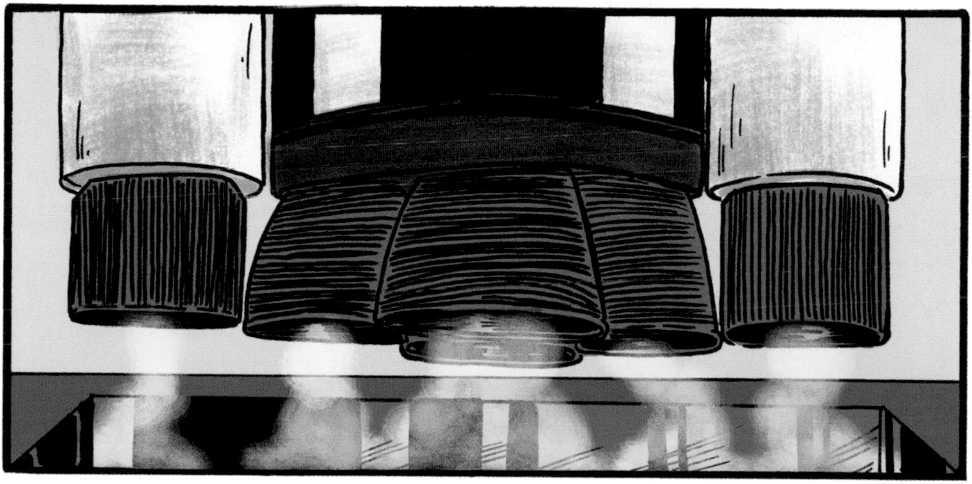

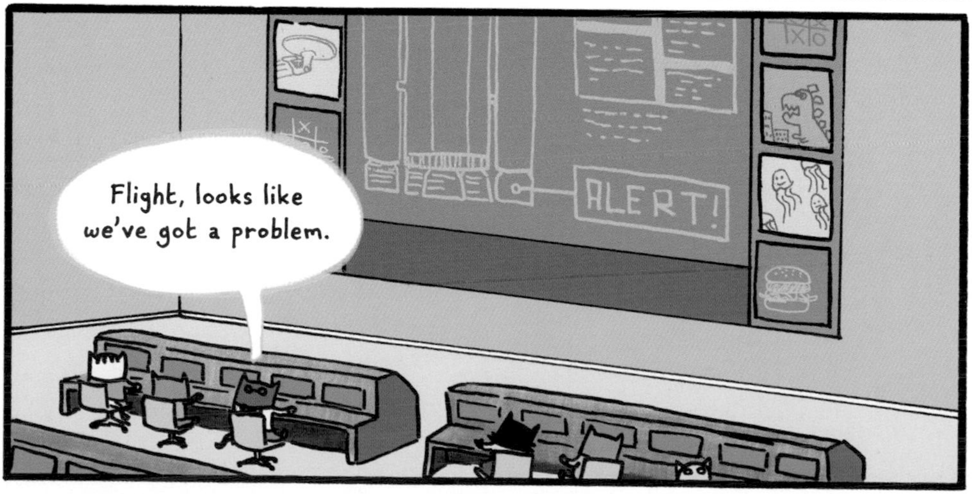
ALERT!
Flight, looks like we've got a problem.

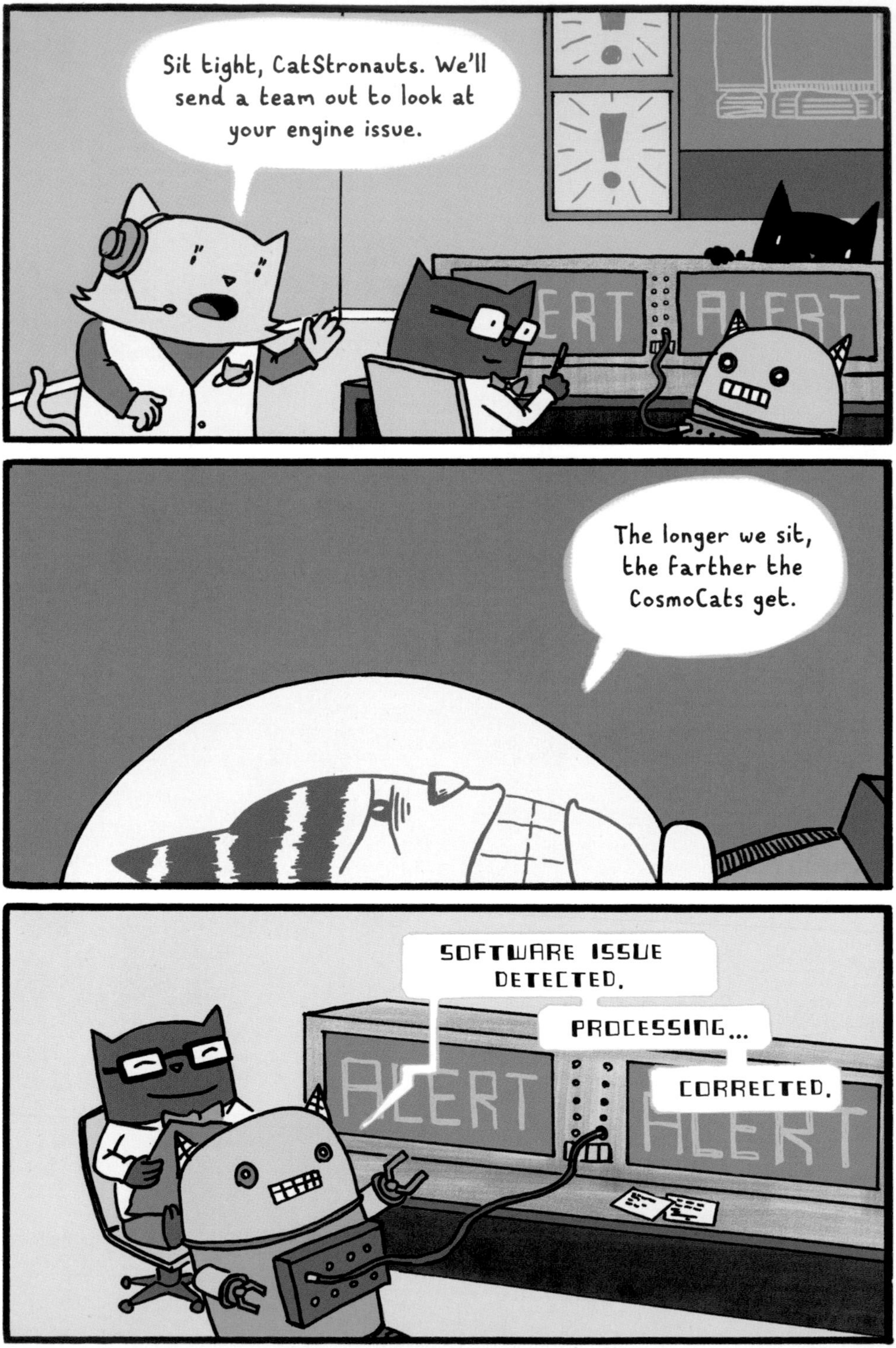
Sit tight, CatStronauts. We'll send a team out to look at your engine issue.
ALERT
ALERT
The longer we sit, the farther the CosmoCats get.
SOFTWARE ISSUE DETECTED.
PROCESSING...
CORRECTED.
ALERT
ALERT

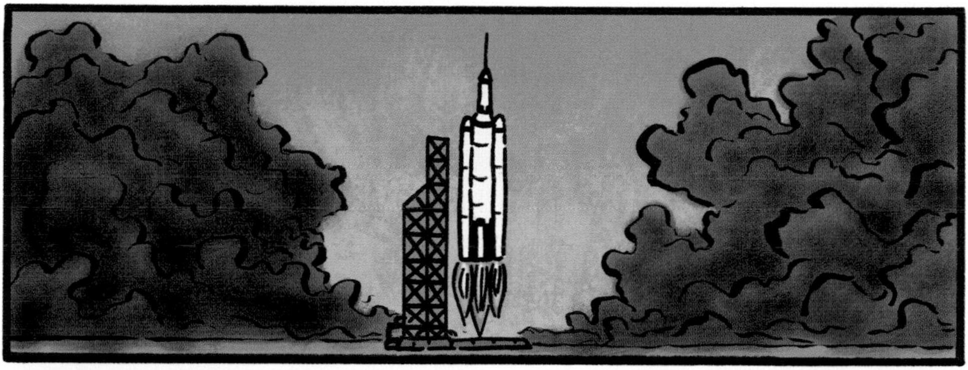

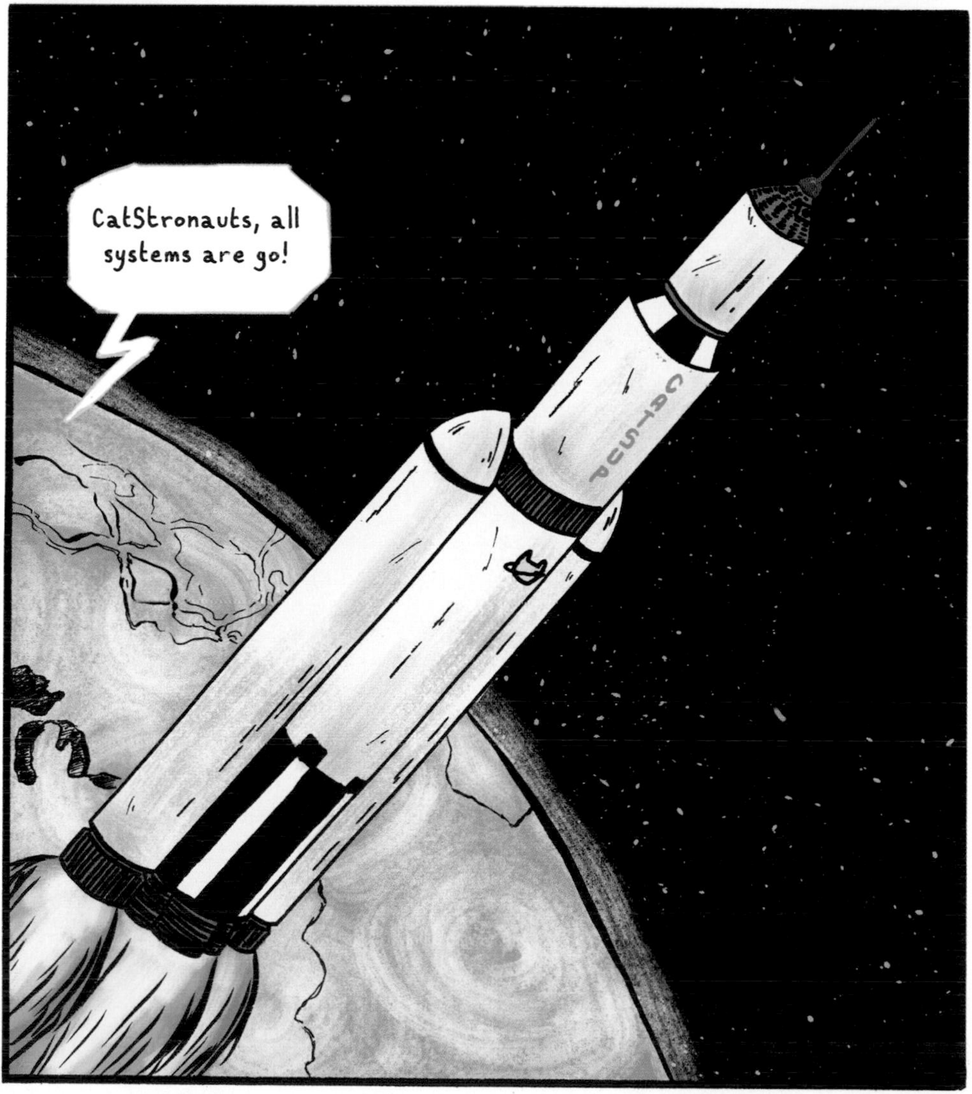
CatStronauts, all systems are go!
CAT-SUP

CHAPTER 6

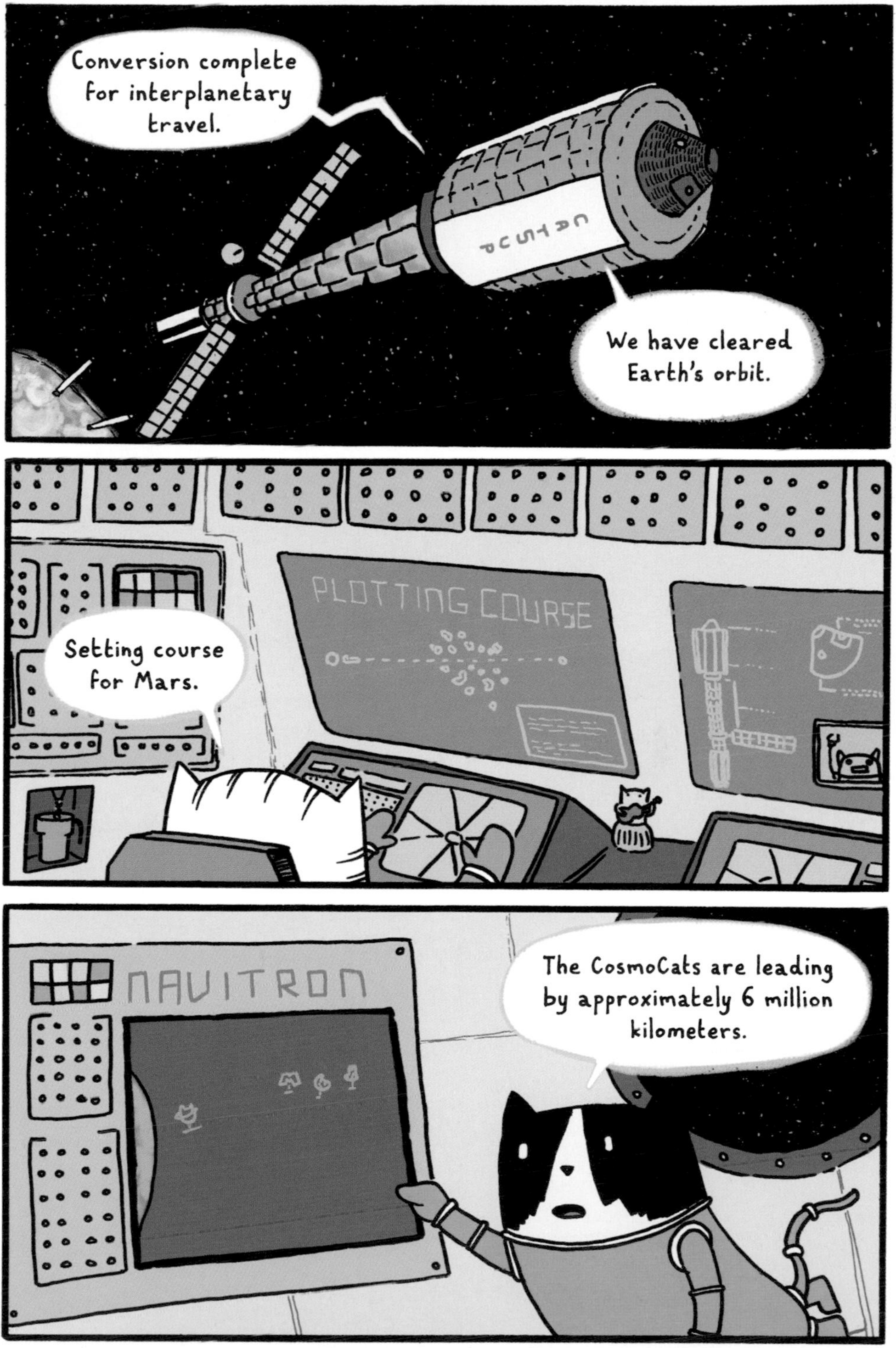
Conversion complete for interplanetary travel.
We have cleared Earth's orbit.
PLOTTING COURSE
Setting course for Mars.
NAVITRON
The CosmoCats are leading by approximately 6 million kilometers.

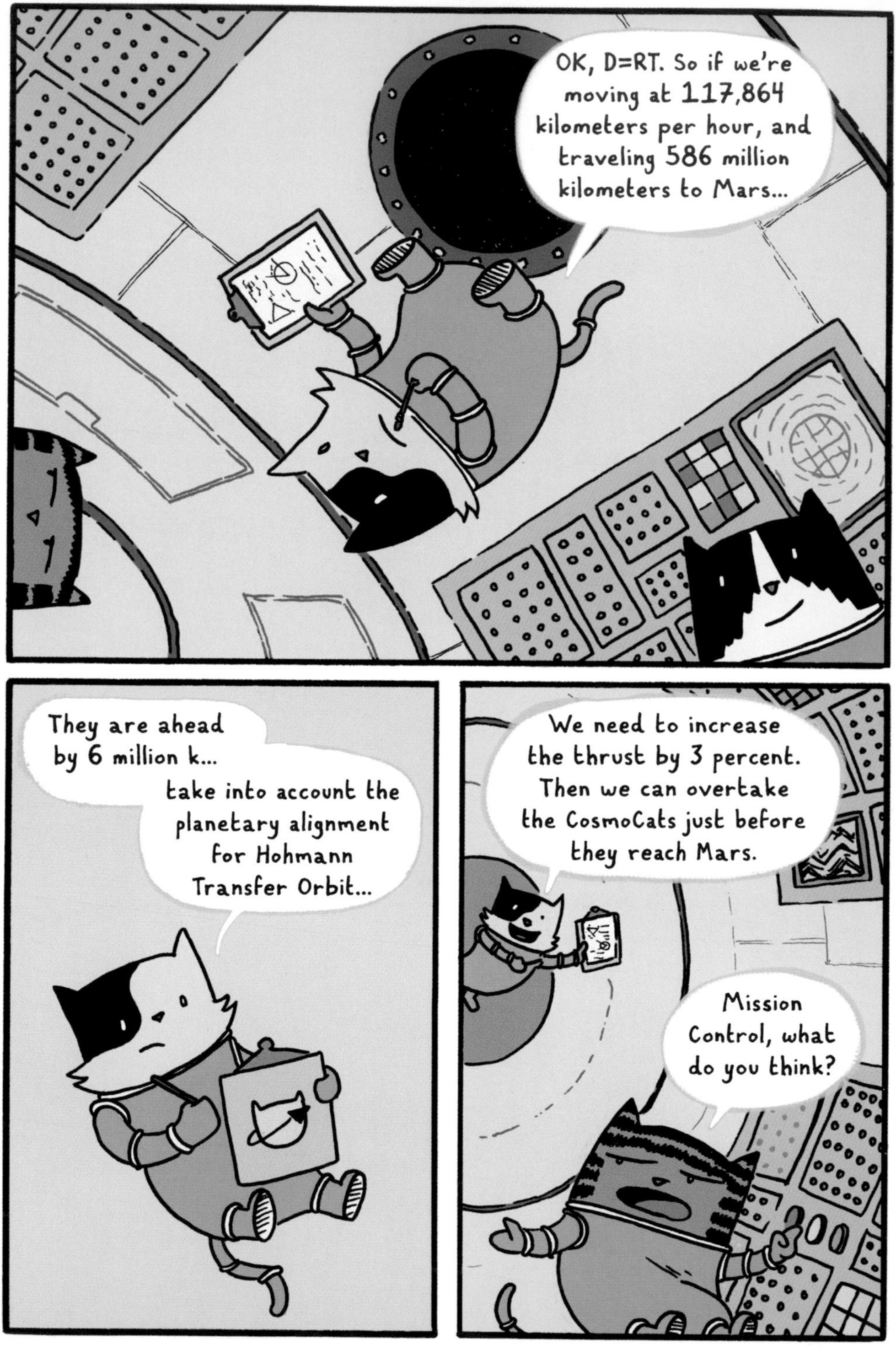
OK, D=RT. So if we're moving at 117,864 kilometers per hour, and traveling 586 million kilometers to Mars...
They are ahead by 6 million k...
take into account the planetary alignment for Hohmann Transfer Orbit...
We need to increase the thrust by 3 percent. Then we can overtake the CosmoCats just before they reach Mars.
Mission Control, what do you think?

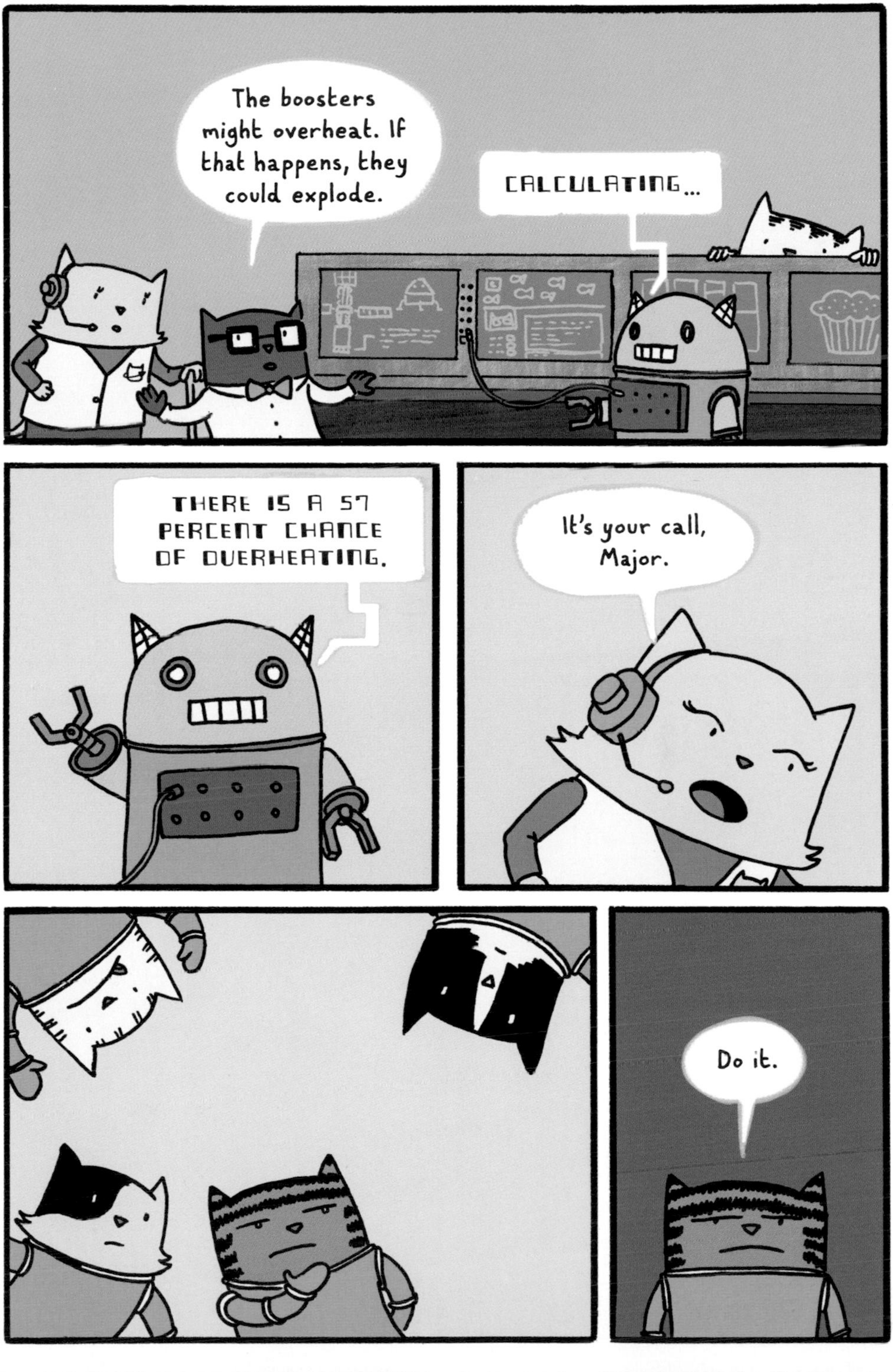
The boosters might overheat. If that happens, they could explode.
CALCULATING...
THERE IS A 57 PERCENT CHANCE OF OVERHEATING.
It's your call, Major.
Do it.

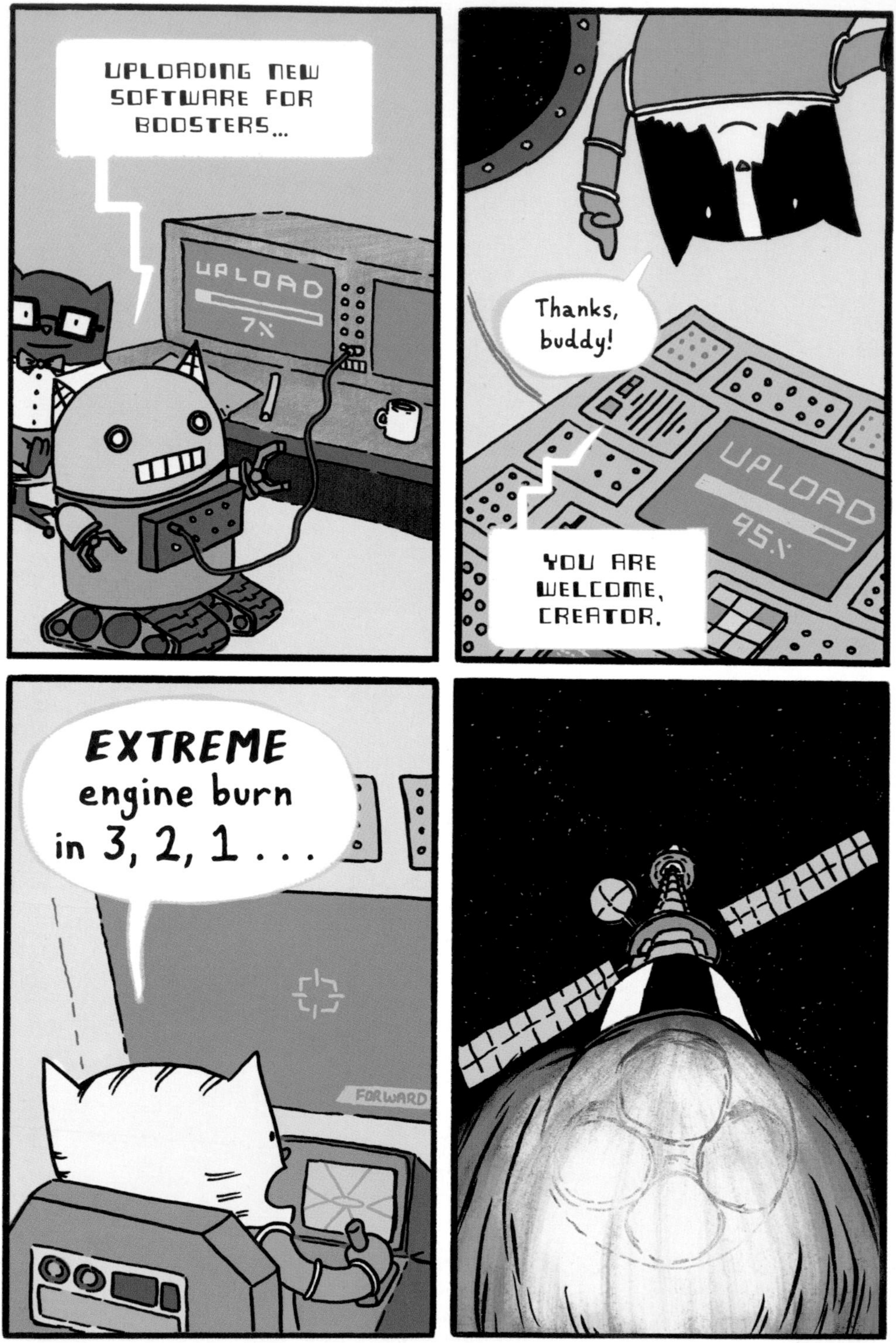
UPLOADING NEW SOFTWARE FOR BOOSTERS...
UPLOAD
7%
Thanks, buddy!
UPLOAD
95%
YOU ARE WELCOME, CREATOR.
EXTREME engine burn in 3, 2, 1 . . .
FORWARD

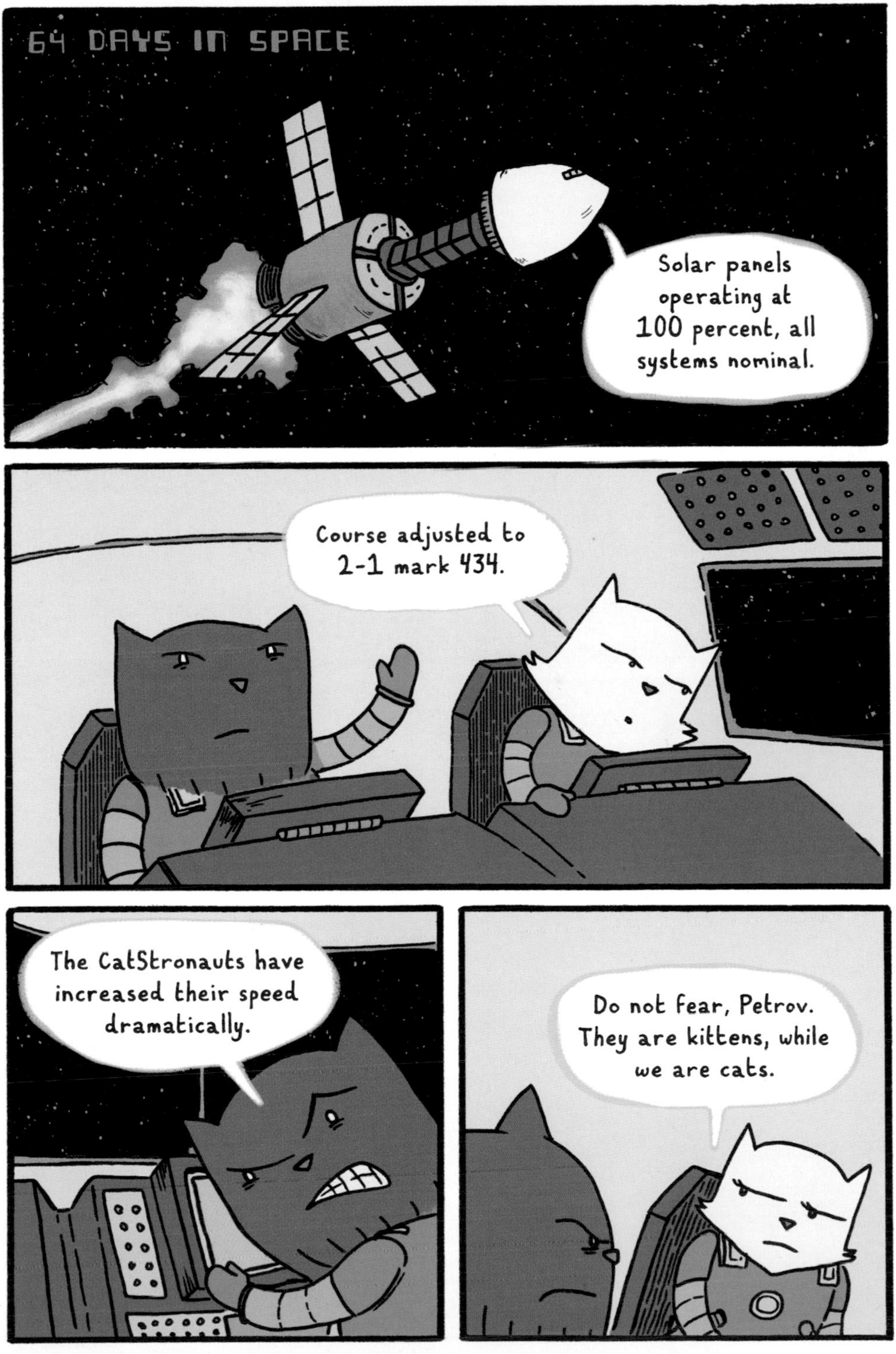
64 DAYS IN SPACE
Solar panels operating at 100 percent, all systems nominal.
Course adjusted to 2-1 mark 434.
The CatStronauts have increased their speed dramatically.
Do not fear, Petrov. They are kittens, while we are cats.

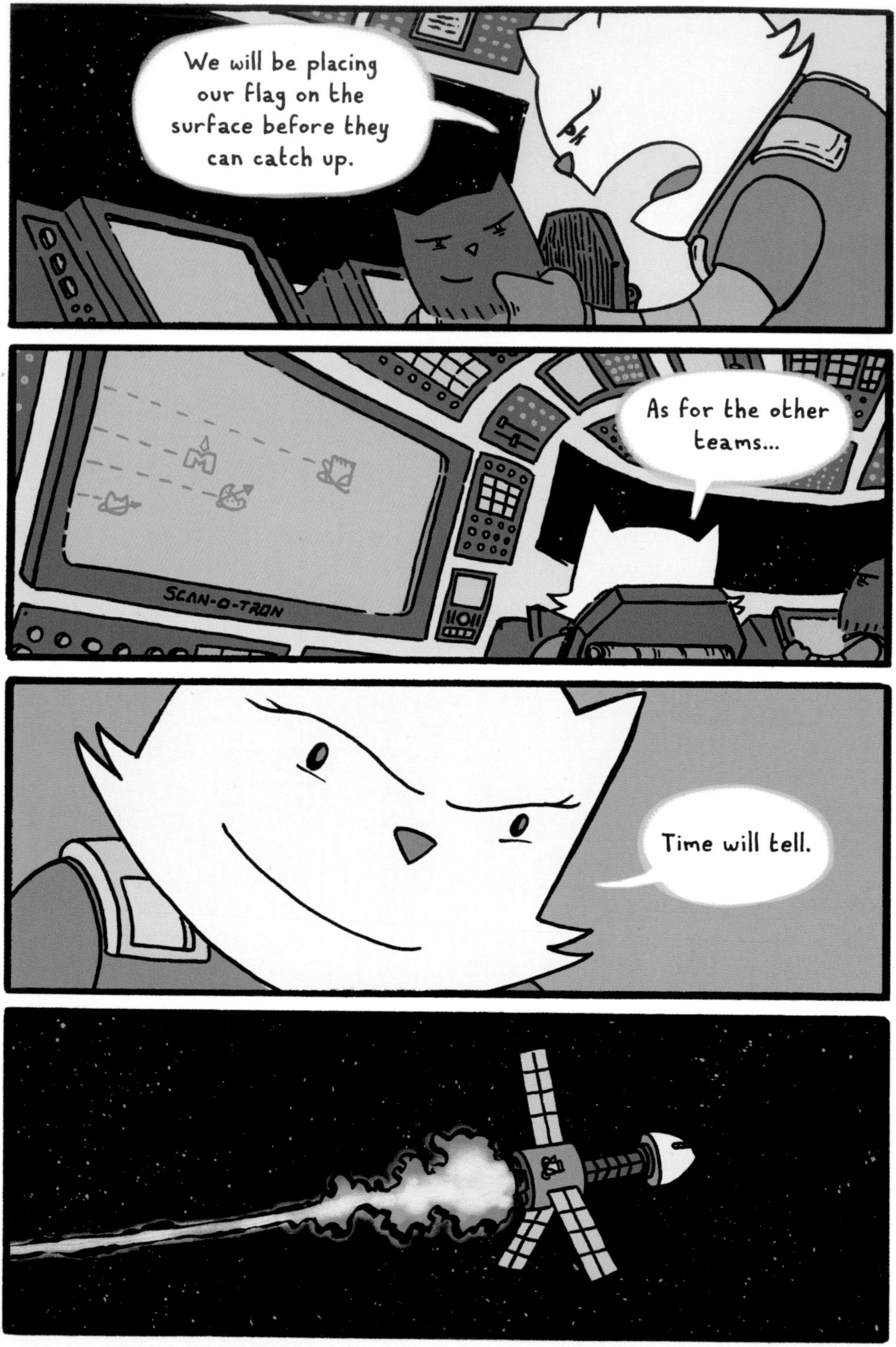
We will be placing our flag on the surface before they can catch up.
As for the other teams...
SCAN-O-TRON
Time will tell.

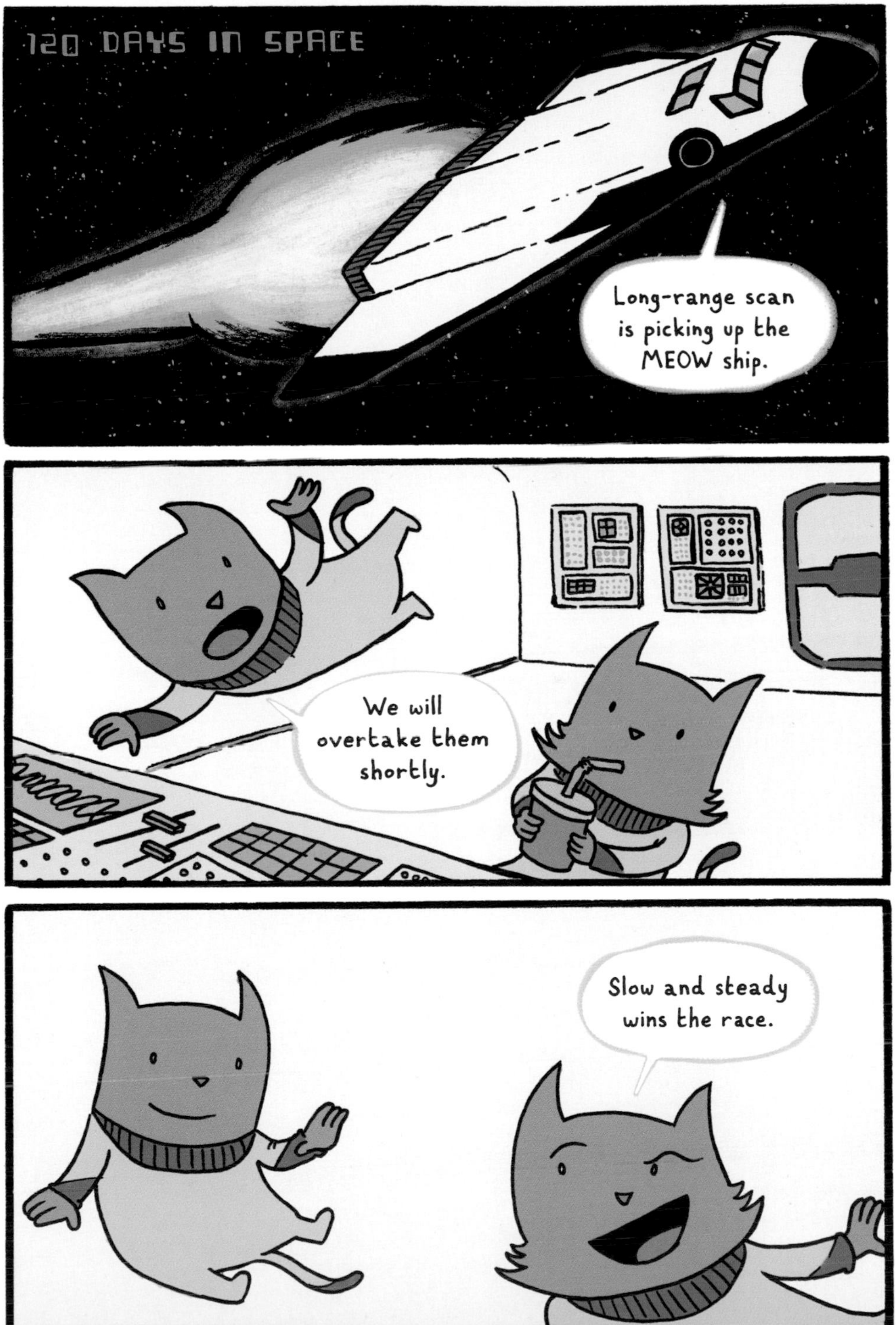
120 DAYS IN SPACE
Long-range scan is picking up the MEOW ship.
We will overtake them shortly.
Slow and steady wins the race.

Tails up, everyone! We are closing in on the others.

Let's see if I can sneak through....

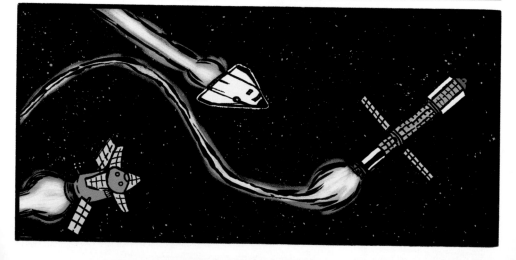

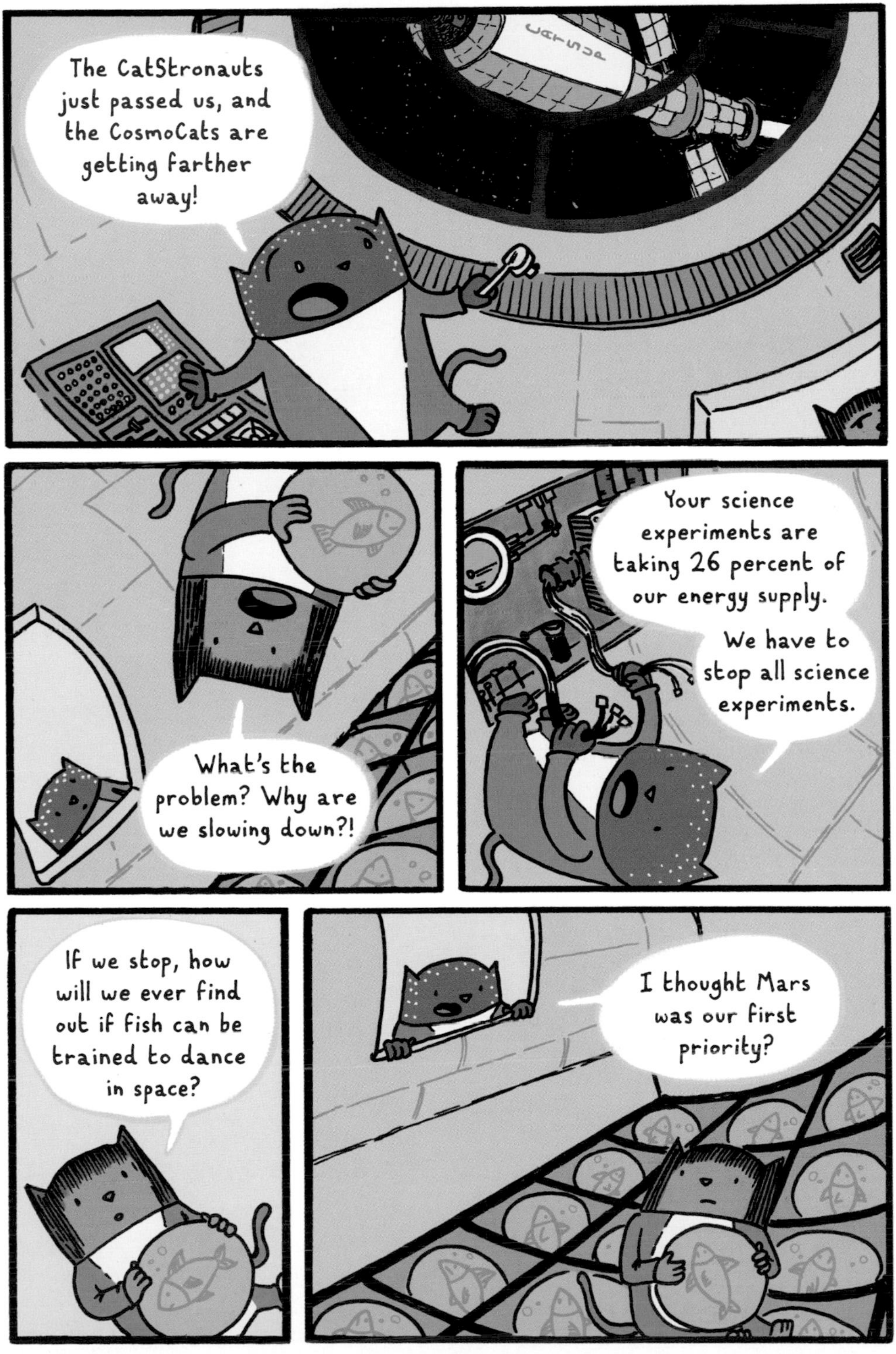
The CatStronauts just passed us, and the CosmoCats are getting farther away!
What's the problem? Why are we slowing down?!
Your science experiments are taking 26 percent of our energy supply.
We have to stop all science experiments.
If we stop, how will we ever find out if fish can be trained to dance in space?
I thought Mars was our first priority?

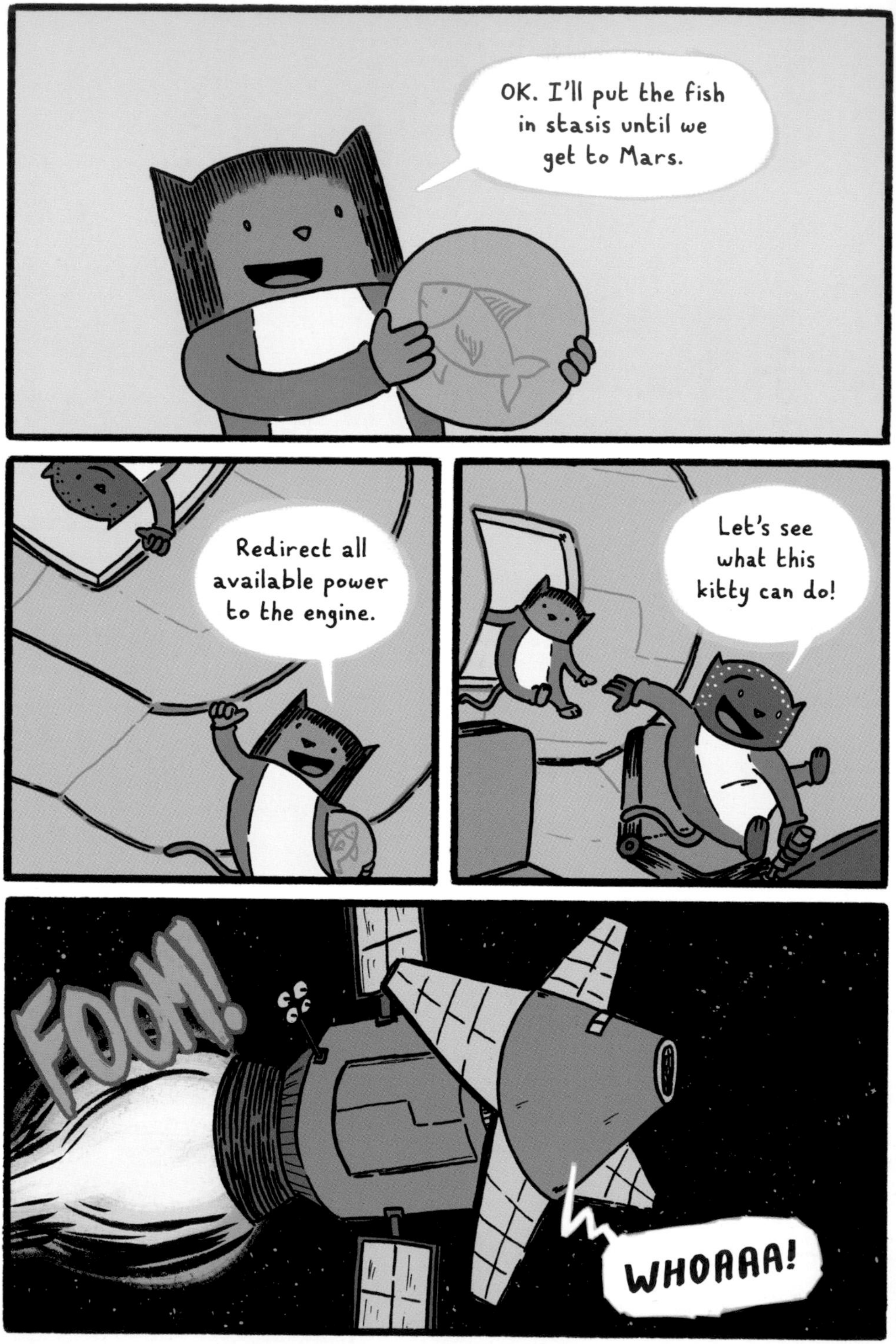
OK. I'll put the fish in stasis until we get to Mars.
Redirect all available power to the engine.
Let's see what this kitty can do!
FOOM!
WHOAAA!

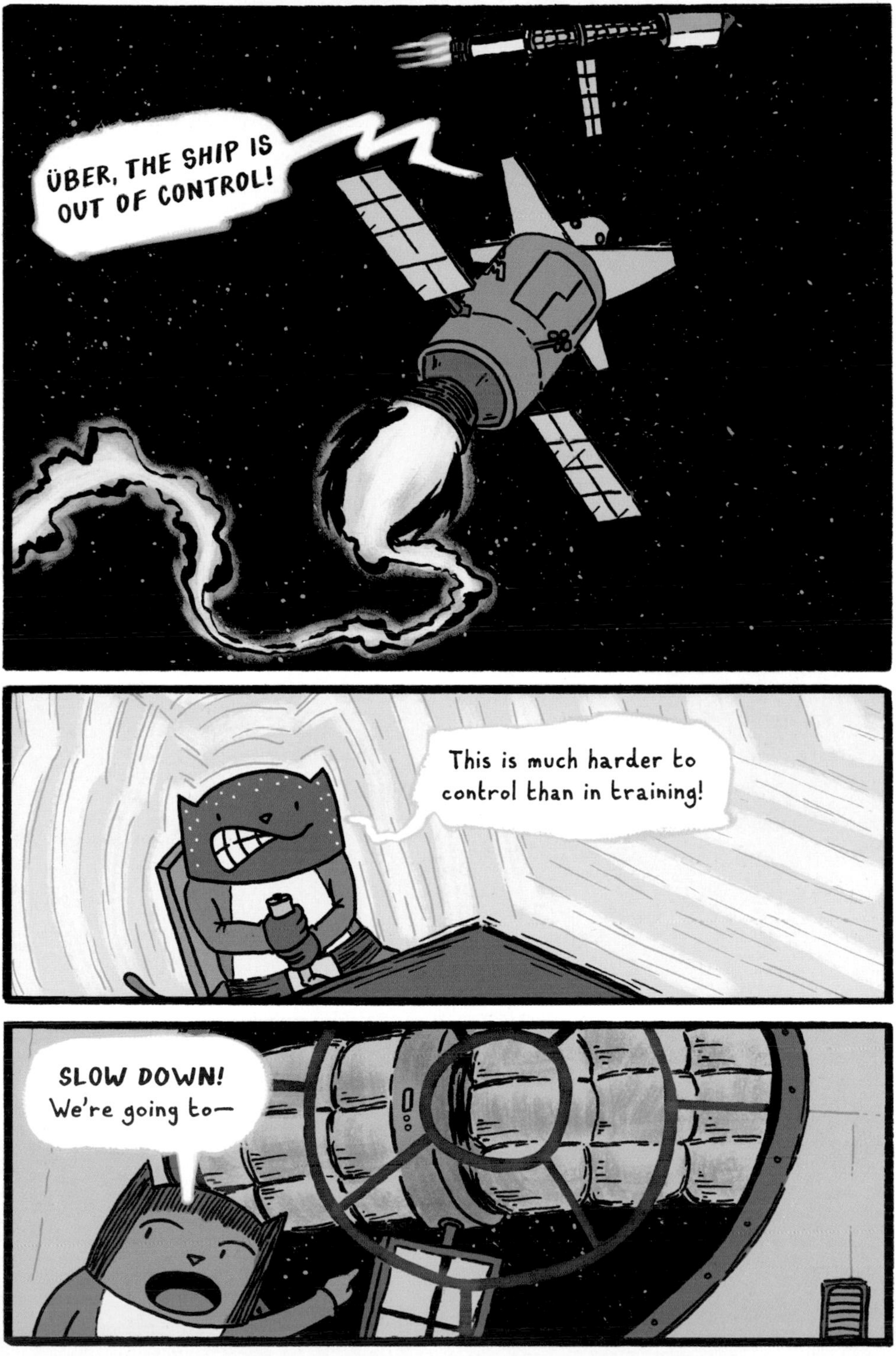
ÜBER, THE SHIP IS OUT OF CONTROL!
This is much harder to control than in training!
SLOW DOWN! We're going to—

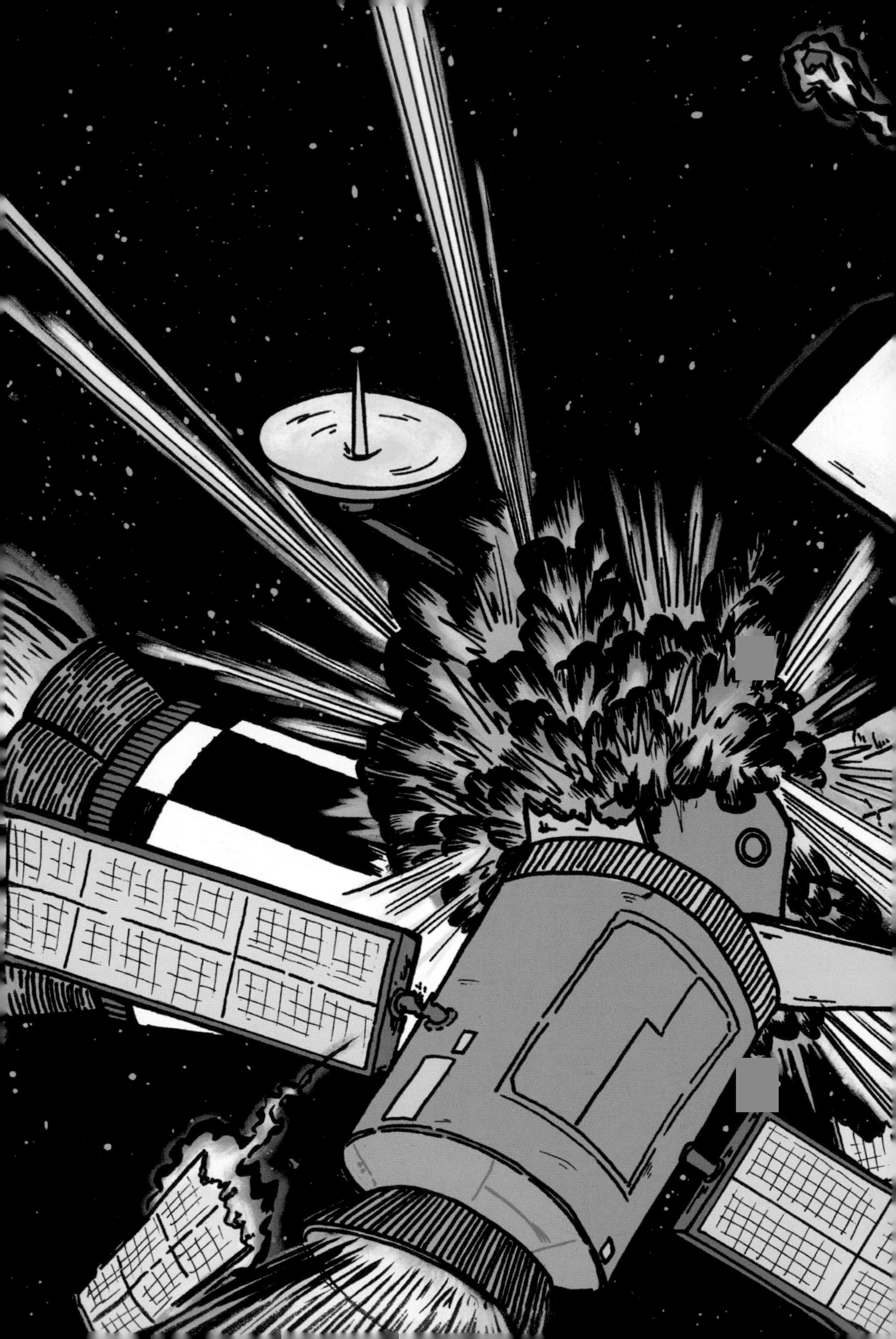

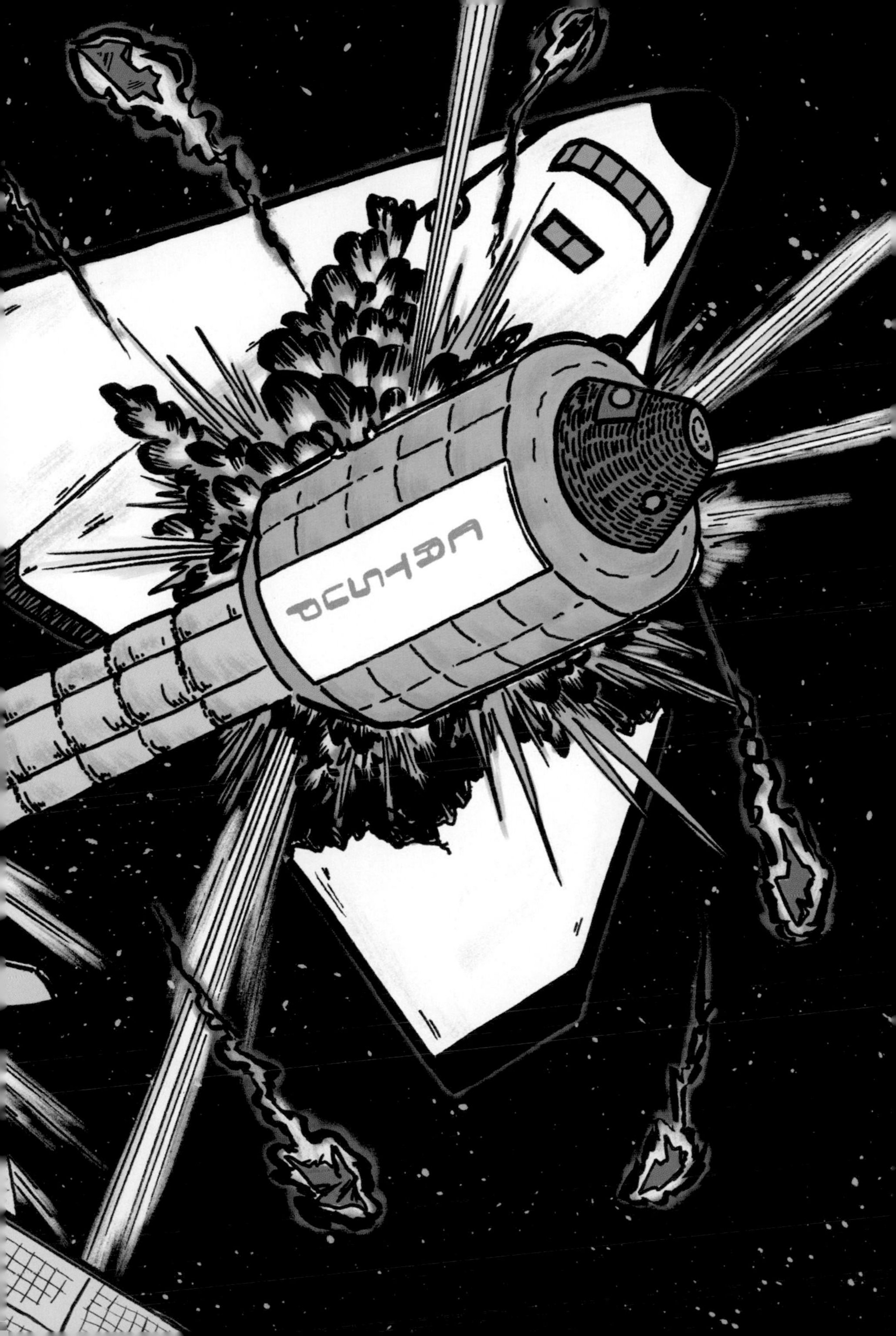

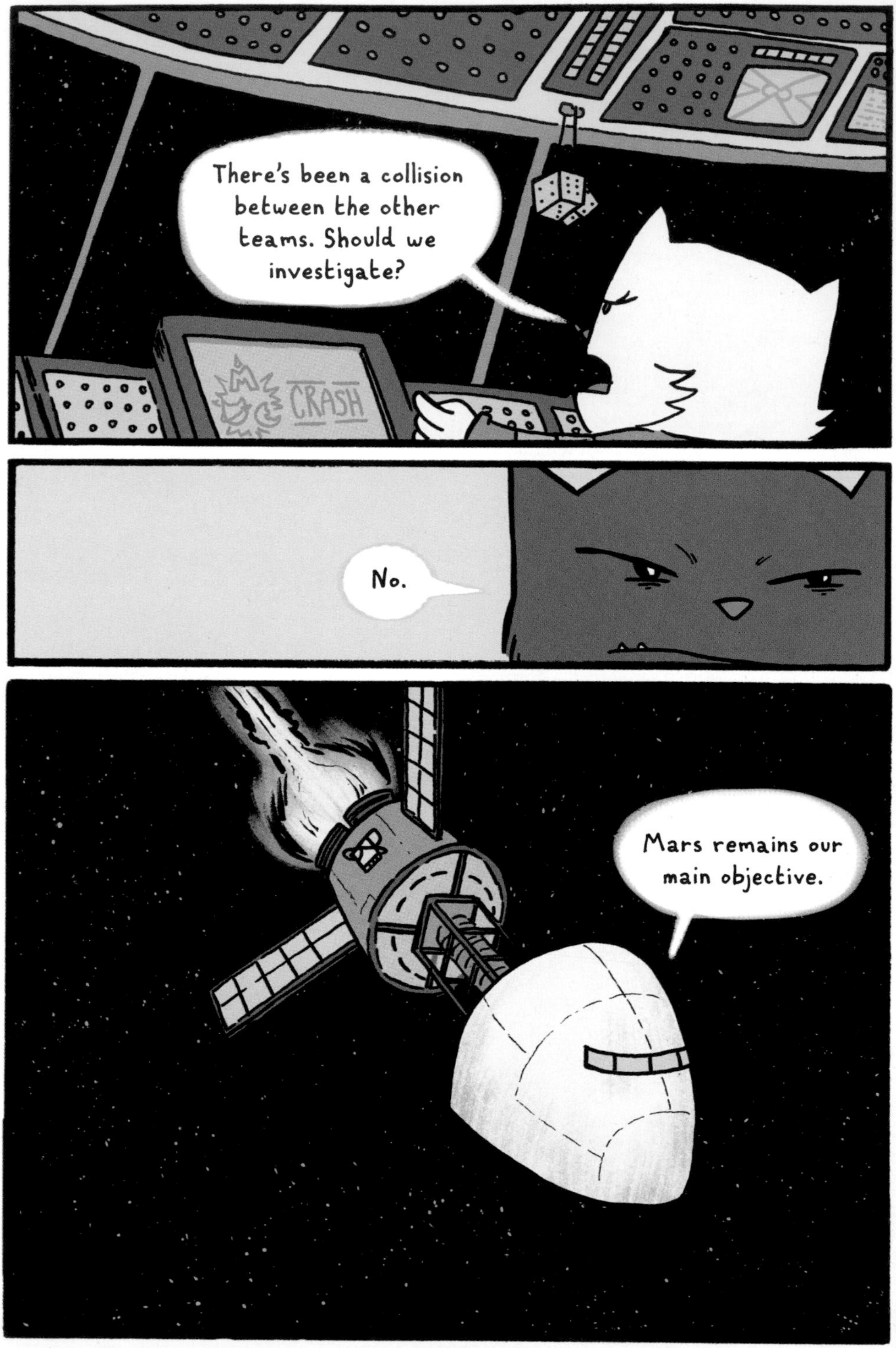
There's been a collision between the other teams. Should we investigate?
CRASH
No.
Mars remains our main objective.

CHAPTER 7

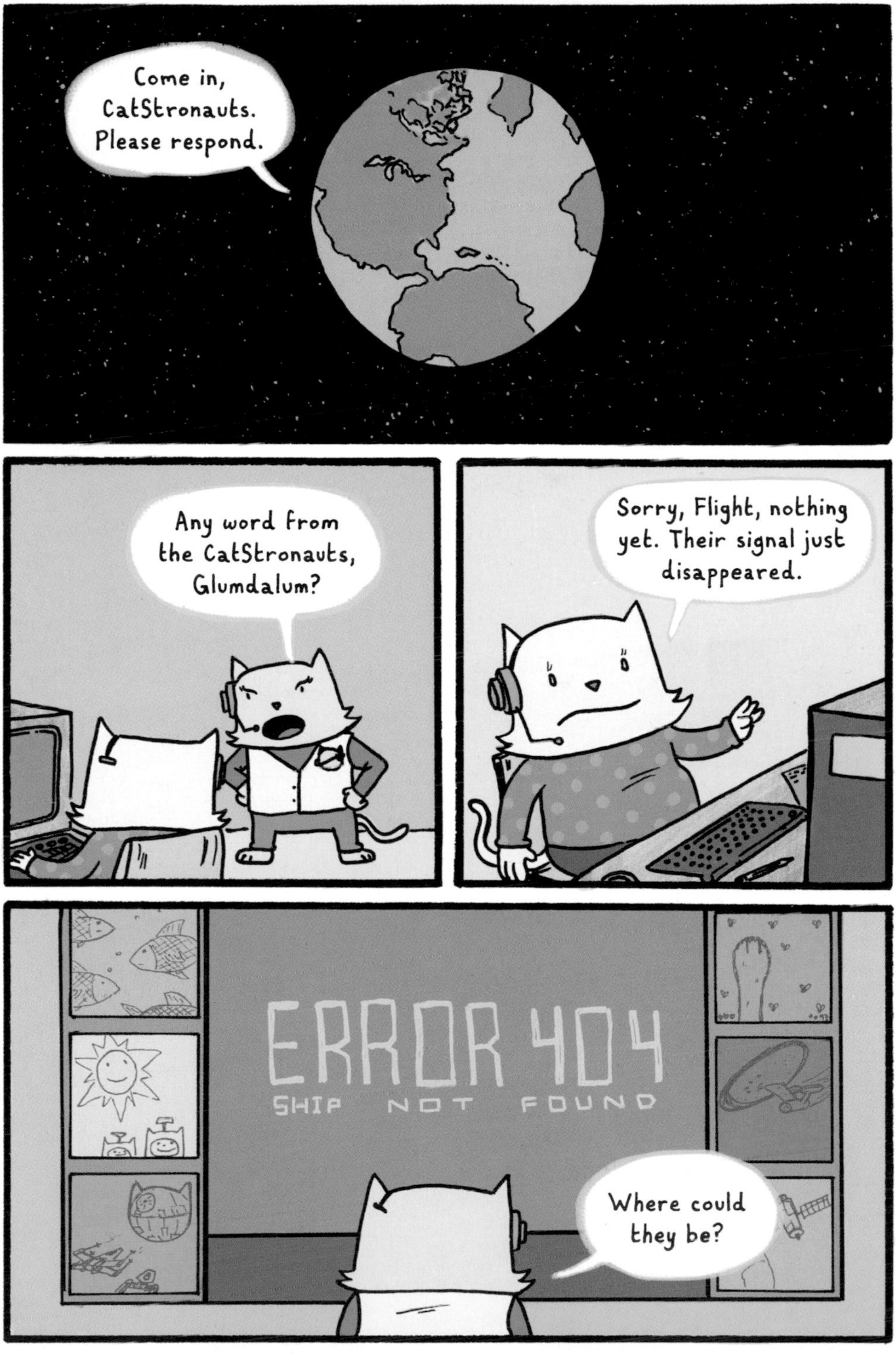
Come in, CatStronauts. Please respond.
Any word from the CatStronauts, Glumdalum?
Sorry, Flight, nothing yet. Their signal just disappeared.
ERROR 404
SHIP NOT FOUND
Where could they be?

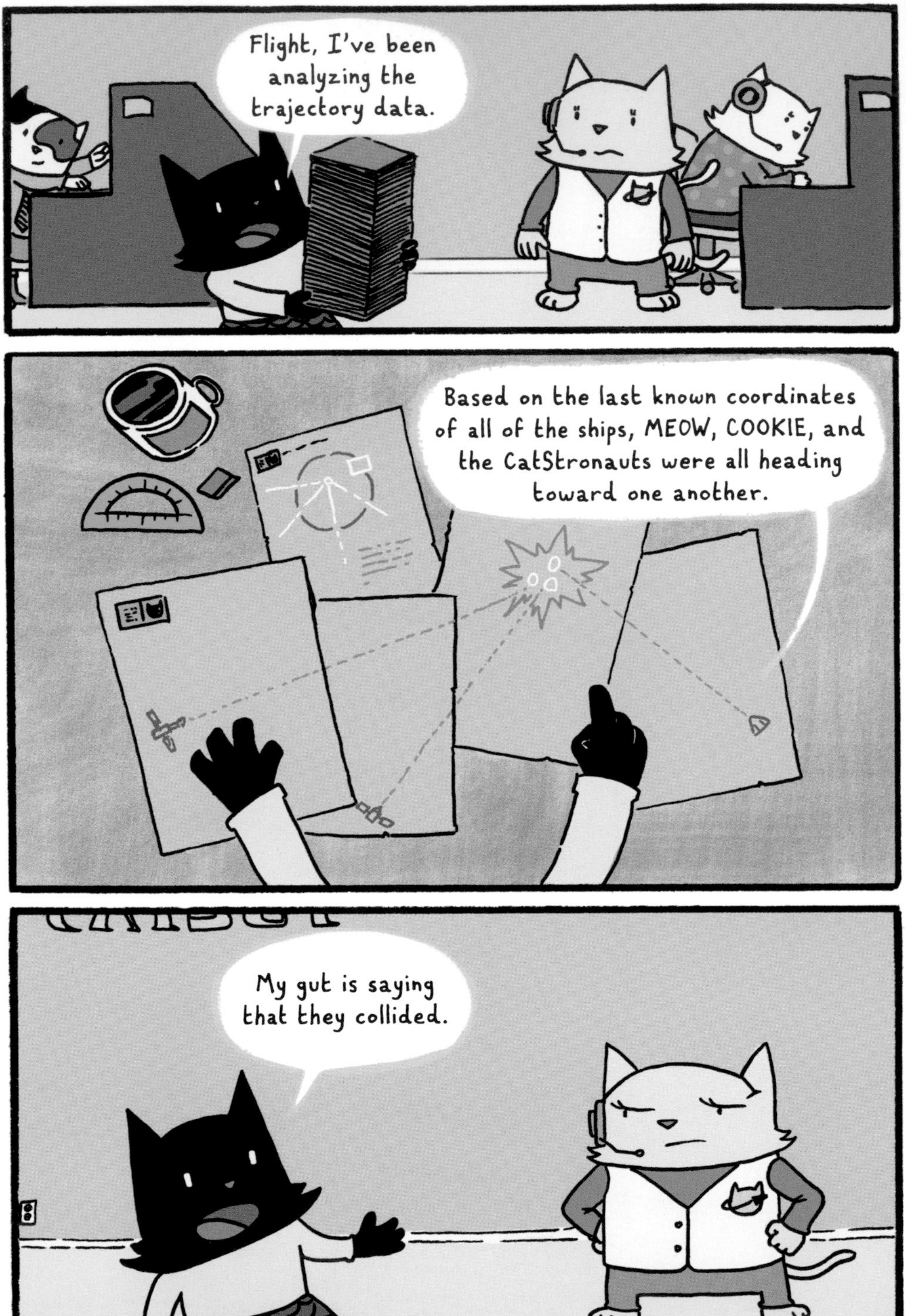
Flight, I've been analyzing the trajectory data.
Based on the last known coordinates of all of the ships, MEOW, COOKIE, and the CatStronauts were all heading toward one another.
My gut is saying that they collided.

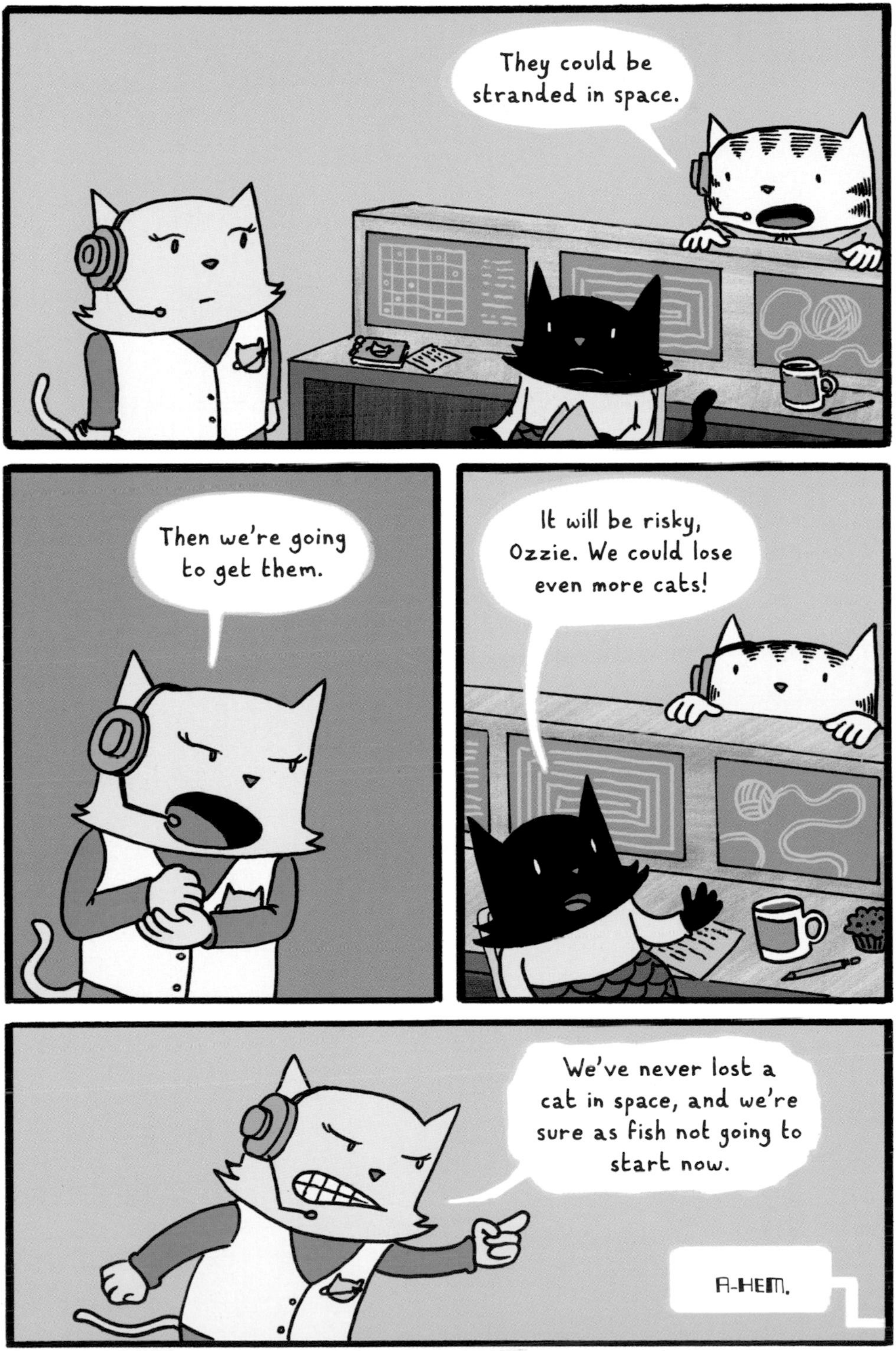
They could be stranded in space.
Then we're going to get them.
It will be risky, Ozzie. We could lose even more cats!
We've never lost a cat in space, and we're sure as fish not going to start now.
A-HEM.

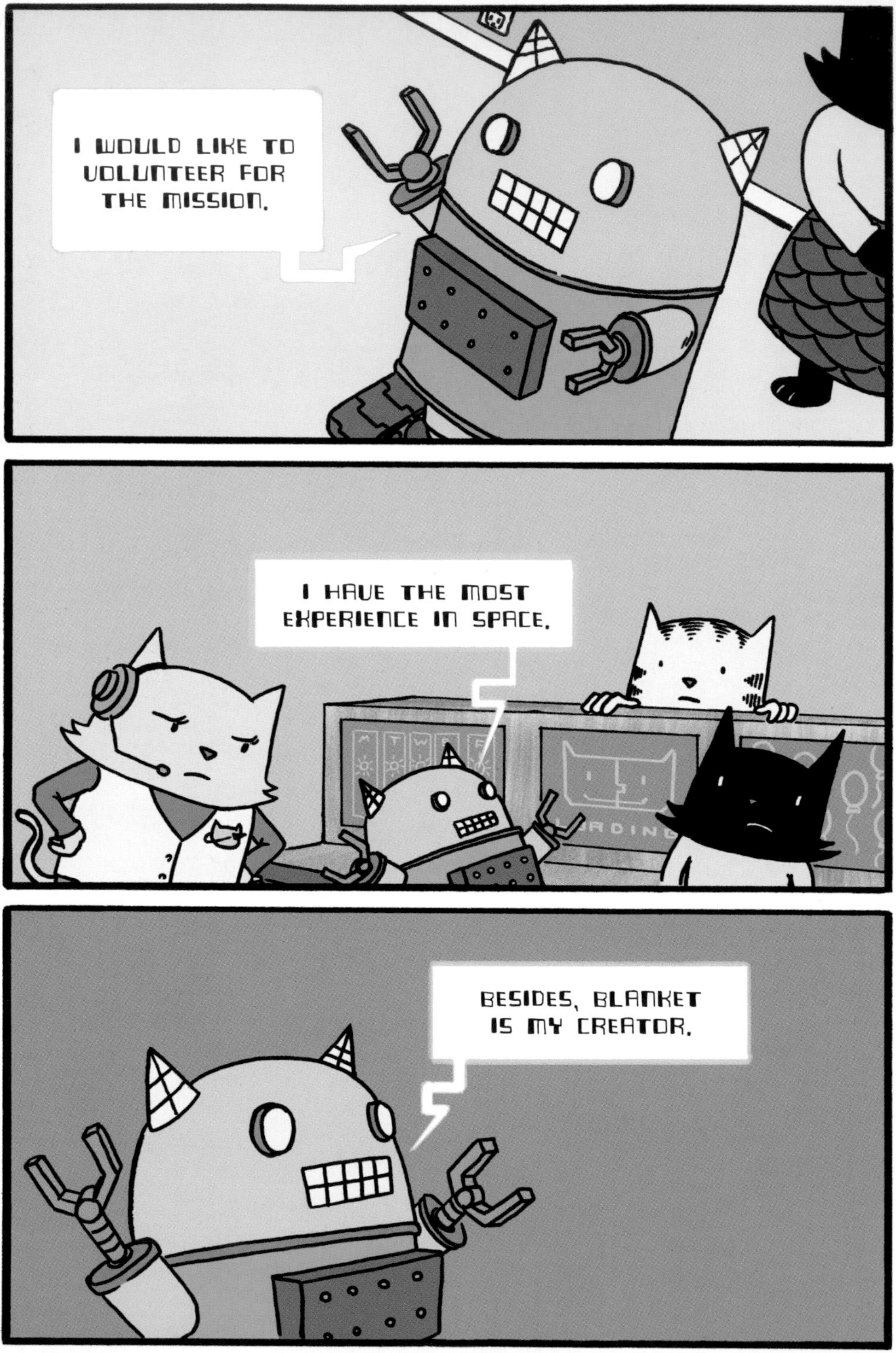
I WOULD LIKE TO VOLUNTEER FOR THE MISSION.
I HAVE THE MOST EXPERIENCE IN SPACE.
BESIDES, BLANKET IS MY CREATOR.

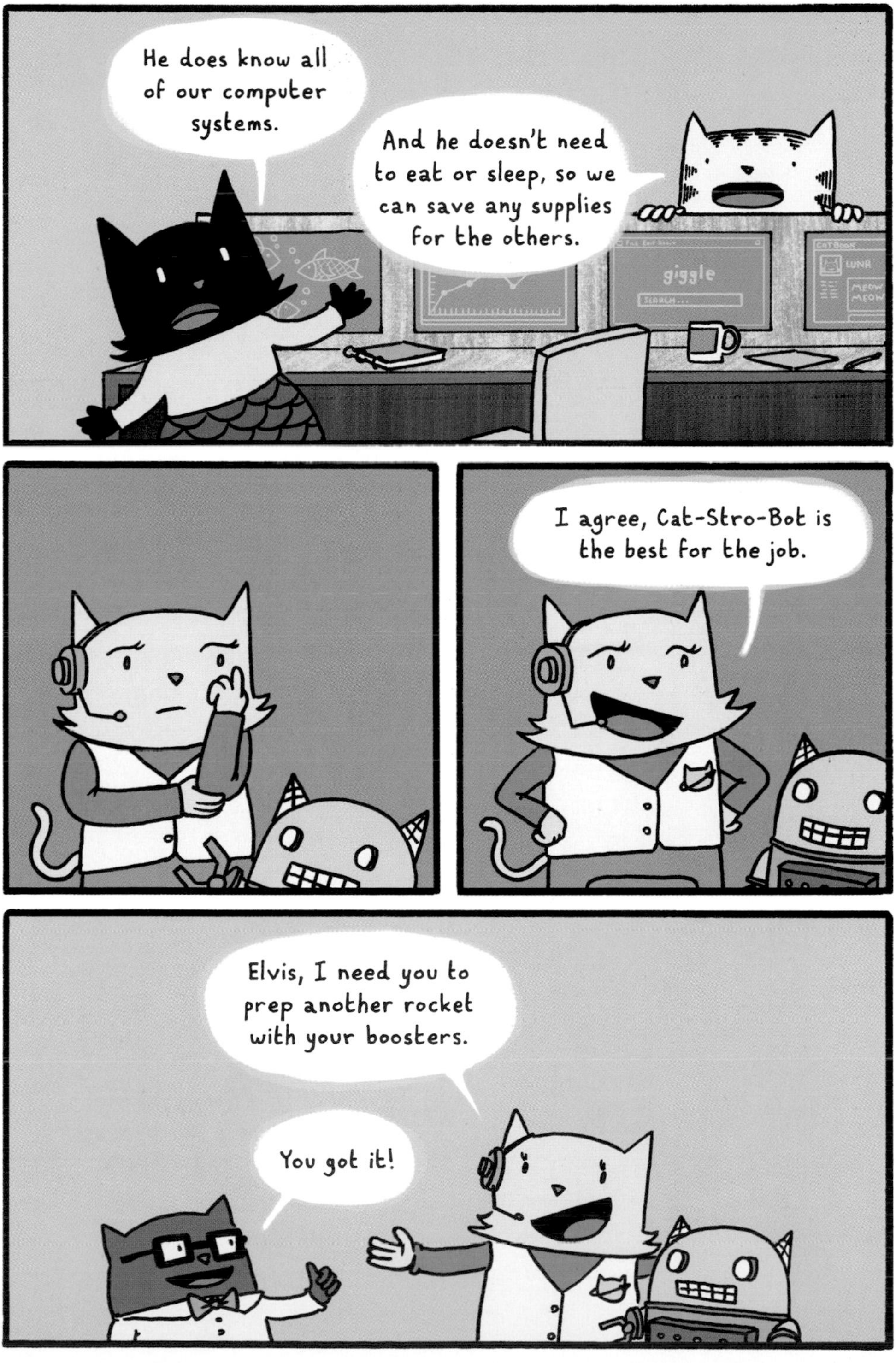

He does know all of our computer systems.
And he doesn't need to eat or sleep, so we can save any supplies for the others.
giggle
I agree, Cat-Stro-Bot is the best for the job.
Elvis, I need you to prep another rocket with your boosters.
You got it!

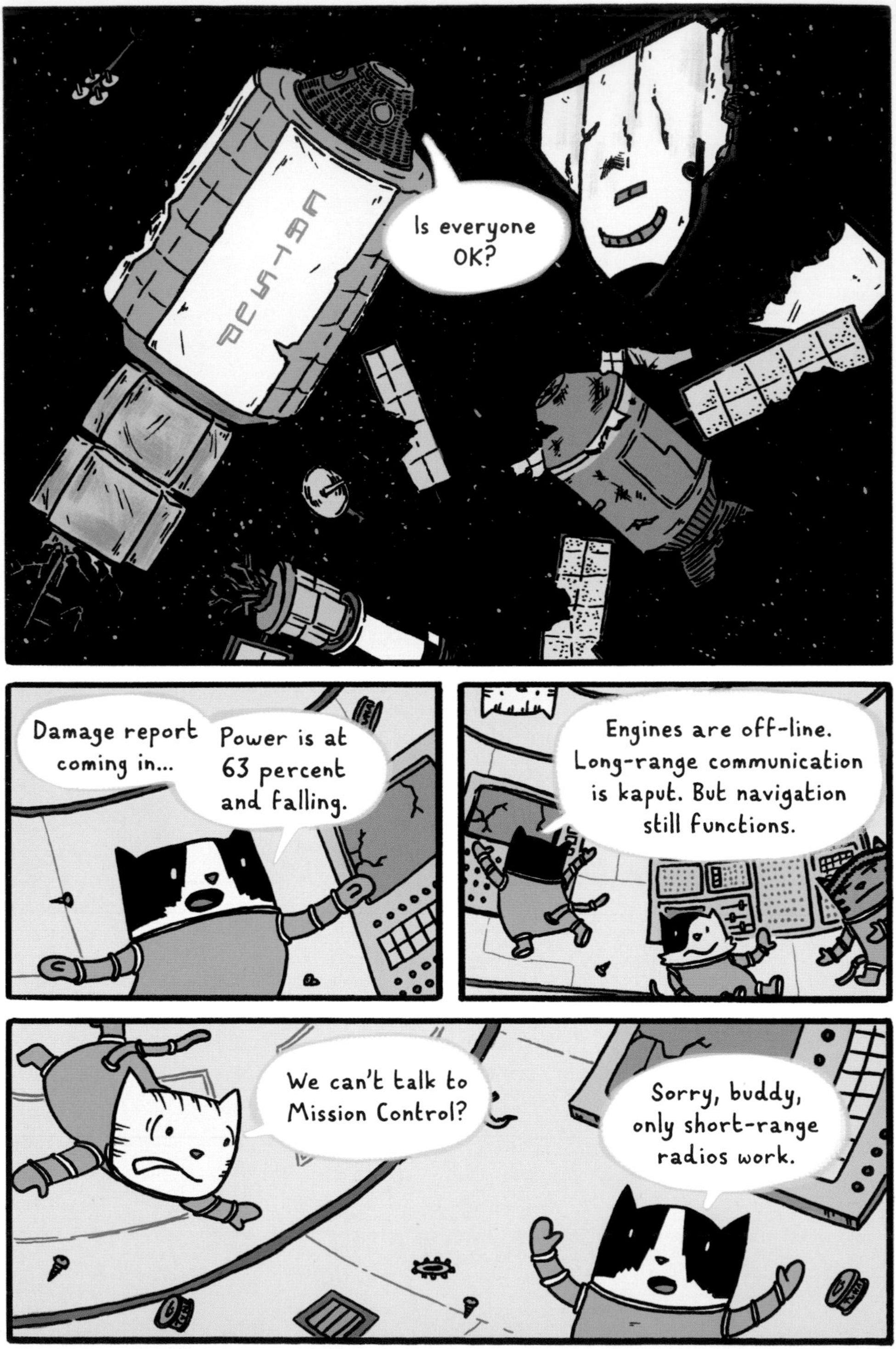
Is everyone OK?
Damage report coming in...
Power is at 63 percent and falling.
Engines are off-line. Long-range communication is kaput. But navigation still functions.
We can't talk to Mission Control?
Sorry, buddy, only short-range radios work.

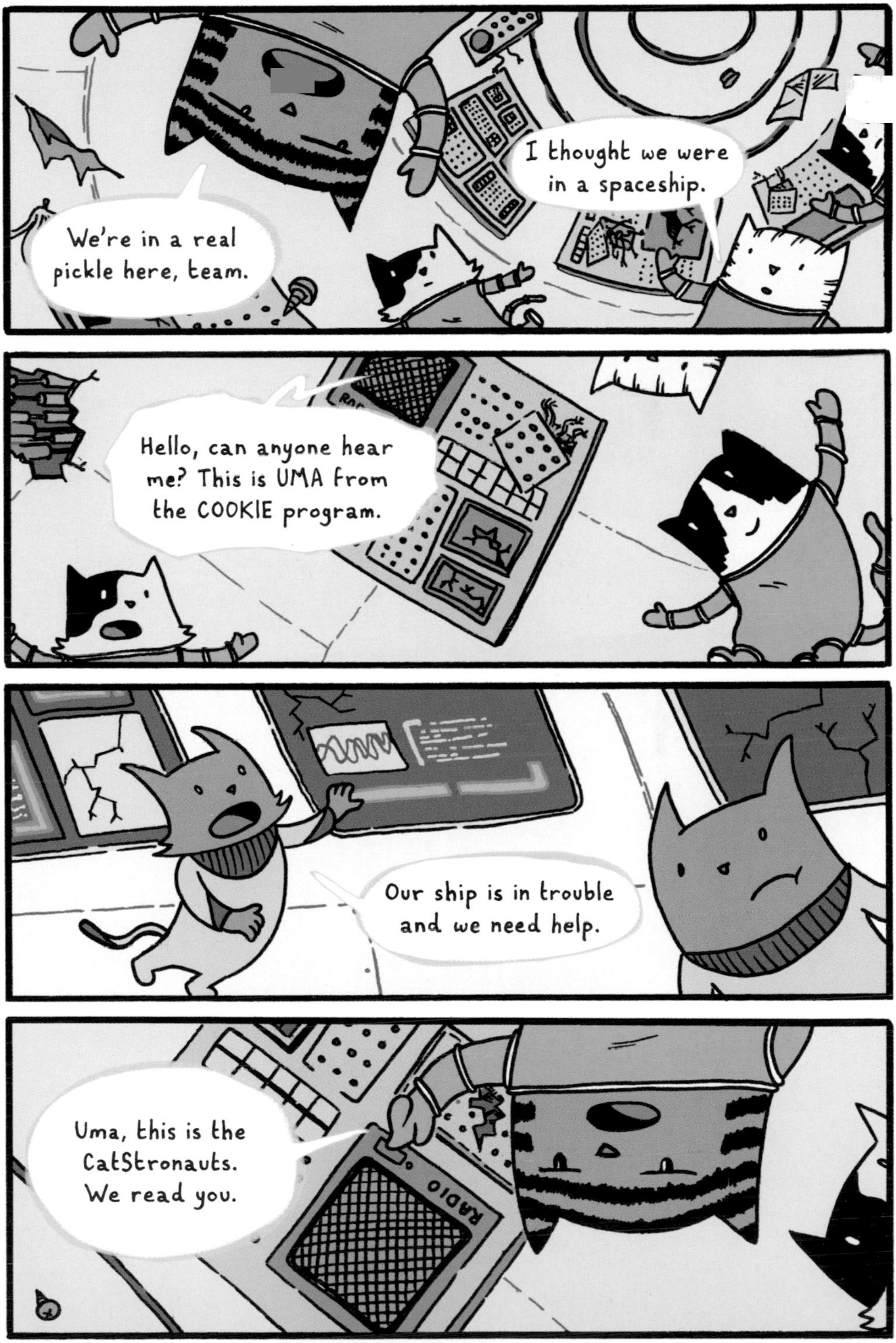
We're in a real pickle here, team.
I thought we were in a spaceship.
Hello, can anyone hear me? This is UMA from the COOKIE program.
Our ship is in trouble and we need help.
Uma, this is the CatStronauts. We read you.
RADIO

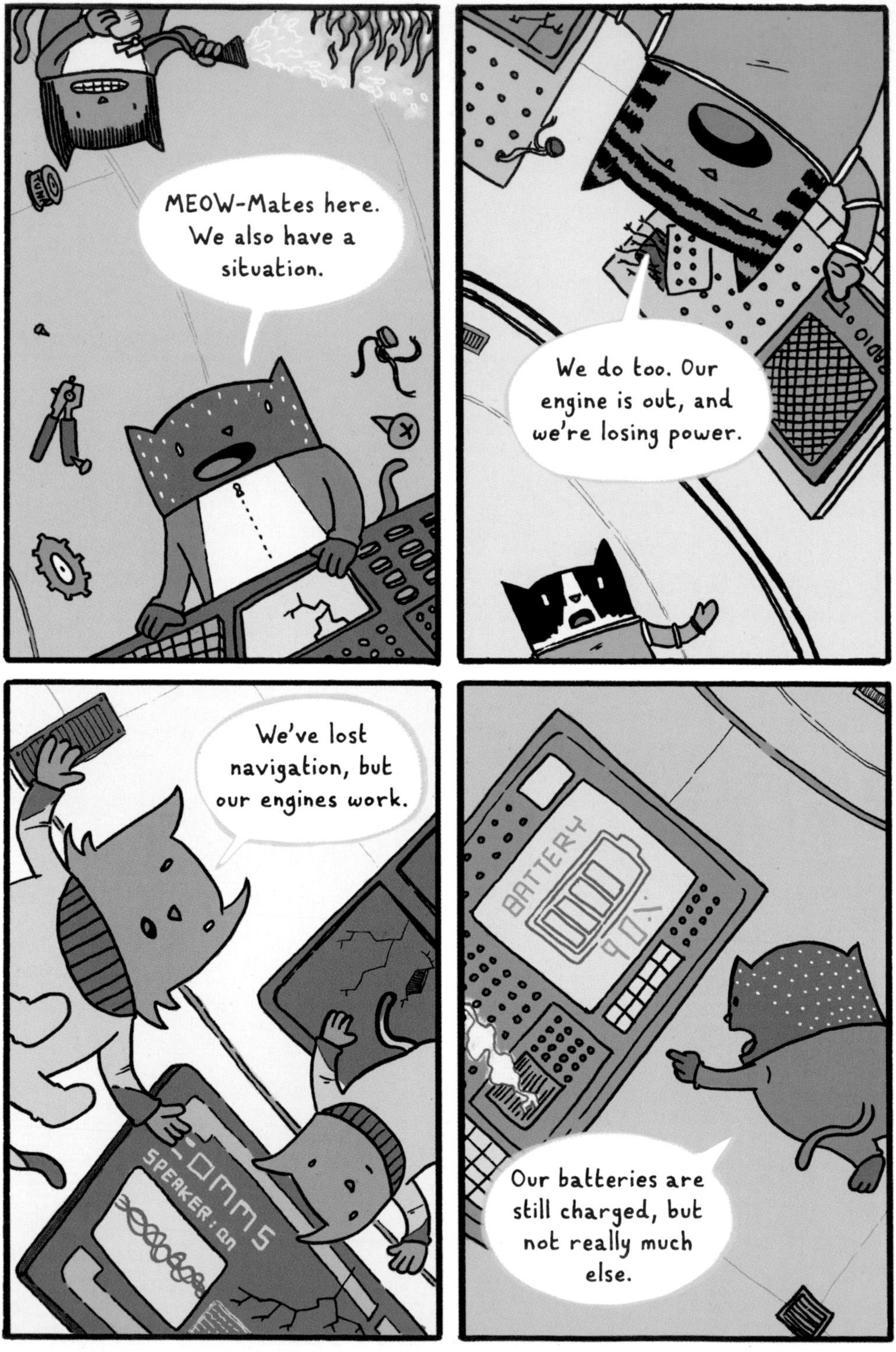
MEOW-Mates here. We also have a situation.
We do too. Our engine is out, and we're losing power.
We've lost navigation, but our engines work.
Our batteries are still charged, but not really much else.
BATTERY
90%
COMMS
SPEAKER: ON
RADIO
TUNA

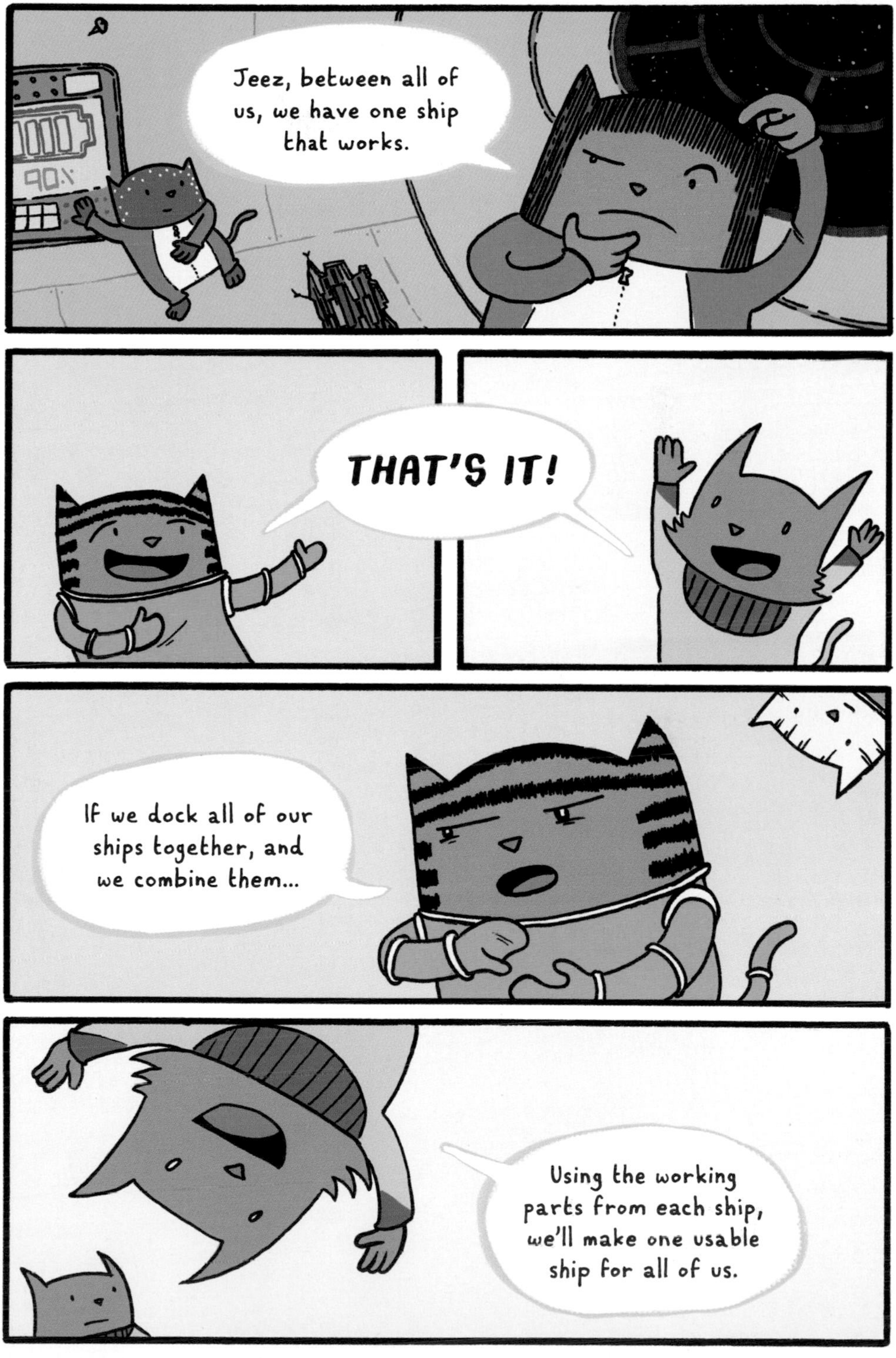
Jeez, between all of us, we have one ship that works.
90%
THAT'S IT!
If we dock all of our ships together, and we combine them...
Using the working parts from each ship, we'll make one usable ship for all of us.

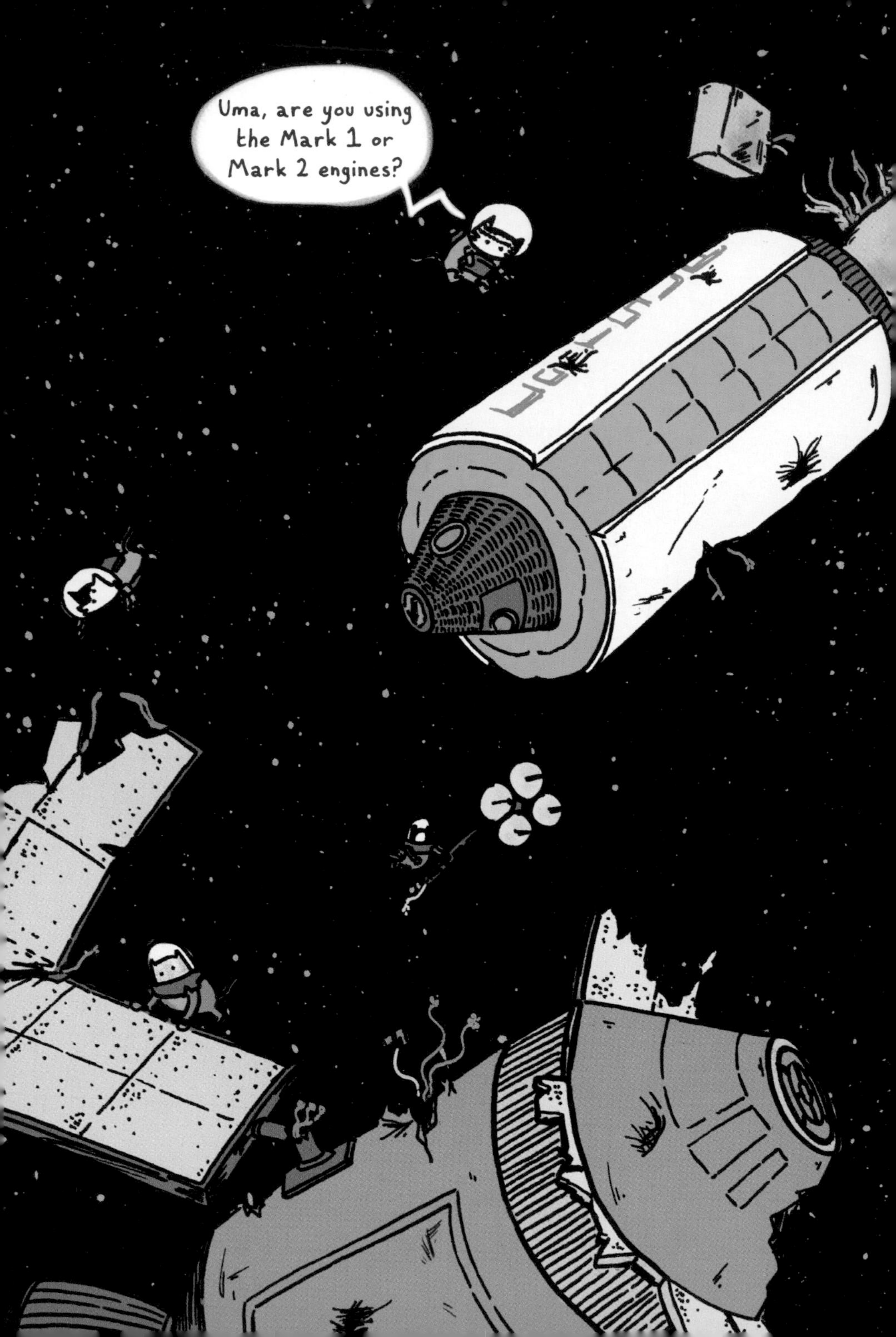
Uma, are you using the Mark 1 or Mark 2 engines?

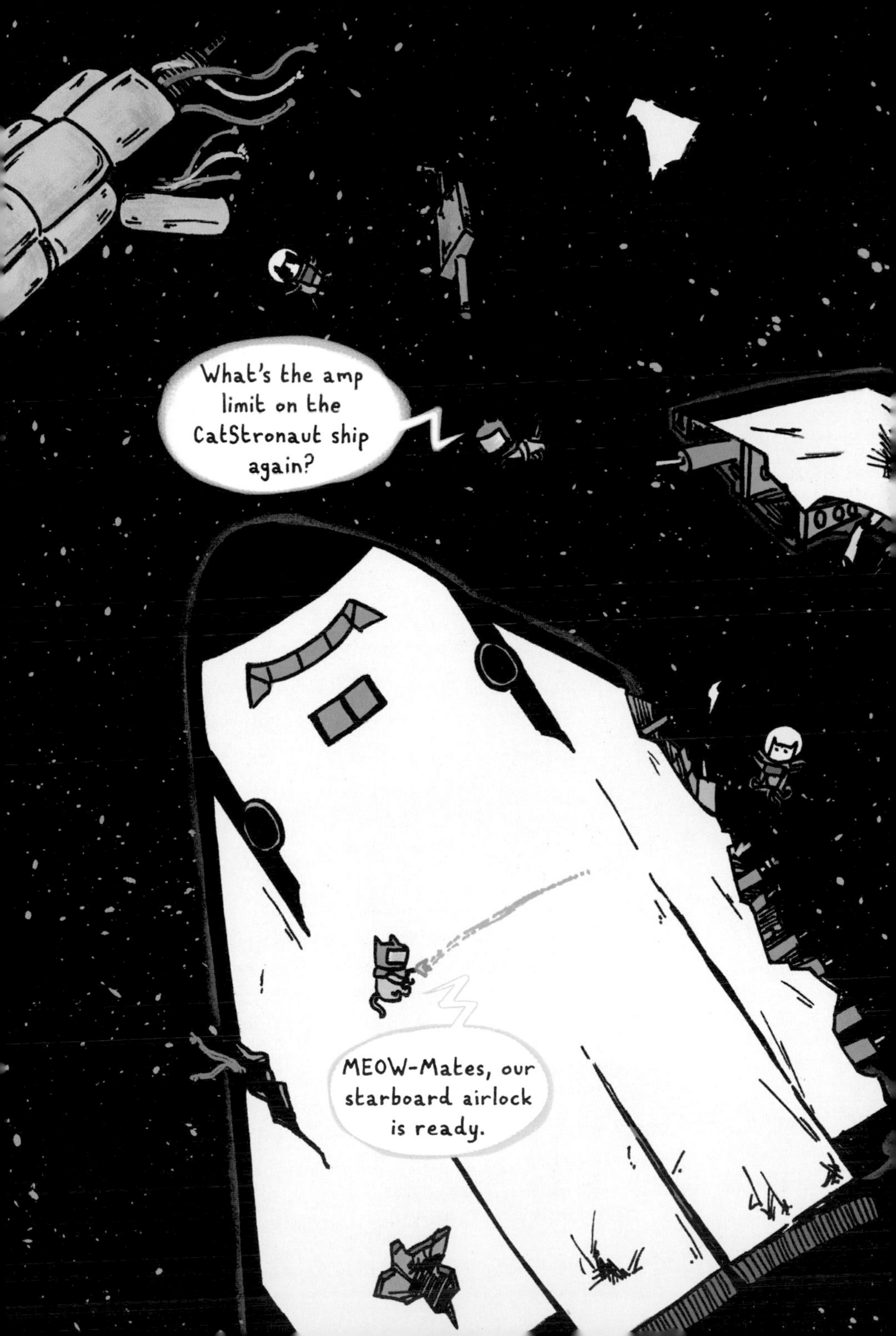
What's the amp limit on the CatStronaut ship again?
MEOW-Mates, our starboard airlock is ready.

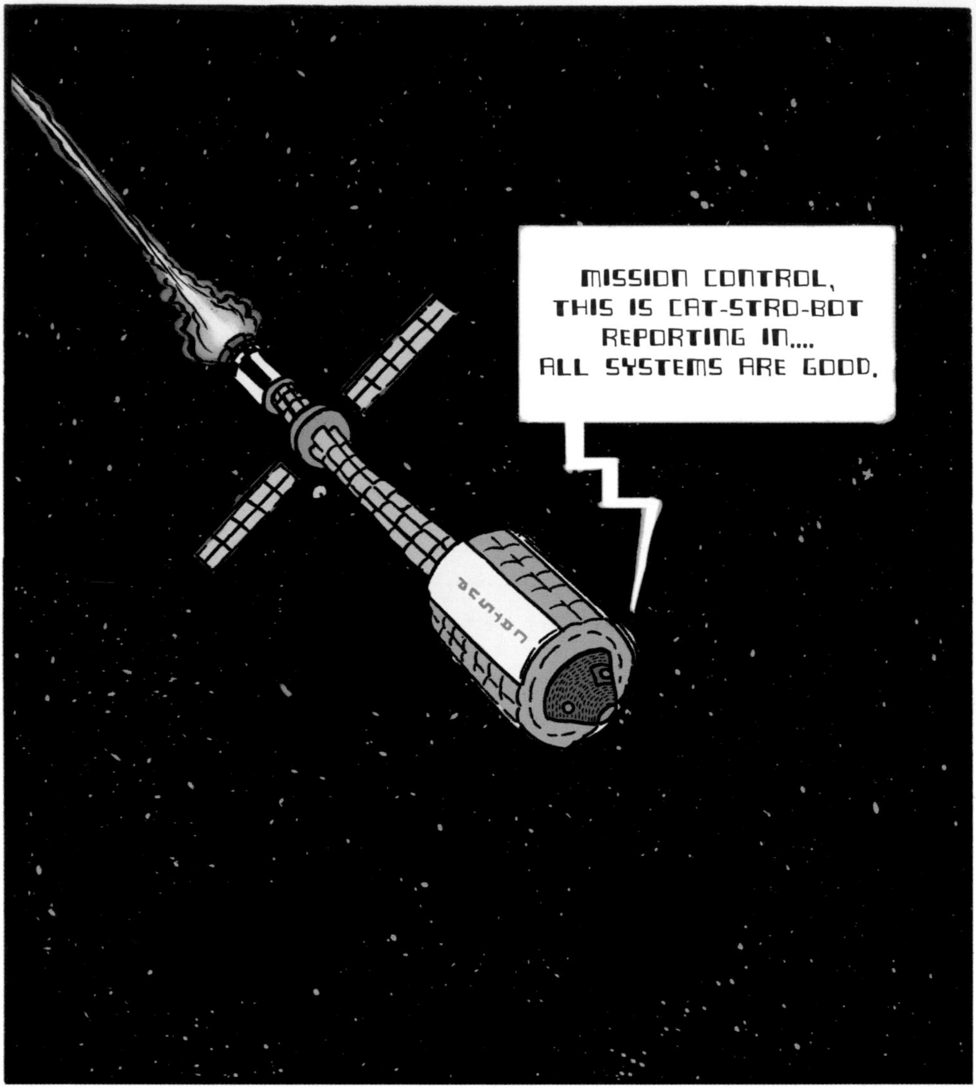
MISSION CONTROL, THIS IS CAT-STRO-BOT REPORTING IN.... ALL SYSTEMS ARE GOOD.

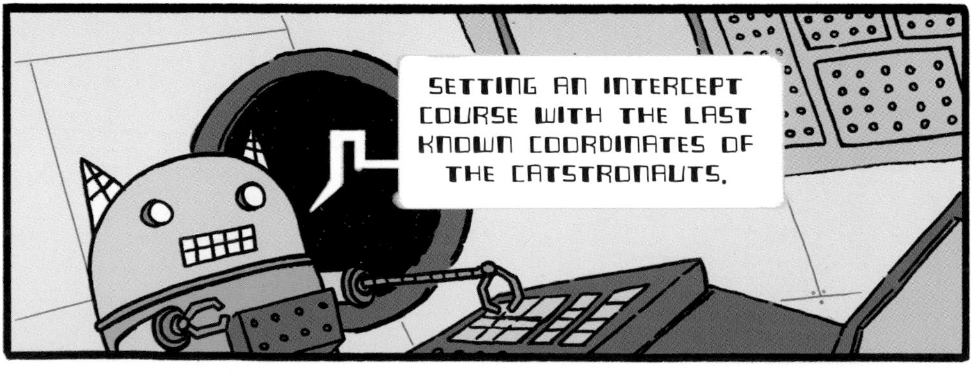
SETTING AN INTERCEPT COURSE WITH THE LAST KNOWN COORDINATES OF THE CATSTRONAUTS.

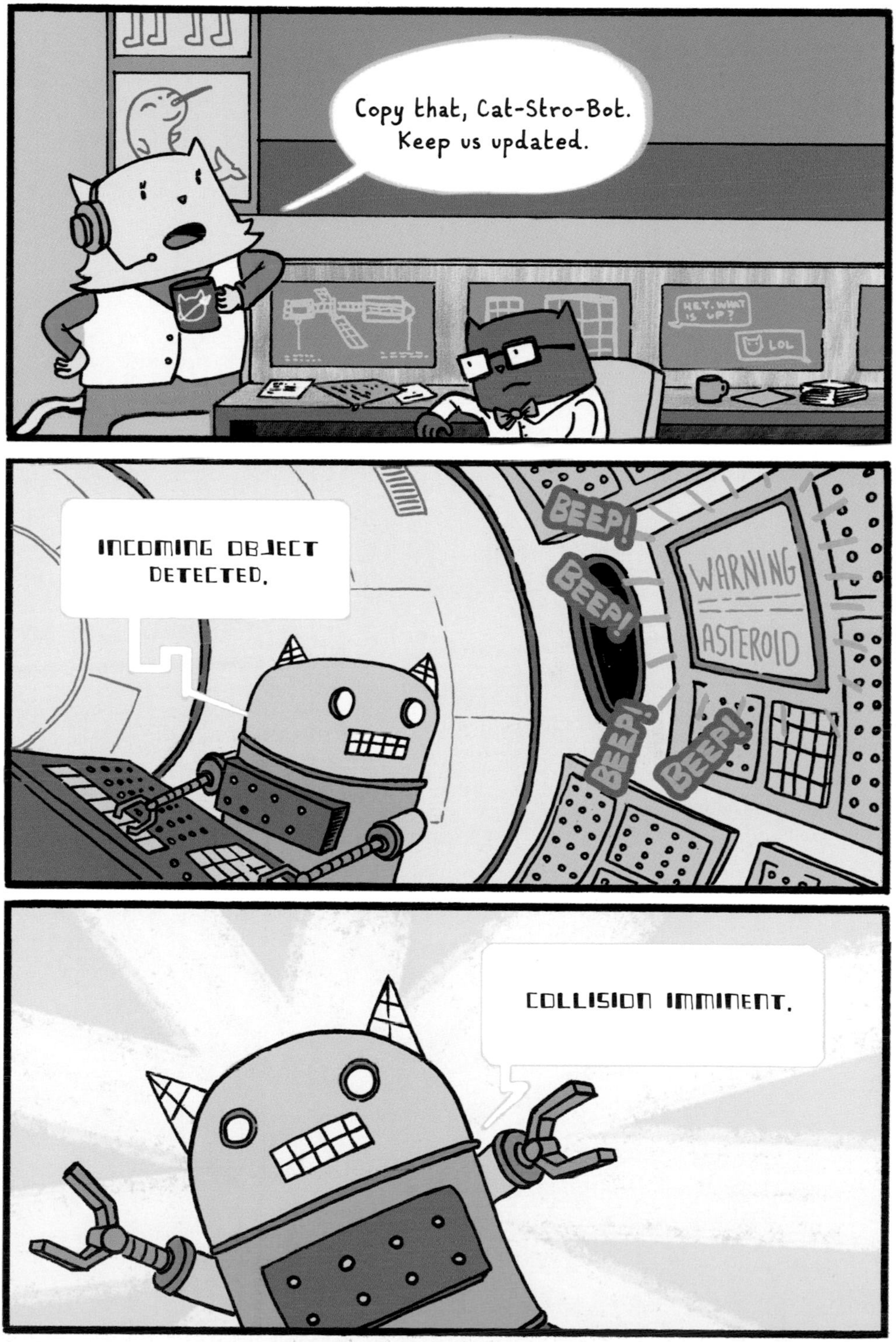
Copy that, Cat-Stro-Bot. Keep us updated.
HEY, WHAT IS UP?
LOL
INCOMING OBJECT DETECTED.
BEEP!
BEEP!
WARNING
ASTEROID
BEEP!
BEEP!
COLLISION IMMINENT.

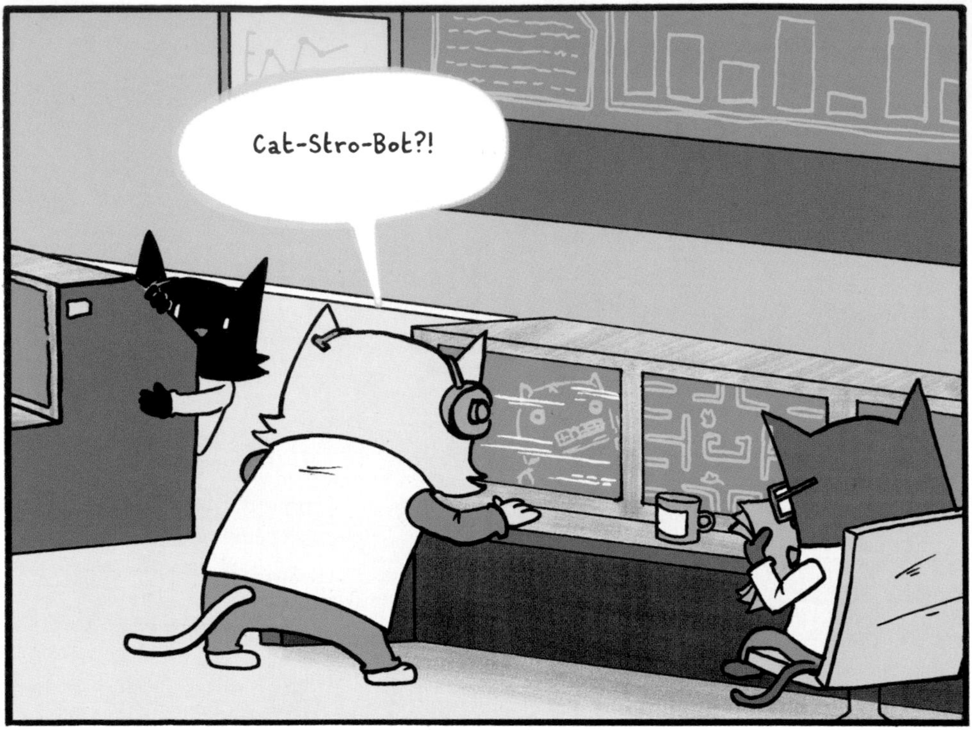
Cat-Stro-Bot?!

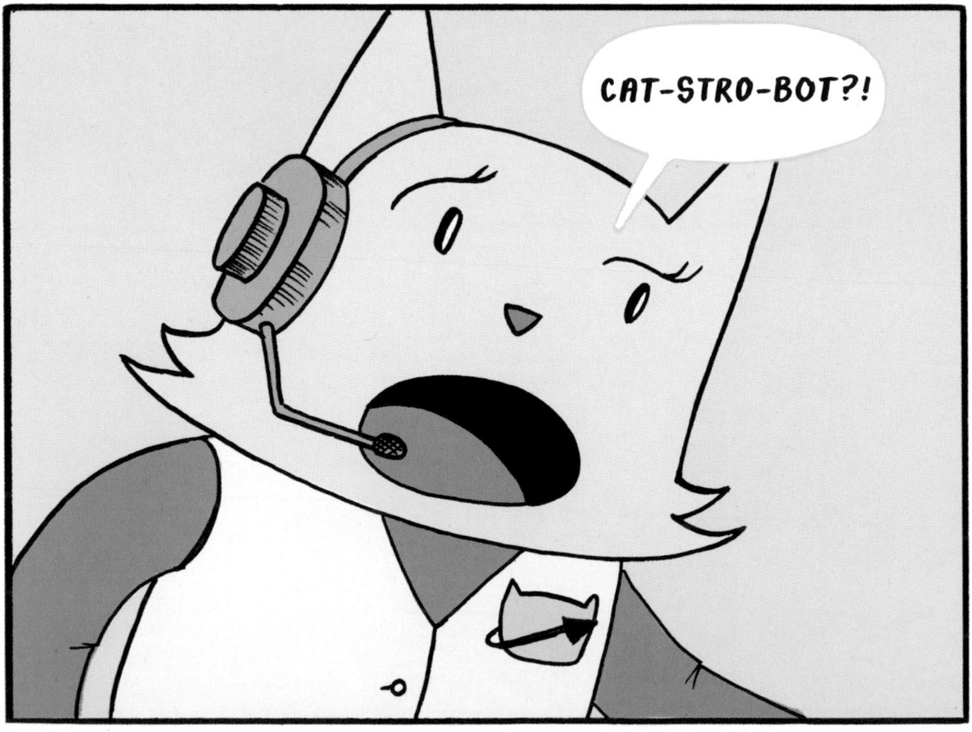
CAT-STRO-BOT?!

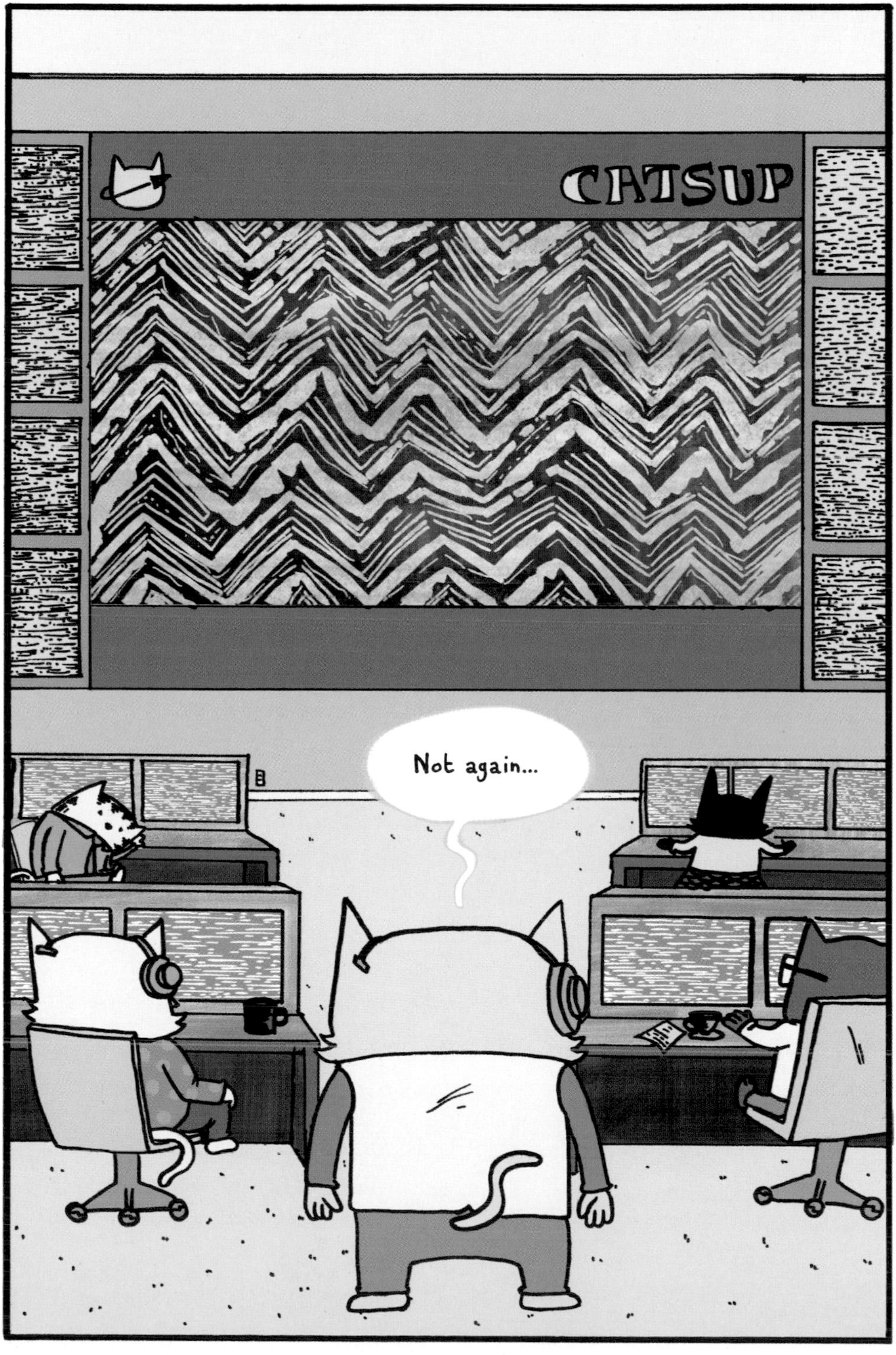
CATSUP
Not again...

CHAPTER 8

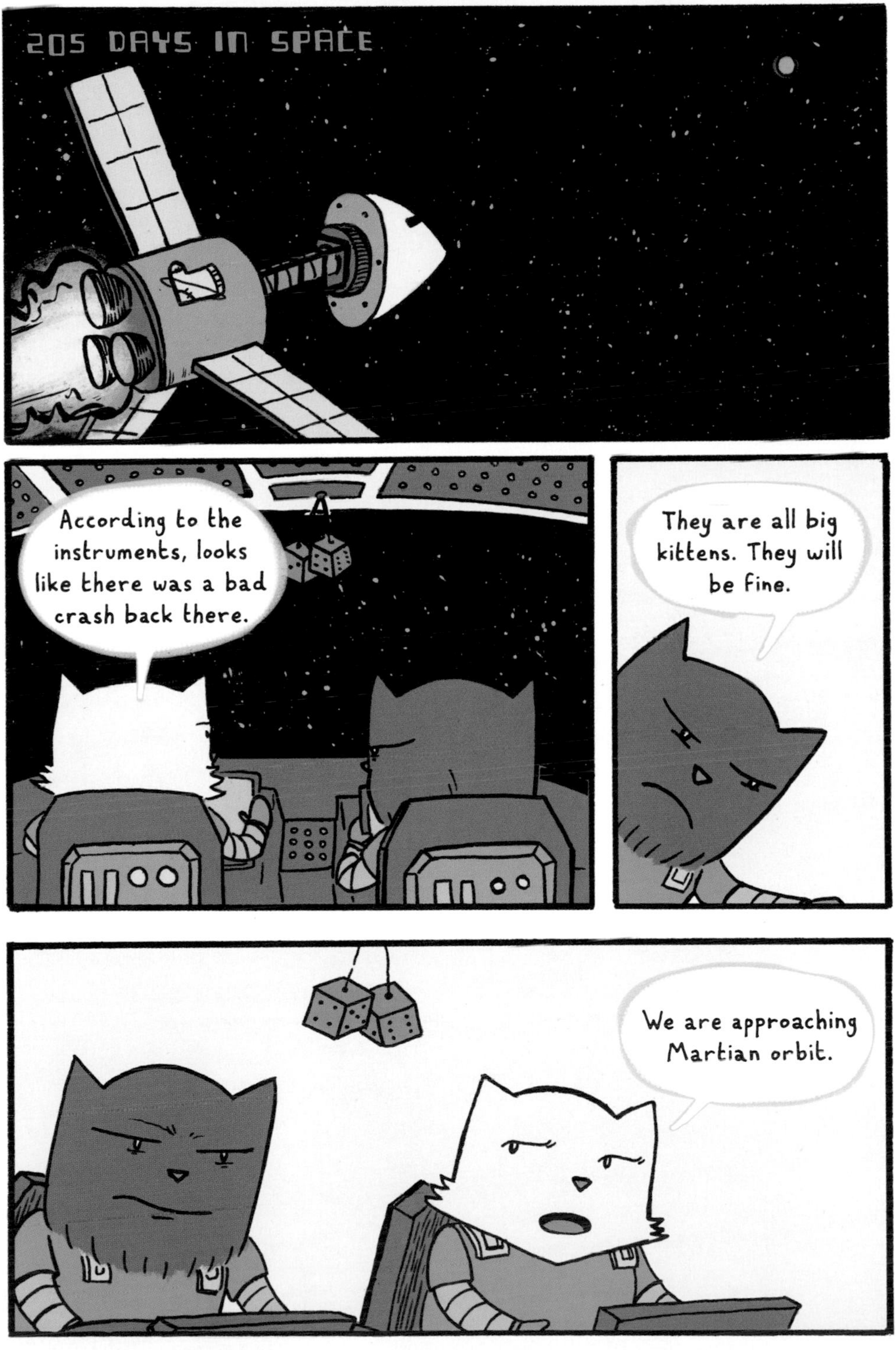
205 DAYS IN SPACE
According to the instruments, looks like there was a bad crash back there.
They are all big kittens. They will be fine.
We are approaching Martian orbit.

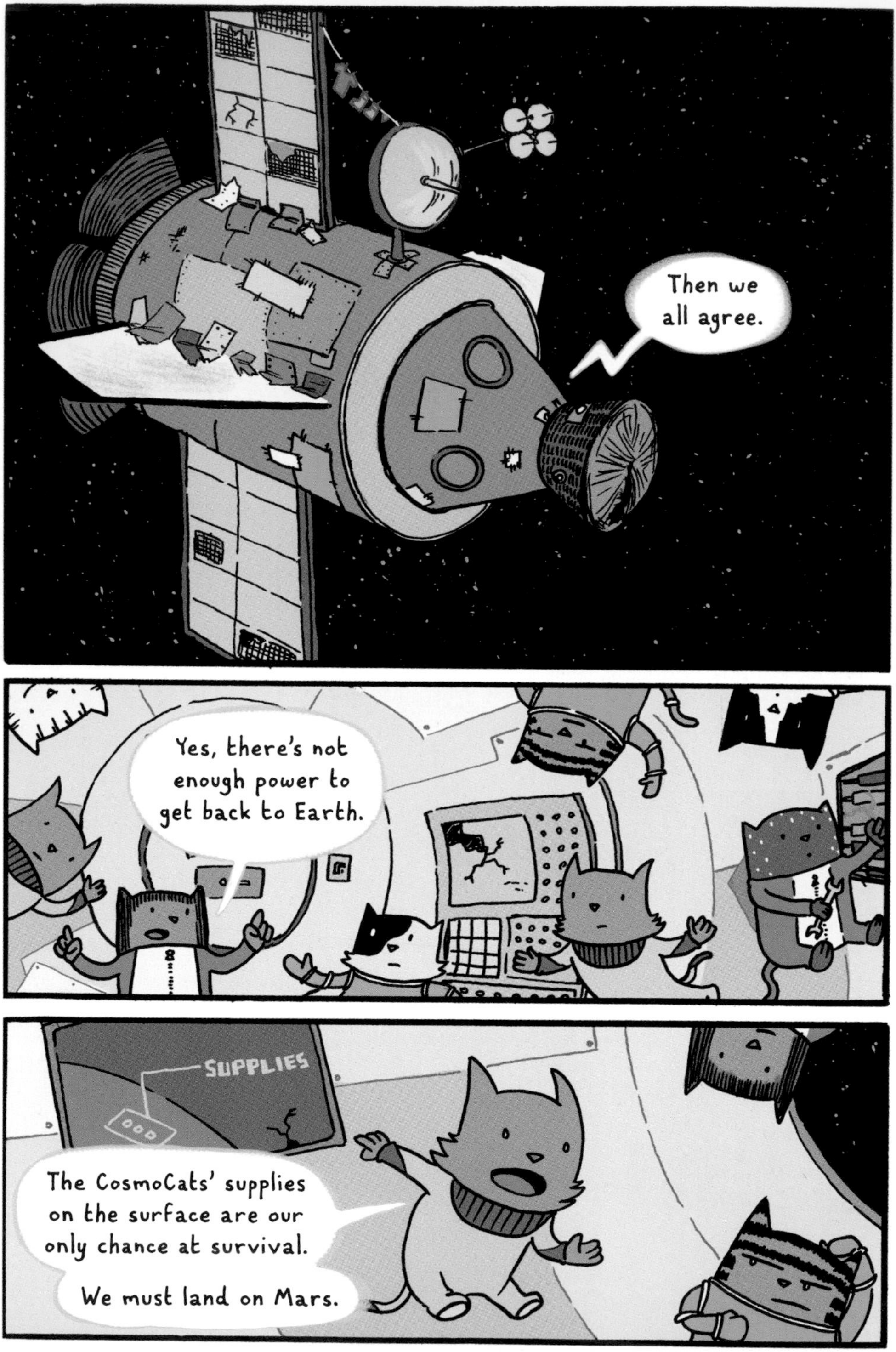
Then we all agree.
Yes, there's not enough power to get back to Earth.
SUPPLIES
The CosmoCats' supplies on the surface are our only chance at survival.
We must land on Mars.

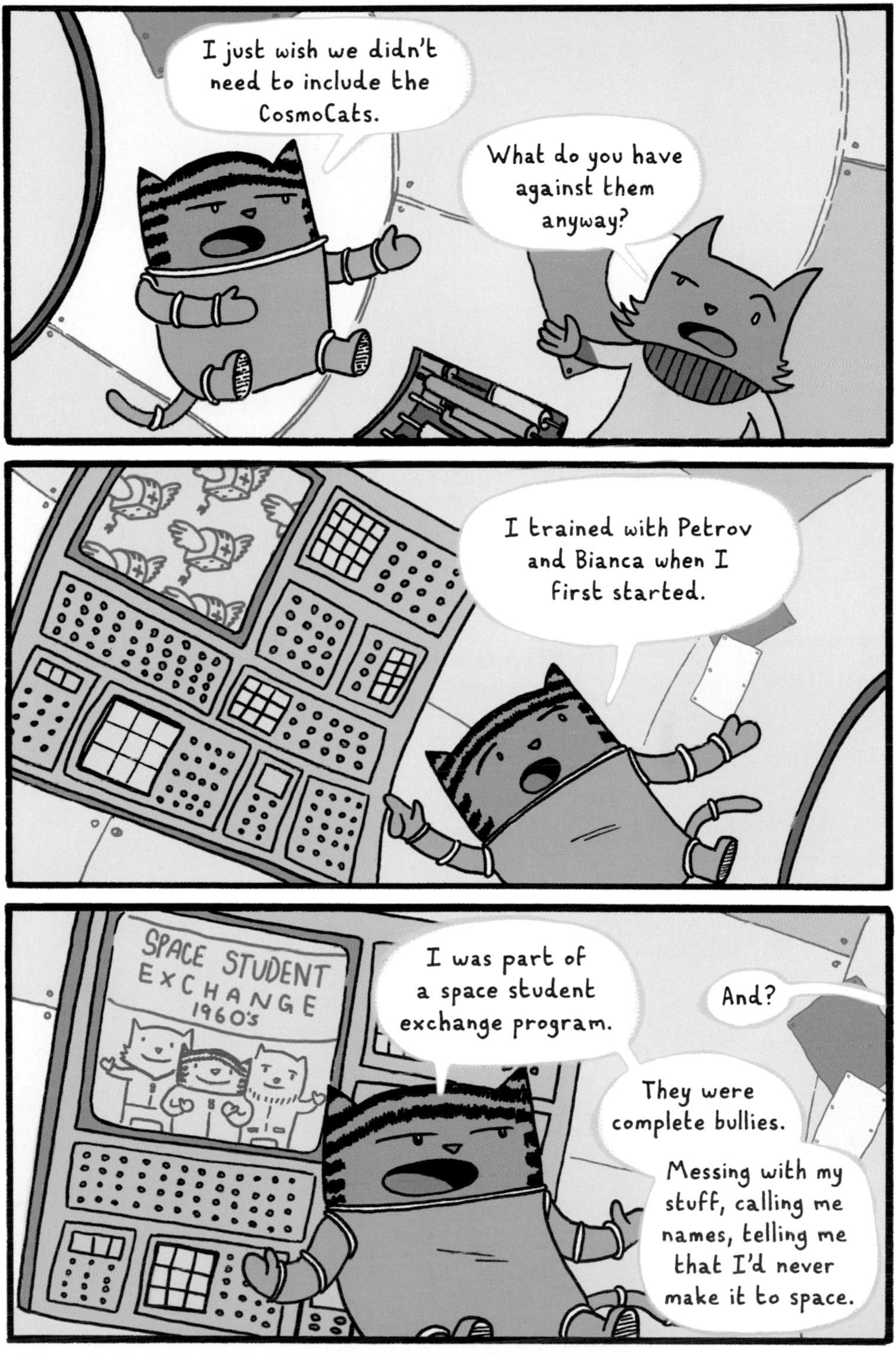
I just wish we didn't need to include the CosmoCats.
What do you have against them anyway?
I trained with Petrov and Bianca when I first started.
SPACE STUDENT EXCHANGE 1960's
I was part of a space student exchange program.
And?
They were complete bullies.
Messing with my stuff, calling me names, telling me that I'd never make it to space.

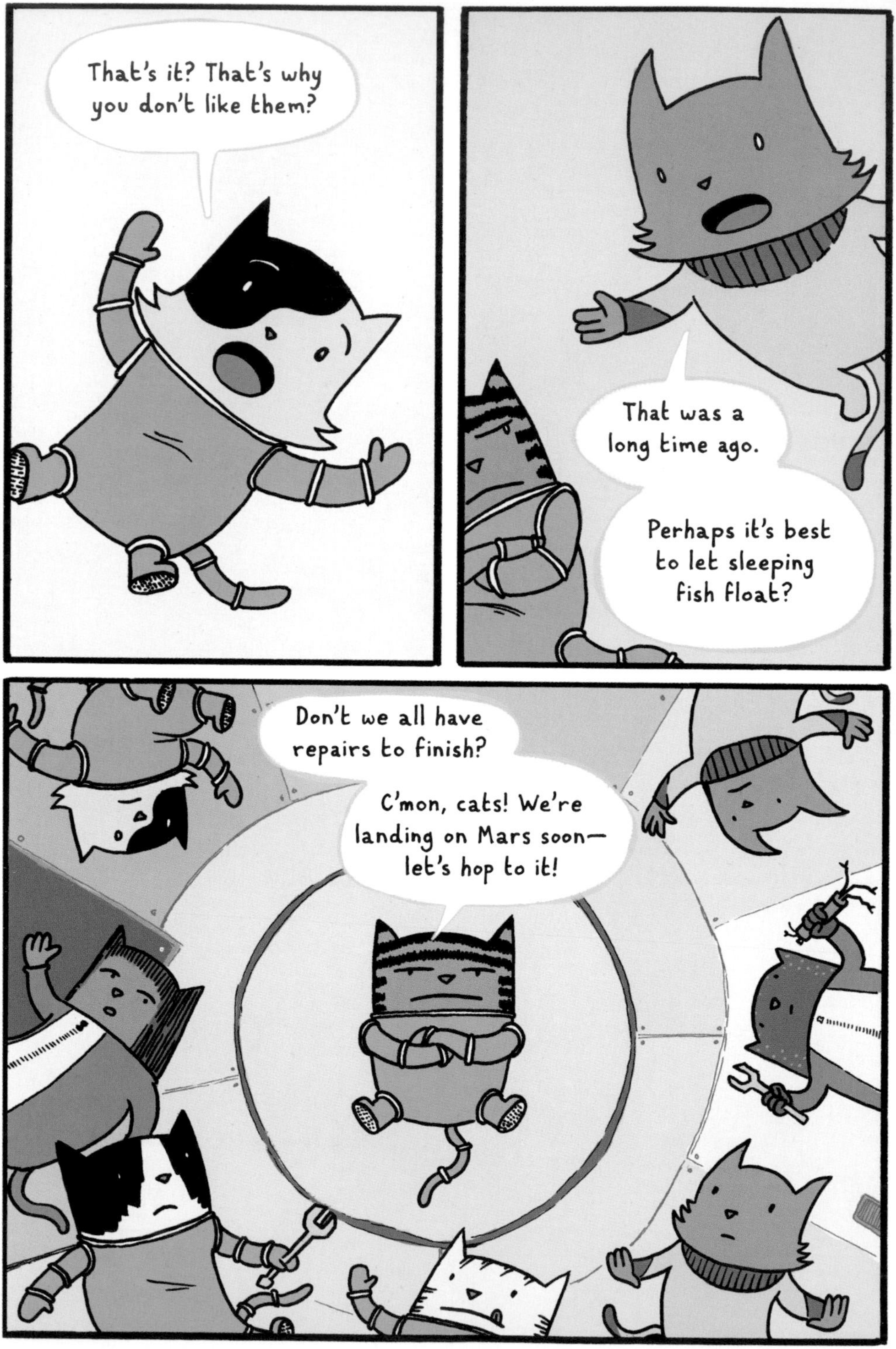
That's it? That's why you don't like them?
That was a long time ago.
Perhaps it's best to let sleeping fish float?
Don't we all have repairs to finish?
C'mon, cats! We're landing on Mars soon—let's hop to it!

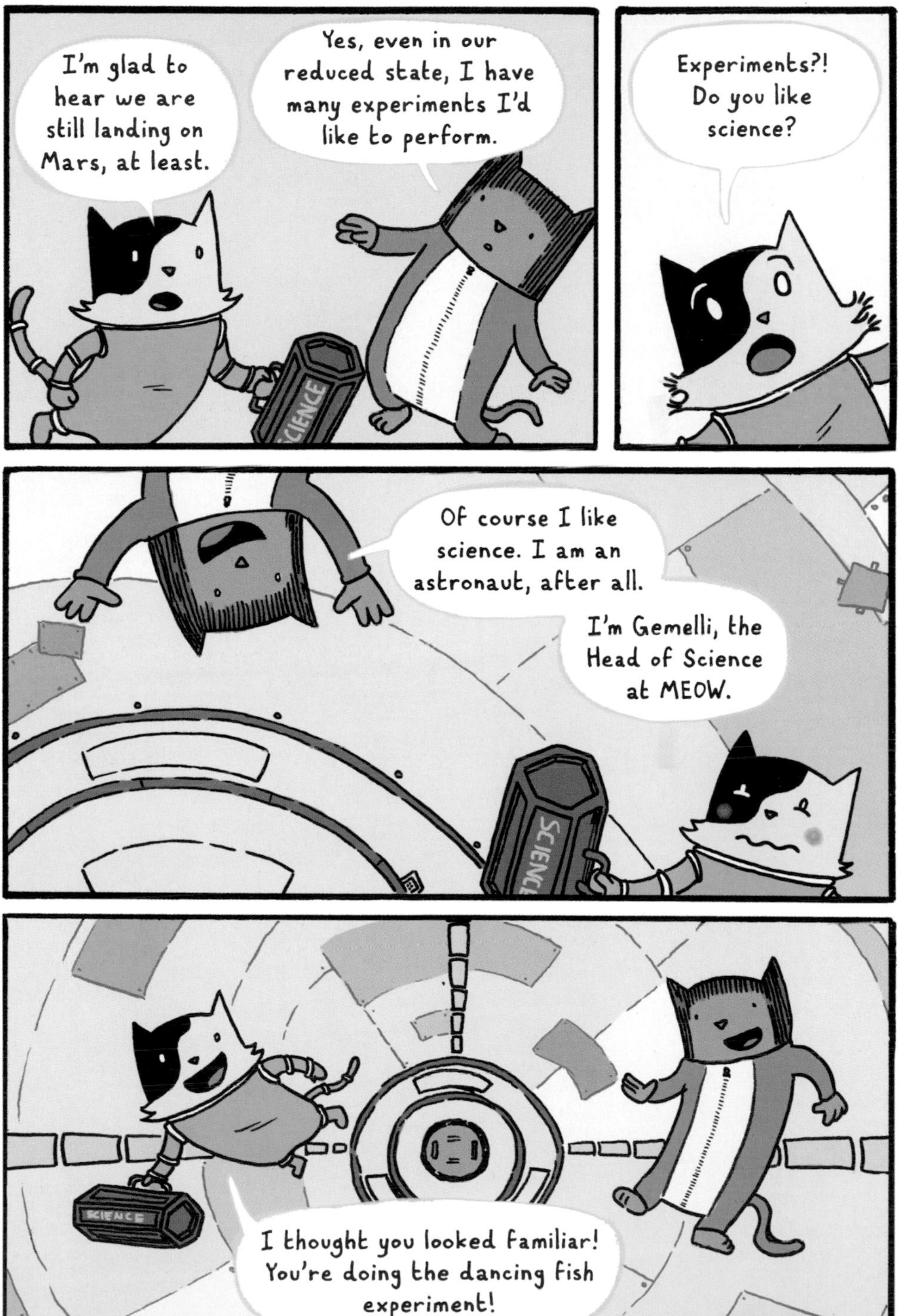
I'm glad to hear we are still landing on Mars, at least.
Yes, even in our reduced state, I have many experiments I'd like to perform.
SCIENCE
Experiments?! Do you like science?
Of course I like science. I am an astronaut, after all.
I'm Gemelli, the Head of Science at MEOW.
SCIENCE
SCIENCE
I thought you looked familiar! You're doing the dancing fish experiment!

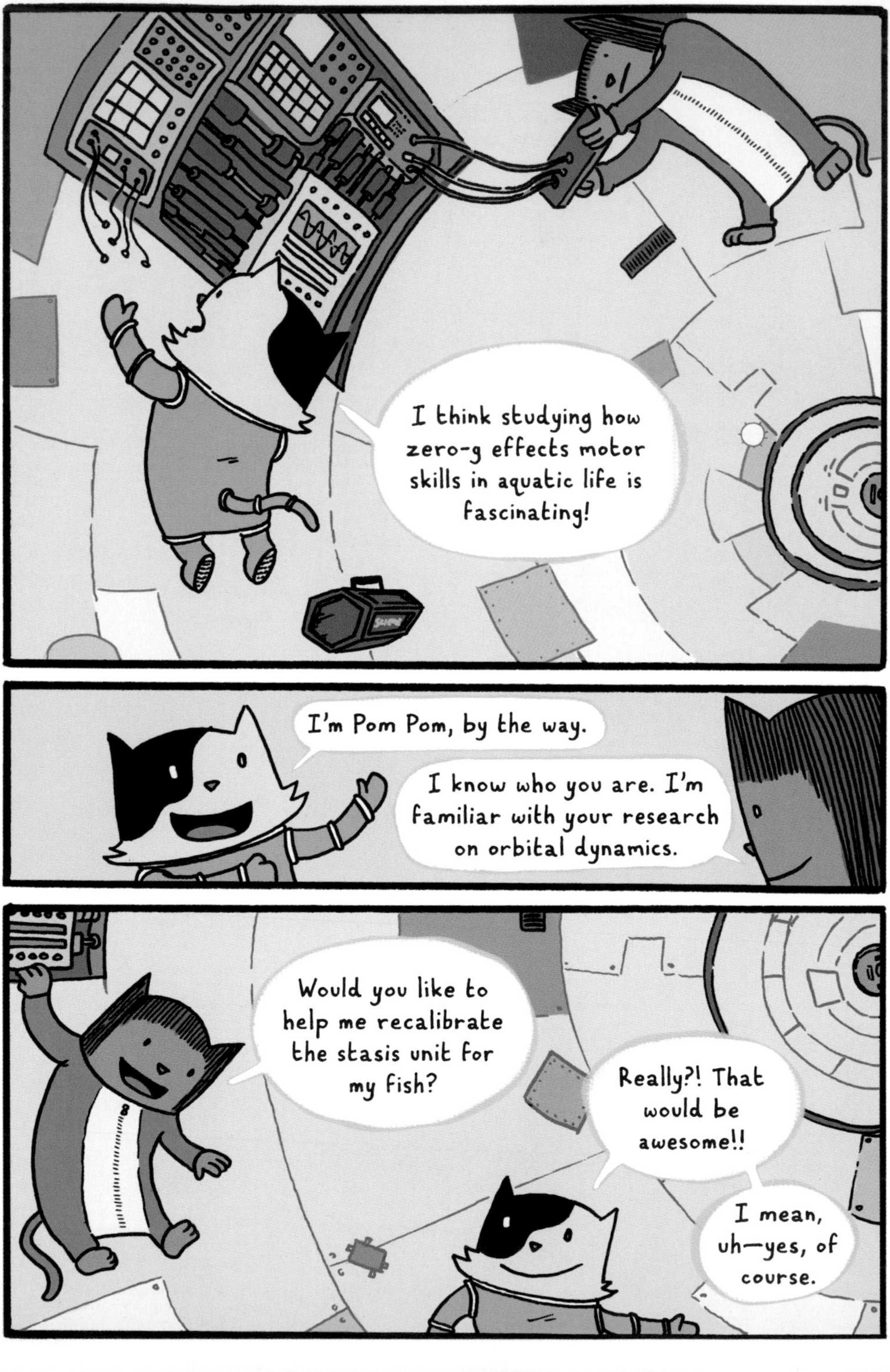

I think studying how zero-g effects motor skills in aquatic life is fascinating!
I'm Pom Pom, by the way.
I know who you are. I'm familiar with your research on orbital dynamics.
Would you like to help me recalibrate the stasis unit for my fish?
Really?! That would be awesome!!
I mean, uh—yes, of course.

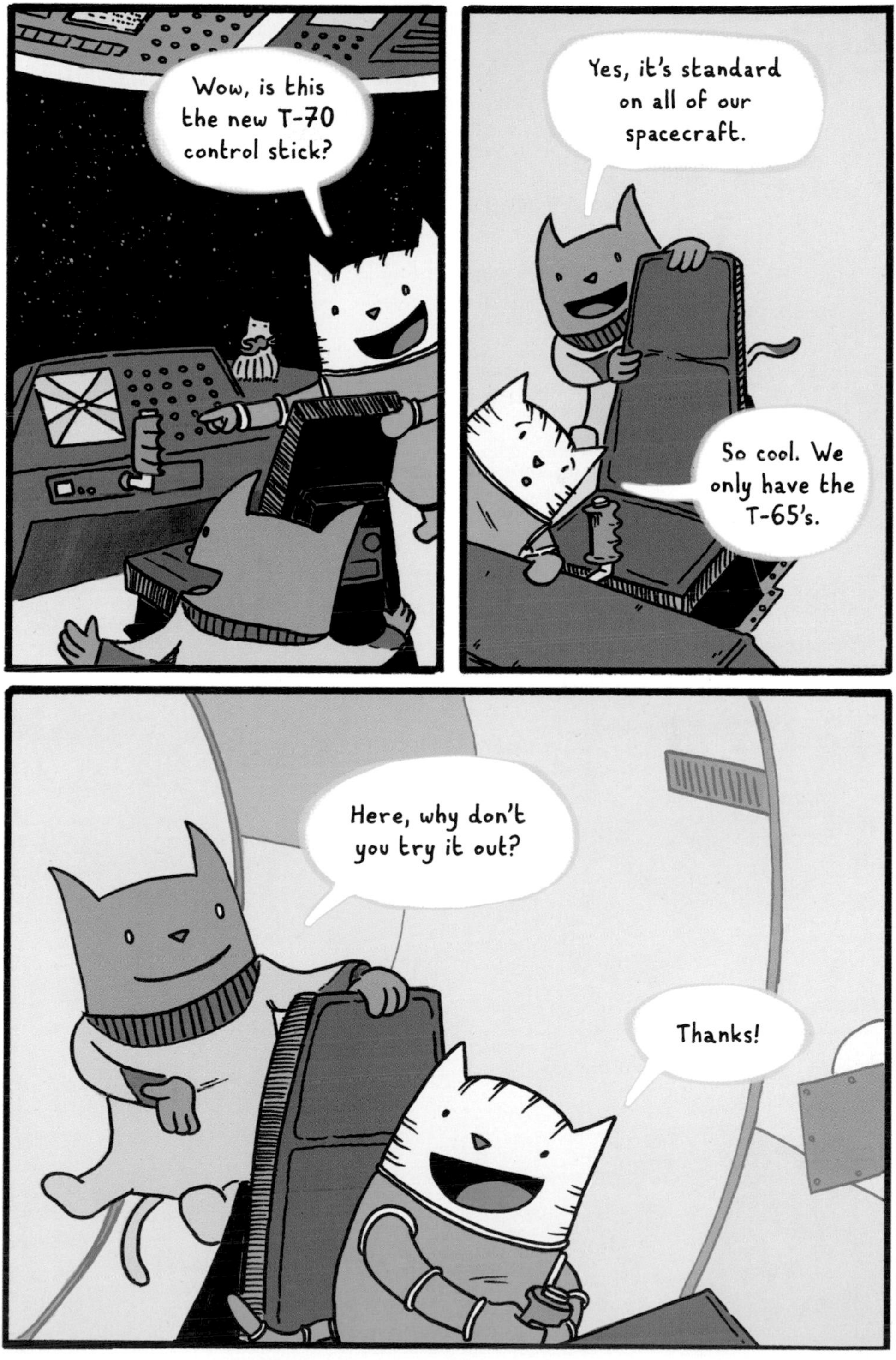
Wow, is this the new T-70 control stick?
Yes, it's standard on all of our spacecraft.
So cool. We only have the T-65's.
Here, why don't you try it out?
Thanks!

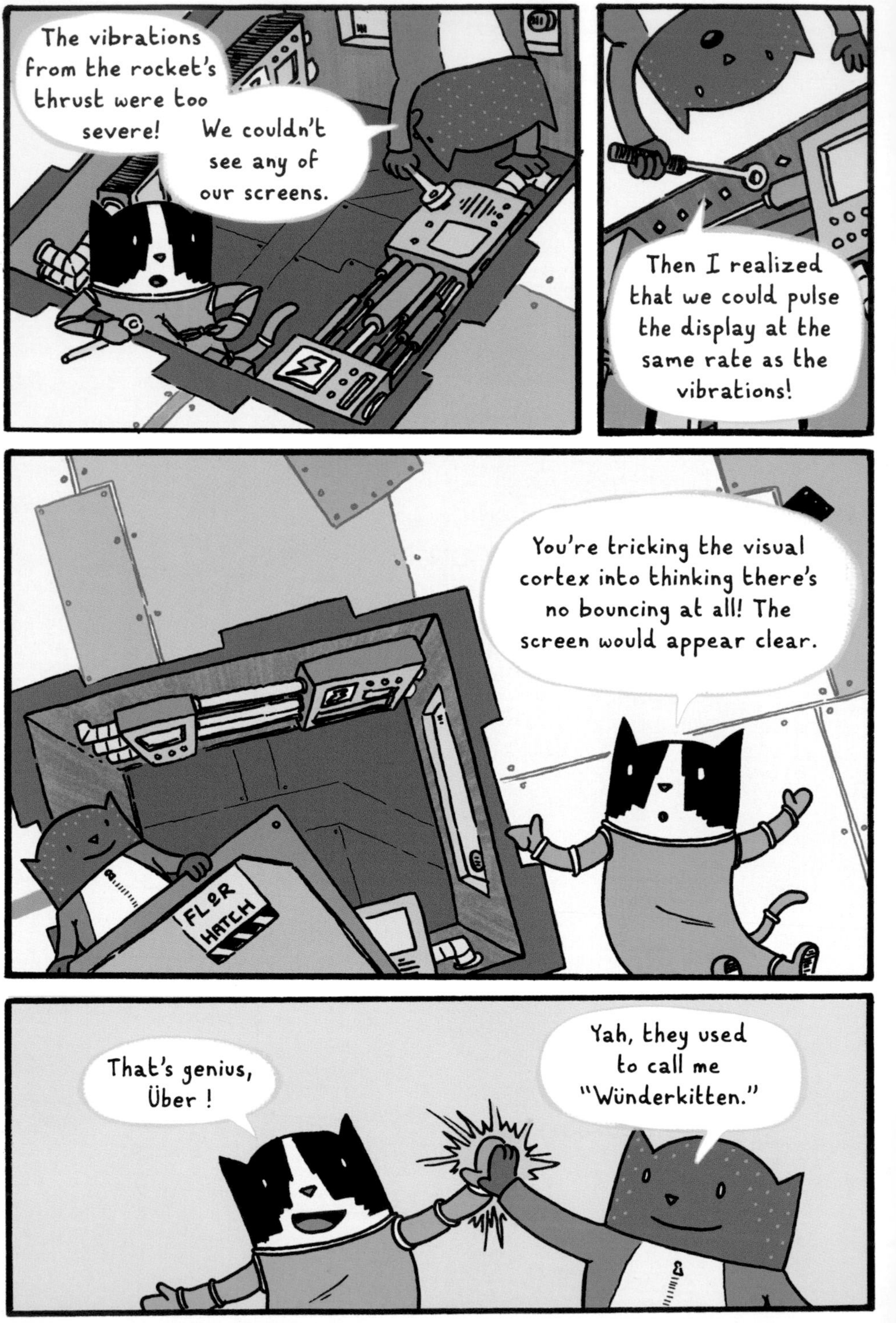
The vibrations from the rocket's thrust were too severe!
We couldn't see any of our screens.
Then I realized that we could pulse the display at the same rate as the vibrations!
You're tricking the visual cortex into thinking there's no bouncing at all! The screen would appear clear.
HATCH
That's genius, Über !
Yah, they used to call me "Wünderkitten."

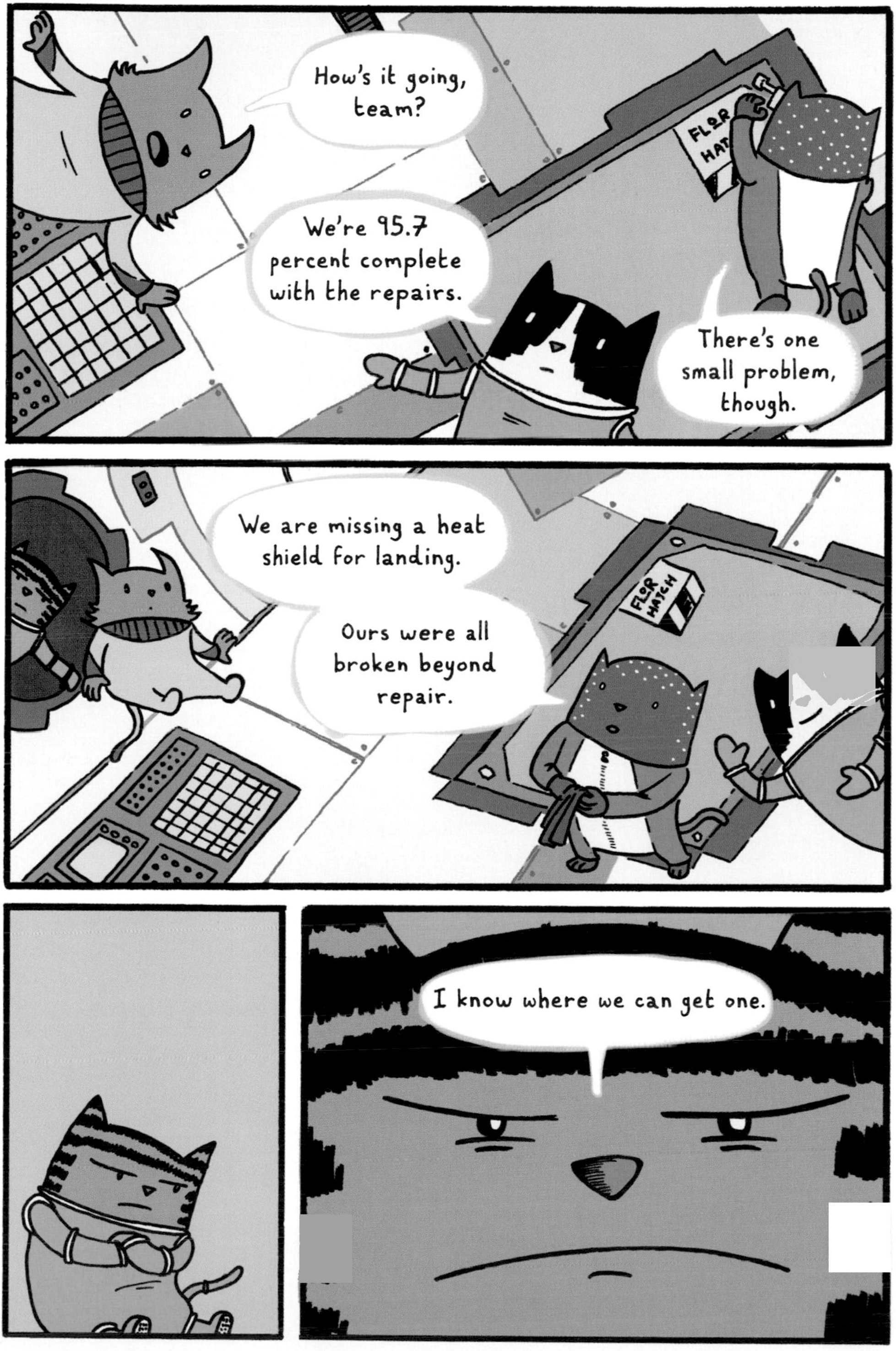
How's it going, team?
We're 95.7 percent complete with the repairs.
There's one small problem, though.
We are missing a heat shield for landing.
Ours were all broken beyond repair.
FLOR HATCH
I know where we can get one.

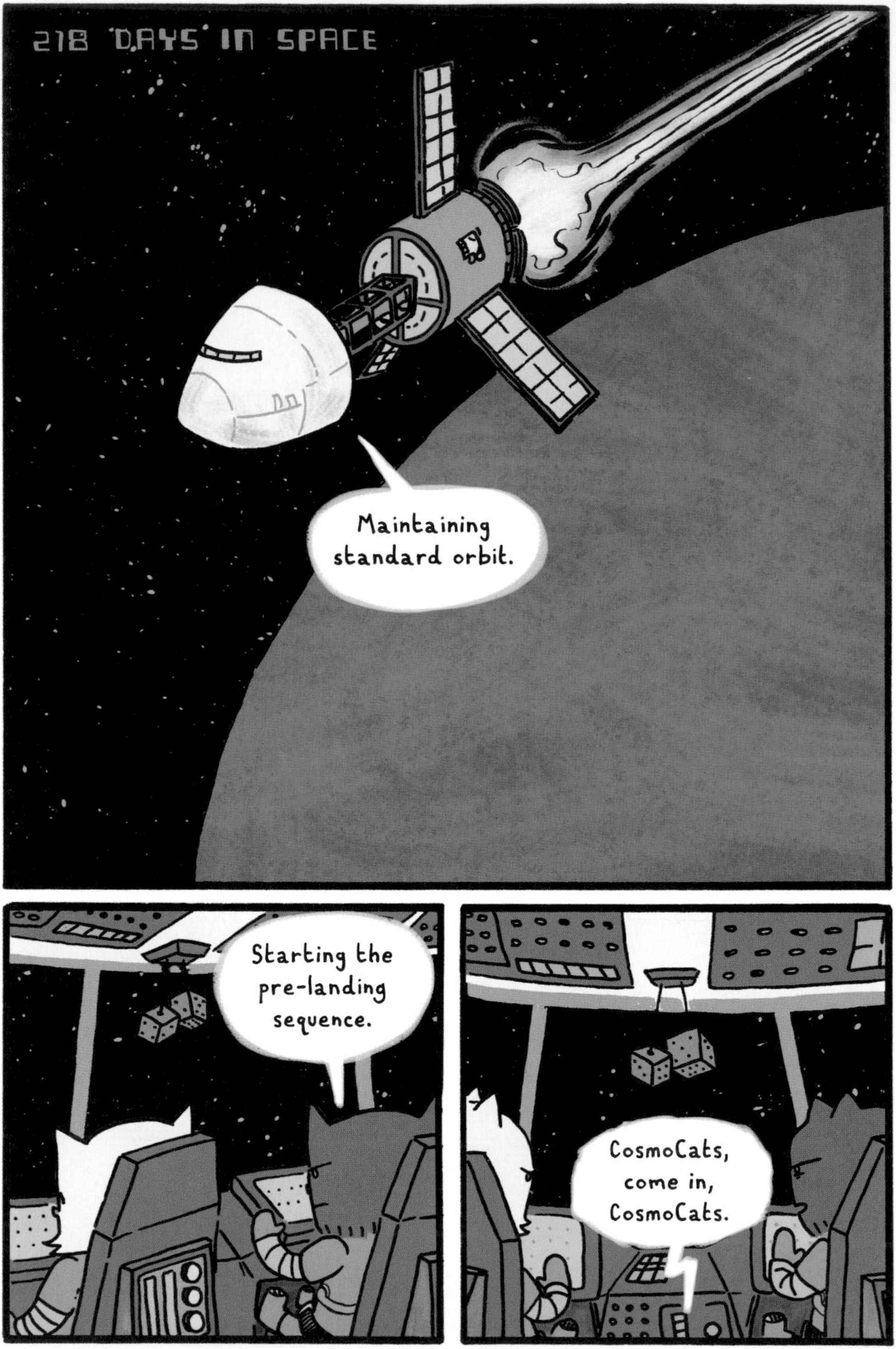
218 DAYS IN SPACE
Maintaining standard orbit.
Starting the pre-landing sequence.
CosmoCats, come in, CosmoCats.

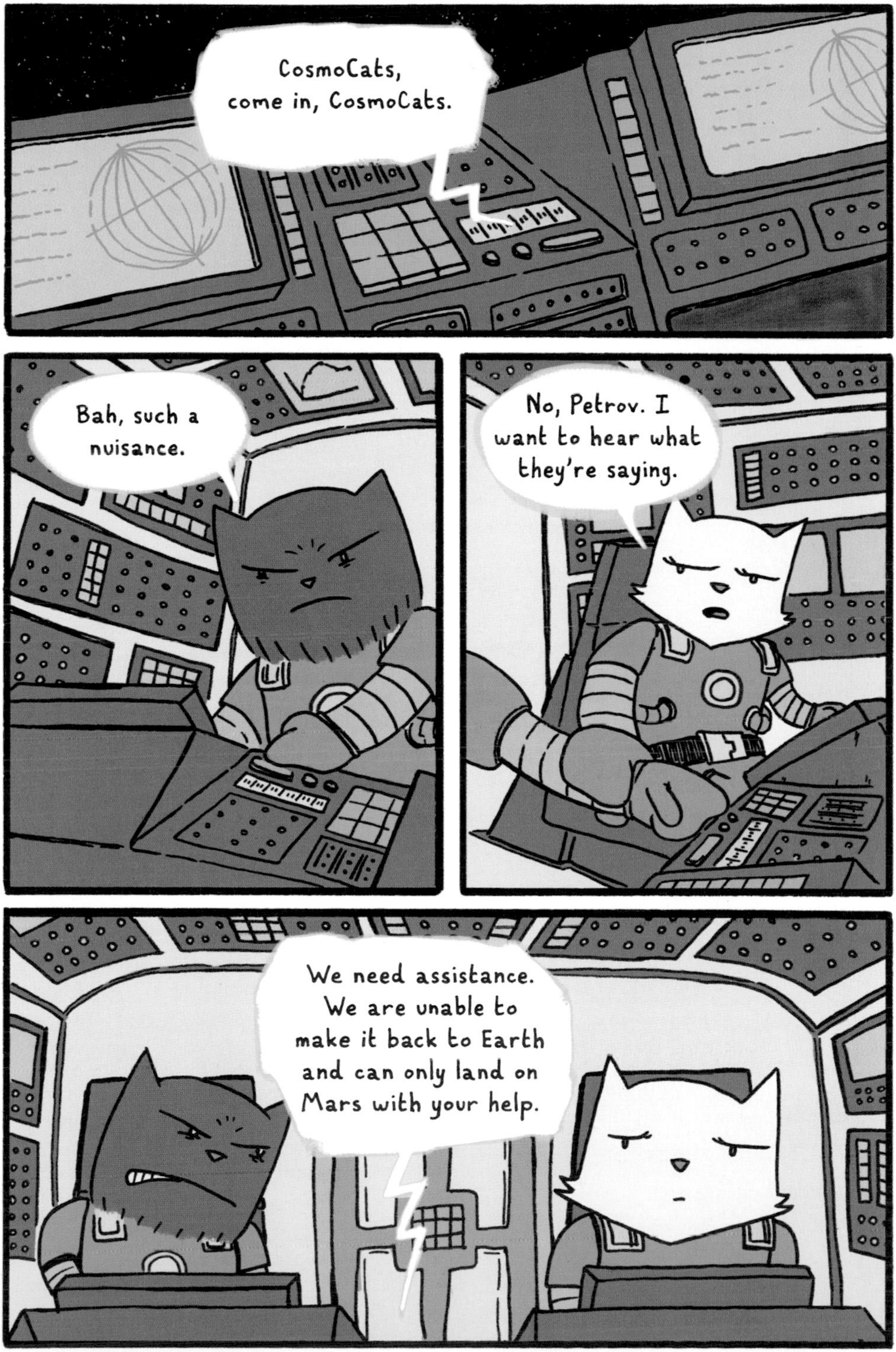
CosmoCats, come in, CosmoCats.
Bah, such a nuisance.
No, Petrov. I want to hear what they're saying.
We need assistance. We are unable to make it back to Earth and can only land on Mars with your help.

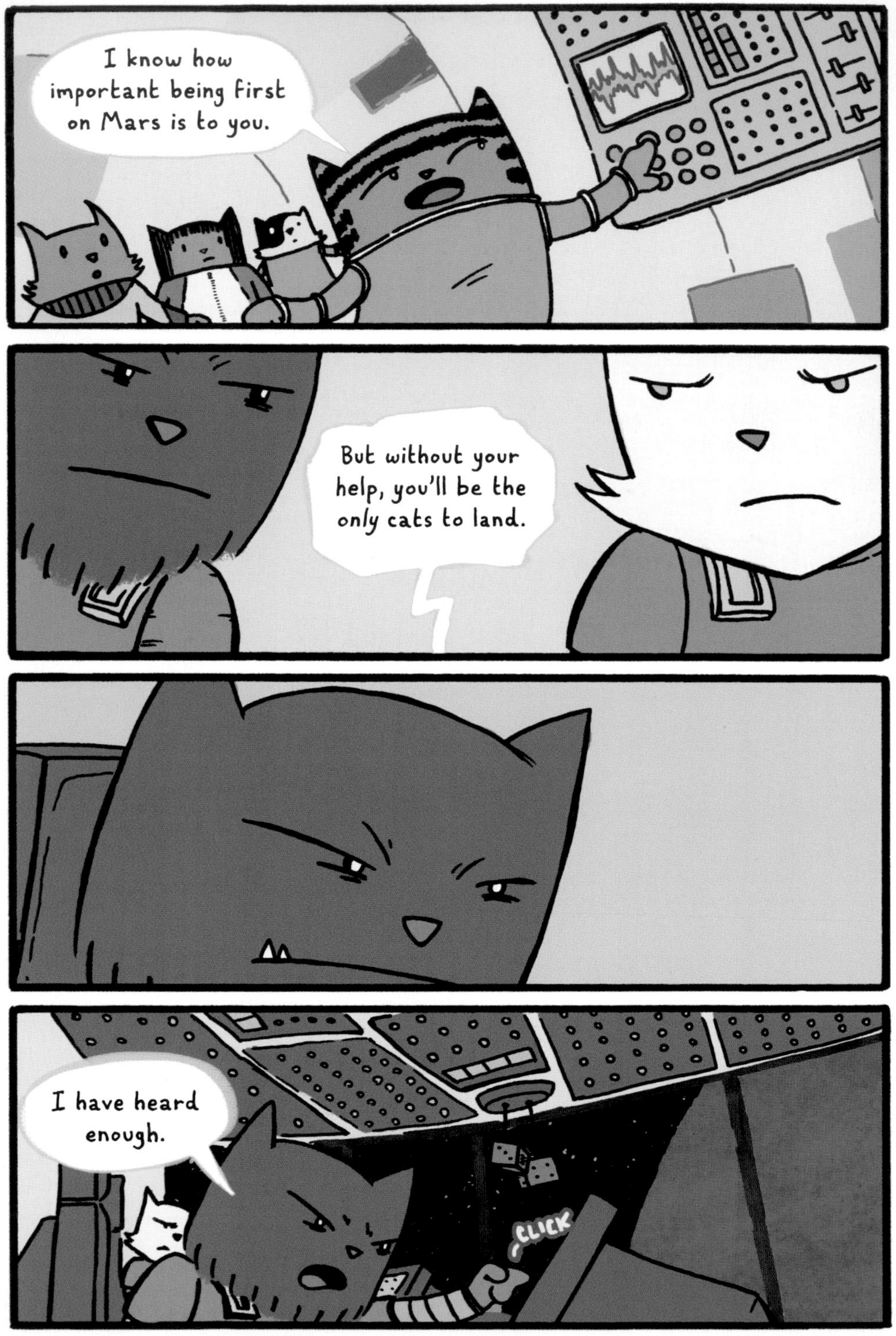
I know how important being first on Mars is to you.
But without your help, you'll be the *only* cats to land.
I have heard enough.
CLICK

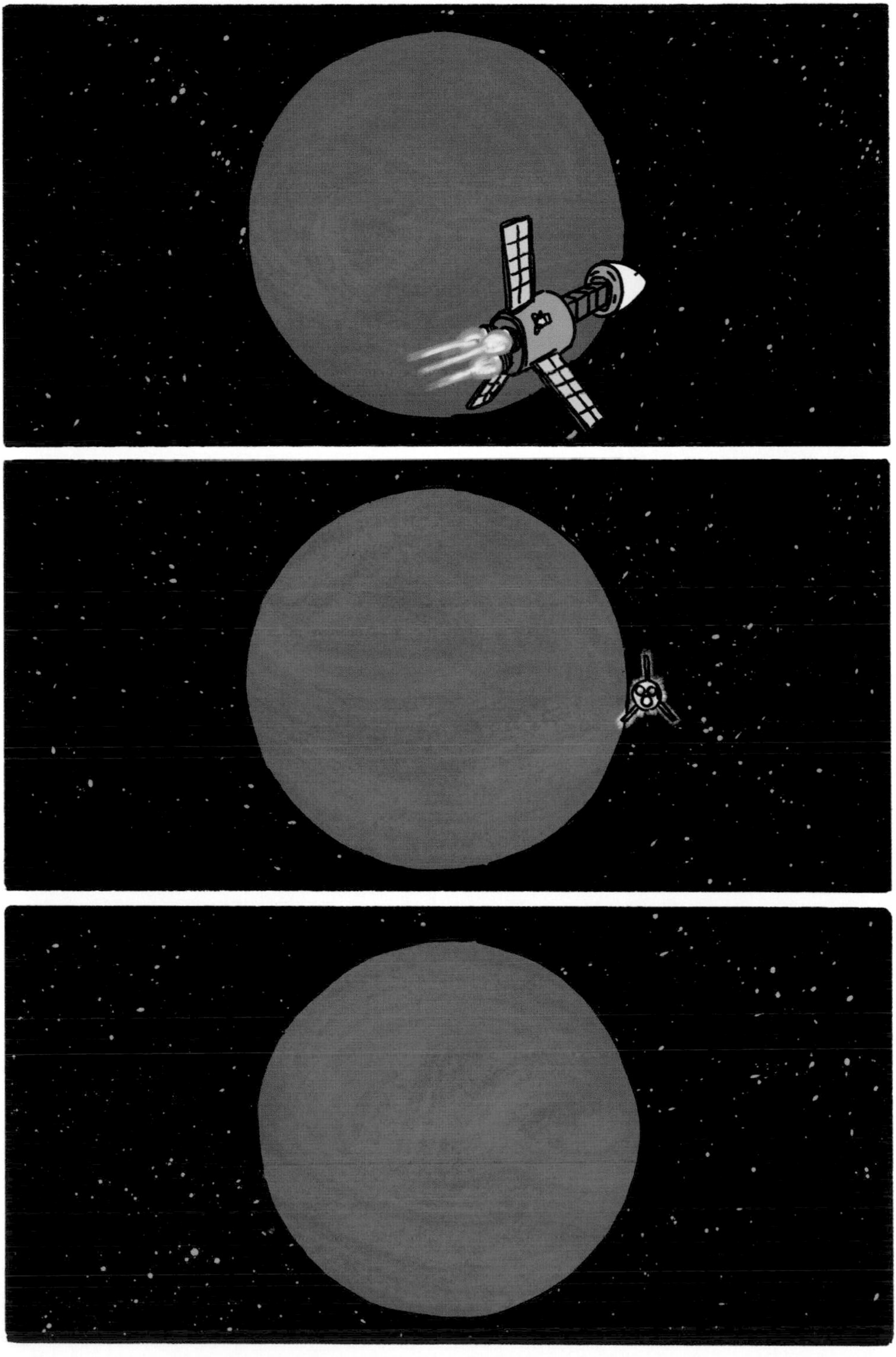

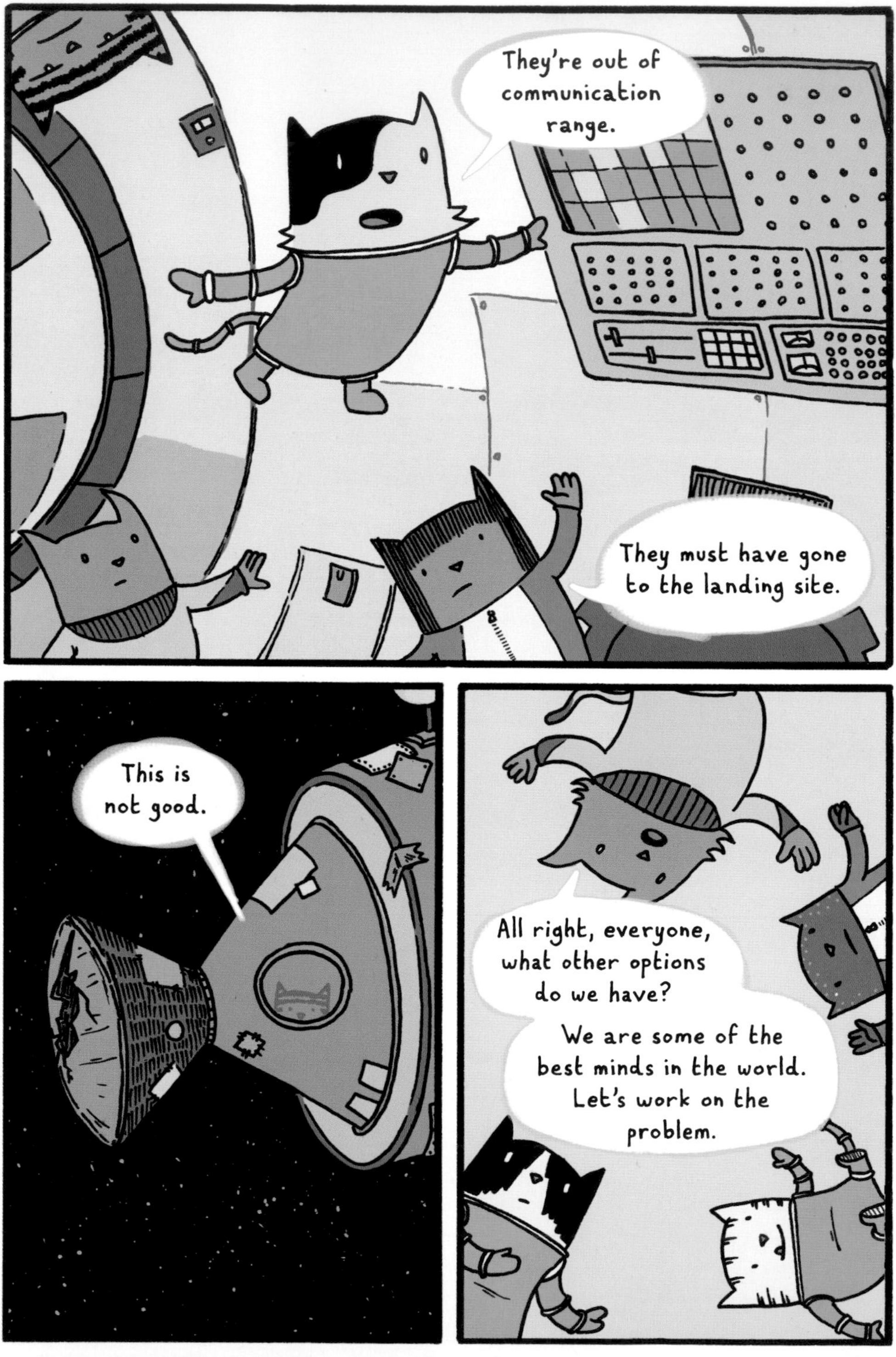
They're out of communication range.
They must have gone to the landing site.
This is not good.
All right, everyone, what other options do we have?
We are some of the best minds in the world. Let's work on the problem.

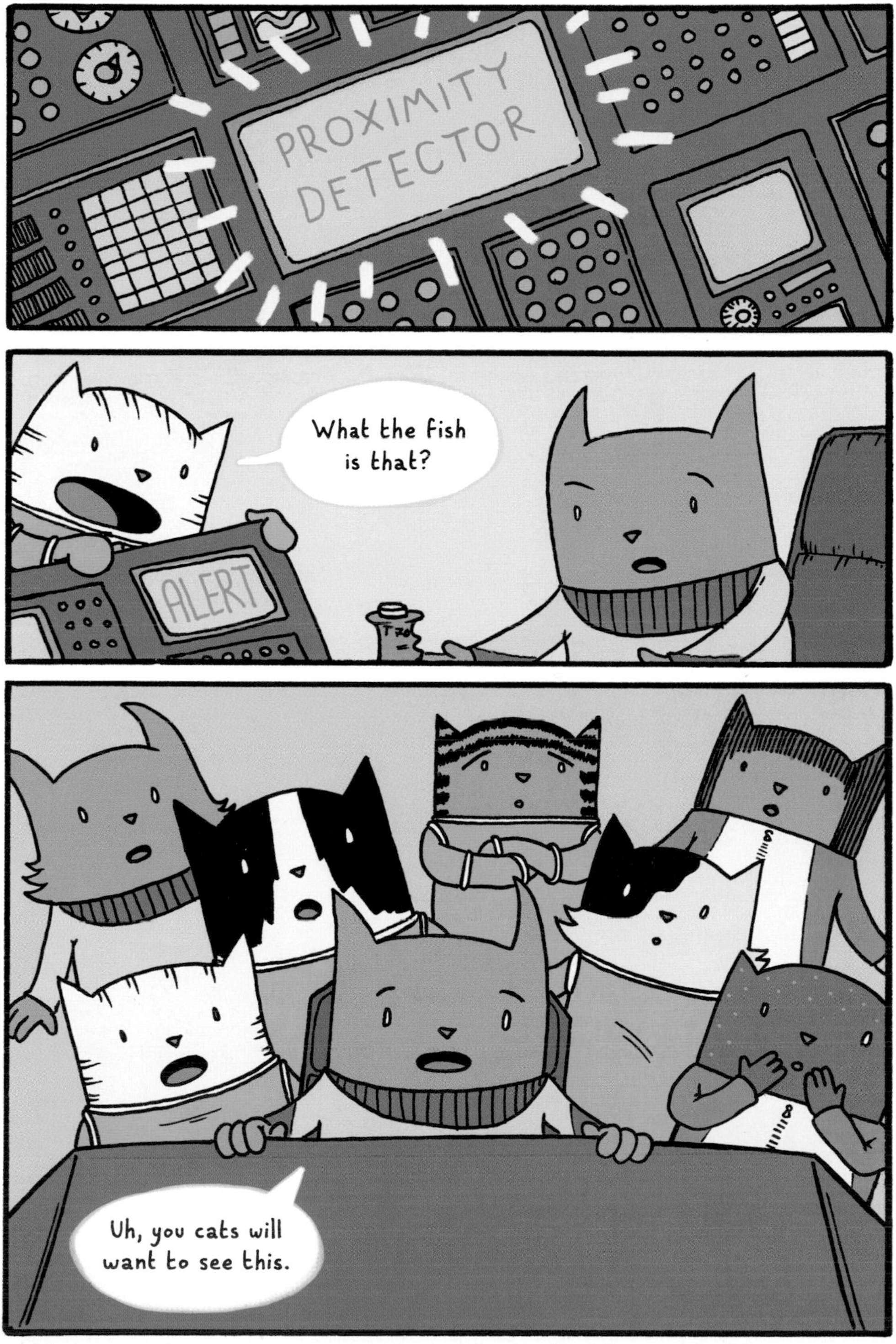
PROXIMITY DETECTOR
What the fish is that?
ALERT
Uh, you cats will want to see this.

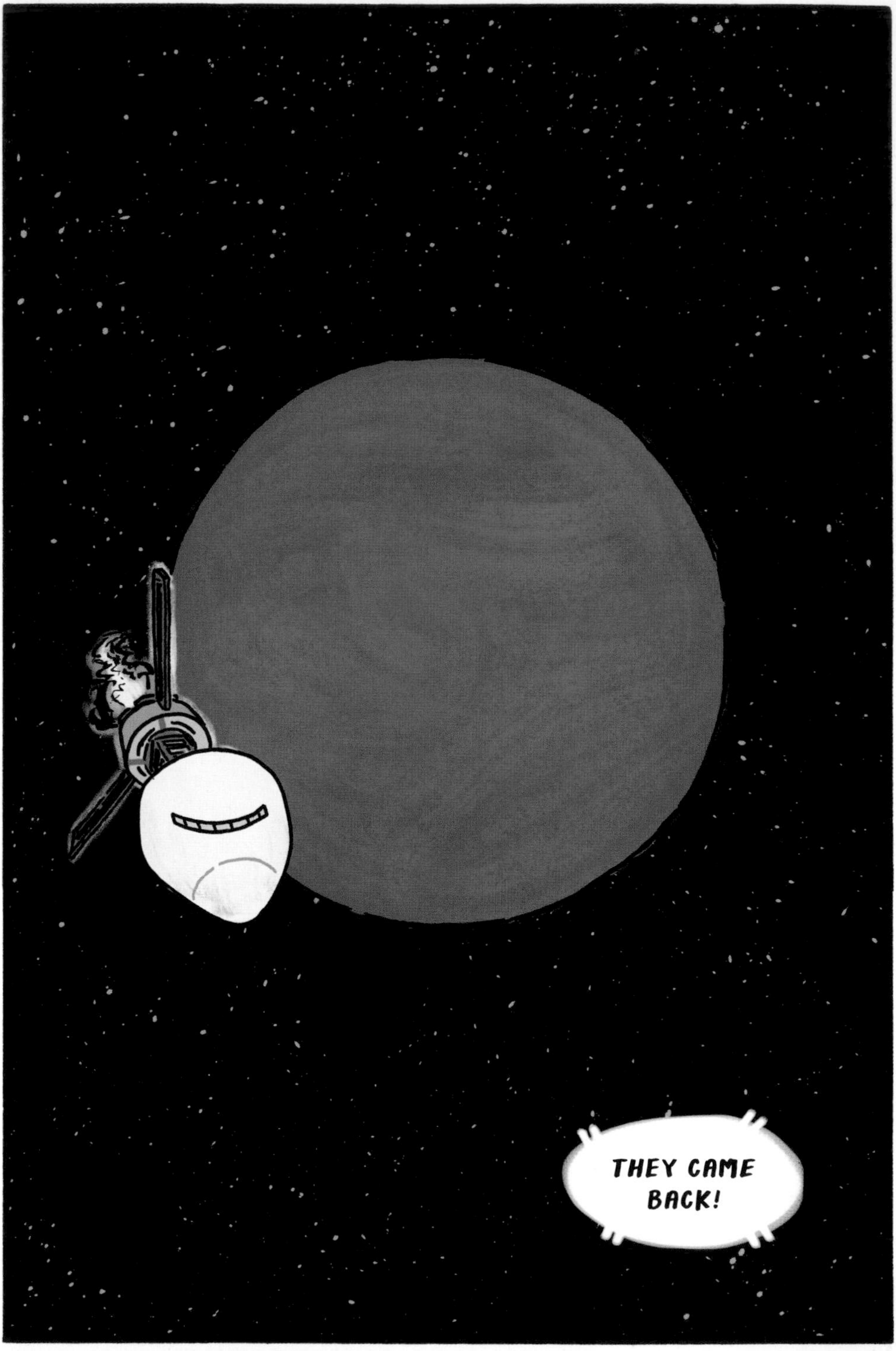
THEY CAME BACK!

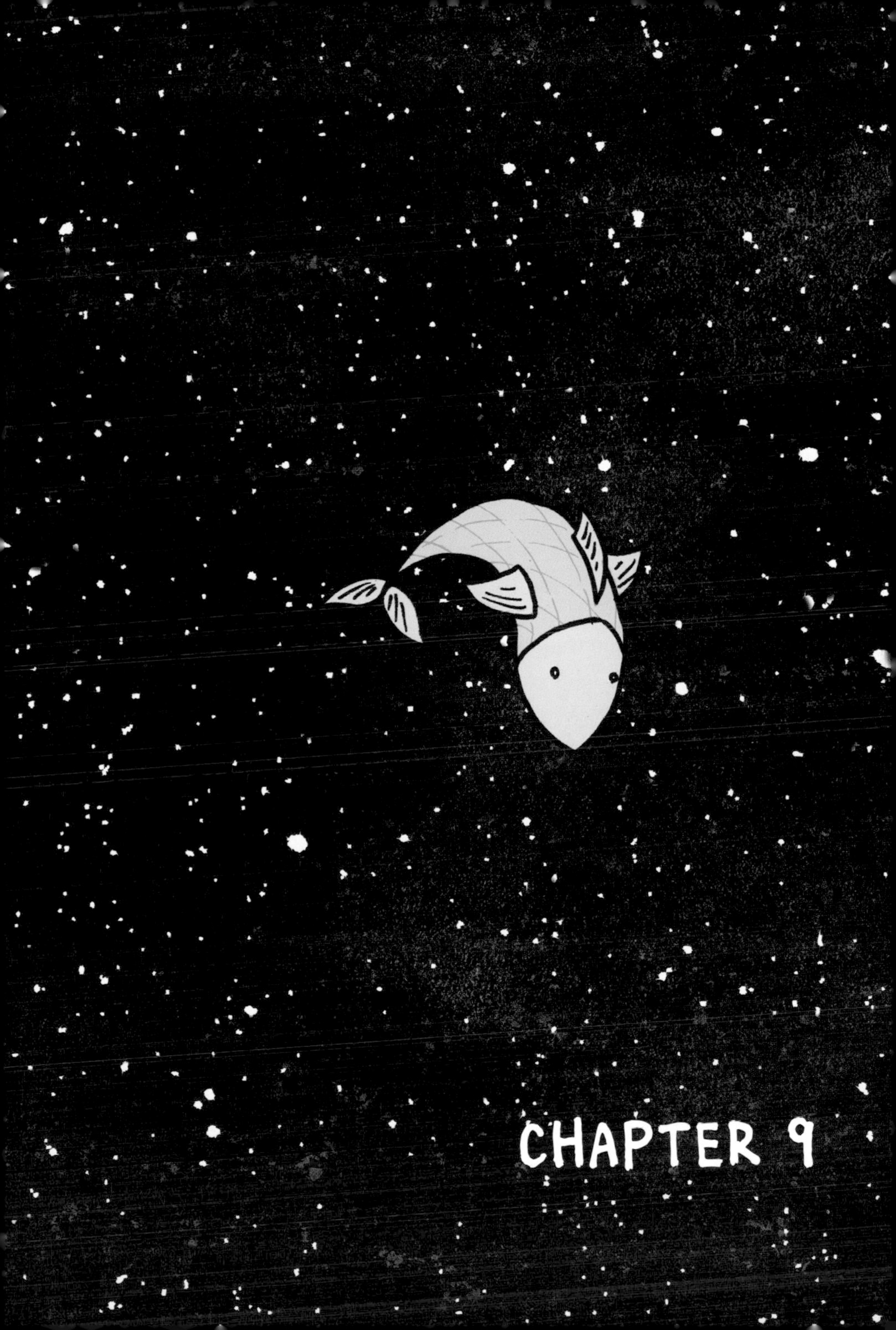

CHAPTER 9

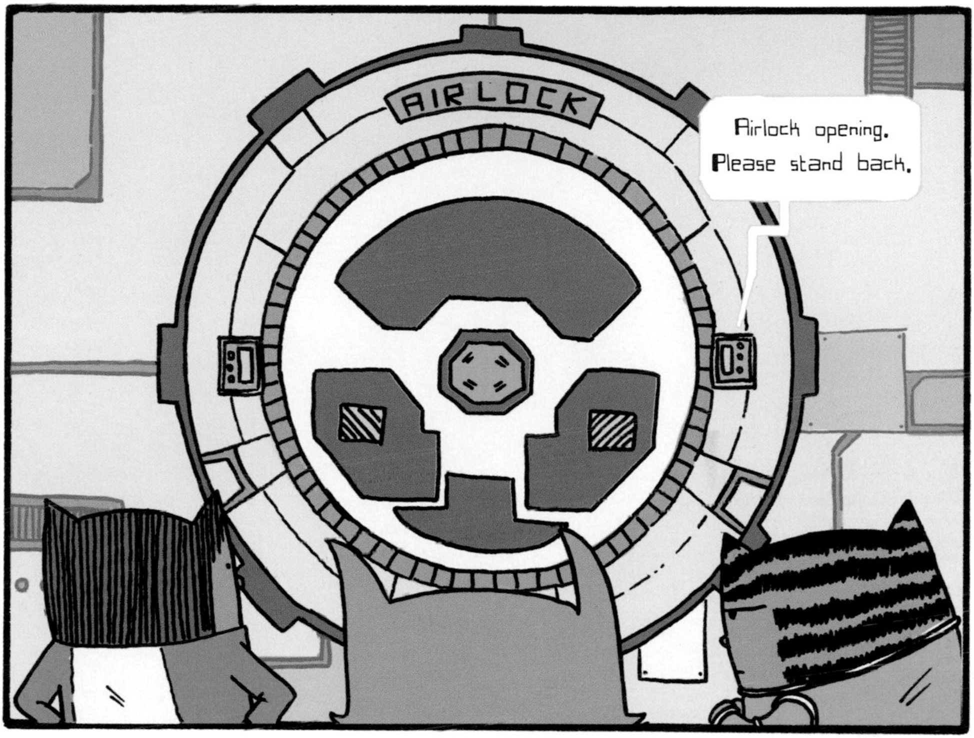
AIRLOCK
Airlock opening. Please stand back.

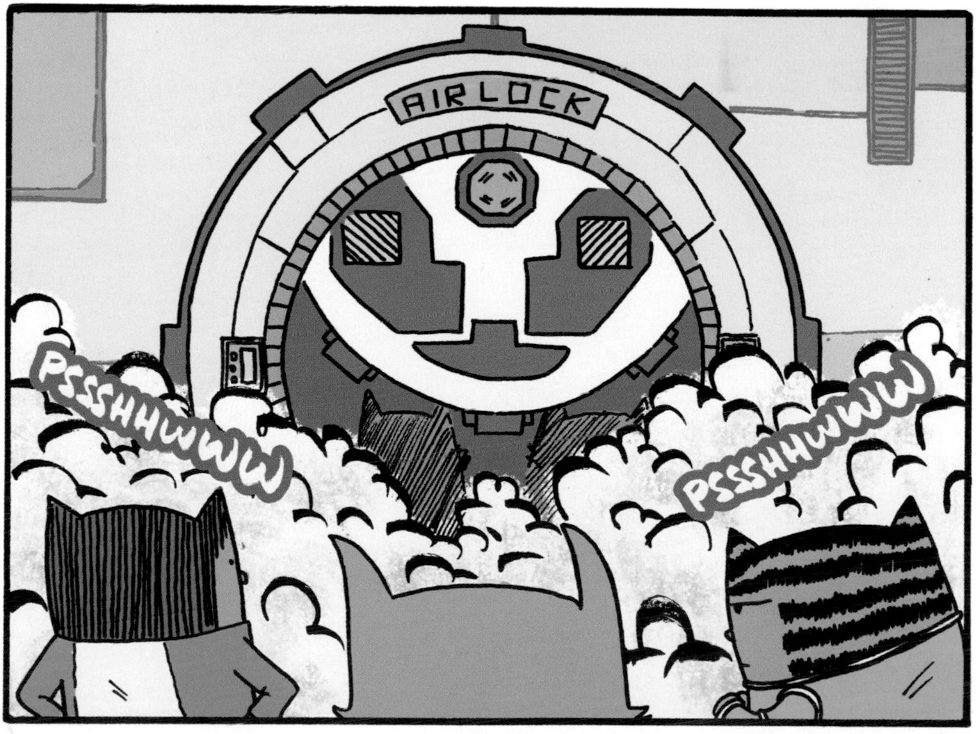
AIRLOCK
PSSSHHWWWW
PSSSHHWWWW

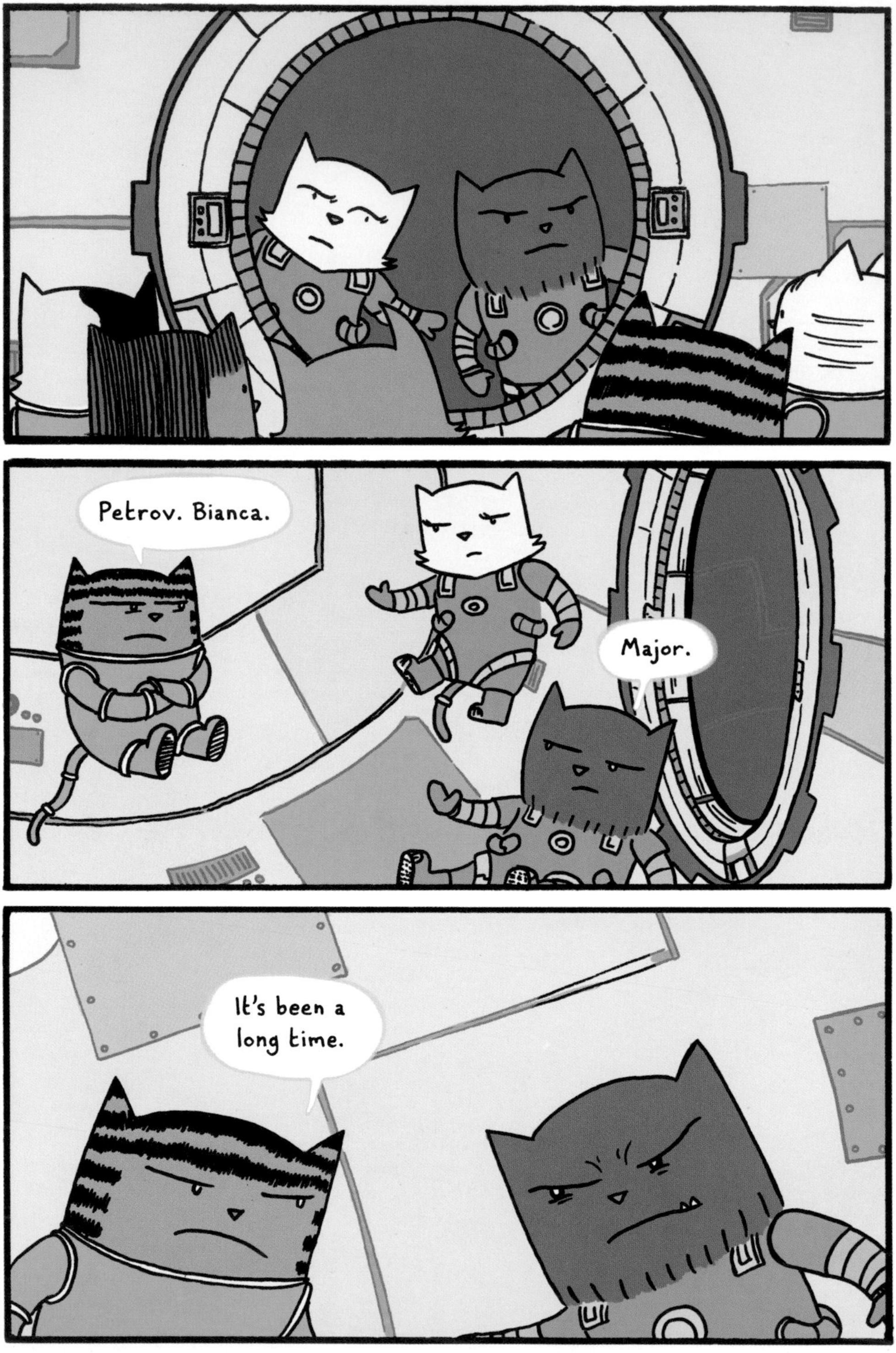
Petrov. Bianca.
Major.
It's been a long time.

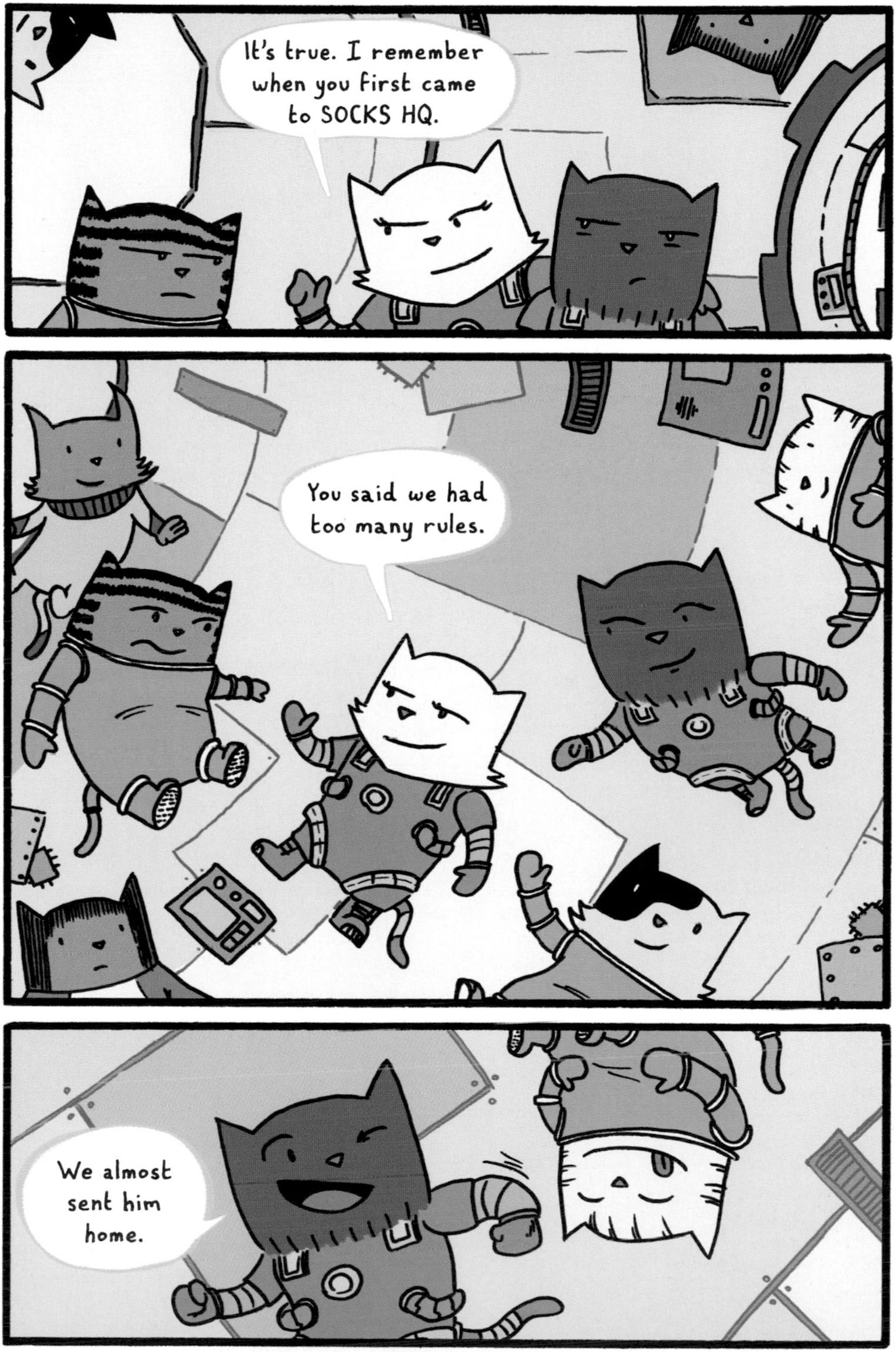
It's true. I remember when you first came to SOCKS HQ.
You said we had too many rules.
We almost sent him home.

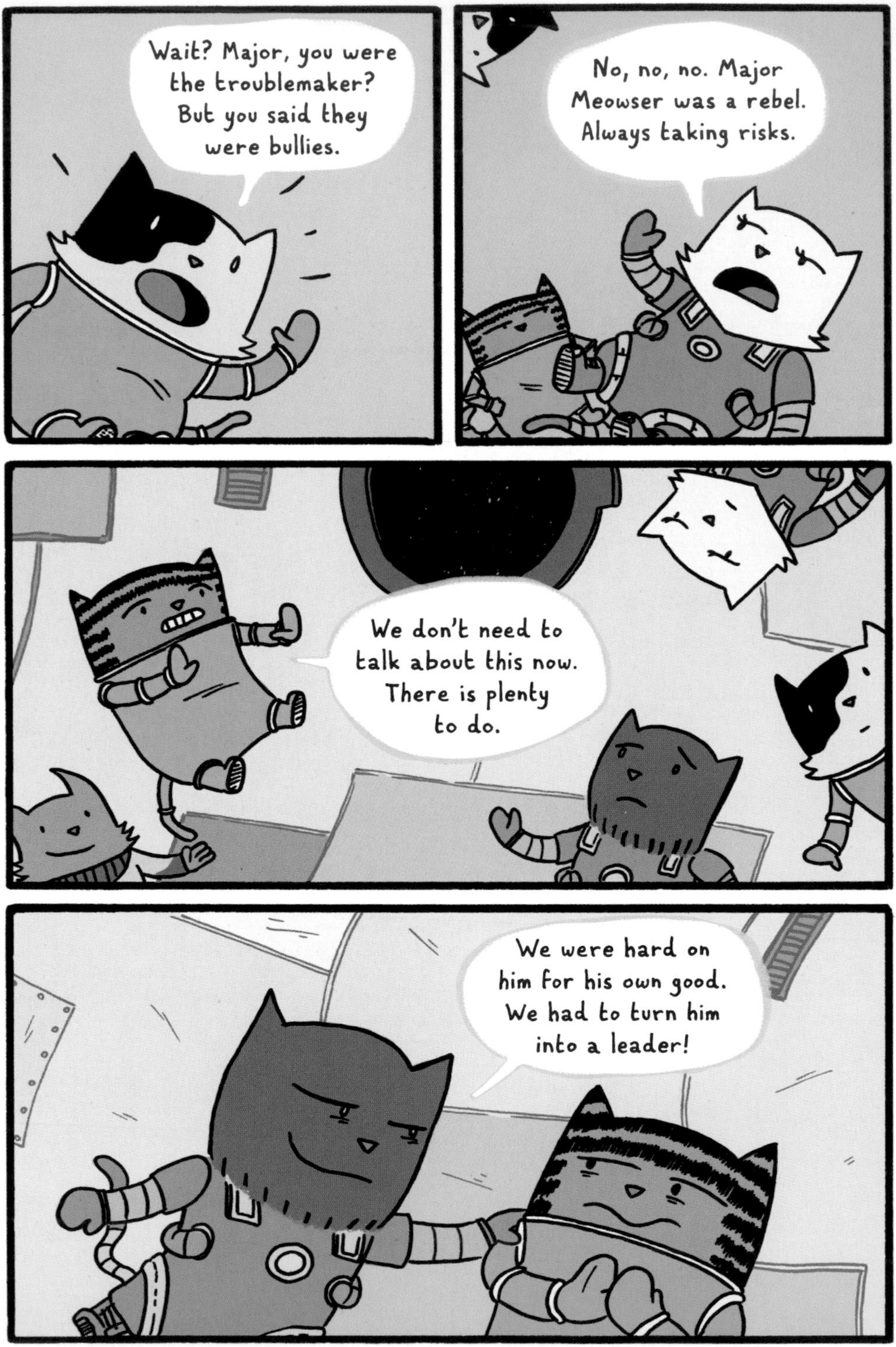
Wait? Major, you were the troublemaker? But you said they were bullies.
No, no, no. Major Meowser was a rebel. Always taking risks.
We don't need to talk about this now. There is plenty to do.
We were hard on him for his own good. We had to turn him into a leader!

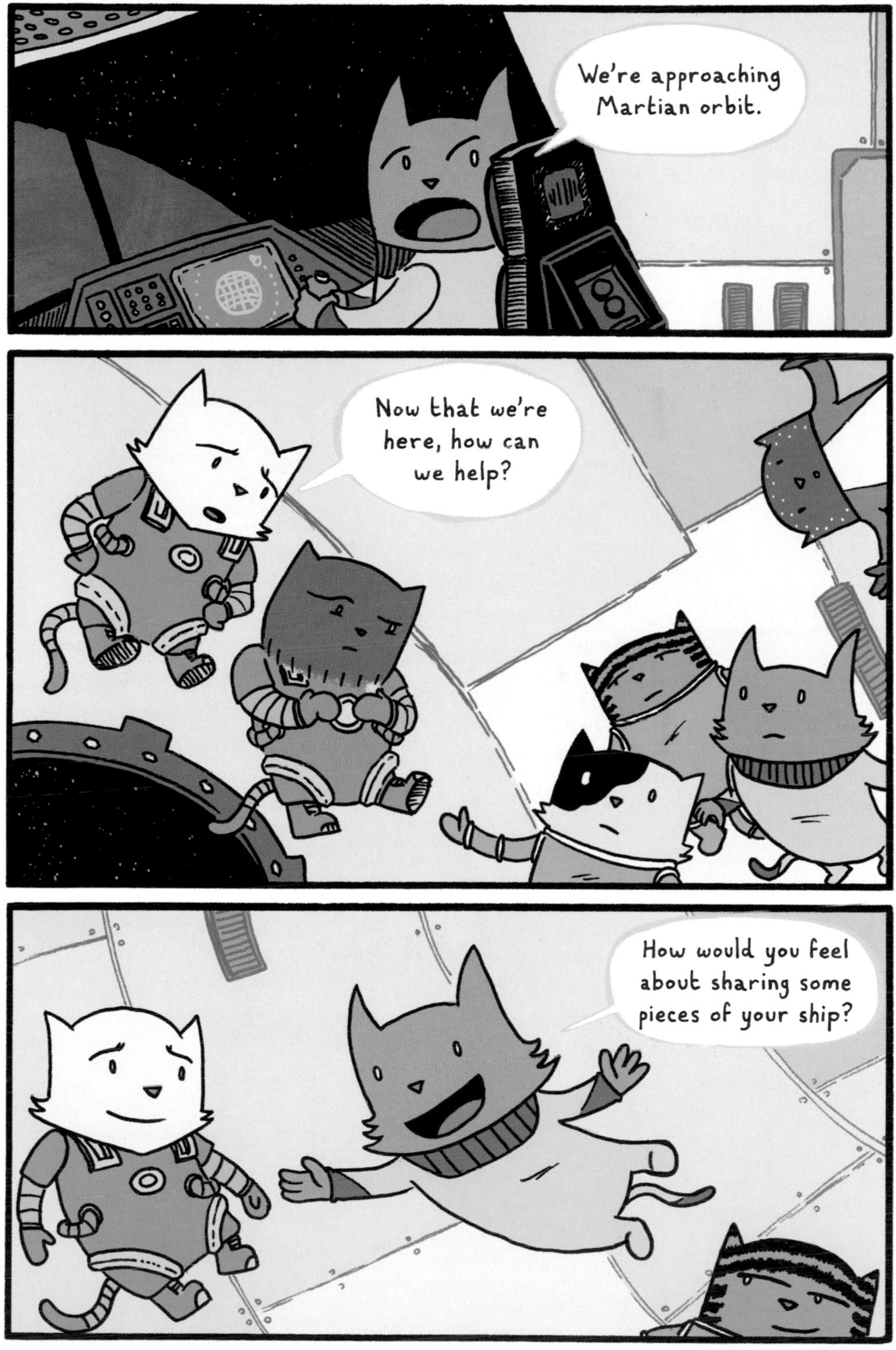
We're approaching Martian orbit.
Now that we're here, how can we help?
How would you feel about sharing some pieces of your ship?

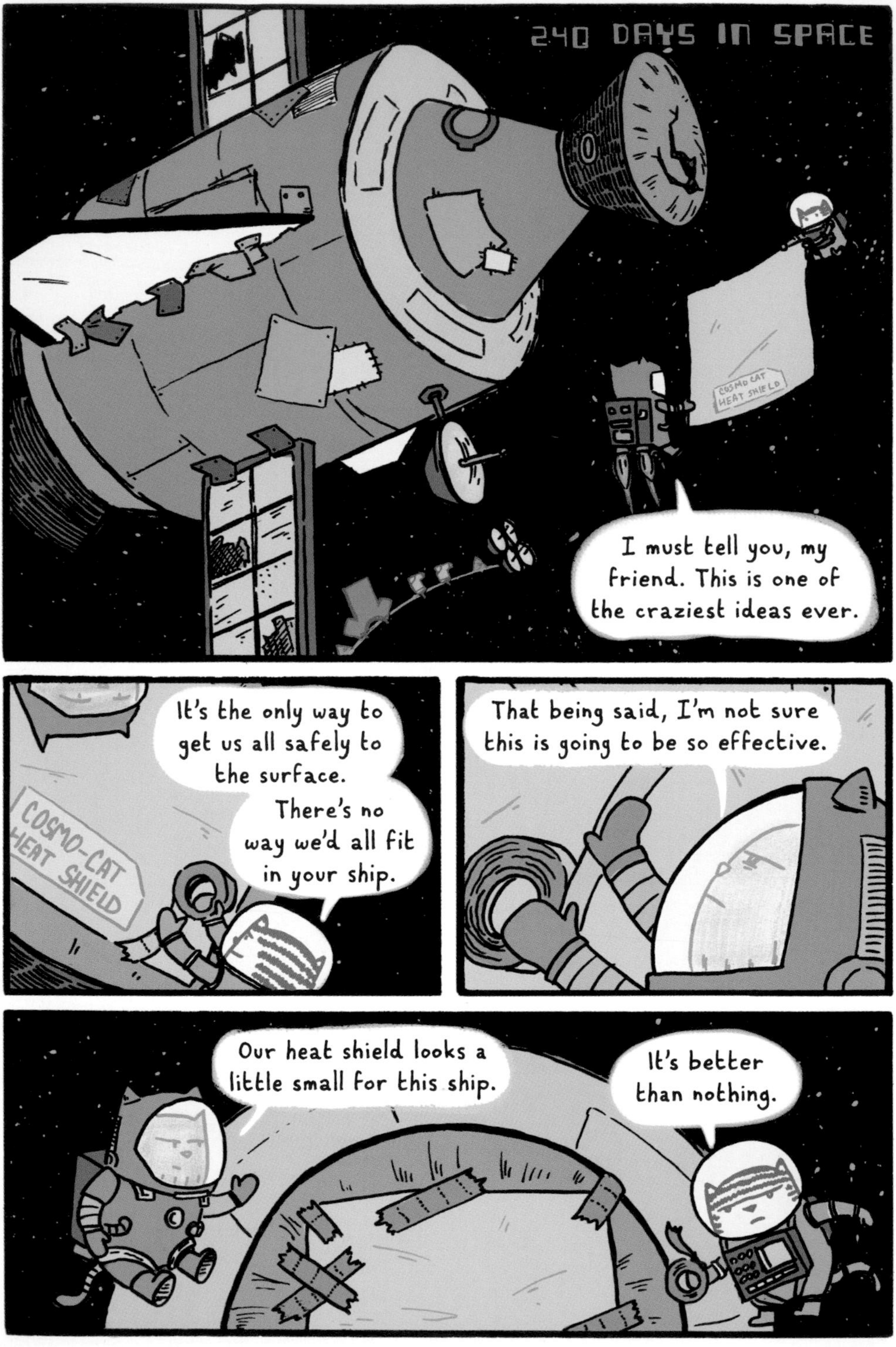
240 DAYS IN SPACE
COSMO CAT HEAT SHIELD
I must tell you, my friend. This is one of the craziest ideas ever.
COSMO-CAT HEAT SHIELD
It's the only way to get us all safely to the surface.
There's no way we'd all fit in your ship.
That being said, I'm not sure this is going to be so effective.
Our heat shield looks a little small for this ship.
It's better than nothing.

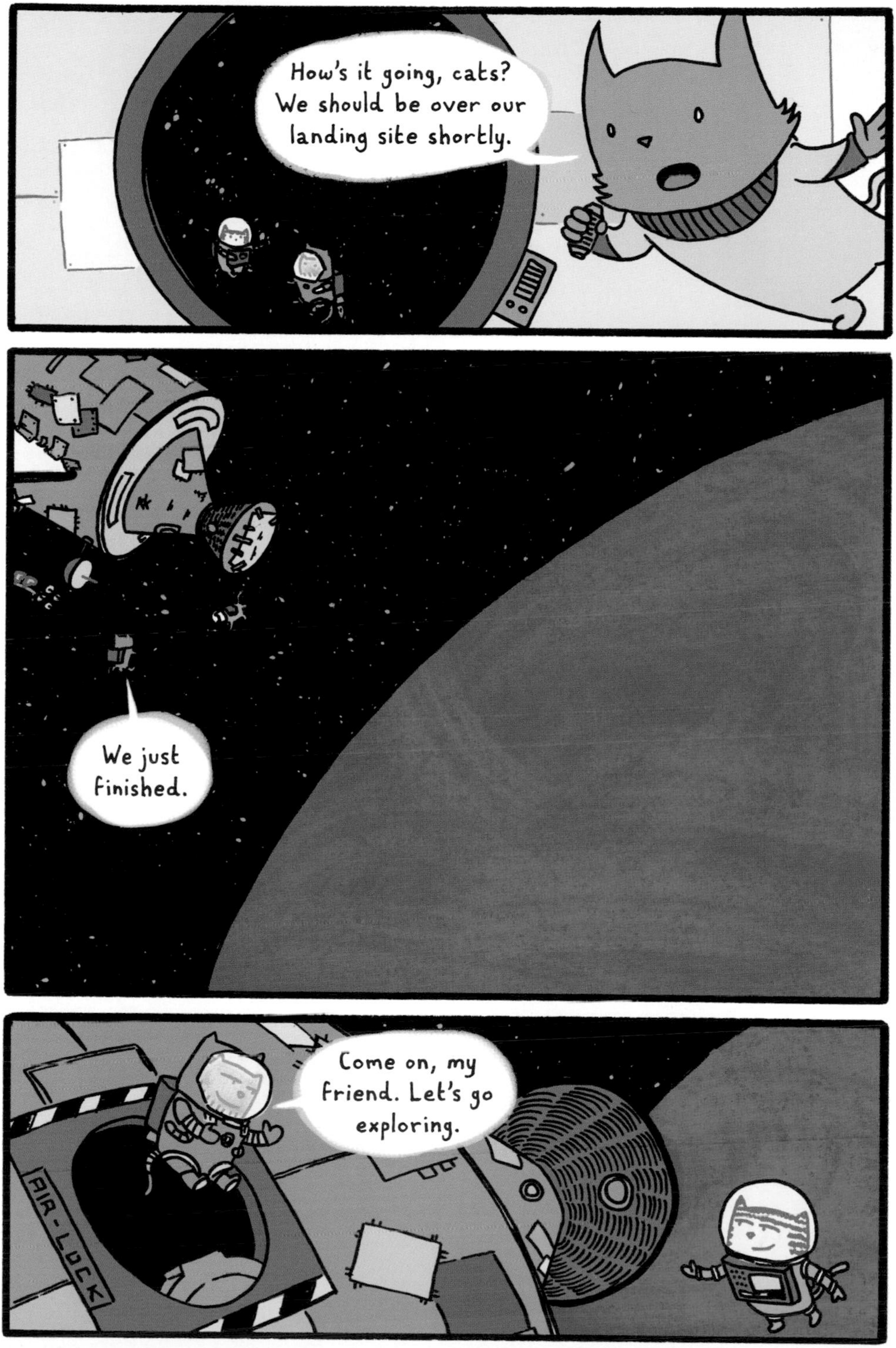
How's it going, cats? We should be over our landing site shortly.
We just finished.
Come on, my friend. Let's go exploring.
AIR-LOCK

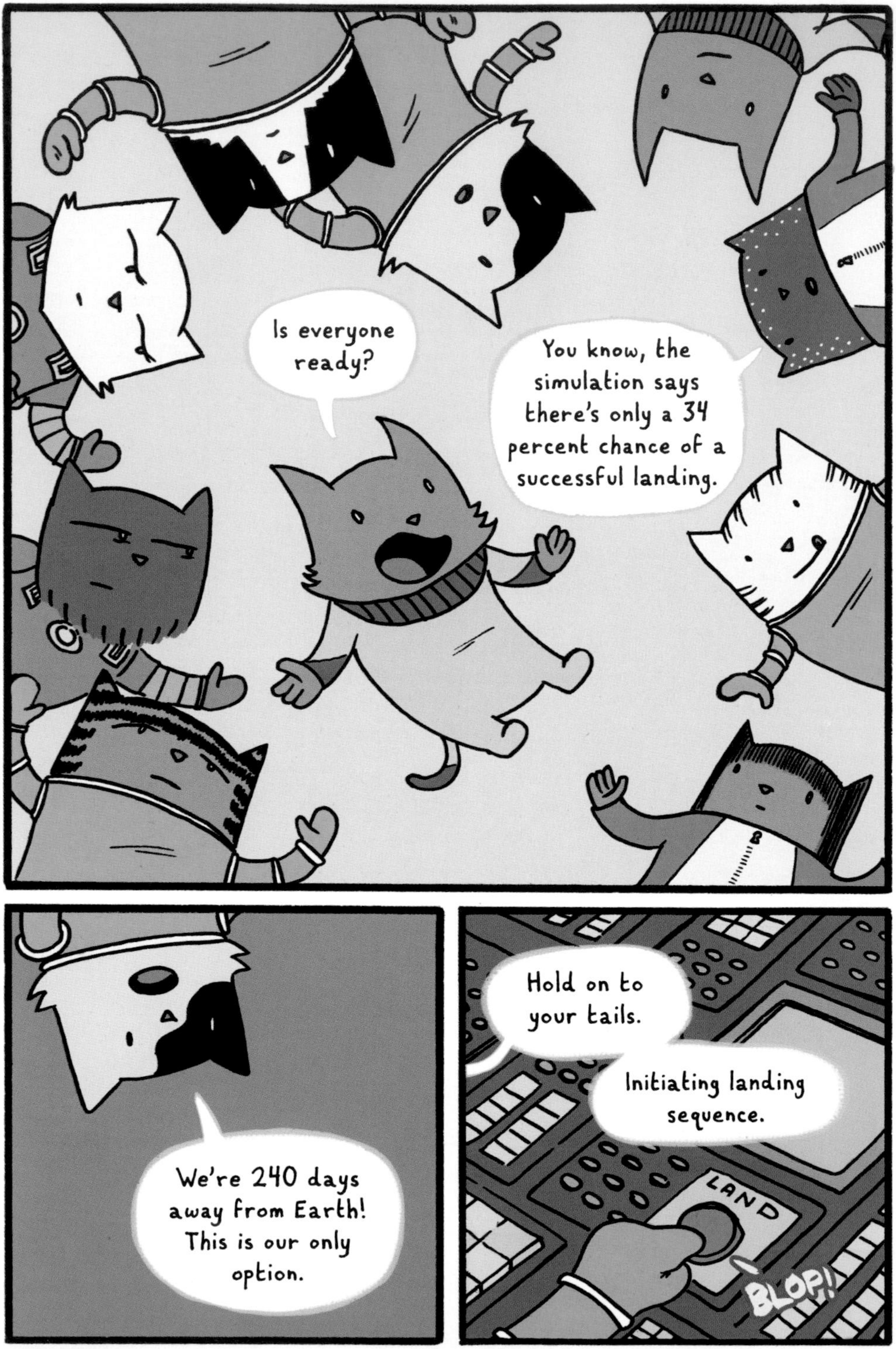
Is everyone ready?
You know, the simulation says there's only a 34 percent chance of a successful landing.
We're 240 days away from Earth! This is our only option.
Hold on to your tails.
Initiating landing sequence.
LAND
BLOP!

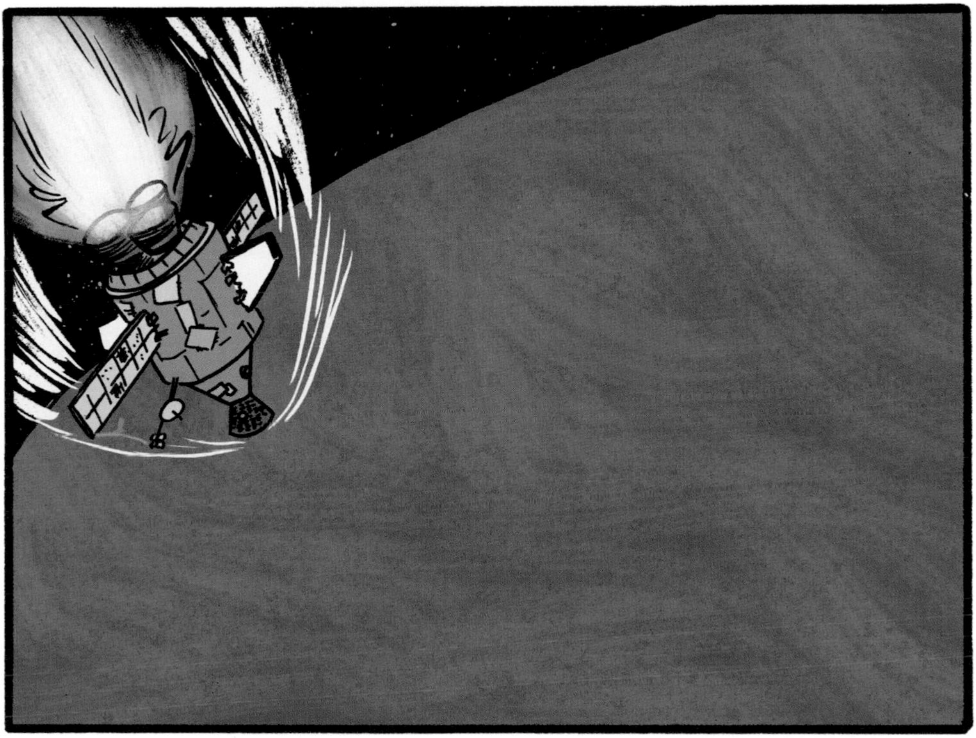
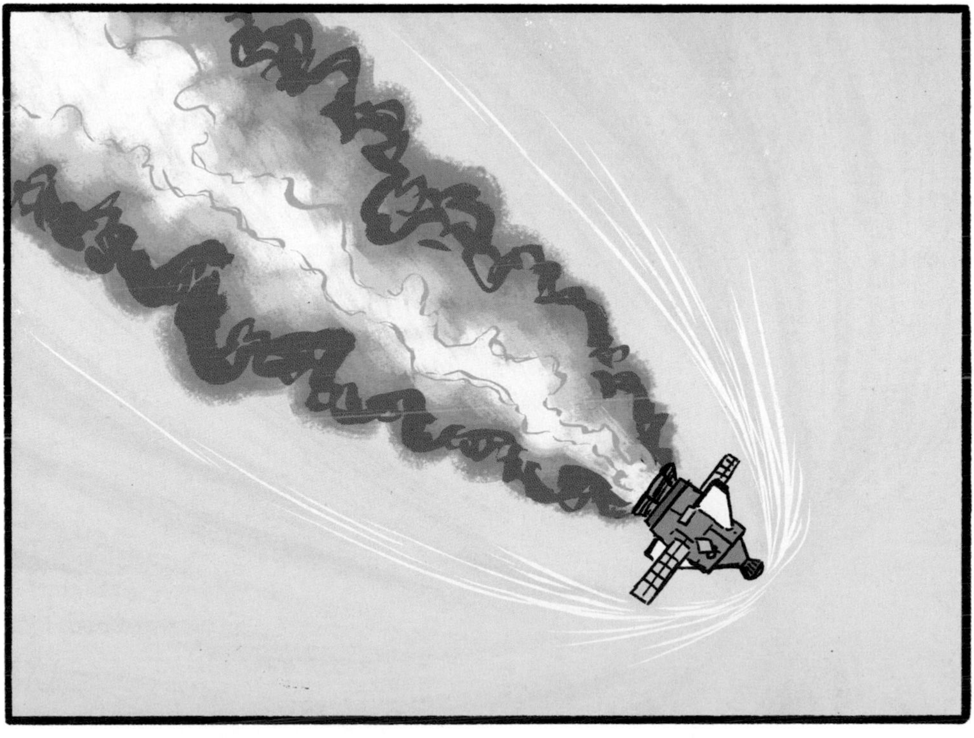

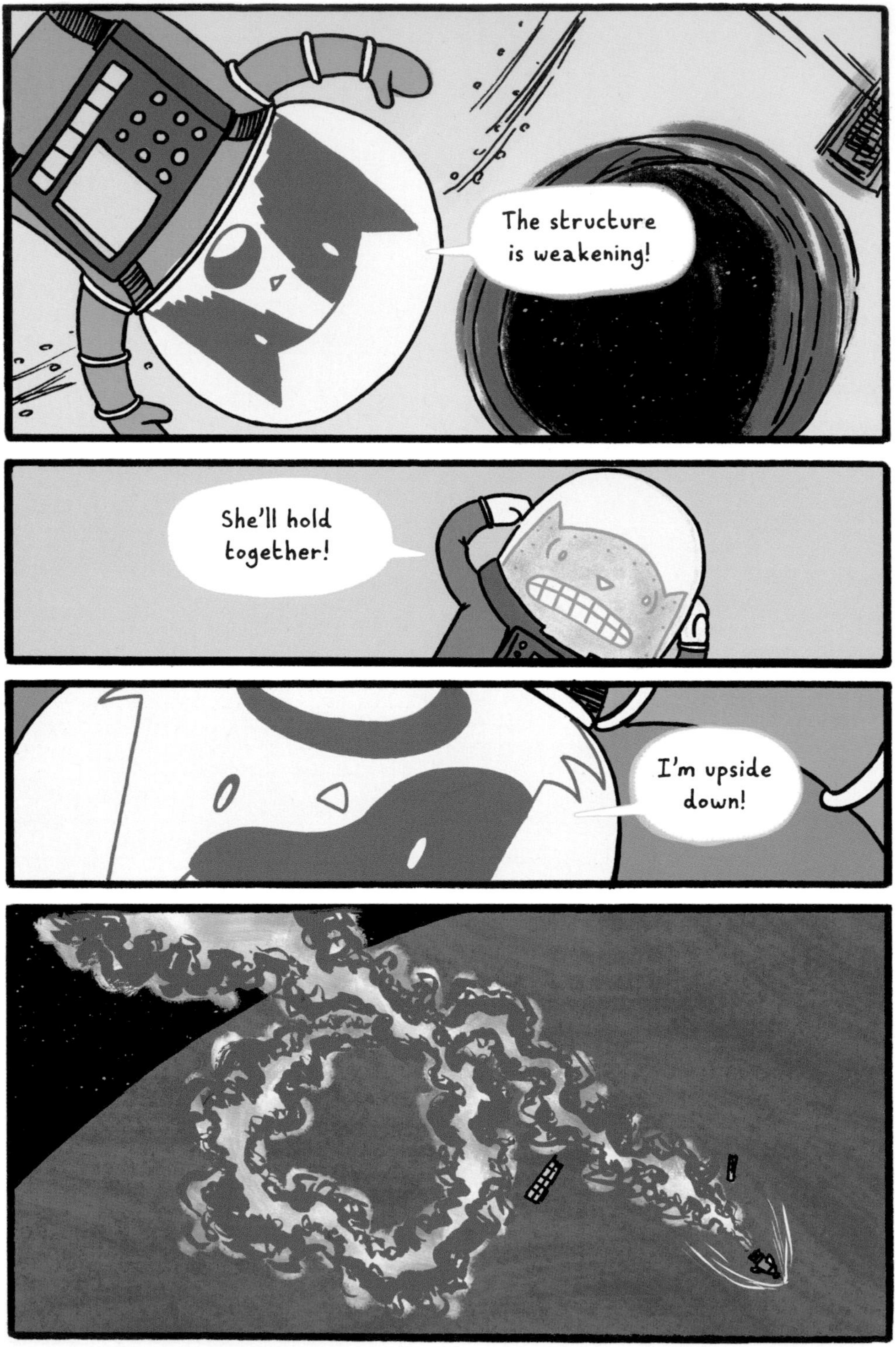
The structure is weakening!
She'll hold together!
I'm upside down!

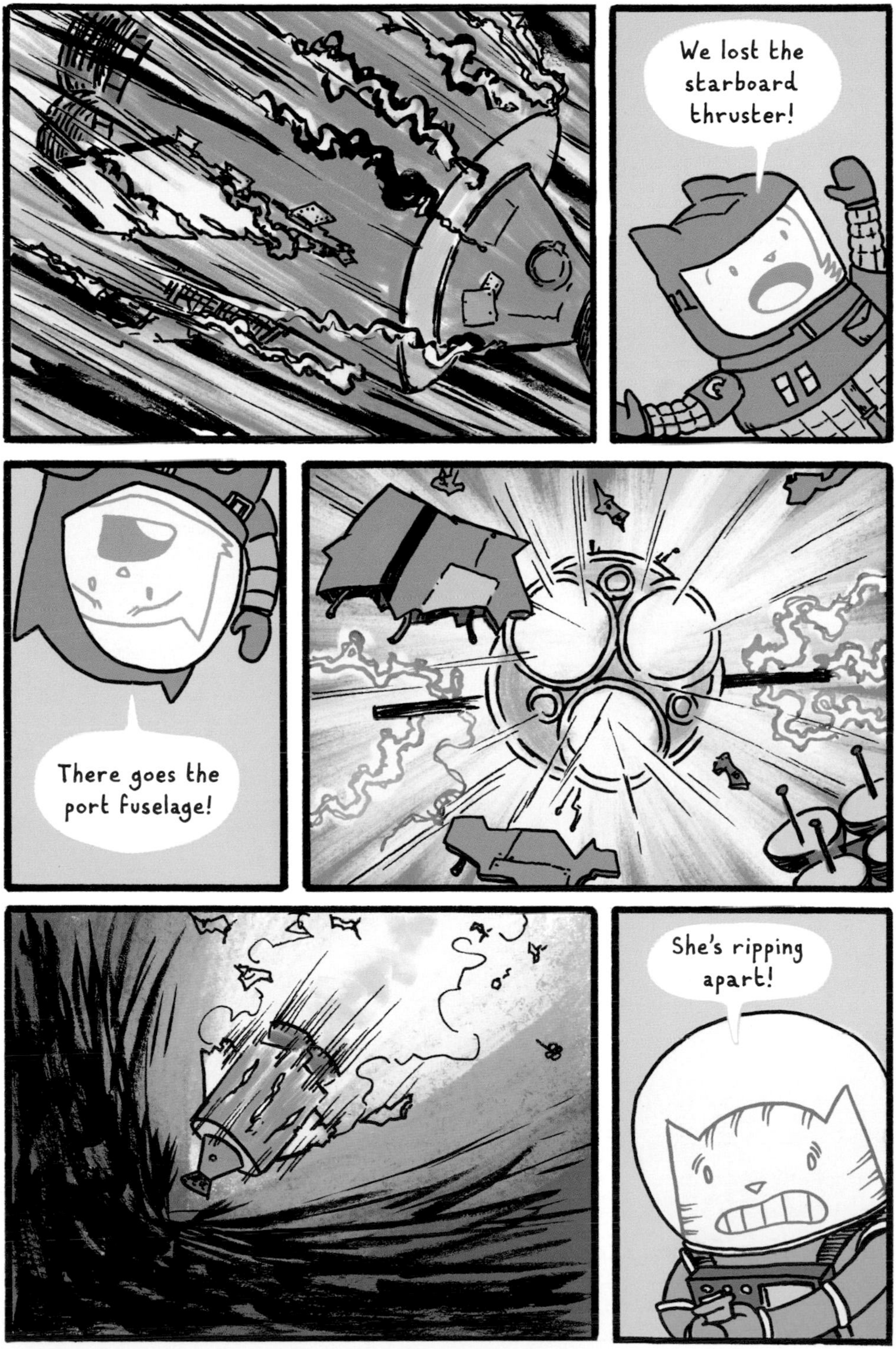
We lost the starboard thruster!
There goes the port fuselage!
She's ripping apart!

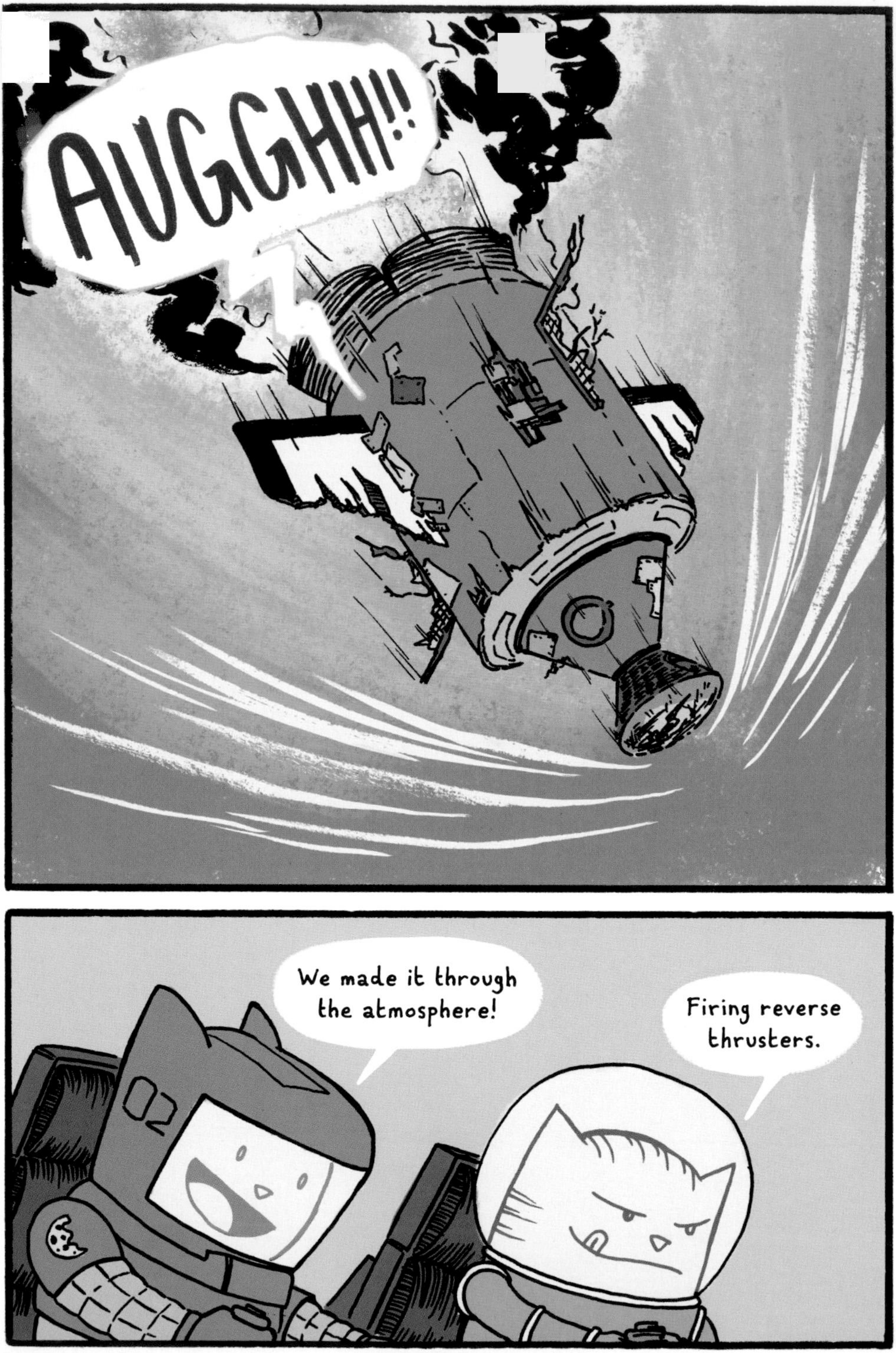
AUGGHH!!
We made it through the atmosphere!
Firing reverse thrusters.

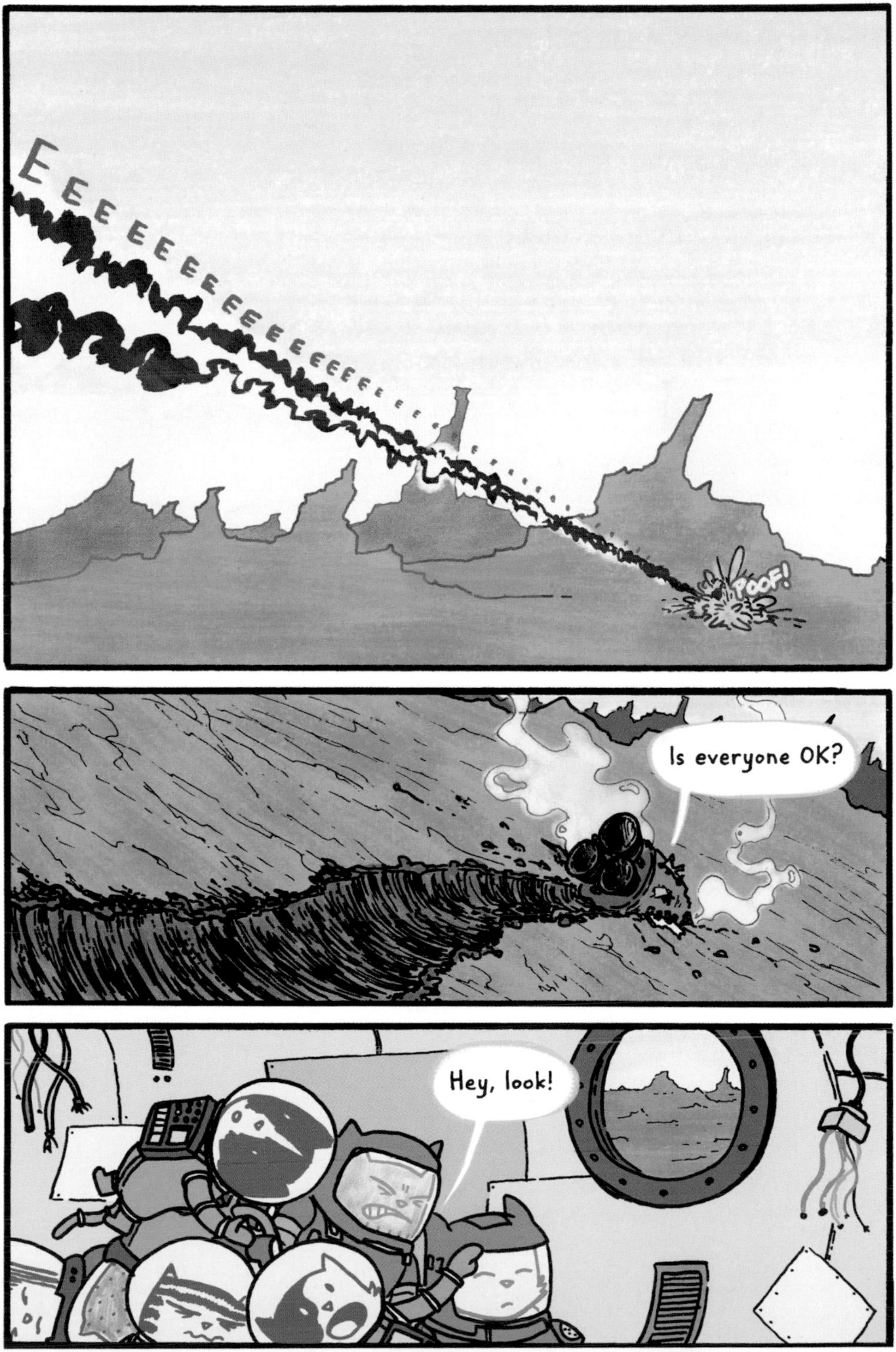
EEEEEEEEEEEEEEEEE
POOF!
Is everyone OK?
Hey, look!

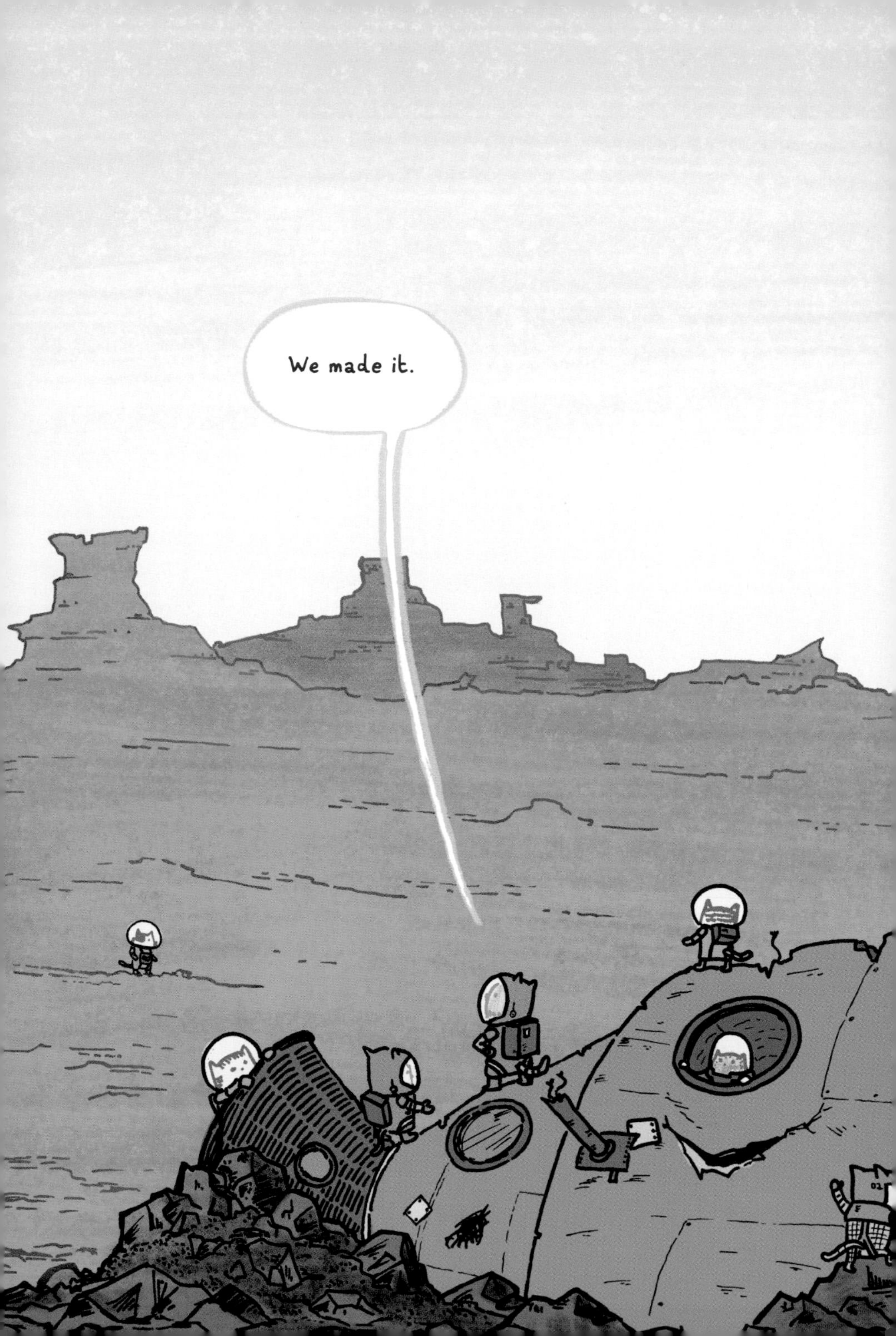
We made it.

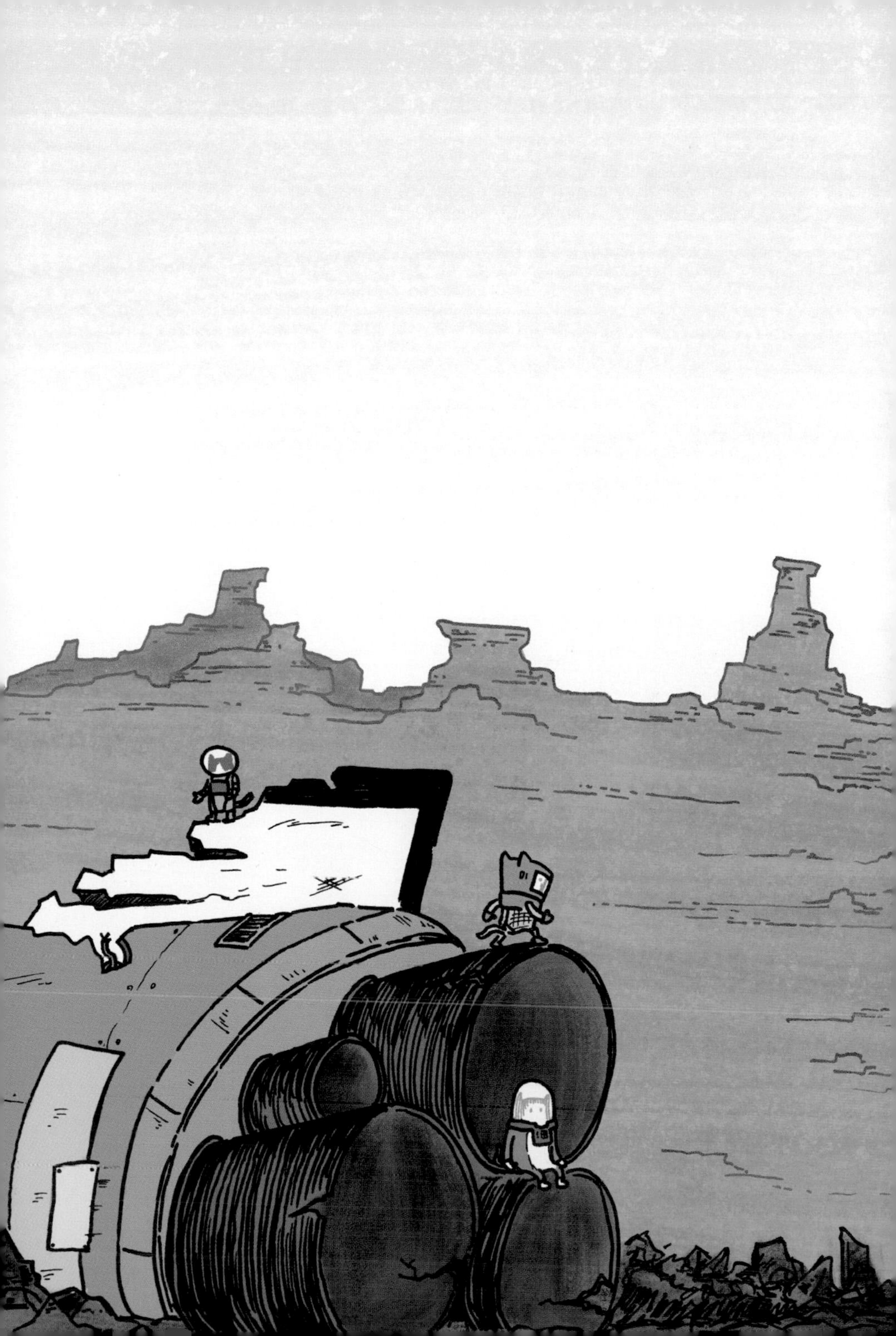

CHAPTER 10

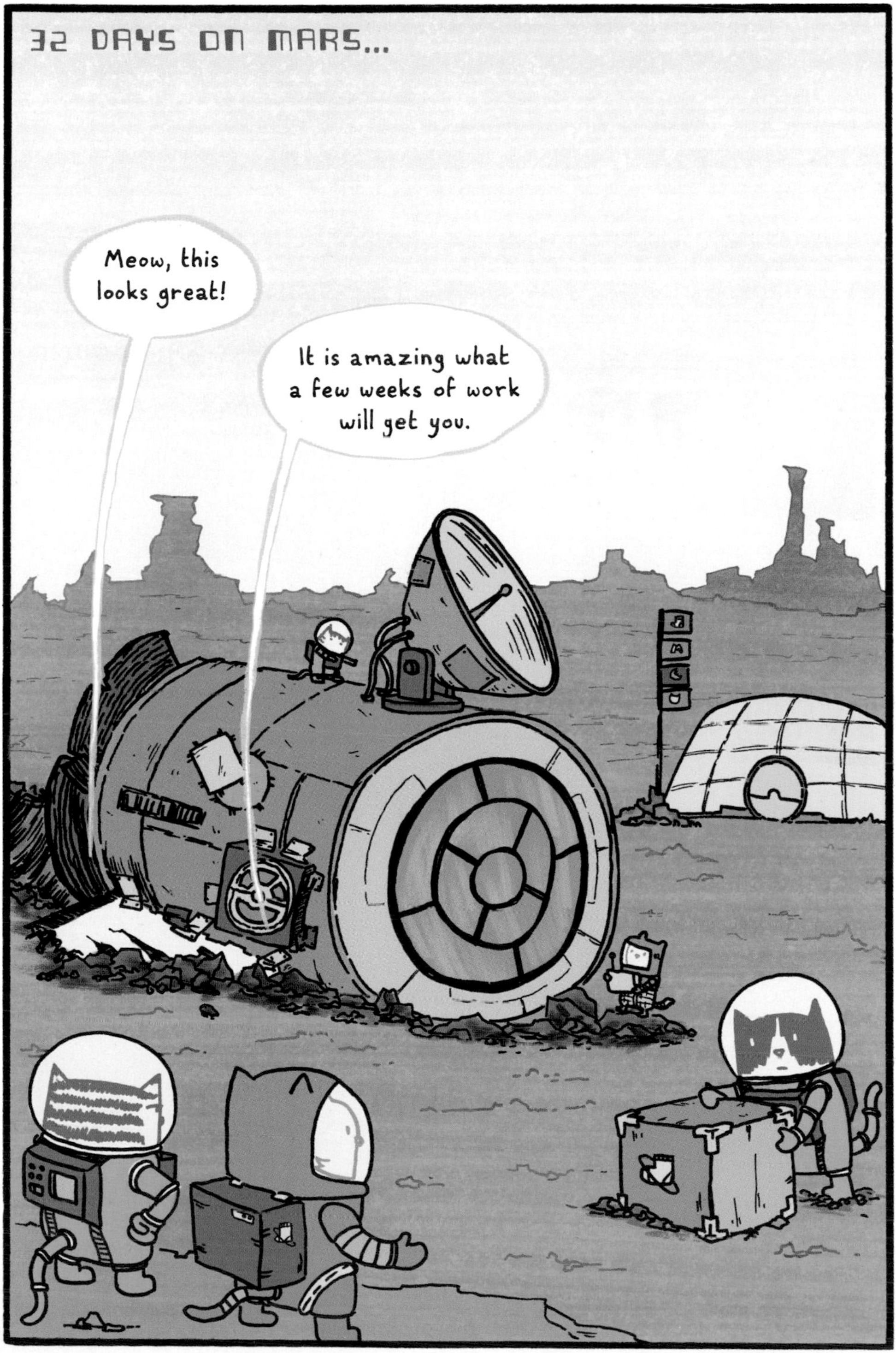
32 DAYS ON MARS...
Meow, this looks great!
It is amazing what a few weeks of work will get you.

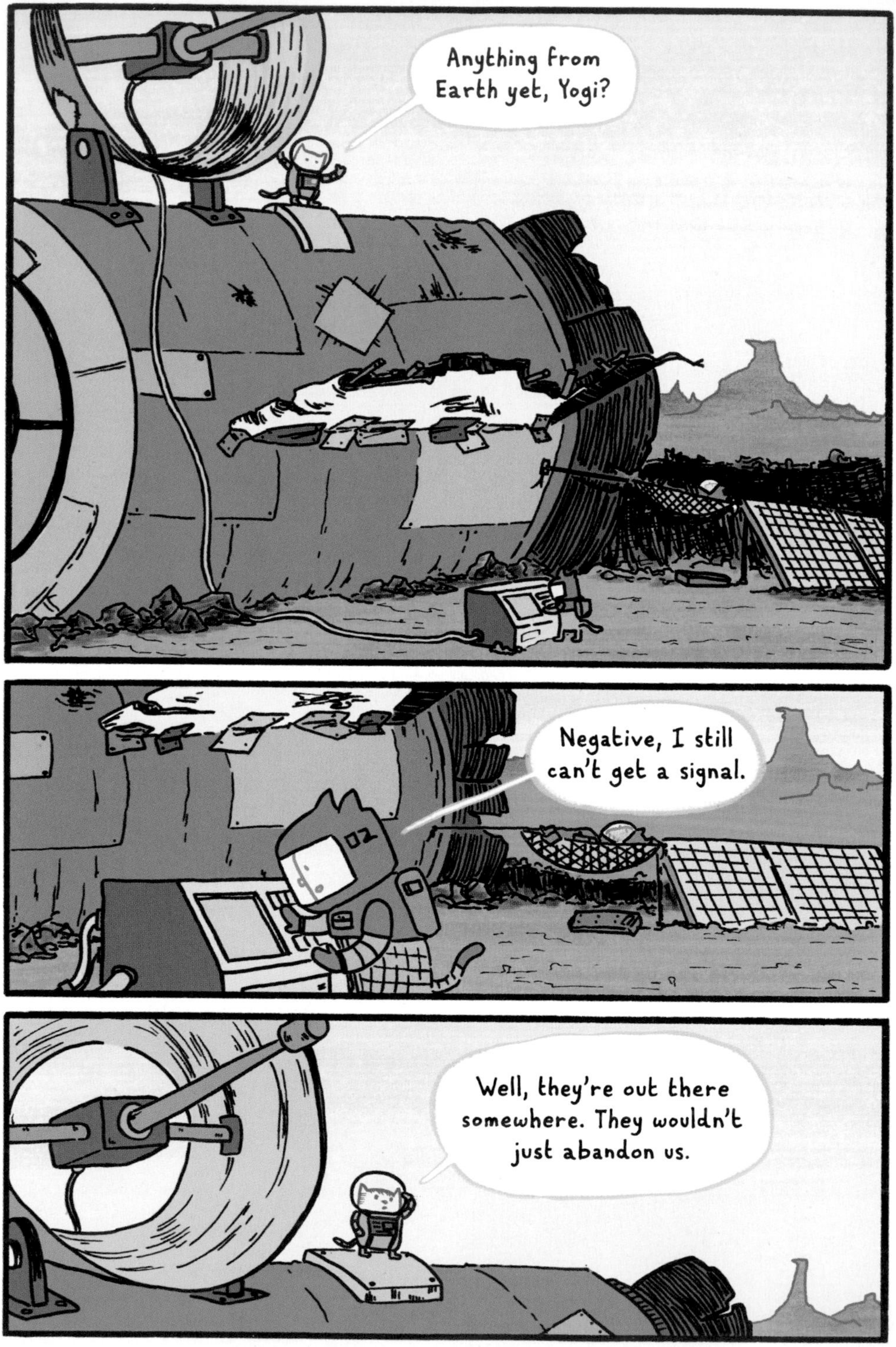
Anything from Earth yet, Yogi?
Negative, I still can't get a signal.
02
Well, they're out there somewhere. They wouldn't just abandon us.

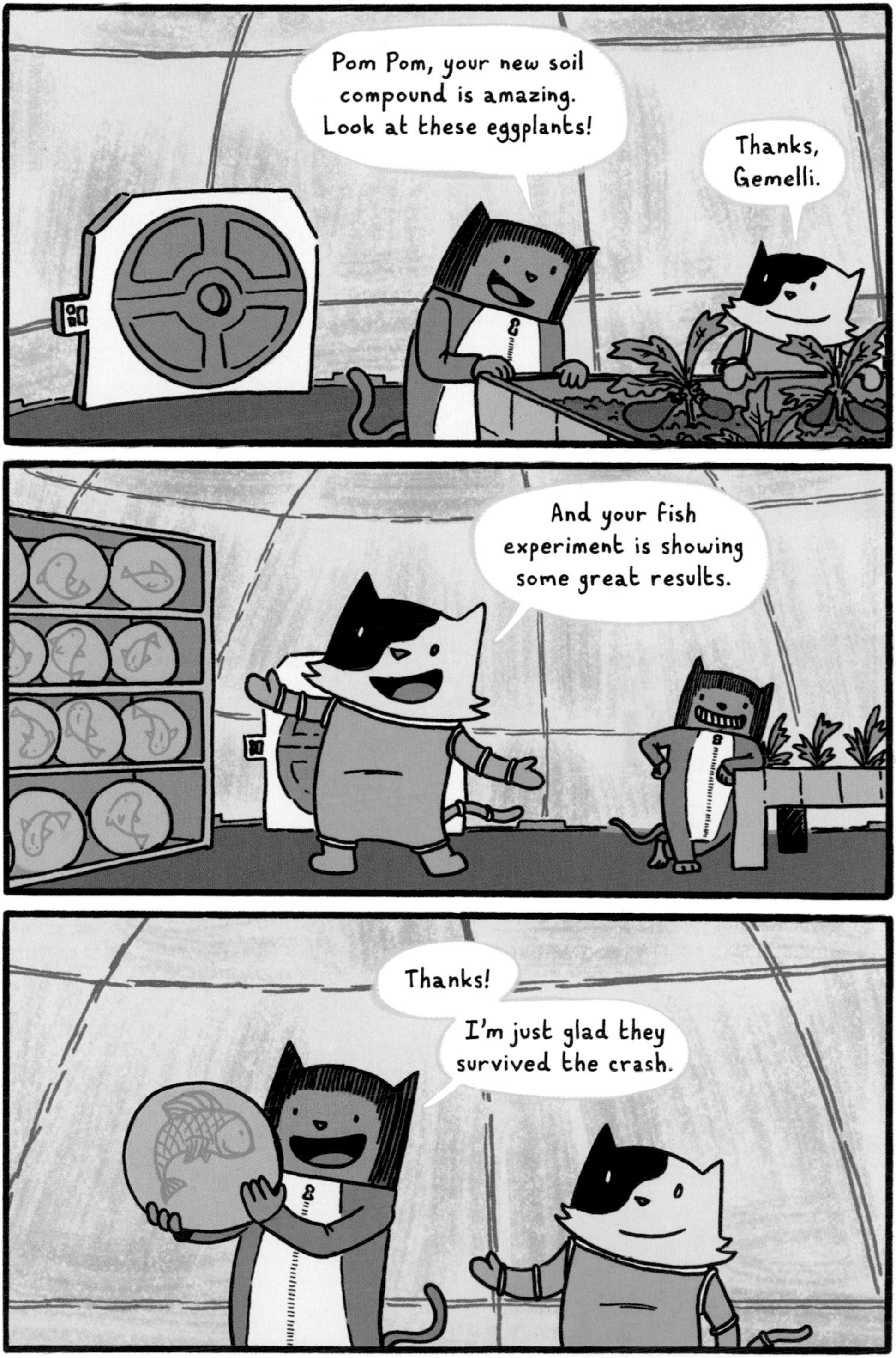
Pom Pom, your new soil compound is amazing. Look at these eggplants!
Thanks, Gemelli.
And your fish experiment is showing some great results.
Thanks!
I'm just glad they survived the crash.

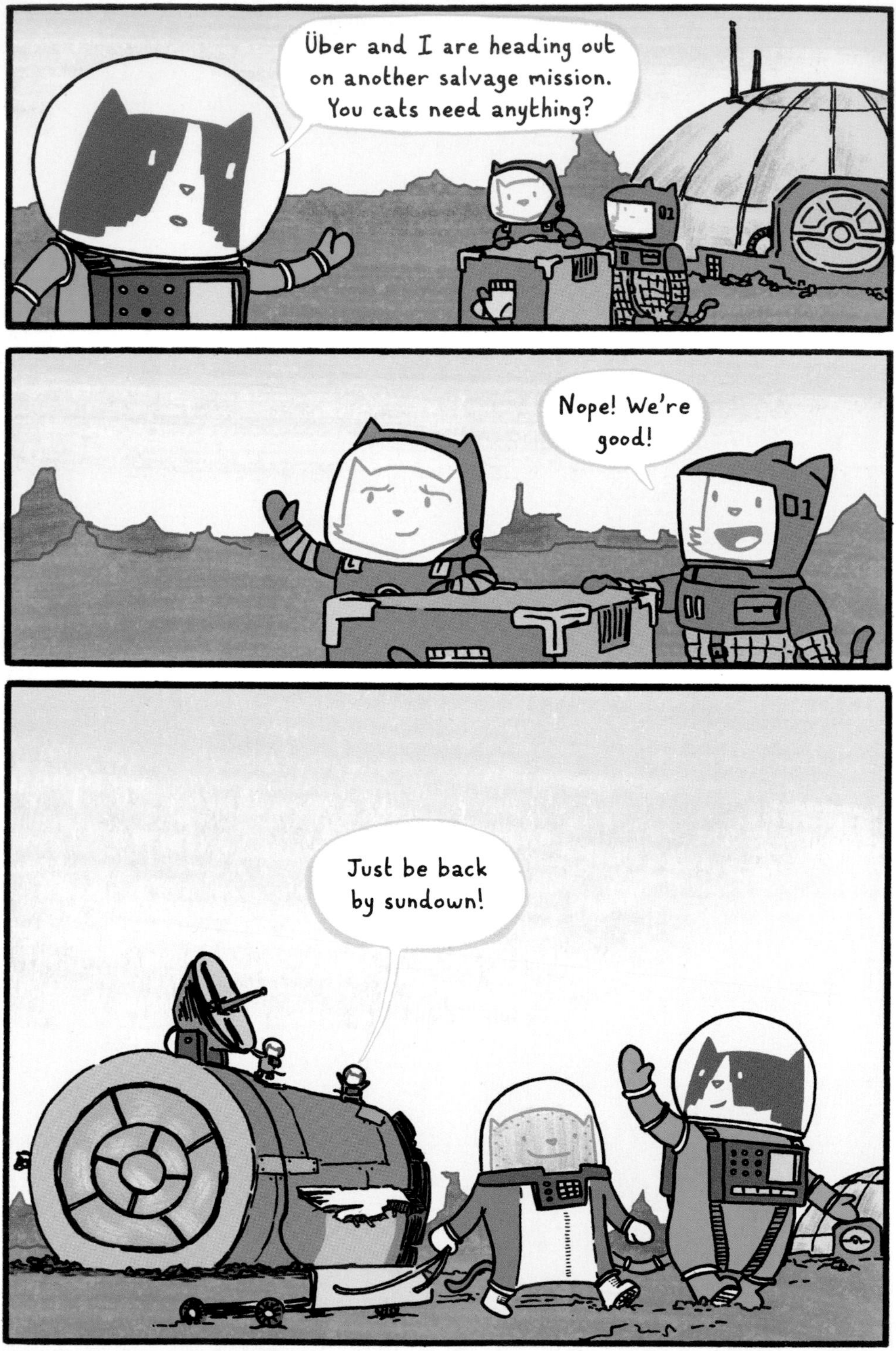
Über and I are heading out on another salvage mission. You cats need anything?
Nope! We're good!
Just be back by sundown!

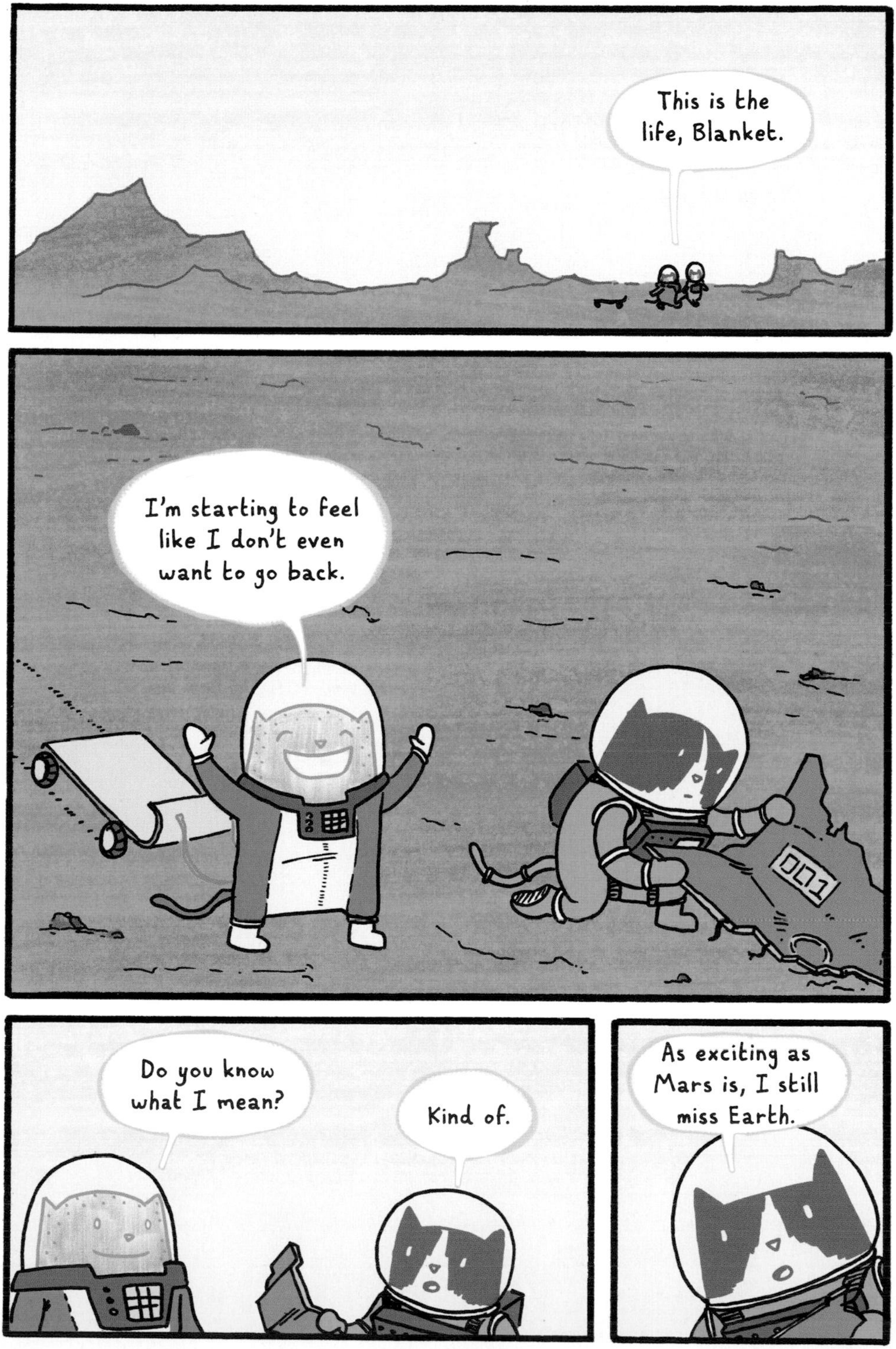
This is the life, Blanket.
I'm starting to feel like I don't even want to go back.
Do you know what I mean?
Kind of.
As exciting as Mars is, I still miss Earth.

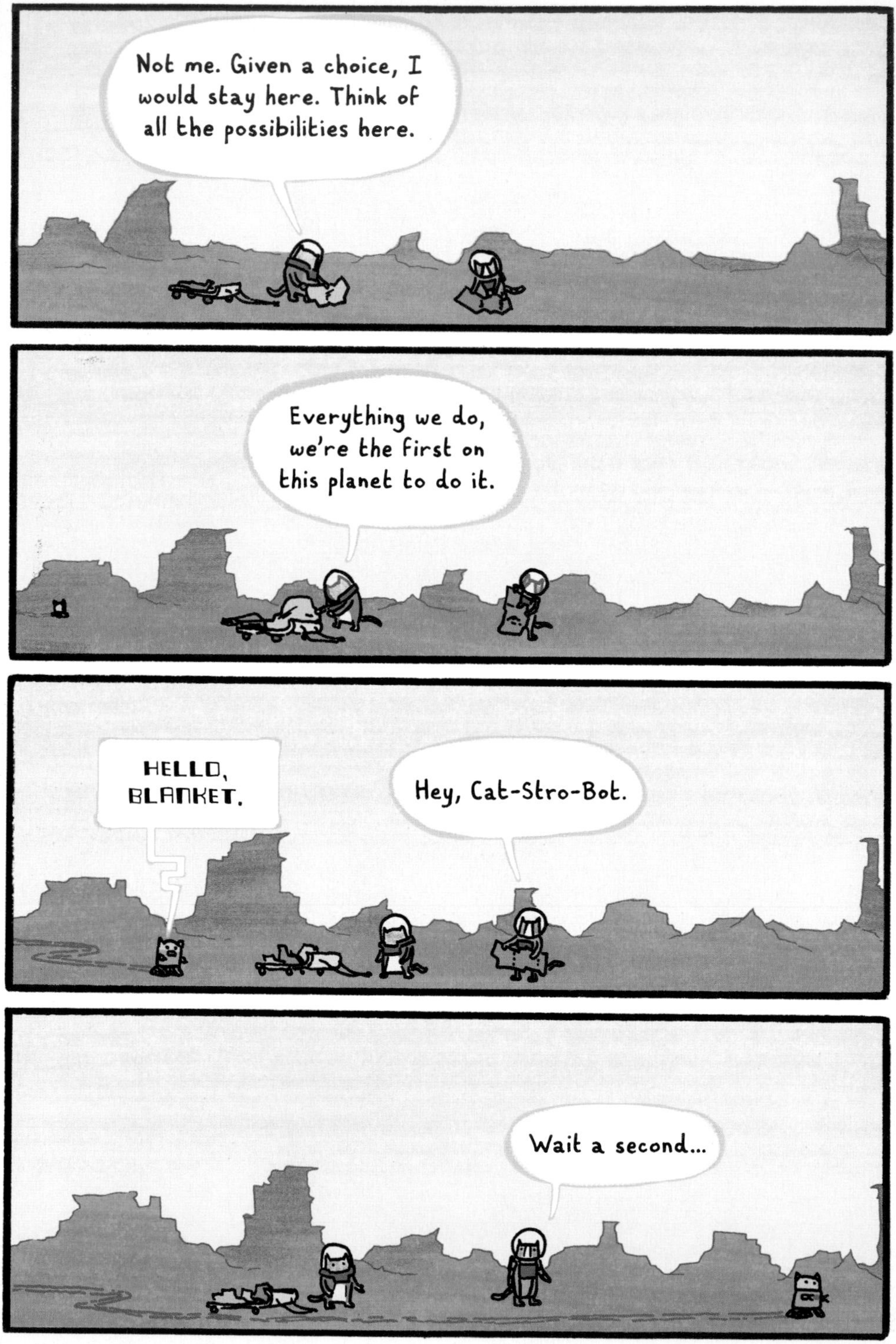
Not me. Given a choice, I would stay here. Think of all the possibilities here.
Everything we do, we're the first on this planet to do it.
HELLO, BLANKET.
Hey, Cat-Stro-Bot.
Wait a second...

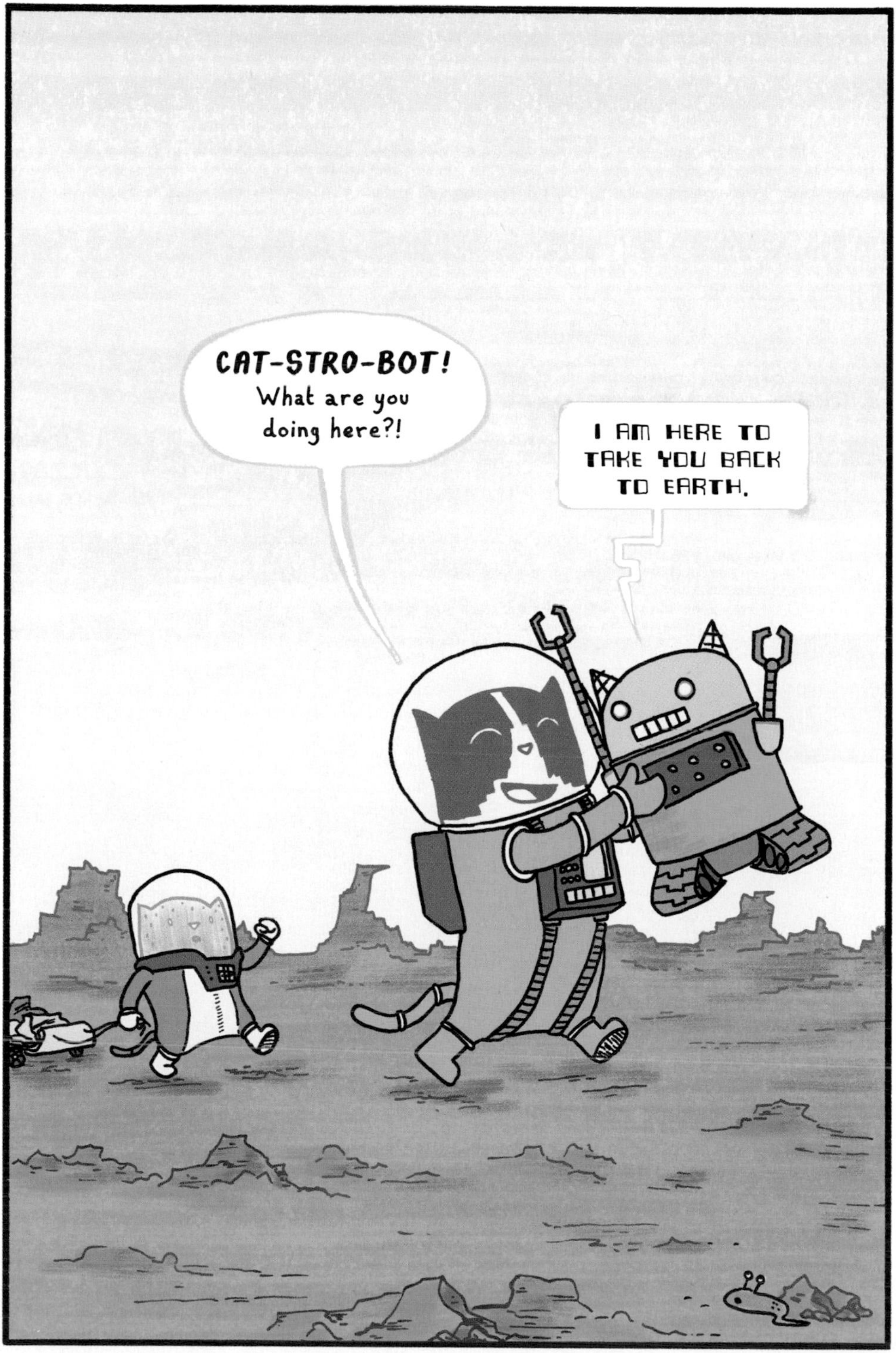
CAT-STRO-BOT! What are you doing here?!
I AM HERE TO TAKE YOU BACK TO EARTH.

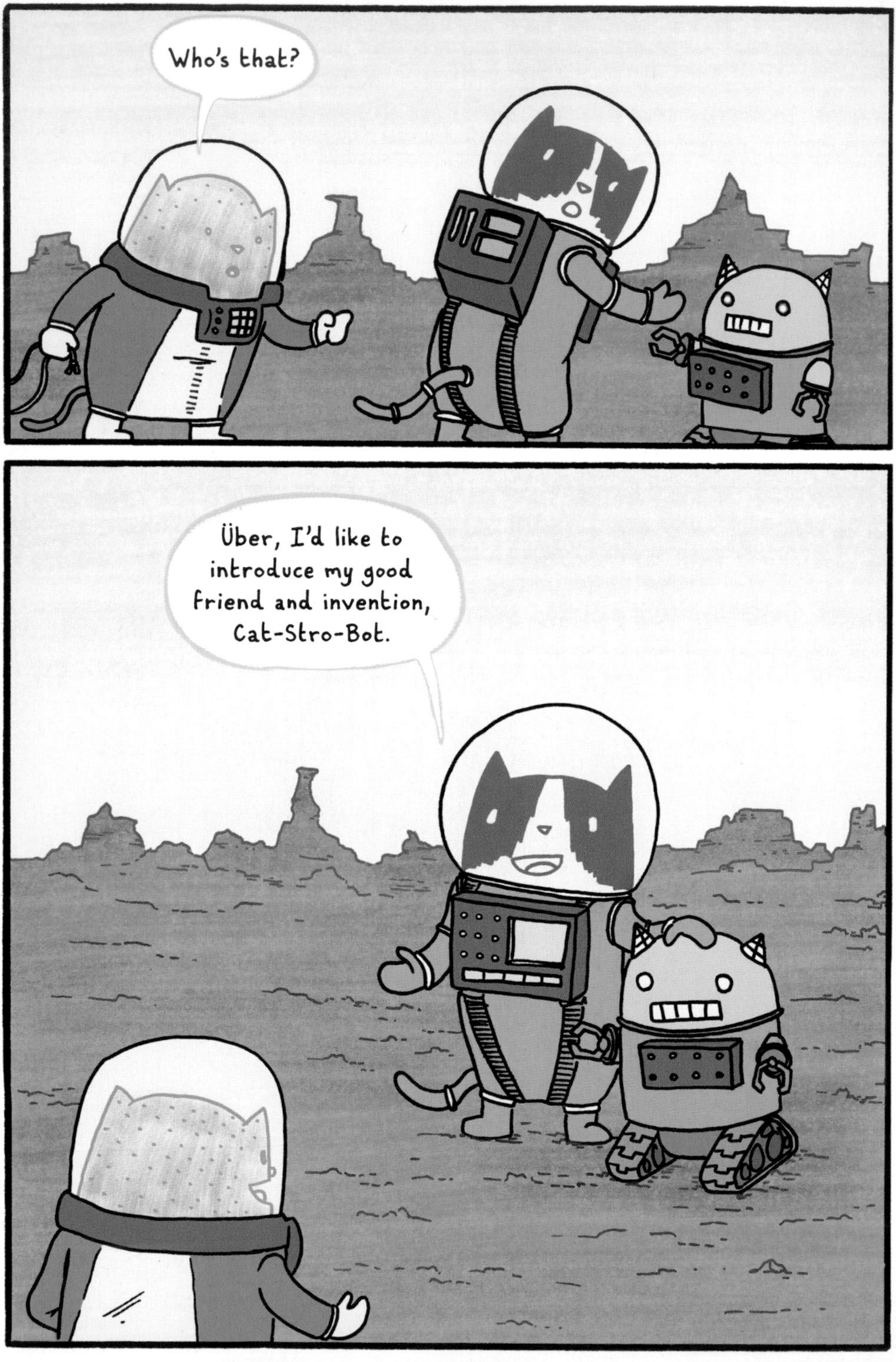
Who's that?
Über, I'd like to introduce my good friend and invention, Cat-Stro-Bot.

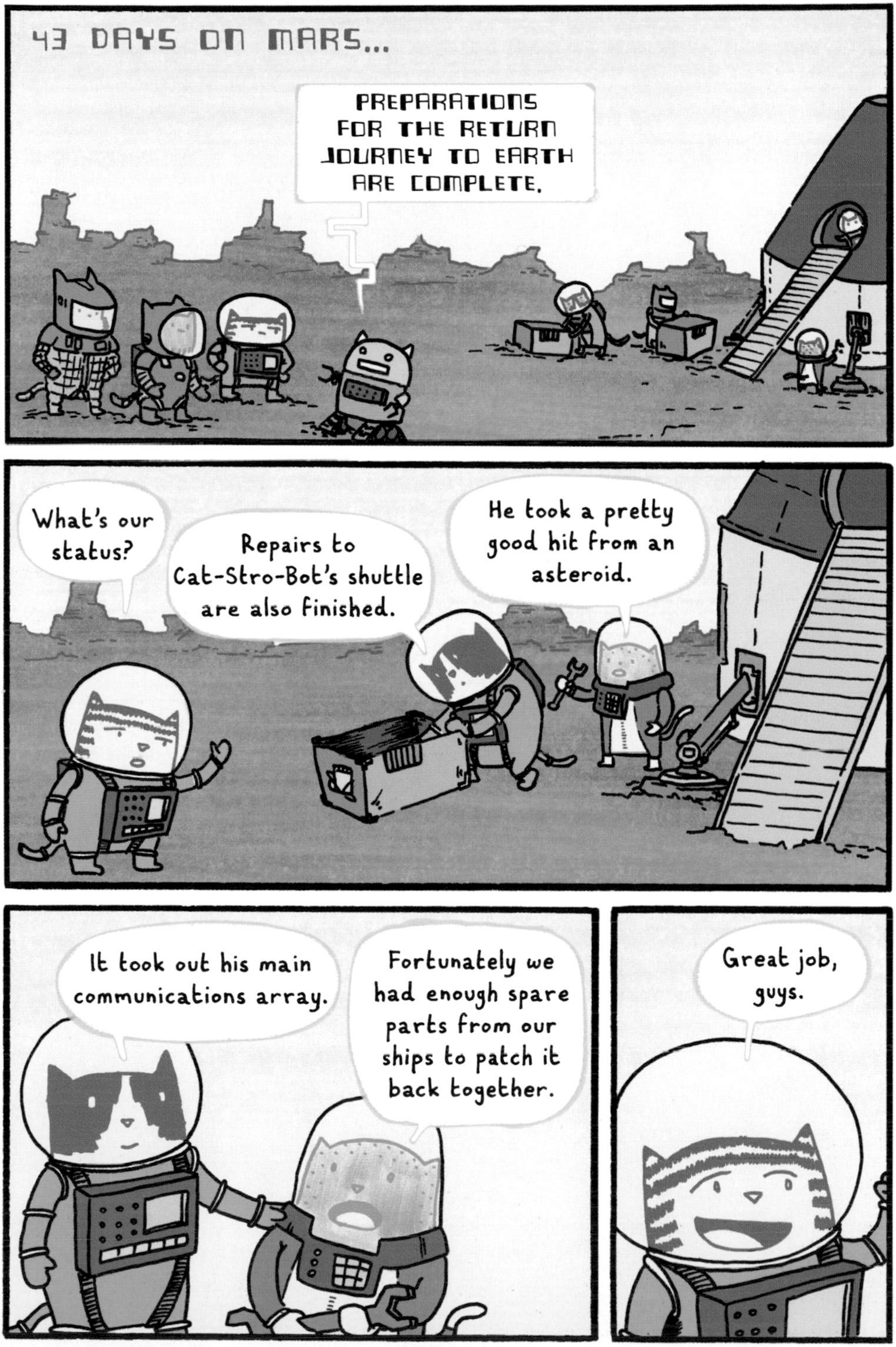
43 DAYS ON MARS...
PREPARATIONS FOR THE RETURN JOURNEY TO EARTH ARE COMPLETE.
What's our status?
Repairs to Cat-Stro-Bot's shuttle are also finished.
He took a pretty good hit from an asteroid.
It took out his main communications array.
Fortunately we had enough spare parts from our ships to patch it back together.
Great job, guys.

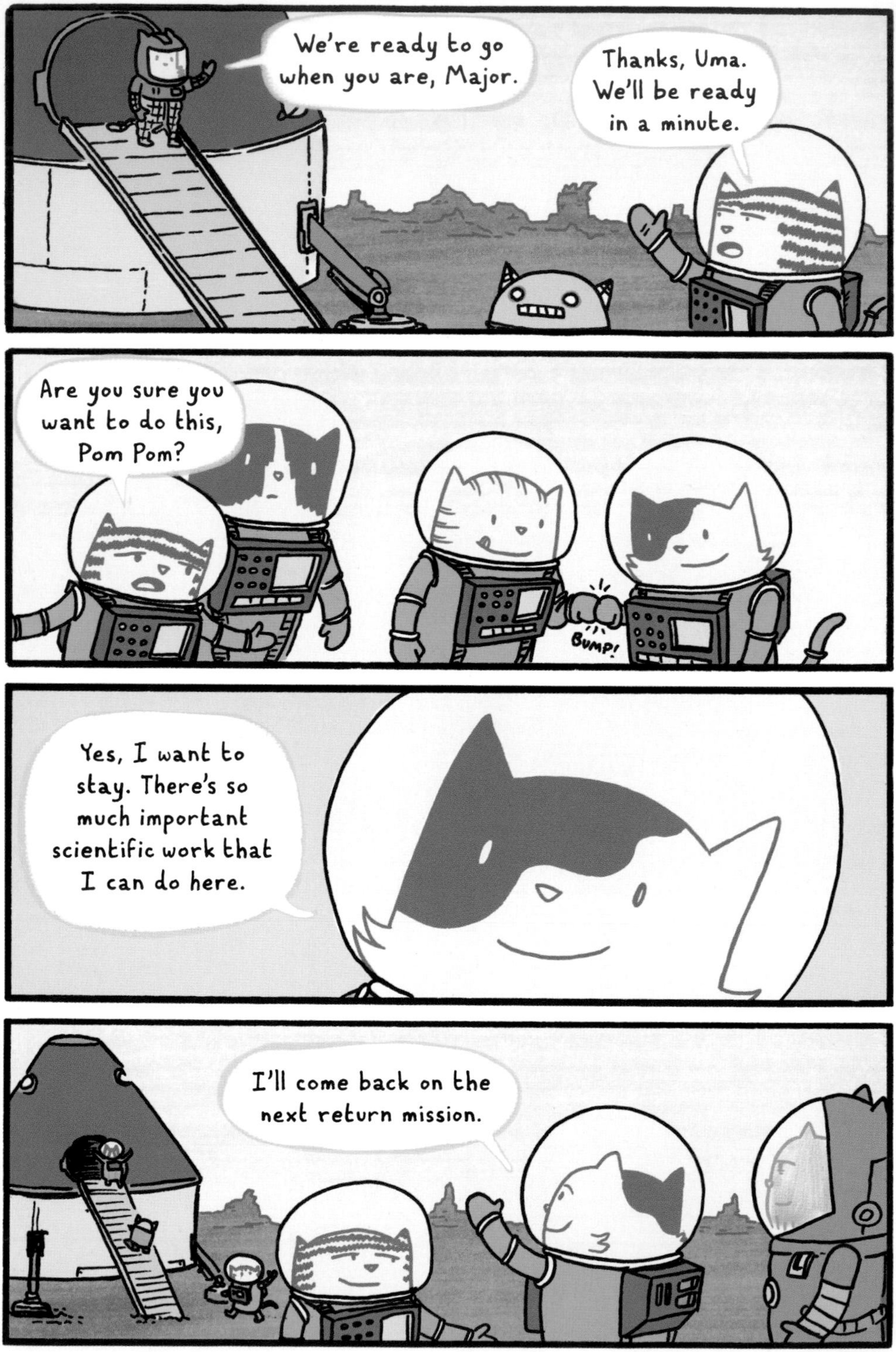
We're ready to go when you are, Major.
Thanks, Uma. We'll be ready in a minute.
Are you sure you want to do this, Pom Pom?
BUMP!
Yes, I want to stay. There's so much important scientific work that I can do here.
I'll come back on the next return mission.

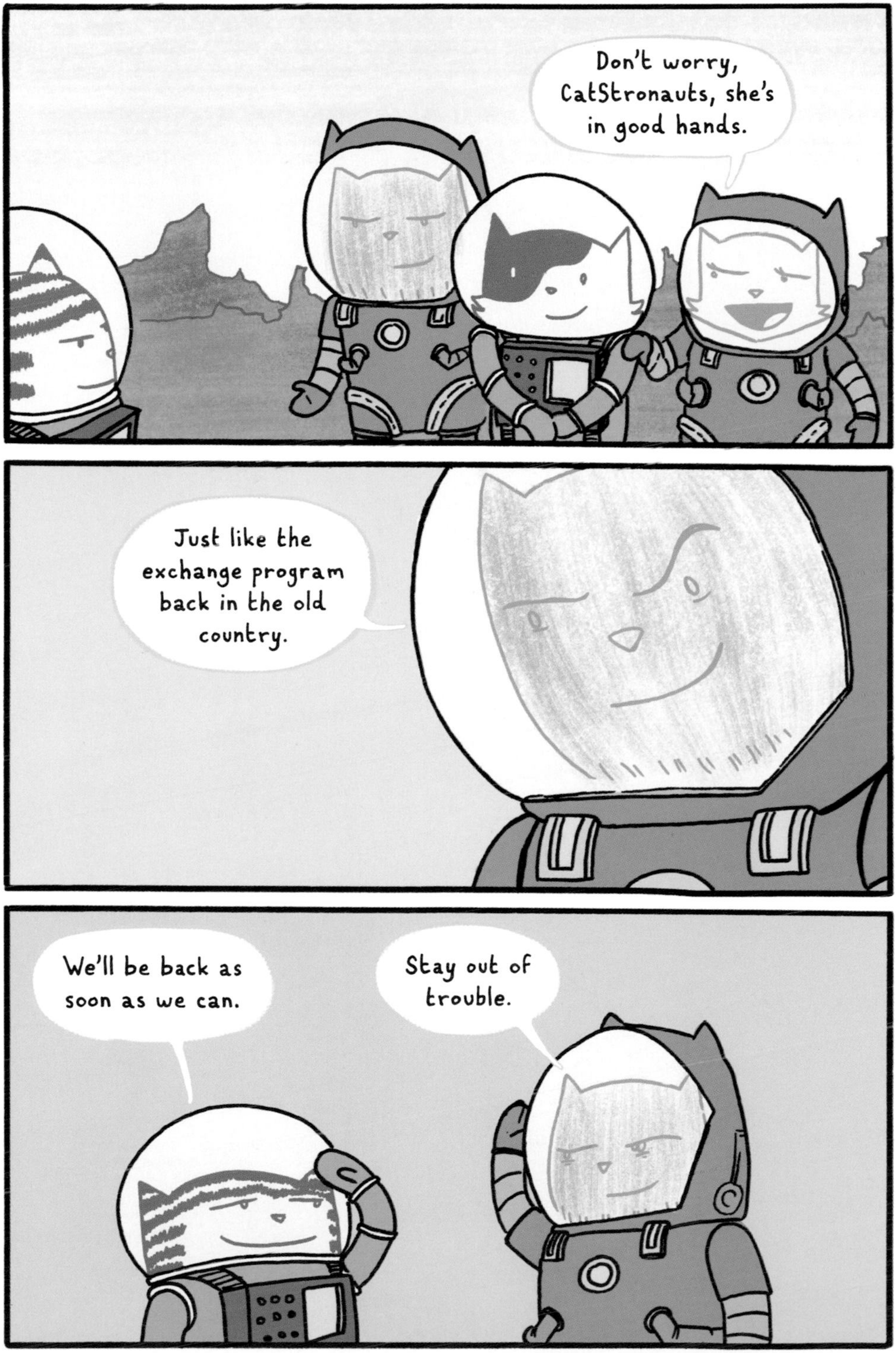
Don't worry, CatStronauts, she's in good hands.
Just like the exchange program back in the old country.
We'll be back as soon as we can.
Stay out of trouble.

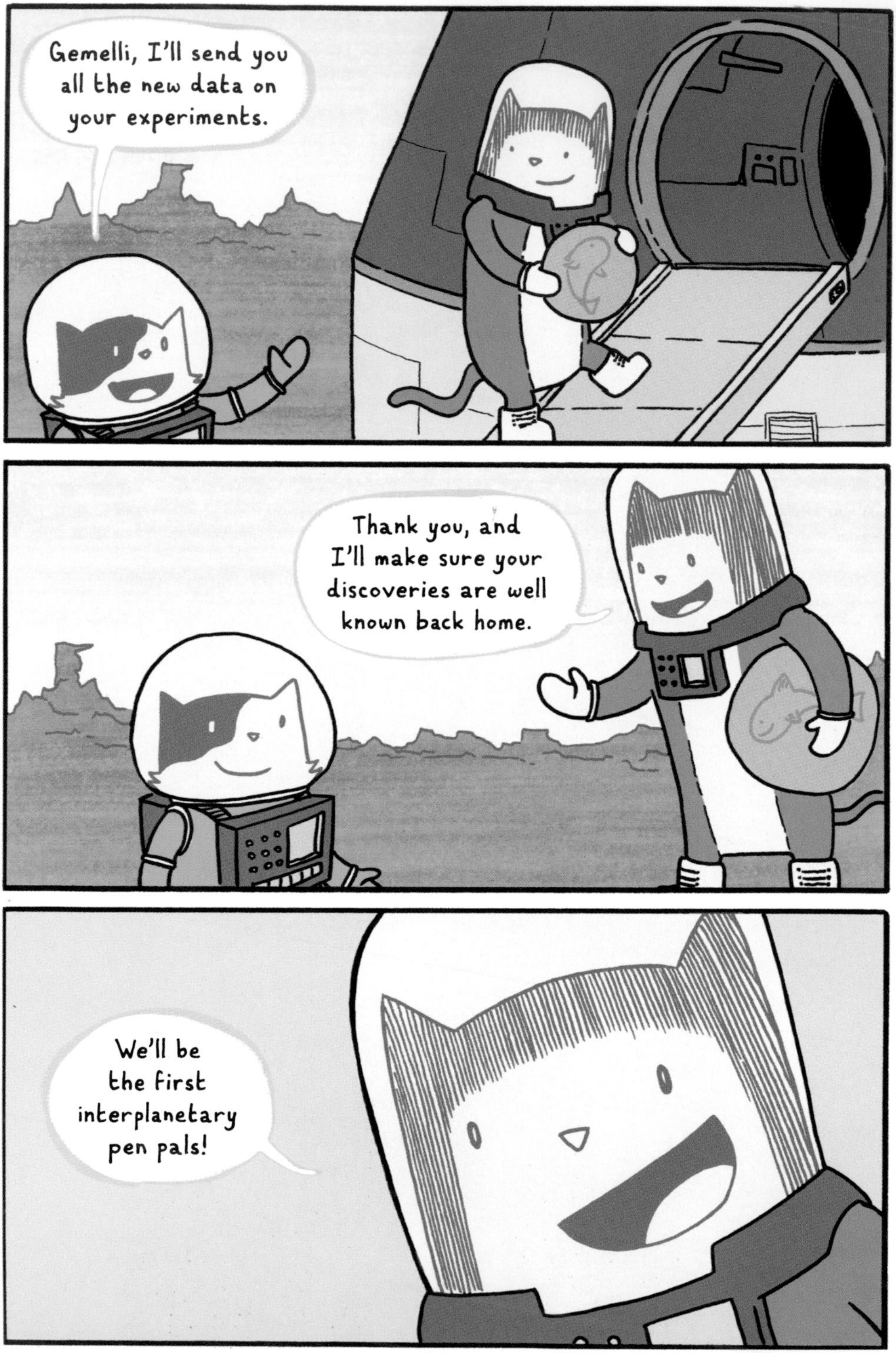
Gemelli, I'll send you all the new data on your experiments.
Thank you, and I'll make sure your discoveries are well known back home.
We'll be the first interplanetary pen pals!

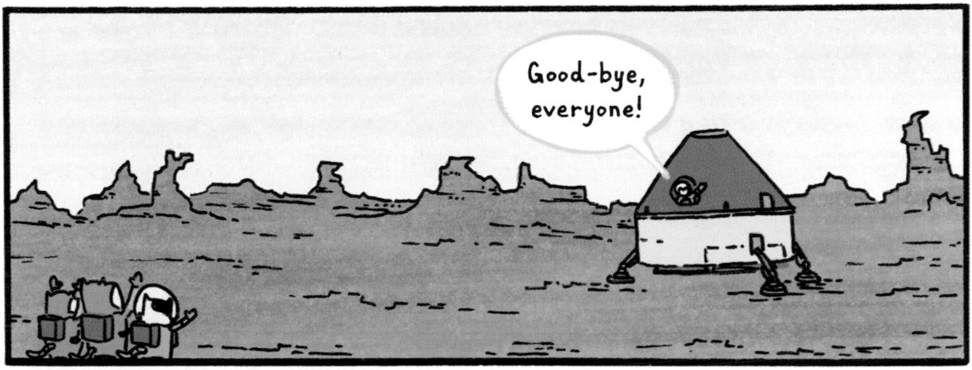
Good-bye, everyone!

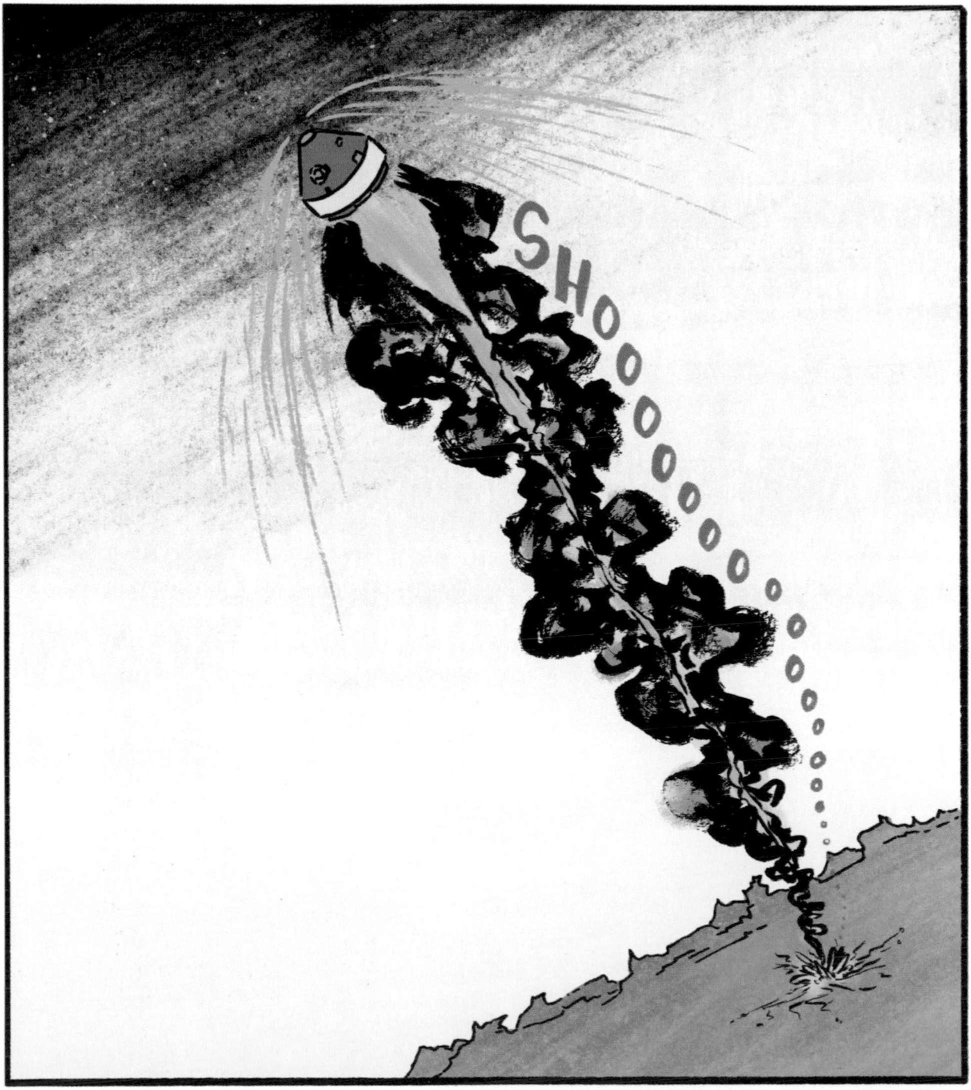
SHOOOOOOOOOOOOOO...

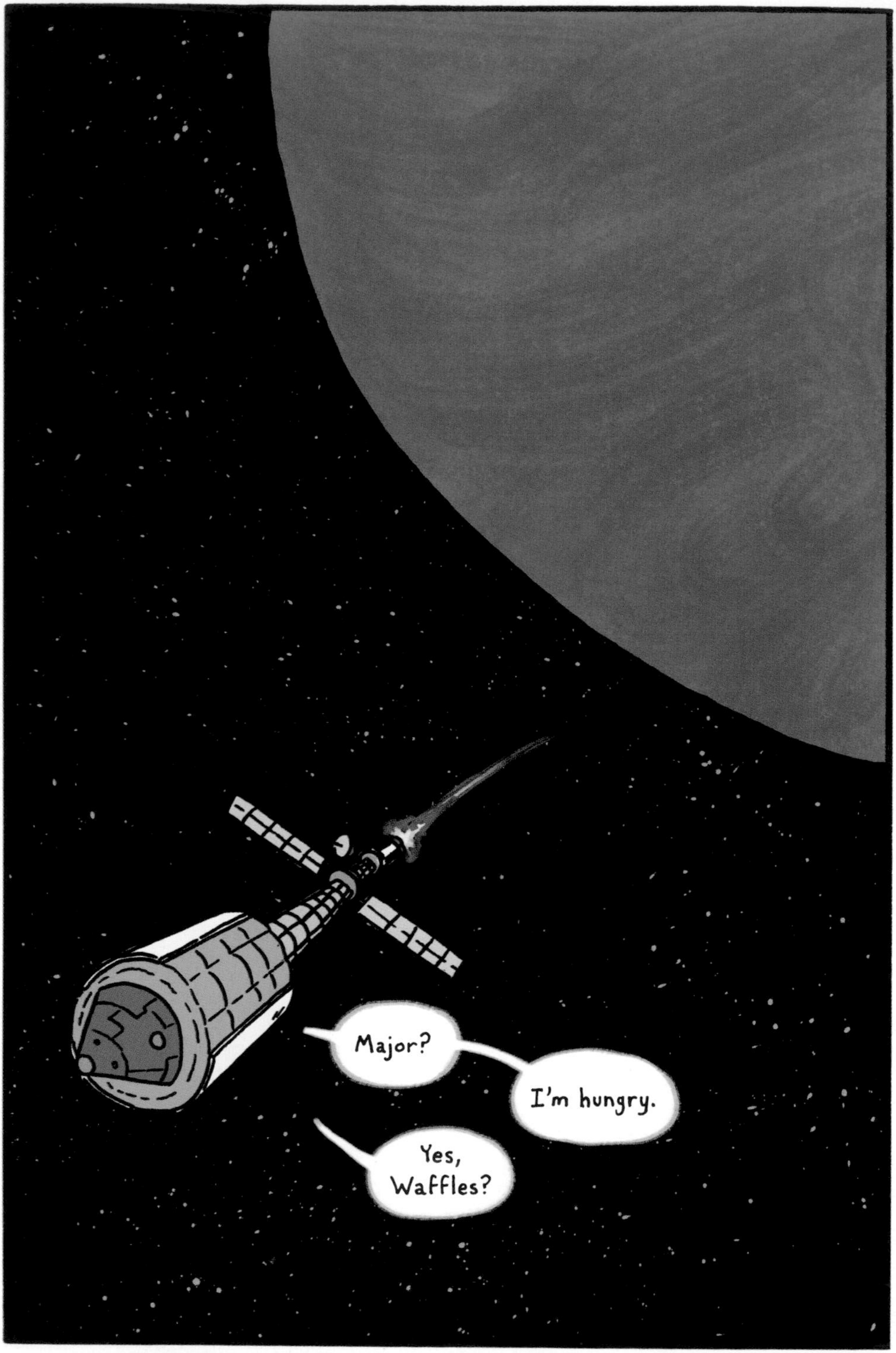
Major?
I'm hungry.
Yes, Waffles?

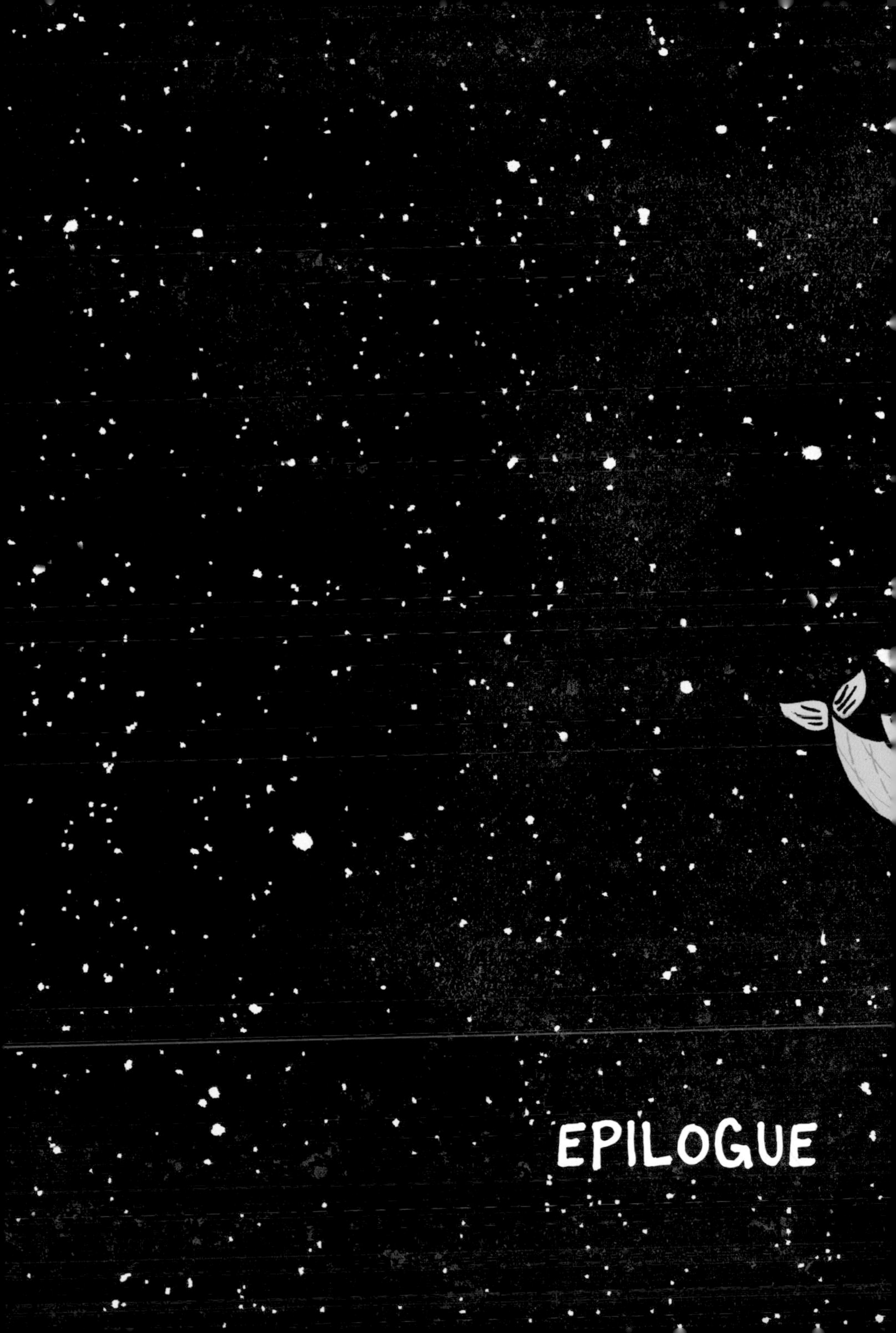
EPILOGUE

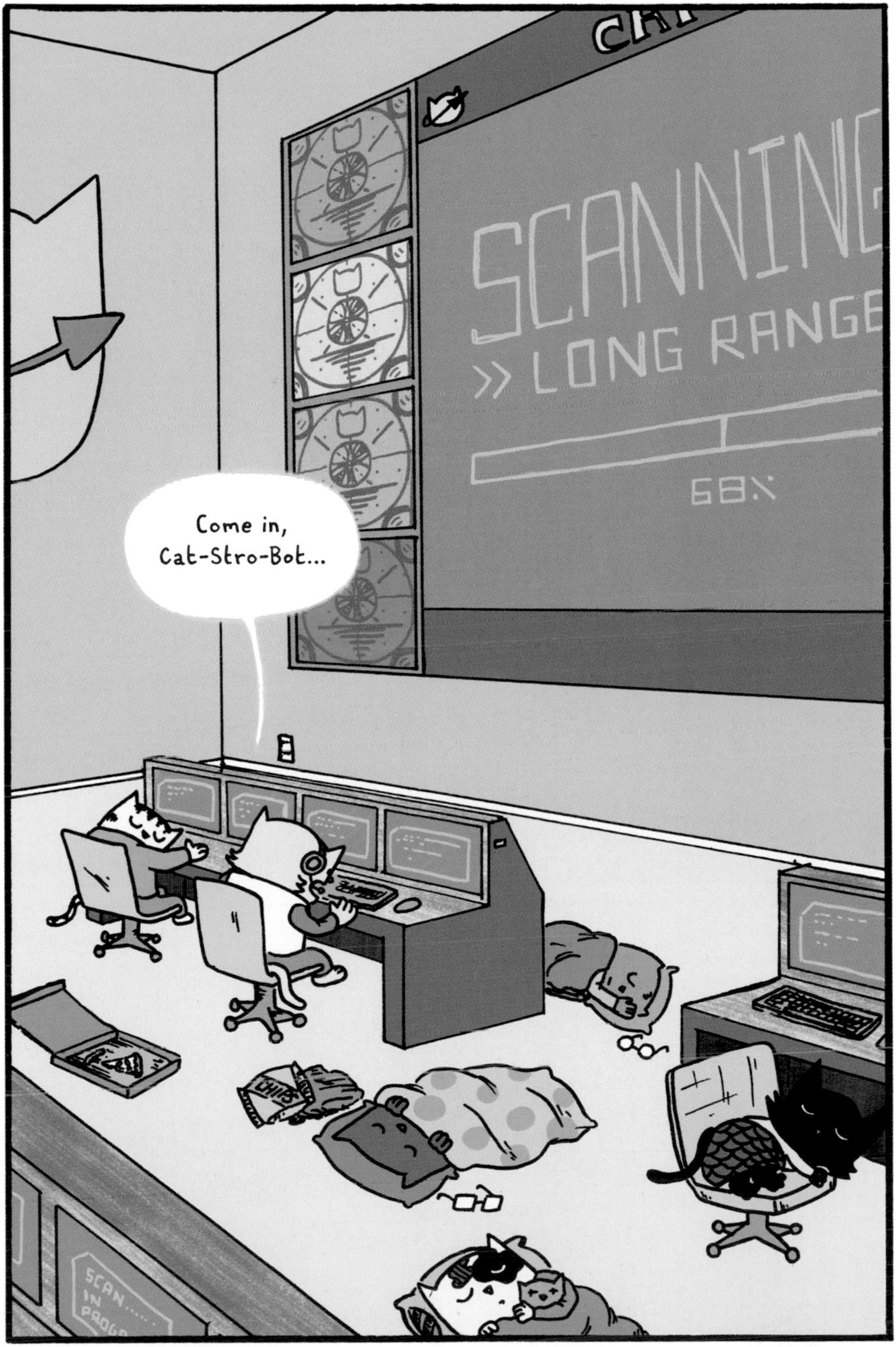
CAT
SCANNING
>> LONG RANGE
68%
Come in, Cat-Stro-Bot...
CHIPS
SCAN...... IN PROG

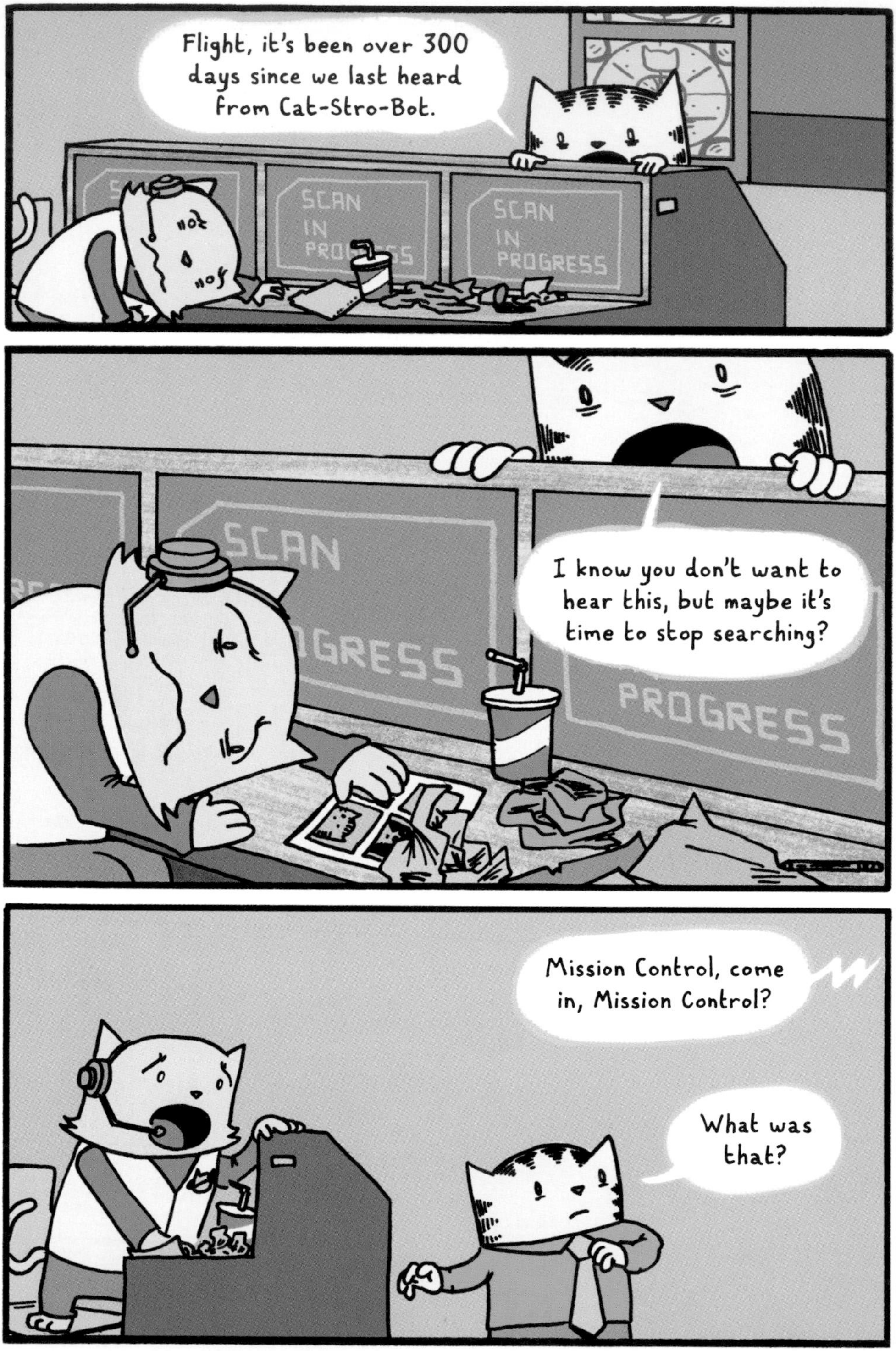
Flight, it's been over 300 days since we last heard from Cat-Stro-Bot.
SCAN IN PROGRESS
SCAN IN PROGRESS
I know you don't want to hear this, but maybe it's time to stop searching?
Mission Control, come in, Mission Control?
What was that?

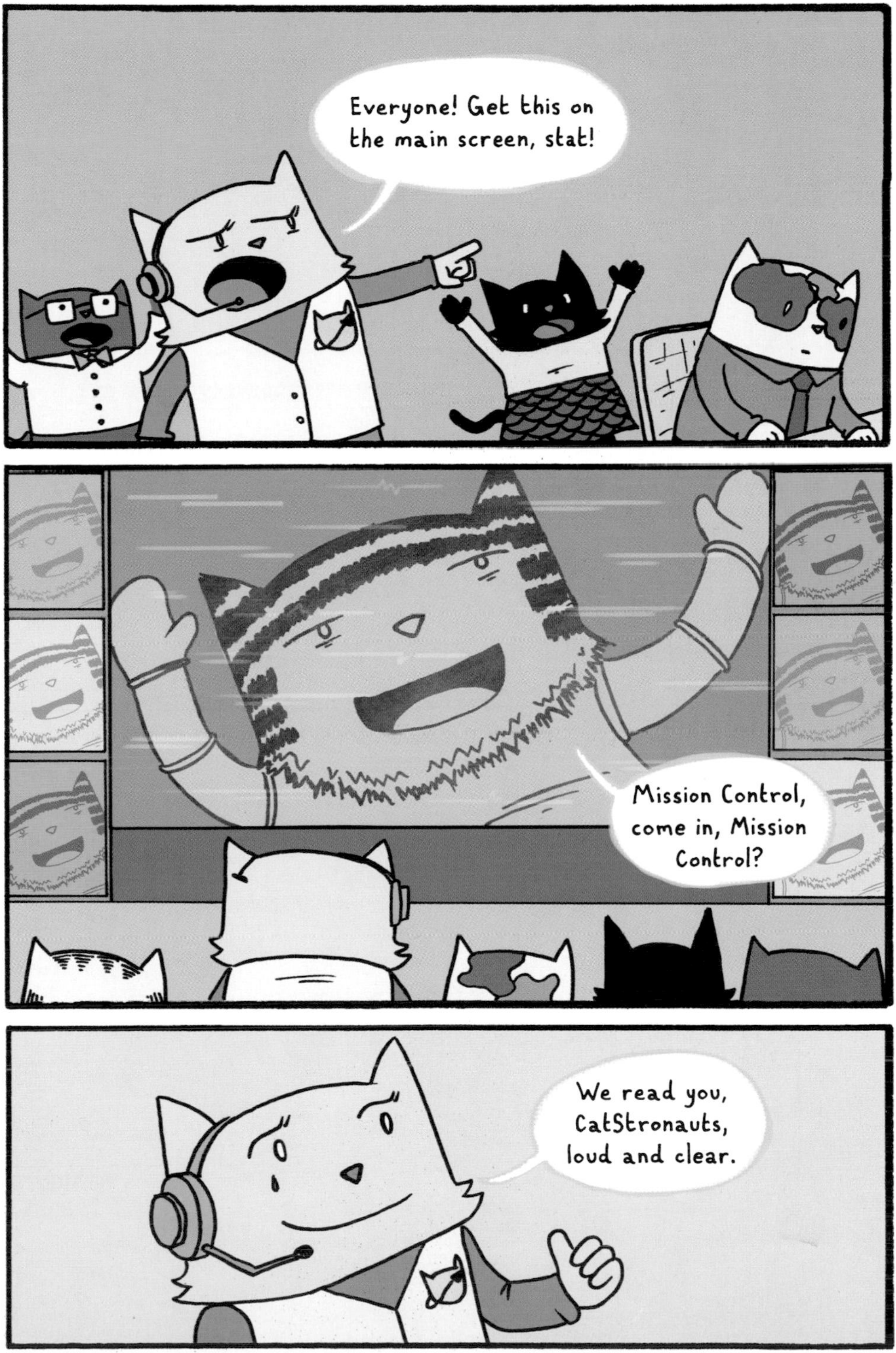
Everyone! Get this on the main screen, stat!
Mission Control, come in, Mission Control?
We read you, CatStronauts, loud and clear.

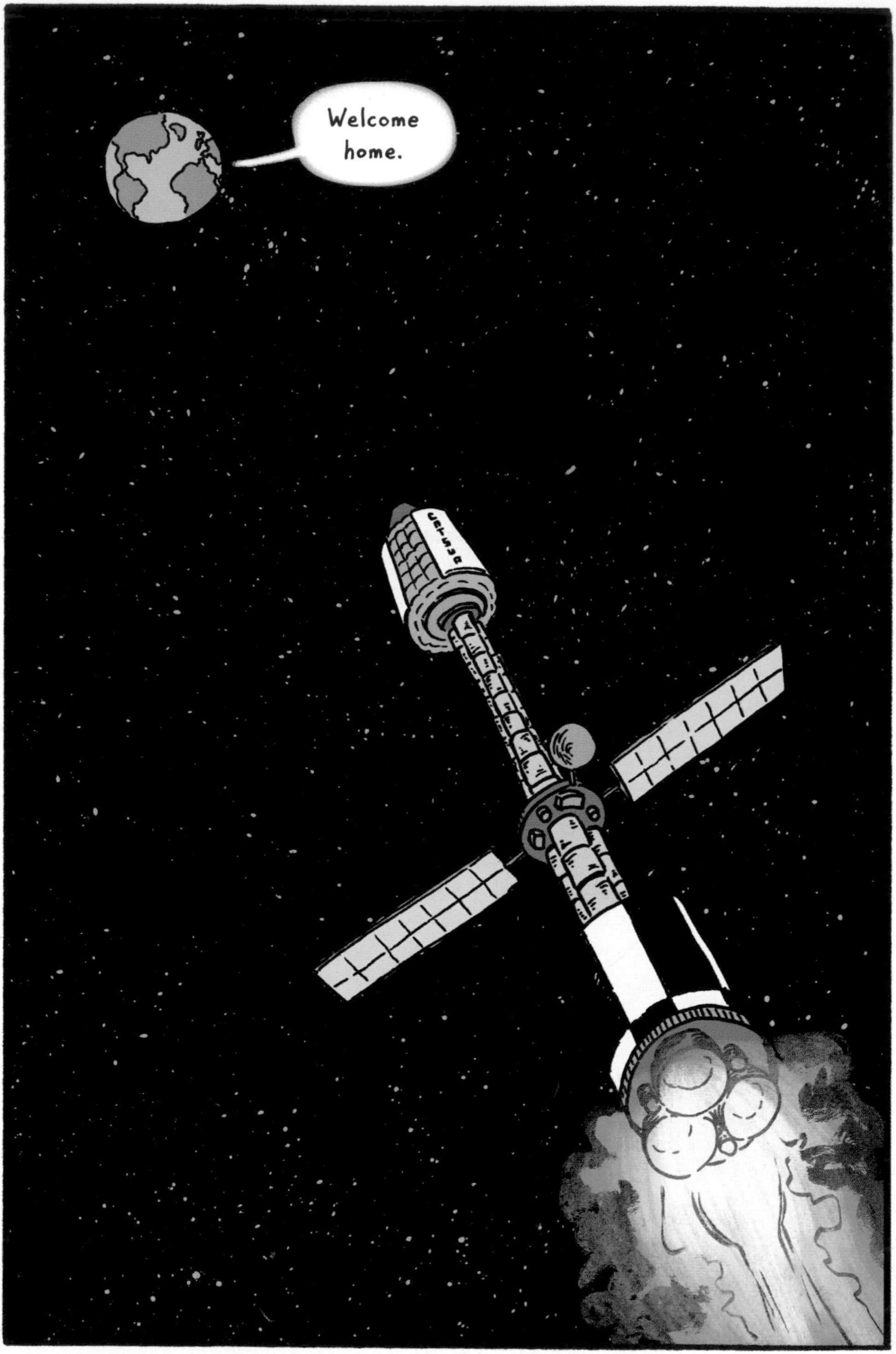
Welcome home.
CATSUA

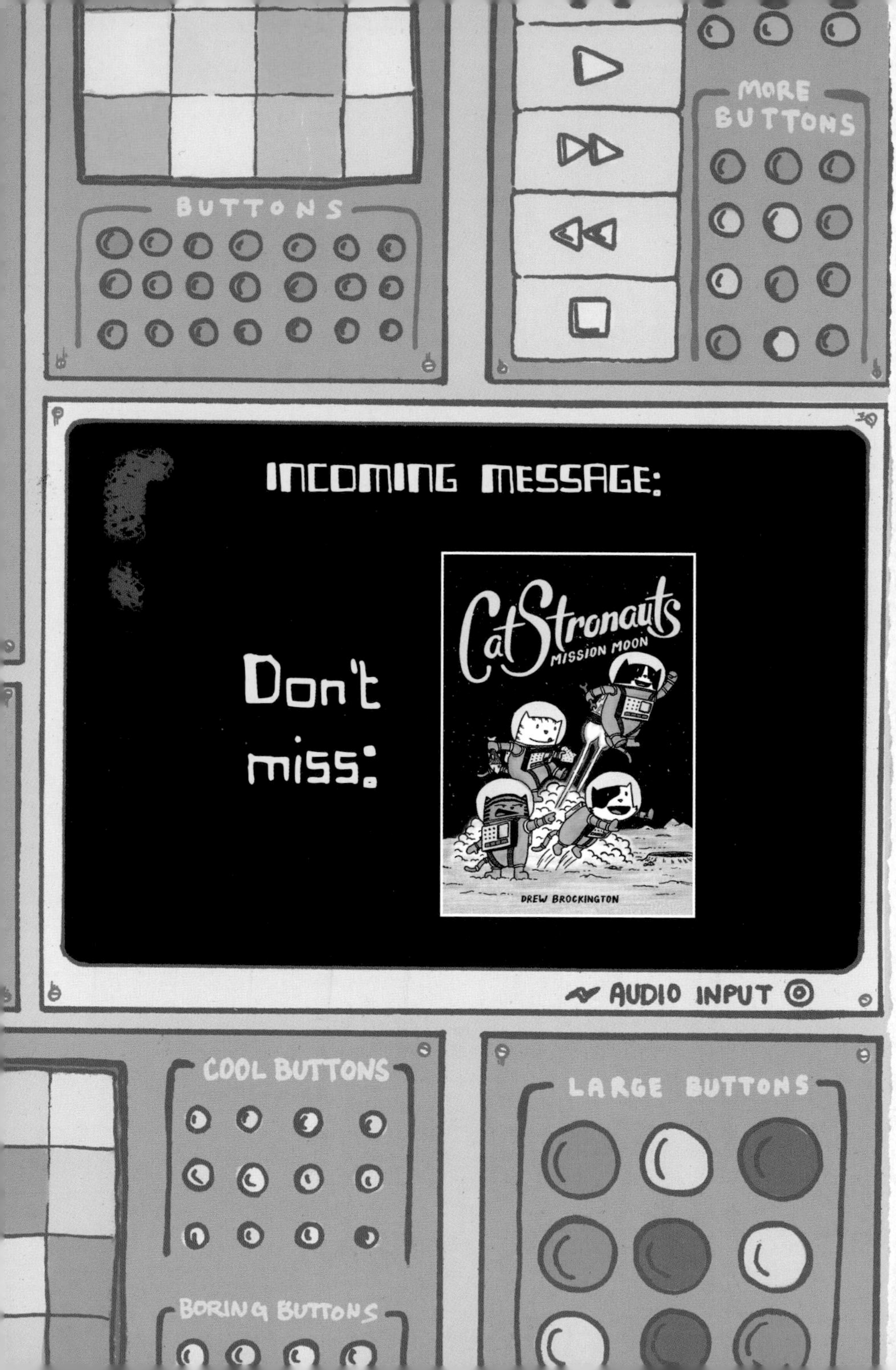
BUTTONS
MORE BUTTONS
INCOMING MESSAGE:
Don't miss:
CatStronauts
MISSION MOON
DREW BROCKINGTON
AUDIO INPUT
COOL BUTTONS
BORING BUTTONS
LARGE BUTTONS